WHOOPS. . . .

General Radescu straightened abruptly, glaring at the Slammers. "But I don't care what they say, gentlemen. I didn't come here to preside over an army sinking into a morass of lethargy and failure. I will remove any officer who seems likely to give only lip service to my commands.

"And—" he paused, for effect but also because the next words proved unexpectedly hard to get out his throat "—and if I give the signal, gentlemen, I expect you to kill everyone else in the room without question or hesitation. I will give the signal—" he twirled the band of his hat on his index finger "—by dropping my hat."

Glittering like a fairy crown in a shaft of sunlight, Radescu's hat spun to the forest floor. The only sound in the copse for the next ten seconds was the shrieking of the animal in the foliage above them.

Hawker walked over to the gilded cap and picked it up with his left hand, the hand which did not hold a submachine gun.

"Here, sir," he said as he handed the hat back to General Radescu. "You may be needing it soon."

—from *At Any Price*

BAEN BOOKS by DAVID DRAKE

DAVID DRAKE

THE BUTCHER'S BILL

This is a work of fiction. All the characters and events portrayed in this book are fictional, and any resemblance to real people or incidents is purely coincidental.

A Baen Books Original

Baen Publishing Enterprises
P.O. Box 1403
Riverdale, NY 10471

ISBN: 0-671-57773-5

Cover art by Charles Keegan

First printing, November 1998

Distributed by Simon & Schuster
1230 Avenue of the Americas
New York, NY 10020

Typeset by Windhaven Press, Auburn, NH
Printed in the United States of America

Contents

Typeset by Windhaven Press, Auburn, NH

Printed in the United States of America

Contents

Becoming a Professional Writer by Way of Southeast Asia

Some years ago my son took an undergraduate history course in the Vietnam Era. He mentioned that his father had been drafted out of law school in 1969. The other students and their 27-year-old professor were amazed; they "knew" that college students weren't drafted.

I was in the Duke Law School Class of 1970 when LBJ removed the graduate student deferment in 1968 and I was drafted along with nine more of its hundred and two guys. There were only two women in our class, a sign of the times that changed abruptly afterwards.

I'd been a history and Latin major as an undergraduate. I'd been against the war in a vague sort of way but I'd never protested or done anything else political except vote–once, since the voting age was 21. There was never any real question about me refusing to serve, though believe me I wasn't happy about it.

While a student I'd sold two fantasy short stories for a total of $85. I used what I knew about: historical settings and monsters based on H. P. Lovecraft's creepie-crawlies. I was proud of the sales, but writing was just a hobby.

Because I scored high on an army language aptitude test I was sent to Vietnamese language school at Fort Bliss, then for interrogation training at Fort Meade. Finally to Nam, where I was assigned to the Military Intelligence detachment

1

of a unit I'd never heard of: the 11th ACR, the Blackhorse Regiment.

My service wasn't in any fashion remarkable, and nothing particularly bad happened to me. I was in the field for a while with 2nd Squadron just after the capture of Snuol; then with 1st squadron; and for the last half of the tour I was back in Di An, probably the safest place in Viet Nam, as unit armorer and mail clerk. The Inspector General was due, and apparently I was the only person in the 541st MID who knew how to strip a .45 down to the frame. (Military Intelligence doesn't seem to get many people who shot in pistol competitions in civilian life.)

And then I went back to the World. 72 hours after I left Viet Nam I was sitting in the lounge of Duke University Law School, preparing to start my fourth semester. Because nothing awful had happened to me, I was honestly convinced that I hadn't changed from when I went over.

As I sat there, two guys I didn't know (my class had already graduated) were talking how they were going to avoid Viet Nam. One of them had joined the National Guard, while the other was getting into the Six and Six program that would give him six months army in the US, followed by five and a half years in the active reserves.

These were perfectly rational plans; I knew better than they did how much Nam was to be avoided. But for a moment, listening to them, I wanted to kill them both.

That gave me an inkling of the notion that maybe I wasn't quite as normal as I'd told myself I was.

I finished law school and got a job lawyering. I kept on writing, which after the fact I think was therapy. I didn't have anybody to talk to who would understand, and I'm not the sort to go to a shrink. I don't drink, either (which I think was a *really* good thing).

I had much more vivid horrors than Lovecraft's nameless ickinesses to write about now. I wrote stories about war in the future, assuming that the important things wouldn't change. The stories weren't like earlier military SF. Instead of brilliant generals or bulletproof heroes, I wrote about troopers doing their jobs the best way they could with tanks that broke down, guns that jammed—and no clue about the Big Picture, whatever the hell that might be. I kept the tone unemotional: I didn't tell the reader that something was horrible, because nobody had had to tell me.

It was very hard to sell those stories because they were different. They didn't fit either of the available molds: "Soldiers are spotless heroes," or the (then-more-popular) "Soldiers are evil monsters." Those seemed to be the only images that civilians had.

But the funny thing is, when the stories were published they gained a following. Part of it was guys who'd been there, "there" being WW II, Korea, and later the Gulf as well as Viet Nam. Some of the fans, though, were civilians who could nonetheless tell the difference between the usual fictions and stories by somebody who was trying to tell the truth he'd seen in the best way he could.

Some civilians really wanted to understand. I guess that as much as anything helped me get my own head straighter over the years.

After I got back to the World I'd just done what was in front of me. I didn't think about the future, because I suppose I'd gotten out of the habit of believing there was one. When I raised my head enough to look around—almost to the day ten years after I rode a tank back from Cambodia—I quit lawyering and got a part-time job driving a city bus while continuing to write. I didn't quit lawyering "to write" (though I'd already had two books published) but because I realized the work was making me sick.

At this point something unexpected happened. Publishers were setting up new SF lines. Editors already knew that I would write them a story that people wanted to read; my first book, *Hammer's Slammers*, had succeeded beyond the editor's wildest dreams. (*I* didn't realize that for some years afterwards.) I got literally all the work I could do. The only limitation on how many books I could sell was the number of books I could write.

I've told you that Nam gave me a need to write and also gave me something real to write about. It gave me a third thing: service with that unit I'd never heard of; the

11th ACR. I'd been part of a professional outfit whose people did their jobs with no excuses, no matter what the circumstances.

There are writers who spend more time making excuses for why they can't write than they do writing. I could've become one of them, but that attitude wouldn't have cut any ice in the Blackhorse. Instead I just got on with my job, and since 1981 I've supported my family as a full-time freelance writer.

I'm successful now because I learned professionalism in the Blackhorse and carried that lesson over to the work I do in civilian life—which happens to be writing SF. The lessons people learned in Nam probably cost more than they were worth—even to the folks like me who got back with nothing worse than a couple boil scars from the time I was in the field. They were valuable lessons nonetheless.

If any of the folks reading this were with Blackhorse, thank you for what you taught me. I'm proud to have been one of you.

Dave Drake
Chatham County, NC

BUT LOYAL TO HIS OWN

"It just blew up. Hammer and his men knew but they didn't say a thing," blurted the young captain as he looked past Secretary Tromp, his gaze compelled toward the milky noonday sky. It was not the sky of Friesland and that bothered Captain Stilchey almost as much as his near-death in the ambush an hour before. "He's insane! They all are."

"Others have said so," the councillor stated with the heavy ambiguity of an oracle replying to an ill-phrased question. Tromp's height was short of two meters by less than a hand's breadth, and he was broad in proportion. That size and the generally dull look on his face caused some visitors looking for Friesland's highest civil servant to believe they had surprised a retired policeman of some sort sitting at the desk of the Secretary to the Council of State.

Tromp did not always disabuse them.

Now his great left hand expanded over the grizzled fringe of hair remaining at the base of his skull. "Tell me about the ambush," he directed.

"He didn't make any trouble about coming to you here at the port," Stilchey said, for a moment watching his fingers writhe together rather than look at his superior. He glanced up. "Have you met Hammer?"

"No, I kept in the background when plans for the Auxiliary Regiment were drafted. I've seen his picture, of course."

5

"Not the same," the captain replied, beginning to talk very quickly. "He's not big but he, he, he moves, he's alive and it's like every time he speaks he's training a gun on you, waiting for you to slip. But he came along, no trouble— only he said we'd go with a platoon of combat cars instead of flying back, he wanted to check road security between Southport and the firebase where we were. I said sure, a couple hours wasn't crucial. . . ."

Tromp nodded. "Well done," he said. "Hammer's cooperation is very important if this . . . business is to be concluded smoothly. And"—here the councillor's face hardened without any noticeable shift of muscles—"the last thing we wanted was for the good colonel to become concerned while he was still with his troops. He is not a stupid man."

Gratification played about the edges of Stilchey's mouth, but the conversation had cycled the captain's mind back closer to the blast of cyan fire. His stomach began to spin. "There were six vehicles in the patrol, all but the second one open combat cars. That was a command car, same chassis and ground-effect curtain, but enclosed, you see? Better commo gear and an air-conditioned passenger compartment. I started toward it but Hammer said, no, I was to get in the next one with him and Joachim."

Stilchey coughed, halted. "That Joachim's here with him now; he calls him his aide. The bastard's queer, he tried to make me when I flew out. . . ."

Puzzlement. "Colonel Hammer is homosexual, Captain? Or his aide, or . . . ?"

"No, Via! Him, not the—I don't know. Via, maybe him too. The bastard scares me, he really does."

To statesmen patience is a tool; it is a palpable thing that can grind necessary information out of a young man whose aristocratic lineage and sparkling uniform have suddenly ceased to armor him against the universe. "The ambush, Captain," Tromp pressed stolidly.

With a visible effort, Stilchey regained the thread of his narrative.

"Joachim drove. Hammer and I were in the back along with a noncom from Curwin—Worzel, his name was. He and Joachim threw dice for who had to drive. The road was supposed to be clear but Hammer made me put on body armor. I thought it was cop, you know—make the staffer get hot and dusty.

"Via," he swore again, but softly this time. "I was at the leftside powergun but I wasn't paying much attention; nothing really to pay attention to. Hammer was on the radio a lot, but my helmet only had intercom so I didn't know what he was saying. The road was stabilized earth, just a gray line through hectares of those funny blue plants you see all over here, the ones with the fat leaves."

"Bluebrights," the older man said dryly. "Melpomone's only export; as you would know from the briefing cubes you were issued in transit, I should think."

"Would the Lord I'd never *heard* of this damned place!" Stilchey blazed back. His family controlled Karob Trading; no civil servant—not even Tromp, the Gray Eminence behind the Congress of the Republic—could cow him. But he was a soldier, too, and after a moment he continued, "Bluebrights in rows, waist high and ugly, and beyond that nothing but the soil blowing away as we passed.

"We were half an hour out from the firebase, maybe half the way to here. The ground was dimpled with frost heaves. A little copse was in sight ahead of us, trees ten, fifteen meters high. Hammer had the forward gun, and on the intercom he said 'Want to double the bet, Blackie?' Then they armed their guns—I didn't know why—and Worzel said, 'I still think they'll be in the draw two kays south, but I won't take any more of your money.' They were laughing and I thought they were going to just . . . clear the guns, you know?"

The captain closed his eyes. He remembered how they had stared at him, two bulging circles and the hollow of his screaming mouth below them, reflected on the polished floorplate of the combat car. "The command car blew up just as we entered the trees. There was a flash like the sun and it *ate* the back half of the car, armor and all. The front flipped over and over into the trees, and the air *stank* with metal. Joachim laid us sideways to follow the part the

mine had left, cutting in right behind when it hit a tree
and stopped. The driver raised his head out of the hatch
and maybe he could have got clear himself . . . but
Hammer jumped off our deck to his and jerked him out,
yanked him up in his armor as small as he is. Then they
were back in our car. They were firing, everybody was
firing, and we turned right, into the trees, into the guns."

"There were Mel troops in the grove, then?" Tromp
asked.

"Must have been," Stilchey replied. He looked straight
at the older man and said, very simply, "I was behind the
bulkhead. Maybe if I'd known what to expect. . . . The
other driver was at my gun, they didn't need me." Stilchey
swallowed once, continued, "Some shots hit on my side.
They didn't come through, but they made the whole car
ring. The empties kept spattering me and the car was
bouncing, jumping downed trees. Everything seemed to be
on fire. We cleared the grove into another field of bluebrights. Shells from the firebase were already landing in
the trees; the place was targeted. And Worzer pulled off
his helmet and he spat and said, 'Cold meat, Colonel, you
couldn't a called it better.' Via!"

"Well, it does sound like they reacted well to the
ambush," Tromp admitted, puzzled because nothing Stilchey
had told him explained the captain's fear and hatred of
Hammer and his men.

"Nice extempore response, hey?" the aide suggested with
bitter irony. "Only Hammer, seeing I didn't know what
Worzer meant, turned to me, and said, 'We let the Mels get
word that me and Secretary Tromp would take a convoy to
Southport this morning. They still had fifty or so regulars here
in Region 4 claiming to be an infantry battalion, and it looked
like a good time to flush them for good and all.'"

Tromp said nothing. He spread his hands carefully on
the citron-yellow of his desk top and seemed to be fixedly
studying the contrast. Stilchey waited for a response. At
last he said, "I don't like being used for bait, Secretary.
And what if you'd decided to go out to the firebase
yourself? I was all right for a stand-in, but do you think

Hammer would have cared if you were there in person? He won't let anything stand in his way."

"Colonel Hammer does seem to have some unconventional attitudes," Tromp agreed. A bleak smile edged his voice as he continued, "But at that, it's rather fortunate that he brought a platoon in with him. We can begin the demobilization of his vaunted Slammers with them."

The dome of the Starport Lounge capped Southport's hundred-meter hotel tower. Its vitril panels were seamless and of the same refractive index as the atmosphere. As a tactician, Hammer was fascinated with the view: it swept beyond the equipment-thronged spaceport and over the shimmering billows of bluebright, to the mountains of the Crescent almost twenty kilometers away. But tankers' blood has in it a turtle component that is more comfortable on the ground than above it, and the little officer felt claws on his intestines as he looked out.

No similar discomfort seemed to be disturbing the other men in the room, all in the black and silver of the Guards of the Republic, though in name they were armor officers. "Had a bit of action today, Colonel?" said a cheerful, fit-looking major. Hammer did not remember him even though a year ago he had been Second in Command of the Guards.

"Umm, a skirmish," Hammer said as he turned. The Guardsman held out to him one of the two thimble-sized crystals he carried. In the heart of each flickered an azure fire. "Why, thank you—" the major's name was patterned in the silver highlights below his left lapel "—Mestern."

"No doubt you have seen much worse with your mercenaries, eh, Colonel?" a voice called mockingly from across the room.

Karl August Raeder lounged in imperial state in the midst of a dozen admiring junior officers. He had been the executive officer of the Guards for the past year— ever since Hammer took command of the foreign regiment raised to smash the scattered units of the Army of Melpomone.

"Mercenaries, Karl?" Hammer repeated. A threat rasped

through the surface mildness of his tone. "Yes, they cash their paychecks. There may be a few others in this room who do, hey?"

"Oh . . ." someone murmured in the sudden quiet, but there was no way to tell what he meant by it. Raeder did not move. The blood had drawn back to yellow his smooth tan, and where the cushions had borne his languid hands they now were dimpled cruelly. Two men in the lounge had reached officer status in the Guards without enormous family wealth behind them. Hammer was one, Raeder was the other.

He strained at a breath. In build, he and Hammer were not dissimilar: the latter brown-haired and somewhat shorter, a trifle more of the hourglass in his shoulders and waist; Raeder blond and trim, slender in a rapier sort of way and quite as deadly. His uniform of natural silk and leather was in odd contrast to Hammer's khaki battledress, but there was nothing of fop or sloven in either man.

"Pardon," the Guardsman said, "I would not have thought this a company in which one need explain patriotism; there are men who fight for their homelands, and then there are the dregs, the gutter-sweepings of a galaxy, who fight for the same reason they pimped and sold themselves before our government—let me finish, please!" (though only Hammer's smile had moved) "—misguidedly, I submit, offered them more money to do what Friesland citizens could have done better!"

"My boys are better citizens than some born on Friesland who stayed there wiping their butts—"

"A soldier goes where he is ordered!" Raeder was standing.

"A *soldier*—"

Dead silence. Hammer's sentence broke like an axed cord. He looked about the lounge at the twenty-odd men, most of them his ex-comrades and all, like Raeder, men who had thought him mad to post out of the Guards for the sake of a combat command. Hammer laughed. He inverted the stim cone on the inside of his wrist and said approvingly, "Quite a view from up here. If it weren't such

a good target, you could make it your operations center."
As if in the midst of a normal conversation, he faced back
toward the exterior and added, "By the way, what sort of
operations are you expecting? I would have said the fighting
here was pretty well over, and I'd be surprised at the
government sending the Guards in for garrison duty."

The whispering that had begun when Hammer turned
was stilled again. It was Raeder who cleared his throat and
said in a tone between triumph and embarrassment,
"Colonel Rijsdal may know. He . . . he has remained in
his quarters since we landed." Rijsdal had not had a sober
day in the past three years since he had acceded to an
enormous estate on Friesland. "No doubt we are to provide
proper, ah, background for such official pronouncements
as the Secretary will make to the populace."

Hammer nodded absently as if he believed the black
and silver of a parade regiment would over-awe the Mels
more effectively than could his own scarred killers, the men
who had rammed Frisian suzerainty down Mel throats after
twelve regiments of regulars had tried and failed. But the
Guards were impressively equipped . . . and all their gear
had been landed.

Five hundred worlds had imported bluebright leaves, with
most of the tonnage moving through Southport. The handful
of Frisian vessels scattered on the field looked lost, but traffic
would pick up now that danger was over. For the moment,
hundreds of Guard vehicles gave it a specious life. In the
broad wedge of his vision Hammer could see two rocket
batteries positioned as neatly as chess pieces on the huge
playing surface. The center of each cluster was an ammunition hauler, low and broad-chassied. Within their thin
armor sheetings were the racks of 150mm shells; everything
from armor-piercing rounds with a second stage to accelerate them before impact, to antipersonnel cases loaded with
hundreds of separate bomblets. The haulers rested on the
field; no attempt had been made to dig them in.

The six howitzers of each battery were sited about their
munitions in a regular hexagon, each joined to its hauler
by the narrow strip of a conveyor. In action the hogs could

kick out shells at five-second intervals, so the basic load of twenty rounds carried by the howitzer itself needed instant replenishment from the hauler's store. Their stubby gun-tubes gave them guidance and an initial boost, but most of the acceleration came beyond the muzzle. They looked grim and effective; still, it nagged Hammer to see that nobody had bothered to defilade them.

"A pretty sight," said Mestern. Conversation in the lounge was back to a normal level.

Hammer squeezed the last of his stim cone into the veins of his wrist and let the cool shudder pass through him before saying, "The Republic buys the best, and that's the only way to go when a battle's hanging on it. Not that you don't need good crews to man the gear."

Mestern pointed beyond the howitzers, toward a wide-spaced ring of gun trucks. "Latest thing in arty defense," he said. "Each of those cars mounts an eight-barrel powergun, only 30mm but they're high-intensity. They've got curst near the range of a tank's 200—thirty, forty kilometers if you've that long a sight line. With our radar hook-up and the satellite, we can just about detonate a shell as soon as it comes over the horizon."

"Nice theory," Hammer agreed. "I doubt you can swing the rig fast enough to catch the first salvo, but maybe placing them every ten degrees like that . . . where you've got the terrain to allow it. The Mels never had arty worth cop anyway, of course."

He paused, not sure he wanted to comment further. The grounded tanks and combat cars of the regiment were in an even perimeter at the edge of the circular field. Their dull iridium armor was in evident contrast to the ocher soil on which they rested. "You really ought to have dug in," Hammer said at last.

"Oh, the field's been stabilized to two meters down," the major protested innocently, "and I don't think the Mels are much of a threat now."

Hammer shook his head in irritation. "Lord!" he snorted, "the Mels aren't any threat at all after this morning. But just on general principles, when you set up in a war zone—

any war zone—you set up as if you were going to be hit. Via, you may as well park your cars on Friesland for all the good they'd do if it dropped in the pot."

"The good colonel has been away from soldiers too long," whipped Raeder savagely. "Major Mestern, would you care to enlighten him as to how operations can be conducted by a real regiment—even though a gutter militia would be incapable of doing so?"

"I don't . . . think . . . ," Mestern stuttered in embarrassment. His fingers twiddled an empty stim cone.

"Very well, then I will," the blond XO snapped. Hammer was facing him again. This time the two men were within arm's length. "The Regiment of Guards is using satellite reconnaissance, Colonel," Raeder announced sneeringly. "The same system in operation when you were in charge here, but we are *using* it, you see."

"We used it. We—"

"Pardon, Colonel, permit me to explain and there will be fewer needless questions."

Hammer relaxed with a smile. There was a tiger's certainty behind its humor. "No, your pardon. Continue."

Hammer had killed two men in semi-legal duels fought on Friesland's moon. Raeder chuckled, unconcerned with his rival's sudden mildness. "So," he continued, "no Mel force could approach without being instantly sighted."

He stared at Hammer, who said nothing. If the Guardsman wanted to believe no produce truck could drop a Mel platoon into bunkers dug by a harvesting crew—spotting the activity was no problem, interpreting it, though—well, it didn't matter now. But it proved again what Hammer had known since before he was landed, that a lack of common sense was what had so hamstrung the regular army that his Slammers had to be formed.

Of course, "common sense" meant to Hammer doing what was necessary to complete a task. And that sometimes created problems of its own.

"Our howitzers can shatter them ninety kilometers distant," Raeder lectured on, "and our tanks can pierce all but the heaviest armor at line of sight, Colonel." He gestured arrogantly toward the skyline behind Hammer. "Anything that can be seen can be destroyed."

"Yeah, it's always a mistake to underrate technology," agreed the man in khaki.

"So," Raeder said with a crisp nod. "It is possible to be quite efficient without being—" his eyes raked Hammer's stained, worn coveralls "—shoddy. When we hold the review tomorrow, it will be interesting to consider your . . . force . . . beside the Guard."

"Via, only two of my boys are in," Hammer said "though for slickness I'd bet Joachim against anybody you've got." He looked disinterestedly at the drink dispenser. "We'll all be back in the field, as soon as I see what Tromp wants. We've got a clean-up operation mounted in the Crescent."

"There is a platoon present now," the Guardsman snapped. "It will remain, as you will remain, until you receive other orders."

Hammer walked away without answering. Bigger men silently moved aside, clearing a path to the dispenser. Raeder locked his lips, murder-tense; but a bustle at the central dropshaft caused him to spin around. His own aide, a fifteen-year-old scion of his wife's house, had emerged when the column dilated. Rather than use the PA system built into the lounge before it was commandeered as an officer's club, messages were relayed through aides waiting on the floor below. Raeder's boy carried a small flag bearing the hollow rectangle of Raeder's rank, his ticket to enter the lounge and to set him apart from the officers. The boy might well be noble, but as yet he did not have a commission. He was to be made to remember it.

He whispered with animation into Raeder's ear, his own eyes open and fixed on the mercenary officer. Hammer ignored them both, talking idly as he blended another stim cone into his blood. The blond man's face slowly took on an expression of ruddy, mottled fury.

"Hammer!"

"The next time you determine where my boys will be, Colonel Raeder, I recommend that you ask me about it."

"You traitorous scum!" Raeder blazed, utterly beyond

curbing his anger. "I closed the perimeter to everyone, *everyone*! And you bull your way through my guards, get them to pass—"

"Pass *my* men, Lieutenant-Colonel!" Hammer blasted as if he were shouting orders through the howling fans of a tank. All the tension of the former confrontation shuddered in the air again. Hammer was as set and grim as one of his war cars.

Raeder raised a clenched fist.

"Touch me and I'll shoot you where you stand," the mercenary said, and he had no need to raise his voice for emphasis. As if only Raeder and not the roomful of officers as well was listening, he said, "You give what orders you please, but I've still got an independent command. As of this moment. That platoon is blocking a pass in the Crescent, because that's what I want it to do, not sit around trying to polish away bullet scars because some cop-head thinks that's a better idea than fighting."

His body still as a gravestone, Raeder spoke. "*Now* you've got a command," he said thickly.

The wing of violence lifted from the lounge. Given time to consider, every man there knew that the battle was in other hands than Raeder's now—and that it would be fought very soon.

The dropshaft hissed again.

Joachim Steuben's dress was identical in design to his colonel's, but was in every other particular far superior. The khaki was unstained, the waist-belt genuine leather, polished to a rich chestnut sheen, and the coveralls themselves tapered to follow the lines of his boyish-slim figure. Perhaps it was the very beauty of the face smoothly framing Joachim's liquid eyes that made the aide look not foppish, but softly feminine.

There was a rich urbanity as well in his careful elegance. Newland, his homeworld, was an old colony with an emphasis on civilized trappings worthy of Earth herself. Just as Joachim's uniform was of a synthetic sleeker and less rugged than Hammer's, his sidearm was hunched high on his right hip in a holster cut away to display the artistry of what it gripped. No weapon in the lounge, even that of Captain Ryssler—the Rysslers on whose land Friesland's second starport had been built—matched that of the Newlander for gorgeous detail. The receiver of the standard service pistol, a 1cm powergun whose magazine held ten charged-plastic disks, had been gilded and carven by someone with a penchant for fleshy orchids. The stems and leaves had been filled with niello while the veins remained in a golden tracery. The petals themselves were formed from a breathtakingly purple alloy of copper and gold. It was hard for anyone who glanced at it to realize that such a work of art was still, beneath its chasing, a lethal weapon.

"Colonel," he reported, his clear tenor a jewel in the velvet silence, "Secretary Tromp will see you now." Neither he nor Hammer showed the slightest concern as to whether the others in the lounge were listening. Hammer nodded, wiping his palms on his thighs.

Behind his back, Joachim winked at Colonel Raeder before turning. The Guardsman's jaw dropped and something mewled from deep in his chest.

It may have been imagination that made Joachim's hips seem to rotate a final purple highlight from his pistol as the dropshaft sphinctered shut.

When the Guards landed, all but the fifteenth story of the Southport Tower was taken over for officers' billets. That central floor was empty save for Tromp, his staff, and the pair of scowling Guardsmen confronting the dropshaft as it opened.

"I'll stay with you, sir," Joachim said. The guards were in dress blacks but they carried full-sized shoulder weapons, 2cm powerguns inferior only in rate of fire to the tribarrels mounted on armored vehicles.

"Go on back to our quarters," Hammer replied. He stepped off the platform. His aide showed no signs of closing the shaft in obedience. "Martyrs' *blood*!" Hammer cursed. "Do as I say!" He wiped his palms again and added, more mildly, "That's where I'll need you, I think."

"If you say so, sir." The door sighed closed behind Hammer, leaving him with the guards.

"Follow the left corridor to the end—sir," one of the big men directed grudgingly. The colonel nodded and walked off without comment. The two men were convinced their greatest worth lay in the fact that they were Guardsmen. To them it was an insult that another man would deliberately leave the Regiment, especially to take service with a band of foreign scum. Hammer could have used his glass-edged tongue on the pair as he had at the perimeter when he sent his platoon through, but there was no need. He was not the man to use any weapon for entertainment's sake.

The unmarked wood-veneer door opened before he could knock. "Why, good afternoon, Captain," the mercenary said, smiling into Stilchey's haggardness. "Recovering all right from this morning?"

"Go on through," the captain said. "He's expecting you."

Hammer closed the inner door behind him, making a soft echo to the thump of the hall panel. Tromp rose from behind his desk, a great gray bear confronting a panther.

"Colonel, be seated," he rumbled. Hammer nodded cautiously and obeyed.

"We have a few problems which must be cleared up soon," the big man said. He looked the soldier full in the face. "I'll be frank. You already know why I'm here."

"Our job's done," Hammer said without inflection. "It costs money to keep the Sl—the auxiliary regiment mobilized when it isn't needed, so it's time to bring my boys home according to contract, hey?"

The sky behind Tromp was a turgid mass, gray with harbingers of the first storm of autumn. It provided the only light in the room, but neither man moved to turn on the wall illuminators. "You were going to say 'Slammers,' weren't you?" Tromp mused. "Interesting. I had wondered if the newscasters coined the nickname themselves or if they really picked up a usage here. . . ."

"The boys started it. . . . It seemed to catch on."

"But I'm less interested in that than another word,"

Tromp continued with the sudden weight of an anvil falling. "'Home.' And that's the problem, Colonel. As you know."

"The only thing I could tell you is what I tell recruits when they sign on," Hammer said, his voice quiet but his forehead sweat-gemmed in the cool air. "By their contract, they became citizens of Friesland with all rights and privileges thereof. . . . Great Dying *Lord,* sir, that's what brought most of my boys here! Look, I don't have to tell you what's been happening everywhere the past ten years, twenty—there are thousands and thousands of soldiers, good soldiers, who wound up on one losing side or another. If everybody that fought alongside them had been as good, and maybe if they'd had the equipment Friesland could buy for them . . . I tell you, sir, there's no one in the galaxy to match them. And what they fight for isn't me, I don't care what cop you've heard, it's that chance at peace, at stability that their fathers had and their father's fathers, but they lost somewhere when everything started to go wrong. They'd *die* for that chance!"

"But instead," Tromp stated, "they killed for it."

"Don't give me any cop about morals!" the soldier snarled. "Whose idea was it that we needed control of bluebright shipments to be sure of getting metals from Taunus?"

"Morals?" replied Tromp with a snort. "Morals be hanged, Colonel. This isn't a galaxy for men with morals, you don't have to tell me that. Oh, they can moan about what went on here and they have—but nobody, not even the reporters, has been looking very hard. And they wouldn't find many to listen if they had been. You and I are paid to get things done, Hammer, and there won't be any blame except for failure."

The soldier hunched his shoulders back against the chair. "Then it's all right?" he asked in wonder. "After all I worried, all I planned, my boys can go back to Friesland with me?"

Tromp smiled. "Over my dead body," he said pleasantly. The two men stared at each other without expression on either side.

"I'm missing something," said Hammer flatly. "Fill me in."

The civilian rotated a flat datavisor toward Hammer and touched the indexing tab with his thumb. A montage of horror flickered across the screen—smoke drifting sullenly from a dozen low-lying buildings; a mass grave, reopened and being inspected by a trio of Frisian generals; another village without evident damage but utterly empty of human life—

"Chakma," Hammer said in sudden recognition. "Via, you ought to thank me for the way we handled that one. I'd half thought of using a nuke."

"Gassing the village was better?" the councillor asked with mild amusement.

"It was quiet. No way you could have kept reporters from learning about a nuke," Hammer explained.

"And the convoy runs you made with hostages on each car?" Tromp asked smilingly.

"The only hostages we used were people we knew—and they knew we knew" —Hammer's finger slashed emphasis— "were related to Mel soldiers who hadn't turned themselves in. We cut ambushes by a factor of ten, and we even had some busted when a Mel saw his wife or a kid riding the lead car. Look, I won't pretend it didn't happen, but I didn't make any bones about what I planned when I put in for transfer. This is bloody late in the day to bring it up."

"Right, you did your duty," the big civilian agreed. "And I'm going to do mine by refusing to open Friesland to five thousand men with the training you gave them. Lord and Martyrs, Colonel, you tell me we're going through a period when more governments are breaking up than aren't—what would happen to *our* planet if we set your animals loose in the middle of it?"

"There's twelve regiments of regulars here," Hammer argued.

"And if they were worth the cop in their trousers, we wouldn't have needed your auxiliaries," retorted Tromp inflexibly. "Face facts."

The colonel sagged. "OK," he muttered, turning his face

toward the sidewall, "I won't pretend I didn't expect it, what
you just said. I owed it to the boys they . . . they believe
when they ought to have better sense, and I owed them to
try. . . ." The soldier's fingers beat a silent tattoo on the
yielding material of his chair. He stood before speaking
further. "There's a way out of it, Secretary," he said.

"I know there is."

"No!" Hammer shouted, his voice denying the flat finality
of Tromp's as he spun to face the bigger man again. "No,
there's a better way, a way that'll work. You didn't want
to hire one of the freelance regiments you could have had
because they didn't have the equipment to do the job fast.
But it takes a government and a curst solvent one to equip
an armored regiment—none of the privateers had that sort
of capital."

He paused for breath. "Partly true," Tromp agreed. "Of
course, we preferred to have a commander—" he smiled
"—whose first loyalty was to Friesland."

Hammer spoke on, choking with his effort to convince
the patient, gray iceberg of a man across from him.
"Friesland's always made her money by trade. Let's go into
another business—let's hire out the best equipped, best
trained—by the Lord, *best*—regiment in the galaxy!"

"And the reason that won't work, Colonel," Tromp
rumbled coolly, "is not that it would fail, but that it would
succeed. It takes a very solvent government, as you noted,
to afford the capital expense of maintaining a first-rate
armored regiment. The Melpomonese, for instance, could
never have fielded a regiment of their own. But if . . .
the sort of unit you suggest was available, they could have
hired it for a time, could they not?"

"A few months, sure," Hammer admitted with an angry
flick of his hands, "But—"

"Nine months, perhaps a year, Colonel," the civilian went
on inexorably. "It would have bankrupted them, but I think
they would have paid for the same reason they resisted what
was clearly overwhelming force. And not even Friesland
could have economically taken Melpomone if the locals were
stiffened by—by your Slammers, let us say."

"Lord!" Hammer shouted, snapping erect, "Of course we wouldn't take contracts against Friesland."

"Men change, Colonel," Tromp replied, rising to his own feet. "Men die. And even if they don't, the very existence of a successful enterprise will free the capital for others to duplicate it. It won't be a wild gamble any more. And Friesland will *not* be the cause of that state of affairs while I am at her helm. If you're the patriot we assumed you were when we gave you this command, you will order your men to come in by platoons and be disarmed."

The smaller man's face was sallow and his hands shook until he hooked them in his pistol belt. "But you can't even let them go then, can you?" he whispered. "It might be all right on Friesland where there wouldn't be any recruiting by outsiders. But if you just turn my boys loose, somebody else will snap them up, somebody else who reads balance sheets. Maybe trained personnel would be enough of an edge to pry loose equipment on the cuff. Life's rough, sure, and there are plenty of people willing to gamble a lot to make a lot more. Then we're where you didn't want us, aren't we? Except that the boys are going to have some notions of their own about Friesland. . . . What do you plan, Secretary? Blowing up the freighter with everybody aboard? Or will you just have the Guards shoot them down when they've been disarmed?"

Tromp turned away for the first time. Lightning was flashing from cloud peak to cloud peak, and the mass that lowered over the Crescent was already linked to the ground by a haze of rain. "They put us in charge of things because we see them as they are, Colonel," Tromp said. The vitril sheet in front of him trembled to the distant thunder. "Friesland got very good value from you, because you didn't avoid unpleasant decisions; you saw the best way and took it—be damned to appearances.

"I would not be where I am today if I were not the same sort of man. I don't ask you to like this course of action—I don't like it myself—but you're a pragmatist too, Hammer, you see that it's the only way clear for our own people."

"Secretary, anything short of having my boys killed, but—"

"Curse it, man!" Tromp shouted. "Haven't you taken a look around you recently? Lives are cheap, Colonel, lives are very cheap! You've got to have loyalty to something more than just men."

"No," said the man in khaki with quiet certainty. Then, "May I be excused, sir?"

"Get out of here."

Tromp was seated again, his own face a mirror of the storm, when Captain Stilchey slipped in the door through which Hammer had just exited. "Your lapel mike picked it all up," the young officer said. He gloated conspiratorially. "The traitor."

Tromp's face forced itself into normal lines. "You did as I explained might be necessary?"

"Right. As soon as I heard the word 'disarmed' I ordered men to wait for Hammer in his quarters." Stilchey's gleeful expression expanded to a smile of real delight. "I added a . . . refinement, sir. There was the possibility that Hammer would—you know how he is, hard not to obey— tell the guards be cursed and leave them standing. So I took the liberty of suggesting to Colonel Raeder that he lead four men himself for the duty. I used your name, sir, but I rather think the colonel would have gone along with the idea anyway."

The captain's laughter hacked loudly through the suite before he realized that Tromp still sat in iron gloom, cradling his chin in his hands.

The room was a shifting bowl of reds and hot orange in which the khaki uniforms of Worzer and Steuben seemed misplaced. The only sound was a faint buzzing, the leakage of the bone-conduction speakers implanted in either man's right mastoid. Hammer, like Tromp, had left his lapel mike keyed to his aides.

"Get us a drink, Joe," Worzer asked. With the Slammers, you either did your job or you left, and nobody could fault Joachim's effectiveness. Still, there was a good deal of ambivalence about the Newlander in a unit made up in large measure of ex-farmers whose religious training had been fundamental if not scholarly. Tense, black-bearded Worzer got along with him better than most, perhaps because it had been a Newland ship which many years before had lifted him from Curwin and the Security Police with their questions about a bombed tax office.

Joachim stood and stretched, his eyes vacant. The walls and floor gave him a satanic cruelty that would have struck as incongruous those who knew him slightly. Yawning, he touched the lighting control, a slight concavity in the wall. The flames dulled, faded to a muted pattern of grays. The room was appreciably darker.

"Wanted you to do that all the time," Worzer grumbled. He seated himself on a bulging chair that faced the doorway.

"I liked it," Joachim said neutrally. He started for the kitchen alcove, then paused. "You'd best take your pistol off, you know. They'll be jumpy."

"You're the boss," Worzer grunts. Alone now in the room, he unlatches his holstered weapon and tosses the rig to the floor in front of him. It is a fixed blackness against the grays that shift beneath it. Glass tinkles in the kitchen. Men on every world have set up stills, generally as their first constructions. Even in a luxury hotel, Worzer's habits are those of a lifetime. Hammer's microphone no longer broadcasts voices.

The door valves open.

"Freeze!" orders the first man through. He is small and blond, his eyes as cold as the silver frosting his uniform. The glowing tab of a master door key is in his left hand, a pistol in his right. The Guardsmen fanning to each side of him swing heavy powerguns at waist level, the muzzles black screams in a glitter of iridium. Two more men stand beyond the door, facing either end of the hallway with their weapons ready.

"Move and you're dead," the officer hisses to Worzer. Then, to his tight-lipped subordinates, "Watch for the other one—the deviate."

The kitchen door rotates to pass Joachim. His left hand holds a silver tray with a fruit-garnished drink on it. Reflections shimmer from the metal and the condensate on the glass. He smiles.

"You foul *beast!*" says the officer and his pistol turns toward the aide of its own seeming will. The enlisted men wait, uncertain.

"Me, Colonel Raeder?" Joachim's voice lilts. He is raising the tray and it arcs away from his body in a gentle movement that catches Raeder's eyes for the instant that the Newlander's right hand dips and—a cyan flash from Joachim's pistol links the two men. Raeder's mouth is open but silent. His eyeballs are bulging outward against the pressure of exploding nerve tissue. There is a hole between them and it winks twice more in the flash of Joachim's shots. Two spent cases hang in the air to the Newlander's right; a third is jammed, smeared across his pistol's ejection port. None of the Guardsmen have begun to fall, though a gout of blood pours from the neck of the right-hand man.

It is two-fifths of a second from the moment Joachim reached for his pistol.

Worzer had been ready. He leaped as Steuben's shots flickered across the room, twisting the shoulder weapon from a Guardsman who did not realize he was already dead. The stocky Curwinite hit the floor on his right side, searching the doorway with the powergun. In the hall, a guard shouted as he spun himself to face the shooting. Joachim's jammed pistol had thudded on the floor but Worzer wasted no interest on what the aide might do—you didn't worry about Joachim in a firefight, he took care of himself. The noncom had been squeezing even as he fell, and only a feather of trigger pressure was left to take up when the Guardsman's glittering uniform sprouted above the sights.

Heated air thumped the walls of the room. The body ballooned under the cyan impact. The big-bore packed enough joules to vaporize much of a man's abdomen at that range, and the Frisian hurtled back against the far wall. His tunic was afire and spilling coils of intestine.

The boots of the remaining Guardsman clattered on the

tile as he bolted for the dropshaft. Joachim snaked his head and the pistol he had snatched from Raeder through the doorway. Worzer and the big gun plunged into the corridor low to cover the other end. The shaft entrance opened even before the Frisian's outflung arm touched the summoning plate. Hammer, standing on the platform, shot him twice in the chest. The Guardsman pitched into the wall. As he did so, Joachim shot him again at the base of the skull. Joachim generally doubted other men's kills, a practice that had saved his life in the past.

Hammer glanced down at the jellied skull of the last Guardsman and grimaced. "Didn't anybody tell you about aiming at the body instead of getting fancy?" he asked Joachim. Neither man commented that the final shot had been aimed within a meter of Hammer.

The Newlander shrugged. "They should've been wearing body armor," he said offhandedly. "Coppy fools."

The colonel scooped up both the powerguns from the corridor and gestured his men back into the room. The air within stank of blood and hot plastic. Death had been too sudden to be prefaced with pain, but the faces of the Guardsmen all held slack amazement. Hammer shook his head. "With five thousand of you to choose from," he said to Joachim, "didn't they think I could find a decent bodyguard?"

The Newlander smiled. After his third quick shot, the expended disk had been too hot to spin out whole and had instead flowed across the mechanism when struck by the jet of ejection gas. Joachim was carefully chipping away at the cooled plastic with a stylus while the pistol he had taken from his first victim lay on the table beside him. Its muzzle had charred the veneer surface. "There isn't enough gas in a handgun ejector to cool the chamber properly," he said, pretending to ignore his colonel's indirect praise.

"Via, you hurried 'cause you wanted all of them." Worzer laughed. He thumbed a loaded round into the magazine of the shoulder gun he had appropriated. "What's the matter—don't you want the colonel to bother bringing me along the next time 'cause I scare away all your pretty friends?"

Hammer forced a smile at the interchange, but it was only a shimmer across lines of fear and anger. On one wall was a communicator, a flat, meter-broad screen whose surface was an optical pickup as well as a display. Hammer stepped in front of it and drew the curtain to blank the remainder of the room. His fingers flicked the controls, bringing Captain Stilchey into startled focus. Tromp's aide blinked, but before he could speak the colonel said, "We've got three minutes, Stilchey, and there's no time to cop around. Put me through."

Stilchey's mouth closed. Without comment he reached out and pressed his own control panel. With liquid abruptness his figure was replaced by the hulking power of Secretary Tromp, seated against the closing sky.

"Tell the Guard to ground arms, Secretary," Hammer ordered in a voice trembling with adrenaline. "Tell them now and I'll get on the horn to my boys—it'll be close."

"I'm sorry for the necessity of your arrest, Colonel," the big man began, "but—"

"Idiot!" Hammer shouted at the pickup, and his arm slashed aside the drapes to bare the room. "I heard your terms—now listen to mine. I've arranged for a freighter to land tomorrow at 0700 and the whole regiment's leaving on it. I'll leave you an indenture for the fair value of the gear, and it'll be paid off as soon as contracts start coming in. But the Lord help you, Tromp, if anybody tries to stop my boys."

"Captain Stilchey," Tromp ordered coolly, "sound general quarters. As for you, Colonel," he continued without taking verbal notice of the carnage behind the small officer, "I assure you that the possibility you planned something like this was in my mind when I ordered the Guards landed with me."

"Secretary, we planned what we'd do if we had to a month and a half ago. Don't be so curst a fool to doubt my boys can execute orders without me to hold their hands. If I don't radio in the next few seconds, you won't have the Guards to send back. Lord and *Martyrs*, man, don't you understand what you see back of me? This isn't some coppy parade!"

"Sir," came Stilchey's thin voice from offscreen, "Fire Central reports all satellite signals are being jammed. The armored units in the Crescent began assembling thirty— Lord! Lord! *Sir!*"

A huge scarlet dome swelled upward across the vitril behind Tromp. The window powdered harmlessly an instant later as the shock wave threw man and desk toward Hammer's image. The entire hotel shuddered to the blast.

"They're blowing up the artillery," the captain bleated. "The ammunition—" His words were drowned in the twin detonations of the remaining batteries.

Hammer switched the communicator off. "Early," he muttered. "Not that it mattered!" His face was set like that of a man who had told his disbelieving mechanic that something was wrong with the brakes, and who now feels the pedal sink to the firewall to prove him fatally correct. "Don't go to sleep," he grunted to his companions. "Tromp knows he's lost, and I'm not sure how he'll react."

But only Worzer was in the room with him.

Though Tromp was uninjured, he rose only to his knees. He had seen Captain Stilchey when the jagged sheet of iridium buzz-sawed into the suite and through him. Scuttling like a stiff-legged bear, the civilian made his way to the private dropshaft built into the room. He pretended to ignore the warm greasiness of the floor, but by the time the platform began to sink his whole body was trembling.

Ground floor was a chaos of half-dressed officers who had been on the way to their units when fire raked the encampment. Tromp pushed through a trio of chattering captains in the branch corridor; the main lobby of bronze and off-planet stonework was packed and static, filled with men afraid to go out and uncertain where to hide. The councillor cursed. The door nearest him was ajar and he kicked it fully open. The furniture within was in sleep-mode, the self-cleaning sheets rumpled on the bed, but

there was no one present. The vitril outer wall had
pulverized; gouges in the interior suggested more than a
shock wave had been responsible for the damage.

Seen through it, the starport had become a raving hell.

Four hundred meters from the hotel, one of the anti-
artillery weapons was rippling sequential flame skyward from
its eight barrels. High in a boiling thunderhead at its radar-
chosen point of aim, man-made lightning flared magenta: high
explosive caught in flight. Almost simultaneously a dart of
cyan more intense than the sun lanced into the Guard vehicle.
Metal heated too swiftly to melt and sublimed in a glowing
ball that silhouetted the gun crew as it devoured them.
Hammer's tanks, bunkered in the Crescent, were using
satellite-computed deflections to rake the open Guard
positions. Twenty kilometers and the thin armor of the lighter
vehicles were no defense against the 200mm powerguns.

Tromp stepped over the low sill and began to run. The
field was wet and a new slash of rain pocked its gleam. Three
shells popped high in the air. He ignored them, pounding
across the field in a half-crouch. For a moment the whistling
beginning to fill the sky as if from a thousand tiny mouths
meant nothing to him either—then realization rammed a
scream from his throat and he threw himself prone. The
bomblets showering down from the shells went off on impact
all across the field, orange flashes that each clipped the air
with scores of fragments. Panic and Hammer's tanks had
silenced the Guard's defensive weaponry. Now the rocket
howitzers were free to rain in wilful death.

But the tanks, Tromp thought as he stumbled to his feet,
they can't knock out the tanks from twenty kilometers and
they can't capture the port while the Guard still has that
punch. The surprise was over now. Lift fans keened from
the perimeter as the great silvery forms of armored vehicles
shifted from their targeted positions. The combatants were
equal and a standoff meant disaster for the mercenaries.

Much of the blood staining Tromp's clothing was his
own, licked from his veins by shrapnel. Incoming shells
were bursting at ten-second intervals. Munitions shortages
would force a slowdown soon, but for the moment anyone

who stood to run would be scythed down before his third step. Even flat on his belly Tromp was being stung by hot metal. His goal, the ten-place courier vessel that had brought him to Melpomone, was still hopelessly far off. The remains, however, of one of the Guard's self-propelled howitzers lay like a cleat-kicked drink-can thirty meters distant. Painfully the councillor crawled into its shelter. Hammer's punishing fire had not been directed at the guns themselves but at the haulers in the midst of each battery. After three shots, the secondary explosions had stripped the Guard of all its ill-sited artillery.

A line of rain rippled across the field, streaking dried blood from Tromp's face and whipping the pooled water. He was not running away. There was one service yet that he could perform for Friesland, and he had to be home to accomplish it. After that—and he thought of it not as revenge but as a final duty—he would not care that reaction would assuredly make him the scapegoat for the catastrophe now exploding all around him. It was obvious that Hammer had ordered his men to disturb the spaceport as little as possible so that the mercenaries would not hinder their own embarkation. The lightly rattling shrapnel crumpled gun crews and the bewildered Guard infantry, but it would not harm the port facilities themselves or the ships docked there.

For the past several minutes no powerguns had lighted the field. The bunkered mercenaries had either completed their programs or ceased fire when a lack of secondary explosions informed them that the remaining Guard vehicles had left their targeted positions. The defenders had at first fired wild volleys at no better target than the mountain range itself, but a few minutes' experience had taught them that the return blasts aimed at their muzzles were far more effective than their own could possibly be. Now there was a lull in the shelling as well.

Tromp eased a careful glance beyond the rim of his shelter, the buckled plenum chamber of the gun carriage. His ship was a horizontal needle three hundred meters distant. The vessel was unlighted, limned as a gray shadow by cloud-hopping lightning. The same flashes gleamed momentarily on the wet turtle-backs of a dozen tanks and combat cars in a nearby cluster, their fans idling. All the surviving Guard units must be clumped in similar hedgehogs across the port.

The big man tensed himself to run; then the night popped and crackled as a Guard tank began firing out into the storm. Tromp counted three shots before a cyan dazzle struck the engaged vehicle amidships and its own ammunition went off with an electric crash. The clustered vehicles were lit by a blue-green fire that expanded for three seconds, dissolving everything within twenty meters of its center. One of the remaining combat cars spun on howling fans, but it collapsed around another bolt before it could pull clear. There were Guardsmen on the ground now, running from their vehicles. Tromp's eyes danced with afterimages of the exploding tank, and for the first time he understood why Stilchey had been so terrified by the destruction of the car he might have ridden in.

Half a dozen shots ripped from beyond the perimeter and several struck home together. All the Guard blowers were burning now, throwing capering shadows beyond the councillor's shelter. Then, threading their way around the pools of slag, the steam and the dying fires, came a trio of tanks. Even without the scarlet wand wavering from each turret for identification, Tromp would have realized these were not the polished beauties of the Guard. The steel skirts of their plenum chambers were rusty and brushworn. One's gouged turret still glowed where a heavy powergun had hit it glancingly; the muzzle of its own weapon glowed too, and the bubbling remains of the perimeter defense left no doubt whose bolts had been more accurately directed. The fighting had been brief, Hammer's platoons meeting the disorganized Guardsmen with pointblank volleys. The victors' hatches were open and as they swept in toward the central tower, Tromp could hear their radios crackling triumphant instructions. Other wands floated across the immense field, red foxfire in the rain.

The shooting had stopped. Now, before the combat cars and infantry followed up the penetrations their tanks had made, Tromp stood and ran to his ship. His career was ruined, of that he had no doubt. No amount of deceit would cover his role in the creation of the Slammers or his leadership in the attempted suppression. All that was left to Nicholas Tromp was the sapphire determination that the national power which he had worked four decades to build should not fall with him. They could still smash Hammer before he got started, using Friesland's own fleet and the fleets of a dozen other worlds. The cost would leave even Friesland groaning, but they could blast the Slammers inexorably from space wherever they were landed. For the sake of his planet's future, the excision had to be made, damn the cost.

And after Tromp fell in disgrace in the next week or two weeks at most, there would be no man left with the power to force the action or the foresight to see its necessity. Panting, he staggered through his vessel's open lock. The interior, too, was unlighted. That was not surprising in view of the combat outside, but one of the three crewmen should have been waiting at the lock. "Where are you?" Tromp called angrily.

The lights went on. There was a body at the big Frisian's feet. From the cockpit forward stretched another hairline of blood still fresh enough to ooze. "I'm here," said a cultured voice from behind.

Tromp froze. Very slowly, he began to turn his head.

"People like you," the voice continued, "with dreams too big for men to fit into, don't see the same sort of world that the rest of us do. And sometimes a fellow who does one job well can see where his job has to be done, even though a better man has overlooked it. Anyhow, Secretary, there always was one thing you and I could agree on—lives *are* cheap."

Surely Joachim's wrists were too slim, Tromp thought, to raise his heavy pistol so swiftly.

AT ANY PRICE

Ferad's body scales were the greenish black of extreme old age, but his brow horns—the right one twisted into a corkscrew from birth—were still a rich gray like the iridium barrel of the powergun he held. The fingertips of his left hand touched the metal, contact that would have been distracting to most of his fellows during the preliminaries to teleportation.

Molt warriors had no universal technique, however, and Ferad had grown used to keeping physical contact with the metallic or crystalline portion of whatever it was that he intended to carry with him. He was far too old to change a successful method now, especially as he prepared for what might be the most difficult teleportation ever in the history of his species—the intelligent autochthons of the planet named Oltenia by its human settlers three centuries before.

The antechamber of the main nursery cave had a high ceiling and a circular floor eighteen meters in diameter. A dozen tunnel archways led from it. Many young Molt warriors were shimmering out of empty air, using the antechamber as a bolthole from the fighting forty kilometers away. The familiar surroundings and the mass of living rock from which the chamber was carved made it an easy resort for relative youths, when hostile fire ripped toward them in the press of battle.

The vaulted chamber was alive with warriors' cries, fear or triumph or simply relief, as they returned to catch their

32

breath and load their weapons before popping back to attack from a new position. One adolescent cackled in splendid glee though his left arm was in tatters from a close-range gunshot: in his right hand the youth carried both an Oltenian shotgun and the mustached head of the human who had owned it before him. The ripe sweat of the warriors mingled with propellant residues from projectile weapons and the dry, arch-of-the-mouth taste of iridium from powerguns which still glowed with the heat of rapid fire.

Sopasian, Ferad's junior by a day and his rival for a long lifetime, sat eighteen meters away, across the width of the chamber. Each of the two theme elders planned in his way to change the face of the three-year war with the humans. Sopasian's face was as taut with strain as that of any post-adolescent preparing for the solo hunt which would make him a warrior.

Sopasian always tried too hard, thought Ferad as he eyed the other theme elder; but that was what worked, had always worked, for Sopasian. In his right hand was not a gun bought from a human trader or looted from an adversary but rather a traditional weapon: a hand-forged dagger, hafted with bone in the days when Molt warriors fought one another and their planet was their own. While Ferad stroked his gunbarrel to permit him to slide it more easily through the interstices of intervening matter, Sopasian's left hand fiercely gripped a disk of synthetic sapphire.

The two elders had discussed their plans with the cautious precision of mutually-acknowledged experts who disliked one another. Aloud, Ferad had questioned the premise of Sopasian's plan. Consciously but unsaid, he doubted his rival or *anyone* could execute a plan calling for so perfect a leap to a tiny object in motion.

Still deeper in his heart, Ferad knew that he was rotten with envy at the very possibility that the other theme elder would succeed in a teleportation that difficult. Well, to be old and wise was not to be a saint; and a success by Sopasian would certainly make it easier for Ferad to gain his ends with the humans.

The humans, unfortunately, were only half the problem—and the result Sopasian contemplated would make his fellow Molts even more intransigent. Concern for the repercussions of his plan and the shouts of young warriors like those who had made the war inevitable merged with the background as Ferad's mind tried to grip the electrical ambience of his world. The antechamber itself was a hollow of energy—the crystalline structure of the surrounding rocks, constantly deforming as part of the dynamic stasis in which every planetary crust was held, generated an aura of piezoelectrical energy of high amplitude.

Ferad used the shell of living rock as an anchor as his consciousness slipped out in an expanding circle, searching to a distance his fellows—even Sopasian—found inconceivable. For the younger warriors, such a solid base was almost a necessity unless their goal was very well-known to them and equally rich in energy flux. As they aged, male Molts not only gained conscious experience in teleportation but became better attuned to their planet on a biological level, permitting jumps of increasing distance and delicacy.

In circumstances such as these, the result was that Molts became increasingly effective warriors in direct proportion to their growing distaste for the glory which had animated them in their hot-blooded youth. By the time they had reached Ferad's age . . .

The last object of which Ferad was aware within the antechamber was an internally-scored five-centimeter disk, the condensing unit for a sophisticated instrument display. The disk came from a disabled combat car, one of those used by the mercenaries whom the human colonists had hired to support them in their war with the Molts.

Sopasian held the crystal in his left hand as his mind searched for a particular duplicate of it: the location-plotter in the vehicle used by Colonel Alois Hammer himself.

"Largo, vector three-thirty!" called Lieutenant Enzo Hawker as Profile Bourne, his sergeant-driver, disrupted the air-condensed hologram display momentarily by firing his powergun through the middle of it.

A bush with leaves like clawing fingers sprawled over a slab of rock a few meters from the Slammers' jeep. Stems which bolts from the submachine gun touched popped loudly, and the Molt warrior just condensing into local existence gave a strangled cry as he collapsed over his own human-manufactured powergun.

"Via!" the little sergeant shouted as he backed the air-cushion jeep left-handed. "Somebody get this rock over here. Blood and martyrs, that's right on top of us!"

An infantryman still aboard his grounded skimmer caught the shimmer of a Molt teleporting in along the vector for which Hawker had warned. He fired, a trifle too early to hit the attacker whose imminent appearance had ionized a pocket of air which the detection apparatus on the jeep had located. The cyan bolt blew a basin the size of a dinnerplate into the rock face on which the Molt was homing. Then the ten-kilo shaped charge which Oltenian engineers had previously placed shattered the rock and the autochthon warrior himself into a sphere of flying gravel and less recognizable constituents.

Ducking against the shower of light stones, a pair of Oltenians gripping another shaped charge and the bracket that would hold it two meters off the ground scuttled toward the slab on which Bourne's victim quivered in death. A trooper on the right flank of the company, controlled by the other detection jeep, missed something wildly and sent a bolt overhead with a hiss-*thump!* which made even veteran Slammers cringe. The two locals flattened themselves, but they got to their feet again and continued even though one of the pair was visibly weeping. They had balls, not like most of the poofs.

Not like the battalion supposedly advancing to support this thrust by a company of Hammer's infantry reinforced by a platoon of Oltenian combat engineers.

"Spike to Red One," said Hawker's commo helmet—and Bourne's, because the tall heavy-set lieutenant had delib-erately split the feed to his driver through the intercom

circuits. Profile was the team's legs; and here on Oltenia
especially, Hawker did not want to have to repeat an order
to bug out. "Fox Victor—" the Oltenian battalion "—is hung
up. Artillery broke up an outcrop, but seems like the Molts
are homing on the boulders even. There's some heavy help
coming, but it'll be a while. Think you might be able to
do some good?"

"Bloody buggerin' *poofs*," Sergeant Bourne muttered as
he bent in anticipation of the charge blasting the nearby
slab, while the pipper on the map display glowed on a
broad gully a kilometer away as "Spike"—the company
commander, Henderson—pinpointed the problem.

The pair of detection jeeps were attached to the infantry
for this operation, but Hawker's chain of command was
directly to Central—Hammer's headquarters—and the idea
wasn't one that Henderson was likely to phrase as an order
even to someone unquestionably under his control. The
Slammers had been on Oltenia for only a few days before
the practice of trusting their safety to local support had
proven to be the next thing to suicide.

But the present fact was that the company was safe
enough only for the moment, with the larger crystalline rocks
within their perimeter broken up. The autochthons could—
given time to approach the position instead of teleporting
directly from some distant location—home on very small
crystals indeed. Unless somebody shook loose Fox Victor, the
troopers in this lead element were well and truly screwed.

Hawker rubbed his face with his big left hand, squeezing
away the prickling caused by Bourne's nearby shots and
the nervous quiver inevitable because of what he knew he
had to say. "All right," he muttered, "all right, we'll be the
fire brigade on this one too."

A hillock six hundred meters distant shattered into
shellbursts turbid with dirt and bits of tree. Waves quivered
across the ground beneath the jeep for a moment before
the blast reached the crew through the air. Bourne cursed
again though the artillery was friendly, the guns trying to
forestall Molt snipers by pulverizing a site to which they
could easily teleport. The attempt was a reminder that no

amount of shelling could interdict all outcrops within the line-of-sight range of a powergun.

"Want an escort, Red One?" asked the company commander, flattened somewhere beside his own jeep while his driver's gun wavered across each nearby spray of vegetation, waiting for the warning that it was about to hold a Molt warrior.

"Profile?" asked Lieutenant Hawker, shouting over the fan whine rather than using the intercom.

"What a bloody copping *mess*," grunted the sergeant as his left hand spun the tiller and the fans spun the jeep beneath them. "Hang on," he added, late but needlessly: Hawker knew to brace himself before he said anything that was going to spark his driver into action. "No, we don't want to bloody babysit pongos!" and the jeep swung from its axial turn into acceleration as smooth as the brightness curve of rheostat-governed lights.

"Cover your own ass, Spike," Hawker reported as the jeep sailed past a trio of grounded infantrymen facing out from a common center like the spokes of a wheel. "We'll do better alone."

The trouble with being a good all-rounder was that you were used when people with narrower capacities got to hunker down and pray. The other detection team, Red Two, consisted of a driver possibly as good as Bourne and a warrant officer who could handle the detection gear at least as well as Hawker. But while no one in the Slammers was an innocent about guns, neither of the Red Two team was the man you really wanted at your side in a firefight. They would do fine, handling detection chores for the entire company during this lull while the autochthones regrouped and licked their wounds.

Red One, on the other hand, was headed for the stalled support force, unaccompanied by skimmer-mounted infantry who would complicate the mad dash Profile intended to make.

Shells passed so high overhead that they left vapor trails and their attenuated howl was lost in the sizzle of brush slapping the jeep's plenum chamber.

"Gimme the push for Fox Victor," Hawker demanded of Central, as his right hand gripped his submachine gun and his eyes scanned the route by which Bourne took them to where the supports were bottlenecked.

The Slammers lieutenant was watching for Molts who, already in position, would not give warning through the display of his detection gear. But if one of those bright-uniformed, totally-incompetent Oltenian general officers suddenly appeared in his gunsights . . .

Enzo Hawker might just decide a burst wouldn't be wasted.

The gorgeous clothing of the officers attending the Widows of the War Ball in the Tribunal Palace differed in cut from the gowns of the ladies, but not in quality or brilliance. General Alexander Radescu, whose sardonic whim had caused him to limit his outfit to that prescribed for dress uniforms in the *Handbook for Officers in the Service of the Oltenian State*, knew that he looked ascetic in comparison to almost anyone else in the Grand Ballroom—his aide, Major Nikki Tzigara, included.

"Well, the lily has a certain dignity that a bed of tulips can't equal, don't you think?" murmured the thirty-two-year-old general as his oval fingernails traced a pattern of lines down the pearly fabric of his opposite sleeve.

Nikki, who had added yellow cuffs and collar to emphasize the scarlet bodice of his uniform jacket, grinned at the reference which he alone was meant to hear in the bustle of the gala. From beyond Tzigara, however, where he lounged against one of the pair of huge urns polished from blue john—columnar fluorspar—by Molt craftsmen in the dim past, Major Joachim Steuben asked, "And what does that leave me, General? The dirt in the bottom of the pot?"

Colonel Hammer's chief of base operations in the Oltenian capital flicked a hand as delicately manicured as Radescu's own across his own khaki uniform. Though all the materials were of the highest quality, Steuben's ensemble had a restrained elegance—save for the gaudily-floral inlays of the pistol, which was apparently as much part of the Slammers dress uniform as the gold-brimmed cap was for an Oltenian general officer. In fact, Major Steuben looked very good indeed in his tailored khaki, rather like a leaf-bladed dagger in an intarsia sheath. Though flawlessly personable, Steuben had an aura which Radescu himself found at best disconcerting: Radescu's mind kept focusing on the fact that there was a skull beneath that tanned, smiling face.

But Joachim Steuben got along well in dealing with his Oltenian counterparts here in Belvedere. The first officer whom Hammer had given the task of liaison and organizing his line of supply from the starport had loudly referred to the local forces as poofs. That was understandable, Radescu knew; but very impolitic.

Nikki, who either did not see or was not put off by the core of Joachim which Radescu glimpsed, was saying, "Oh, Major Steuben, *you* dirt?" when the string orchestra swung into a gavotte and covered the remainder of the pair's smalltalk.

Every man Radescu could see in the room was wearing a uniform of some kind. The regulars, like Nikki Tzigara, modified the stock design for greater color; but the real palm went to the "generals" and "marshals" of militia units which mustered only on paper. These were the aristocratic owners of mines, factories, and the great ranches which were the third leg of human success on Oltenia. They wore not only the finest imported natural and synthetic fabrics, but furs, plumes, and—in one case of strikingly poor taste, Radescu thought—a shoulder cape flayed from the scaly hide of an adolescent Molt. Officers of all sorts spun and postured with their jeweled ladies, the whole seeming to the young general the workings of an ill-made machine rather than a fund-raiser for the shockingly large number of relicts created in three years of war.

Radescu lifted his cap and combed his fingers through the pale, blond hair which was plastered now to his scalp by perspiration. The second blue john vase felt cool to his back, but the memories it aroused increased his depression. The only large-scale celebrations of which the autochthons, the Molts, had not been a part were those during the present war. While not everyone—yet—shared the general's opinion that the war was an unmitigated disaster, the failure of this gathering to include representatives of the fourteen Molt themes made it less colorful in a way that no amount of feathers and cloth-of-gold could repair.

A gust of air, cool at any time and now balm in the steaming swamps, played across the back of Radescu's neck and the exposed skin of his wrists. He turned to see a scarlet Honor Guard disappearing from view as he closed a door into the interior of the Tribunal Palace. The man who had just entered the ballroom was the Chief Tribune and effective ruler of Oltenia, Grigor Antonescu.

"Well met, my boy," said the Chief Tribune as he saw General Radescu almost in front of him. There was nothing in the tone to suggest that Antonescu felt well about anything, nor was that simply a result of his traditional reserve. Radescu knew the Chief Tribune well enough to realize that something was very badly wrong, and that beneath the wall of stony facial control there was a mind roiling with anger.

"Good evening, Uncle Grigor," Radescu said, bowing with more formality than he would normally have shown his mother's brother, deferring to the older man's concealed agitation. "I don't get as much chance to see you as I'd like, with your present duties."

There were factory owners on the dance floor who could have bought Alexander Radescu's considerable holdings twice over; but there was no one with a closer path to real power if he chose to travel it.

"You have good sense, Alexi," Antonescu said with an undertone of bitterness that only an ear as experienced as Radescu's own would have heard.

The Chief Tribune wore his formal robes of office, spotlessly white and of a severity unequaled by even the functional uniform of Joachim Steuben . . . who seemed to have disappeared. Another man in Grigor Antonescu's position might have designed new regalia more in line with present tastes or at least relieved the white vestments' severity with jewels and metals and brightly-patterned fabrics rather the way Nikki had with his uniform (and where *was* Nikki?). Chief Tribune Antonescu knew, however, that through the starkness of a pure neutral color he would draw eyes like an ax blade in a field of poppies.

"It's time," Antonescu continued, with a glance toward the door and away again, "that I talk to *someone* who has good sense."

On the dance floor, couples were parading through the steps of a sprightly *contre-danse*—country dance—to the bowing of the string orchestra. The figures moving in attempted synchrony reminded Alexander Radescu now of a breeze through an arboretum rather than of a machine. "Shall we . . . ?" the general suggested mildly with a short, full-hand gesture toward the door through which his uncle had so recently appeared.

The man-high urns formed an effective alcove around the door, while the music and the bustle of dancing provided a sponge of sound to absorb conversations at any distance from the speakers. Chief Tribune Antonescu gave another quick look around him and said, gesturing his nephew closer, "No, I suppose I need to show myself at these events to avoid being called an unapproachable dictator." He gave Radescu a smile as crisp as the glitter of shears cutting sheet metal: both men knew that the adjective and the noun alike were more true than not.

"Besides," Antonescu added with a rare grimace, "if we go back inside we're likely to meet my esteemed colleagues—" Tribunes Wraslov and Deliu "—and having just spent an hour with their inanity, I don't care to repeat the dose for some while."

"There's trouble, then?" the young general asked, too softly in all likelihood to be heard even though he was stepping shoulder to shoulder as the older man had directed.

There was really no need for the question anyway, since Antonescu was already explaining, "The great offensive that Marshal Erzul promised has stalled. Again, of course."

A resplendent colonel walked past, a young aide on his

arm. They both noticed the Chief Tribune and his nephew and looked away at once with the terrified intensity of men who feared they would be called to book. Radescu waited until the pair had drifted on, then said, "It was only to get under way this morning. Initial problems don't necessarily mean—"

"Stalled. Failed. Collapsed totally," Antonescu said in his smooth, cool voice, smiling at his nephew as though they were discussing the gay rout on the dance floor. "According to Erzul, the only units which haven't fallen back to their starting line decimated are those with which he's lost contact entirely."

"Via, he *can't* lose contact!" Radescu snapped as his mind retrieved the Operation Order he had committed to memory. His post, Military Advisor to the Tribunes, was meant to be a sinecure. That General Radescu had used his access to really study the way the Oltenian State fought the autochthones was a measure of the man, rather than of his duties. "Every *man* in the forward elements has a personal radio to prevent just that!"

"Every man alive, yes," his uncle said. "That was the conclusion I drew, too."

"And—" Radescu began, then paused as he stepped out from the alcove to make sure that he did not mistake the absence of Major Steuben before he completed his sentence with, "and Hammer's Slammers, were they unable to make headway also? Because if they were . . ." He did not go on by saying, ". . . then the war is patently unwinnable, no matter what level of effort we're willing to invest." Uncle Grigor did not need a relative half his age to state the obvious to him.

Antonescu gave a minute nod of approval for the way his nephew had this time checked their surroundings before speaking. "Yes, that's the question that seems most frustrating," he replied as the *contre-danse* spun to a halt and the complex patterns dissolved.

"Erzul—he was on the screen in person—says the mercenaries failed to advance, but he says it in a fashion that convinces me he's lying. I presume that there has been another failure to follow up thrusts by Hammer's units."

The Chief Tribune barked out a laugh as humorless as the stuttering of an automatic weapon. "If Erzul were a better commander, he wouldn't *need* to be a good liar," he said.

The younger man looked at the pair of urns. At night functions they were sometimes illuminated by spotlights beamed down on their interiors, so that the violet tinge came through the huge, indigo grains and the white calcite matrix glowed with power enchained. Tonight the stone was unlighted, and only reflections from the smooth surfaces belied its appearance of opacity.

"The trouble is," Radescu said, letting his thoughts blend into the words his lips were speaking, "that Erzul and the rest keep thinking of the Molts as humans who can teleport and therefore can never be caught. That means every battle is on the Molts' terms. But they *don't* think the way we do, the way humans do, as a society. They're too individual."

The blue john urns were slightly asymmetric, proving that they had been polished into shape purely by hand instead of being lathe-turned as any human craftsman would have done. That in itself was an amazing comment on workmanship, given that the material had such pronounced lines of cleavage and was so prone to splinter under stress. Even the resin with which the urns were impregnated was an addition by the settlers to whom the gift was made, preserving for generations the micron-smooth polish which a Molt had achieved with no tool but the palms of his hands over a decade.

But there was more. Though the urns were asymmetric, they were precise mirror images of one another.

"If we don't understand the way the Molts relate to each other and to the structure of their planet," said Alexander Radescu with a gesture that followed the curve of the right-hand urn without quite touching the delicate surface, "then we don't get anywhere with the war.

"And until then, there's no chance to convince the Molts to make peace."

❖   ❖   ❖

The ambience over which Ferad's mind coursed was as real and as mercurial as the wave-strewn surface of a sea. He knew that at any given time there were hundreds, perhaps thousands, of his fellows hurling themselves from point to point in transfers which seemed instantaneous only from the outside. There was no sign of others in this universe of stresses and energy, a universe which was that of the Molts uniquely.

That was the key to the character of male Molts, Ferad had realized over the more than a century that he observed his race and the human settlers. Molt females cooperated among themselves in nurturing the young and in agriculture—they had even expanded that cooperation to include animal husbandry, since the human settlement. The prepubescent males cooperated also, playing together even when the games involved teleportation for the kilometer or so of which they and the females were capable.

But with the hormonal changes of puberty, a male's world became a boundless, vacant expanse that was probably a psychological construct rather than a 'real' place— but which was no less real for all that.

In order to transport himself to a point in the material landscape, a Molt had to identify his destination in the dreamworld of energy patterns and crystal junctions that depended both on the size of the object being used as a beacon and on its distance from the point of departure. Most of all, however, finding a location depended on the experience of the Molt who picked his way across the interface of mind and piezoelectrical flux.

That focus on self deeply affected the ability of males to consider anything but individual performance. Hunters, especially the young who were at pains to prove their prowess, would raid the herds of human ranchers without consideration of the effect that had on settler-autochthon relations. And, even to the voice of Ferad's dispassionate experience, it was clear that there would be human herds and human cities covering the planet like studded leather upholstery if matters continued as they began three centuries before.

But while the war might be a necessary catalyst for change, no society built on continued warfare would be beneficial to Man or Molt.

The greater questions of civilization which had been filling Ferad's time in the material world were secondary now in this fluid moment. Crystals which he knew—which he had seen or walked across or handled—were solid foci within the drift. They shrank as the theme elder's mind circled outward, but they did not quickly lose definition for him as they would have done decades or a century earlier.

The psychic mass of the powergun Ferad held created a drag, but his efforts to bring the weapon into tune with his body by stroking the metal now worked to his benefit. He handled the gun in teleporting more easily than he did its physical weight in the material world. His race had not needed the bulk and power of human hunters because their pursuit was not through muscular effort and they struck their quarry unaware, not aroused and violent. Besides that, Ferad was very old, and gravity's tug on the iridium barrel was almost greater than his shrunken arms could resist.

He would hold the weapon up for long enough. Of that he was sure.

Ferad's goal was of unique difficulty, not only because of the distance over which he was teleporting but also due to the nature of the objects on which he was homing. He had never seen, much less touched them; but an ancestor of his had spent years polishing the great urns from solid blocks of blue john. That racial memory was a part of Ferad, poised in momentary limbo between the central cave system of his theme and the Tribunal Palace in Belvedere.

A part of him like the powergun in his hands.

"Shot," called the battery controller through the commo helmets, giving Hawker and Bourne the warning they would have had a few seconds earlier had the rush of their passage not shut off outside sounds as slight as the first pop of the firecracker round. The initial explosion was only large enough to split the twenty-centimeter shell casing short of the impact point and strew its cargo of five hundred bomblets like a charge of high-explosive buckshot.

"Via!" swore the sergeant angrily, because they were in a swale as open as a whore's cunt and the hologram display which he could see from the corner of his eye was giving a warning of its own. The yellow figures which changed only to reflect the position of the moving jeep were now replaced by a nervous flickering from that yellow to the violet which was its optical reciprocal, giving Lieutenant Hawker the location at which a Molt warrior was about to appear in the near vicinity. It was a lousy time to have to duck from a firecracker round.

But Via, they'd known the timing had to be close to clear the ridge before the jeep took its position to *keep* the bottleneck open. Bourne knew that to kill forward motion by lifting the bow would make the slowing jeep a taller target for snipers, while making an axial 180° turn against the vehicle's forward motion might affect the precision with which the Loot called a bearing on the teleporting autochthon. The driver's left hand released the tiller and threw the lever tilting the fan nacelles to exhaust at full forward angle.

His right hand, its palm covered with a fluorescent tattoo which literally snaked all the way up his arm, remained where it had been throughout the run: on the grip of his submachine gun.

"Splash," said the battery controller five seconds after the warning, and the jeep's inertia coasted it to a halt in the waving, head-high grain. A white glow played across the top of the next rise, mowing undergrowth and stripping bark and foliage from the larger trees. The electrical crackle of the bomblets going off started a second later, accompanied by the murderous hum of an object flung by the explosions, a stone or piece of casing which had not disintegrated the way it should have—deadly in either case, even at three hundred meters, had it not missed Bourne's helmet by a hand's breadth.

"Loot!" the driver called desperately. The burring fragment could be ignored as so many dangers survived had been ignored before. But the Molt warrior who by now was in full control of his body and whatever weapon he held, somewhere beyond the waving curtain of grain . . . "Which *way*, Loot, which way!"

"Hold it," said Lieutenant Hawker, an order and not an answer as he jumped to his full meter-ninety height on the seat of the jeep with his gun pointing over the driver's head. There was a feral hiss as Hawker's weapon spewed plastic casings from the ejection port and cyan fire from the muzzle. Profile Bourne's cheeks prickled, and a line of vegetation withered as the burst angled into the grain.

There was a scream from downrange. The sergeant slammed his throttle and the nacelle angle into maximum drive even as his teammate dropped back into a sitting position, the muzzle of his powergun sizzling as it cooled from white to lambent gray. The scream had been high-pitched and double, so that the driver did not need to hear Hawker say, "*Cop!* It was a female and a kid, but I thought she had a bloody satchel charge!"

It wasn't the sort of problem that bothered Bourne a whole lot, but he didn't like to see the Loot so distressed.

The reason Fox Victor was having problems—beyond the fact that they were poofs who couldn't be trusted in a rainstorm, much less a firefight—was obvious on this, the reverse slope of the gully which formed the actual choke-point for the support column. Low retaining walls curved back into the sloping hillside like arms outstretched by the arched opening in their center: the entrance to what the Oltenians called a Molt nursery cave.

In fact, the underground constructs of which this was a small example were almost never true caves but rather tunnels carved into igneous and metamorphic rocks of dense crystalline structure. The sedimentary rocks which could be cut or leached away into caves by groundwater were of no use as beacons for teleporting autochthons—and thus of no use in training young Molts to use their unique abilities.

By being surrounded from earliest infancy with living

rock whose crystals were in a constant state of piezoelectrical flux, Molts—male and female alike—began to
teleport for short distances before they could crawl. As they
grew older, prepubescents played in the near vicinity of
their nurseries and gained a familiarity with the structure
of those rocks which was deeper than anything else they
would meet in life.

And when called to do so by military need, Molt
warriors could home on even the smallest portions of the
particular locality in which they had been raised. Shelling that broke up the gross structure of a slab did not
affect the ability of warriors to concentrate, though the
damage would ordinarily have at least delayed younger
Molts trying to locate it for teleportation. The result, at
least for poofs without the instruments to detect warriors
before the shooting started, would be disastrous.

Now, while the pair of Slammers were flat out with
nothing but a 15° slope to retard the jeep, the possibility of a Molt teleporting to point-blank range beside them
was the least of Profile Bourne's worries. The bolt that
snapped into the hillside thirty meters away, fluffing and
dimming shell-set grass-fires in its momentary passage, was
a more real danger. The microfragments from the firecracker round had cleared the crest and face of the ridge,
but a Molt somewhere out there, far from the immediate battle scene, continued to snipe at the jeep unde-
terred. The autochthons were not, in the main, good
marksmen, and the vehicle's speed made it a chance target
anyway to a gunman a kilometer distant.

But the chance that let the bolt blow a divot from the
soil and splinters from the rock close beneath might easily
have turned the jeep into a sizzling corona as electrical
storage cells shorted through driver and passenger. It was
nothing to feel complacent about, and there was no way
to respond while the jeep was at speed.

If only they were about to join one of the Slammers'
tank companies instead of a poof battalion! Snipers would
learn that they, like dogs, got one bite—and that a second
attempt meant the ground around them glowed and

bubbled with the energy released by a tank's main gun or a long burst from a tribarrel.

That didn't, of course, always mean that the first bite had not drawn blood. . . .

A less skilled driver would have let his jeep lift bow-high at the crest where the ridge rolled down its other slope. Bourne angled his fan nacelles left, throwing the vehicle into a sideslip which cut upward velocity without stalling the jeep as a target silhouetted in two directions. The grass and low brush of the crest were scarred by the bomblets, and a lump half-hidden by the rock which had sheltered it might have been a warrior caught by the shrapnel.

While Bourne concentrated on his own job, Lieutenant Hawker had been on the horn with the poof battalion commander, their Central-relayed conversation audible to the driver but of no particular interest. All Sergeant Bourne cared was that the Oltenian troops not add their fire to that of the Molts already sniping at the jeep. Men so jumpy from being ripped without recourse might well fire at any target they could hit, even when the intellectual levels of their brains knew that it was the wrong target.

"Profile, a hundred and fifty!" the lieutenant ordered. His left arm reached out through the flashing hologram display in the air before him, converting its digital information into a vector for his driver's gun.

The sergeant grounded the jeep in a stony pocket far enough below the crest to be clear of the Molt marksman who had fired as they climbed the back slope. Molts could teleport in within touching distance, but this time that was the plan; and the rocks jumbled by a heavy shell provided some cover from distant snipers.

Bourne did not fire. He knew exactly where the Molt was going to appear, but spraying the area a hundred and fifty meters down the wash would have been suicidal.

Like most of Hammer's troopers, Sergeant Bourne had seen the wreckage Molt warriors made of Oltenian assaults. He hadn't really appreciated the ease with which disaster happened until he saw what now took place in the swale.

The watercut depression in a fold between crystalline ridges was now studded with rubble cracked from both faces by armor-piercing shells and the blazing remains of half a dozen Oltenian vehicles. The human bodies blended into the landscape better than did equipment marked out by pillars of smoke and sometimes a lapping overlay of kerosene flames, though the corpse halfway out of the driver's hatch of an armored car was obvious with his lifted arms and upturned face—brittle as a charcoal statue.

The single firecracker round had been intended only to clear the Molts briefly from the area. A poof armored car and armored personnel carrier were trying to make a dash across the gully during the lull, however, instead of waiting for the Slammers to get into position as Hawker had directed. Some might have said that showed exemplary courage, but Profile Bourne couldn't care less about fools who died well—which was all this crew was managing.

The automatic weapon in the car's turret traversed the slope toward which the vehicle advanced, making a great deal of dust and racket without affecting in the least the warrior who must have teleported directly between the car and the personnel carrier. Bourne didn't fire at the Molt, knowing that the armored vehicles shielded their attacker and that the poofs across the swale would respond to the submachine gun's 'attack' on their fellows, no matter *how* good their fire discipline might be.

"Via! Three more, Profile," Lieutenant Hawker said, his pointing arm shifting 15° to the right as the swale rang with the sound of a magnetic limpet mine gripping the steel side of the vehicle against which it had been slapped.

Rock broken by heavy shells, brush smoldering where the bursting charges of the antipersonnel bomblets had ignited it. No target yet, but Profile loosed a three-round burst to splash the boulders twenty meters from the oncoming APC and warn the poofs.

The armored car dissolved in a sheet of flame so intense that the shock wave a fraction of a second later seemed a separate event. A trio of Molts froze out of the air where

Hawker had pointed and Bourne's own shots had left glazed scars on the stone a moment before.

He had a target now and he fired over open sights, two rounds into the back of the first warrior and three at the second, who leaped up into the last bolt when molten stone sprayed from the boulder sheltering him. A storm of fire from at least twenty Oltenian guns broke wildly on the general area. The Loot was shouting, "*Close* Profile!" his big arm pointing behind the jeep, but nothing this side of Hell was going to keep Bourne from his third kill—the Molt crouched behind his steaming powergun, firing into the APC as fast as his finger could pull the trigger.

Only when that Molt crumpled did the sergeant spin to shoot over the racked electronics modules replacing the jeep's back seat. Bourne lifted the heat-shivering muzzle of his gun even as his finger took up slack in the trigger. If he had fired as he intended into the center of mass of the warrior coalescing a meter away, the satchel charge the Molt was clutching to his chest would have gone off and vaporized the jeep. Instead, the distorted face of the autochthon dissolved in a burst so needlessly long that even Profile knew that he had panicked.

"Seventy-five," the Loot was saying, and Bourne rotated toward the new target while the decapitated remains of his previous victim toppled backwards. In the swale below, the APC crackled with what sounded like gunfire but was actually the explosion of ammunition within its burning interior. Seventy-five meters, a rough figure but there was a tangled clump of ground cover at about that distance in the direction the Loot was pointing, a flat-topped block jutting like a loggia garden into the gully. Bourne squeezed off what was intended to be a two-round burst alerting the poofs deployed on the further side.

There was a single cyan flicker from the submachine gun—he'd emptied the magazine on the previous Molt, leaving only one lonely disk in the loading pan.

Cursing because the warrior homing on the block was going to get a shot in for sure and the Loot was already pointing another vector, the sergeant swapped magazines.

His eyes were open and searching the terrain for the new target, two hundred meters to the front and closer to the Oltenian battalion than to the jeep. The right handgrip enclosed the magazine well, and a veteran like Bourne had no need to look down for hand to find hand in an operation as familiar as reloading.

He had no need to worry about the warrior his shot had marked, as it turned out.

The standard poof shoulder weapon, a stubby shotgun, did not, with its normal load of flechettes, have the range of the target. The outside surface of the guntube could be used as the launching post for ring-airfoil grenades, however, like the one that hurled a pair of Molts in opposite directions from its yellow flash in the center of the target. Turret guns from armored vehicles were raking the blasted area as well, even hitting the corpses as they tumbled.

Could be some a' the poofs had sand in their craws after all.

A powergun too distant to be a target for Bourne under these circumstances was emptied in the direction of the jeep as fast as some warrior could pull the trigger. The bolts weren't really close—some of them were high enough for their saturated blue-green color to be lost in the sunlight. The trio that spattered rock eighty meters from the jeep— forty meters, twenty—were not less terrifying, however, for the fact that the next three missed by more than the sergeant could track.

Bourne's burst toward the Loot's latest warning was careless if not exactly frightened. He couldn't see anything and it was less of a threat than the snipers now ranging on them anyway . . . and then, when the Molt leaped into his vision while poof guns chopped furiously, the sergeant realized that the warrior was hiding from *him*, from the jeep, and fatally ignoring the Oltenians.

"Fox Victor," Lieutenant Hawker ordered, "roll 'em," and the bolt that shattered a boulder into fist-sized chunks ringing on the jeep came from the angle opposite the previous sniper.

"Loot, it's—" the driver said, reaching for the throttle left-handed. A hilltop barely visible puffed white, shells answering a satellite report of sniping, but that alone wouldn't be enough to save their ass. The trucks and armored vehicles of the poof battalion were rumbling from cover; a couple autochthons fired at them, missing badly. Via! If they could miss the broad, flat sides of an APC, how did they get so bloody close to the sheltered jeep?

"Right," said Hawker as he glanced at his display, still and yellow as it vainly awaited more teleporting autochthons, "let's ro—" and the last word was swept away by his driver's fierce acceleration out of the pocket of stone which had become an aiming point for the enemy far off.

The Loot was on Central's push, now, calling for panzers and a salvo of artillery, while Bourne jinked back up and away and the air winked with ill-aimed sniper fire. The bastards didn't need to be good, just lucky, and the bolt that fried sod a millisecond before the jeep's skirts whisked across it was almost lucky enough. Central was answering calmly, dryly—*their* butts weren't on the line!—but that wasn't something the sergeant had time for anyway. They'd done their job, done it bleedin' *perfectly*, and now it looked like they'd be lucky to get out with a whole skin.

Well, that was what happened when you tried to support the poofs.

As the jeep topped the ridge a second time but in the opposite direction, a bolt snapped past it from the far side of the grain field and coincidentally a truck blew up in the swale behind. The detection team could not prevent the support battalion from taking casualties when it traversed open ground. What the Loot's warnings—and Profile's own submachine gun, its barrel reeking with sublimed iridium and the finish it burned from the breastplate to which the elastic sling held it—*had* accomplished was to eliminate the warriors who knew the terrain so well that they could place themselves within millimeters of an opponent in the gully. There were surely other Molts with a nursery association with this area, but the autochthons—thank the Lord!— didn't have the organization to make a massed response to a sudden threat.

They didn't need to, of course, since a handful of

warriors could stall a poof battalion, and weeks of long-range sniping eroded the Slammers' strength to no human purpose.

The shock wave from a six-tube salvo skewed the jeep even though the shells impacted on the far side of the ridge and none closer than a half kilometer to the course down which Bourne was speeding to escape. The Loot was having the Slammers' hogs blast clear the flanks of the Oltenian battalion, crumbling rocks that would otherwise stand as beacons for Molts bouncing closer to shoot down the axis of the swale. The poofs should've done that themselves, but their artillery control wasn't up to civilized standards, and their gun crews minced around in a funk fearing a Molt with a satchel charge would teleport aboard an ammo transporter. Which had happened often enough to give anybody the willies, come to think.

The warrior who had snapped shots at them earlier now had at least a pair of supporters—one of whom was too bloody good. Bourne spun and braked his vehicle, fearing the brief pause during which their original downhill velocity was precisely balanced by thrust in the new direction. Lord help 'em if the Loot's request for heavy armor didn't come through the way the artillery support had done.

Though Colonel Hammer didn't leave his people hanging if there was any way around it.

The dark arch of the nursery tunnel into which Bourne headed the jeep was a perfect aiming point—hitting the center of a large target is easier than nailing a small one. The sergeant expected the entrance to be criss-crossed by the dazzling scatter of bolts squeezed off with all the care of which Molt marksmen were capable. He figured he had no hope save the autochthons' bad aim or bad timing. That there were no shots at all was as pleasant a surprise as he'd had since the night a whore tried to kill him with what turned out to be an empty gun. . . .

The tunnel was three meters wide and of simple design, an angled gallery rather than a labyrinth of interconnected chambers. The same purpose was achieved either way: the encouragement of the very young to teleport to points separated from them by solid barriers.

The same stone angles were just what the doctor ordered to block sniper fire—and as for anybody teleporting directly into the cave, they were cold meat as soon as the Loot's equipment picked them up.

"Safe!" the driver cried happily as he yanked the tiller left at the first 60° break, an edge of polished black granite that had not been dulled by rubbing shoulders as it would have been in a structure occupied by humans.

The warrior just around that corner pointed his Oltenian shotgun squarely at Profile's face.

Molt cave systems were not unlighted—the autochthons actually saw less well in dim conditions than humans did. The roof of this particular tunnel was painted with a strip of—imported—permanent fluorescent, powered by the same piezoelectrical forces which made the rock a beacon for teleporters. It gave off only a pale glow, however, inadequate for irises contracted by the sun outside, so it was in the jeep's front floods that the Molt's eyes gaped. His shadow against the gleaming stone was half again his real height, and the muzzle of the gun seemed broad as the tunnel.

Bourne fluffed his front fans to full screaming lift with his right hand.

He could have shot, have killed the warrior. Man and Molt were equally surprised, and Profile Bourne's reflexes were a safe bet against just about anybody's in those situations.

And then the charge of flechettes, triggered by the warrior's dying convulsion, would have shredded both men from the waist upward.

Lieutenant Hawker shouted as he fired through the hologram display which had failed to warn him. The Molt was already within the tunnel before the jeep entered, so there were no indicia of teleportation for the apparatus to detect. They should have thought of that, but the lightning-swift danger of the snipers outside had made the cave mouth a vision of safety like none since Mother's bosom.

That was the sort of instinctive error that got your ass killed thought Hawker as his energy bolts scarred long ovals across the ceiling's fluorescence, ricocheting further down the tunnel in diminishing deadliness, and the Molt's shotgun blasted deafeningly into the uplifted skirt and plenum chamber of the jeep.

The screech of the jeep striking and skidding along the tunnel wall at a 45° angle was actively painful to Profile Bourne. You didn't get to be as good a driver as he was without empathy for your vehicle, and the shriek of metal crumpling was to the sergeant comparable to skidding along a hard surface himself. But he'd done that too, thrown himself down on gravel when shots slammed overhead. You do what you gotta do; and anyway, the Molt's body when the jeep hit it provided a pretty fair lubricant.

Their forward velocity had been scrubbed off by the contact rather than killed by the vectored fans in normal fashion. Bourne chopped the throttle so that the braking thrust would not slam them back against the far wall. The jeep slumped down onto its skirts again, its back end ringing on the stone a moment before the whole vehicle came to rest.

The sergeant knew that he ought to be watching the next angle in case another warrior, prepared by the racketing death of the first, came around it shooting. Instead he closed his eyes for a moment and squeezed his hands together hard enough to make the thin flesh start up around the print of each fingertip. Lord, he'd almost pissed himself!

When he opened his eyes, he saw the tiny, glittering dimple in the steel flooring just between his boots. It was a flechette from the shotgun charge which had come within a millimeter of doing the warrior's business—or half of it—despite the fact that the roof of the plenum chamber was in the way.

Lord and martyrs!

"Lord and martyrs," muttered Lieutenant Hawker as he stepped out of the vehicle, and curst if he didn't seem as shook as the driver felt. "Don't worry, got it on aural," he added with a nod toward the hologram display and a left-handed tap on the earpiece of his commo helmet. The data relayed through the headset was less instantly assimilable than what his eyes could intake through the holograms—but there were only two directions from which an attack could come in the tunnel.

Anyhow, Profile figured that he needed to walk out the wobbles he could feel in his legs. Maybe the Loot was the same.

Before the sergeant left the jeep, he switched off the headlights which would otherwise be only a targeting aid to whatever Molts were around. The rock quivered when he stepped onto it, an explosion somewhere, and he cursed or prayed—who knew?—at the thought that another salvo of penetrators on the back slope of the ridge might bring the bloody ceiling down and accomplish what the autochthons had failed to do. What the hell, nobody'd ever told him he'd die in bed.

Bourne skidded at his first step. He glanced down, thinking that the stone beneath his boots must have a glass-smooth polish. It wasn't that—and the Molt with the shotgun deserved worse, it'd been too cursed quick for him.

The two Slammers used handsignals at the next angle, five meters further down the tunnel. They could as easily have subvocalized the plan on the intercom, but Profile's quick tap on his own breastplate and the Loot's grimace of acceptance was all that it took anyway.

Bourne put a single shot against the facing wall, the bolt crackling like shattered brick as it bounced from the stone. A fraction of a second later, the sergeant himself went in low.

The shot might have drawn a reflexive return from anyone poised to meet them around the angle—but there was no one, no adult at least: they were in the nursery itself, a circular room no wider than the tunnel from which it was offset to the left, just around the second angle. There were eighteen reed and moss creches like the pips on an instrument dial, and about half of them still squirmed with infant Molts.

"S'all right, Loot!" Bourne shouted as he rolled into a sitting position; and for all the encouragement of his words, his ankles were crossed in a firm shooter's rest beneath him. "S'all clear, just the babes."

The flash of the shot was still a retinal memory to Bourne as he glanced around the chamber, blinking as if to wash the spreading orange blot from the black surface of his eyeballs. The scars of the ricochet were marked by powdered stone at a constant chest height along the circular wall. No significant amount of energy would have sprayed the infants, but they were mewing fearfully anyway.

The Loot came in behind the muzzle of his gun—you didn't leave decisions of safety to somebody else, even Sergeant Bourne, not in a place like this.

The Molt in the creche closest to Bourne teleported neatly into his lap, scaring the sergeant into a shout and a leap upward that ended with the infant clamped hard against him and the muzzle of Lieutenant Hawker's submachine gun pointed dead on. The little Molt squealed even more loudly.

"Let's get the cop outa here before the locals put a flame gun down the tunnel and investigate later," Hawker said as he ported his weapon again, making no apology for aiming it toward a teleporting autochthon, even one in Bourne's lap. "Doesn't seem those Molts'll snipe at us here, what with the little ones in the line of fire."

"Right," said his driver, kneeling to put the infant back in its—his? her?—creche. There were air shafts cut from the chamber's ceiling to the surface twenty or thirty meters above. Through them now sank, competing with the powergun's ozone prickliness, not only the ash and blast residues of the shelling but the stomach-turning sweetness of diesel fumes. The vehicles of Fox Victor had gained the ridge and should by now be advancing down the reverse slope, covered by shellfire against likely sniper positions.

"No, here," said Lieutenant Hawker, reaching out with a left hand that seemed large enough to encircle the infant Molt which he took from Bourne. "You need to drive. We'll clear these out and then get a squad a' engineers to blow the place before it causes more trouble."

Little bastards looked less human than the adults, Bourne thought as he strode quickly back to the jeep, calm again with the tension of battle released by two sudden shocks within the tunnel. You could only be so scared, and then it all had to let go—or you cracked, and Profile Bourne didn't crack. The limbs of the young Molt were very small, more like those of a newt or lizard than of a human baby. Even as adults, the autochthons were shorter and more lightly built than most humans, but after a few years of age there was no difference in proportions.

"I suppose it's because the ones that crawl least do the other—teleport—better," said the Loot as he swung his big frame into the seat behind the displays, still holding the infant Molt. Via, maybe he *could* read his driver's mind; they'd worked through some curst tight places in the past few years. But it was a natural thing to wonder about if you saw the little ones up close like this, and the Loot was smart, he figured out that sort of thing.

Right now, the only thing Bourne really wanted to figure out was how to find a quiet spot where nobody would try to blow him away for a while. He'd given enough gray hairs to this buggering planet and its buggered poof army already!

There was a centimeter's clearance front and rear to turn the jeep in the tunnel's width, but the sergeant did not even consider backing after he tested his eyeball guestimate with a brief tap on the throttle as he twisted the tiller to bring the vehicle just short of alignment. Sure that it was going to make it, he goosed the fans again and brought the detection vehicle quickly around, converting spin into forward motion as the bow swung toward the first angle and the entrance. If it could be done with a ground effect vehicle, Profile would do it without thinking. Thinking wasn't his strong suit anyway.

The mercenaries' commo helmets brightened with message traffic as the jeep slid back down the initial leg of the gallery. Even a satellite relay squarely overhead didn't permit radio communication when one of the parties was deep beneath a slab of rock. Ground conduction signals were a way around that, but a bloody poor one when all your troops were mounted on air cushion vehicles.

Might be nice to have a portable tunnel to crawl into, now and again. When some poof circus needed to have its butt saved again, for instance.

The tunnel mouth gave them a wedge of vision onto the far slope, expanding as the jeep slid smoothly toward the opening where the driver grounded it. Sparkling chains of fire laced the air above the valley, bubbling and dancing at a dozen points from which snipers might have fired earlier.

" 'Bout bloody time!" the driver chortled, though support from the Slammers' big blowers had come amazingly quickly, given the care with which the expensive vehicles had to travel on this hostile terrain. "About *bloody* time!"

The tribarreled powerguns raking Molt hiding places with counterfire cycled so quickly that, like droplets of water in a fountain, the individual cyan flashes seemed to hang in the air instead of snapping light-quick across the valley. Afterimages strobed within Bourne's dark-adapted eyes: on a sunny day, the bursts of two-centimeter fire imposed their own definition of brightness. Snipers were still safe if they fired and fled instantly; but if a warrior paused to take a breath or better aim, heat sensors would lock on the glowing barrel of his powergun and crisscrossing automatic fire would glaze the landscape with his remains.

The support was combat cars, not the panzers—the tanks—that Bourne had been hoping for. This'd do, but it'd be nice to see a whole bloody hillside go up in a blue flash!

Lieutenant Hawker, holding the Molt, stepped from the jeep and the tunnel mouth, his gun hand raised as if he were hailing a cab in a liberty port. It wasn't the safest thing in the world, on this world, to do, what with autochthons still firing at the oncoming poof battalion and those locals themselves dangerously trigger-happy. Still, the Molts had proven unwilling to shoot toward their infants, and the poofs were more likely to pitch a bunker-buster into the tunnel mouth than they were to shoot at a Slammer in battledress, three times the size of any Molt who ever lived. Shrugging, Bourne butted the jeep a couple meters further forward to take a look himself.

The leading elements of Fox Victor had reformed on the ridge crest and were advancing raggedly abreast in a mounted assault line. There were thirty or so vehicles in the first wave, armored cars and APCs with a leavening of all-terrain trucks taking the place of armored vehicles destroyed earlier in the operation.

The nearest vehicle was one of the light trucks, this one equipped with a pintle-mounted machine gun instead of carrying a squad of engineers with blasting charges the way the mercenaries had hoped. The Loot signalled it over peremptorily while his tongue searched the controller of his commo helmet for the setting that would give him Fox Victor's intervehicle push—Hawker's previous radio contact had been with the battalion commander, pointless right now.

The truck, still fifty meters upslope, wavered in its course and did not immediately slow; its driver and vehicle commander, as well as the rest of the six Oltenians aboard, obviously had doubts about the idea of halting on open ground pocked with glassy evidence of Molt gunfire. They *did*, however, turn squarely toward the entrance of the nursery tunnel while the independent axles permitted the four wheels to bobble in nervous disorder over the irregularities of the terrain.

Most important, nobody took a shot at the two Slammers. Profile's tattooed gunhand had swung his own weapon minutely to track the Oltenians; now he relaxed it somewhat. Allies, sure, but curse it, they only had to *look* like they were planning to fire and they were *gone*. . . .

The truck braked to a halt beside the notch in the slope which formed the tunnel entrance. Everybody aboard but the gunner leaped out with the spraddle-legged nervousness of dogs sniffing a stranger's territory. Dust, thrown up by treads that were woven in one piece with the wheel sidewalls from ferrichrome monocrystal, continued to drift downhill at a decreasing velocity.

"Who'n blazes're you!" demanded the close-coupled Oltenian captain who presumably commanded more than the crew of this one truck. Additional vehicles were rolling over the ridge, some of them heavy trucks; and, though the artillery was still crunching away at distant locations, fire from the combat cars in crest positions had slackened for lack of targets.

"We're the fairy godmothers who cleared the back slope for you," said Lieutenant Hawker, pumping his submachine gun toward, and by implication over, the ridge. "Now, I want you guys to go in there and bring out the rest of these, the babies."

He joggled the Molt infant that his left hand held to his breastplate; the little creature made a sound that seemed more like a purr than a complaint. "We get them out—there's maybe a dozen of 'em—and we can pack the tunnel with enough explosives to lift the top off the whole bloody ridge. Let's see 'em use it to snipe from then!"

"You're crazy," said one of the poofs in a tone of genuine disbelief.

"We aren't doing any such thing," agreed his captain. "Just shove the explosives in on top—there'll be plenty room still."

"They're *babies*," Lieutenant Hawker said with the kind of edge that made Bourne smile, not a nice smile, as he checked the damage to the jeep's front skirt. "I didn't risk *my* hide to get a lot of lip from you boys when I saved your bacon. Now, hop!"

Lord knew what the chain of command was in a ratfuck like this situation, but it was a fair bet that the Loot couldn't by protocol give direct orders to a higher-ranking local. Hawker didn't wear rank tabs, nobody did when the Slammers were in a war zone; and no poof with a lick of sense was going to argue with somebody the size and demeanor of the mercenary officer. The captain's short-barrelled shotgun twitched on his shoulder where he leaned it, finger within the trigger guard; but it was to the locals around him that he muttered, "Come on, then," as he strode within the lighted tunnel.

The skirt wasn't damaged badly enough to need replacement, but Profile hoped he'd have a chance soon to hose it down. The slime which glittered with Molt scales was already beginning to stink.

The Loot talked to Central, business that Bourne's mind tuned out as effectively as a switch on his helmet could've done. It was relaxing, standing in the sunlight and about as safe as you could be on this bloody planet: there were still the sounds of combat far away, but the jeep was now lost in the welter of other military vehicles, a needle among needles. The Molts were reeling, anyway, and the few hundred casualties this operation had cost them must be a very high proportion of the fighting strength of the theme involved.

Lieutenant Hawker was absently stroking the back of the infant with the muzzle of his submachine gun. In the minutes since the gun was last fired, the iridium had cooled to the point that the little Molt found its warmth pleasurable—or at least it seemed to: its eyes were closed, its breathing placid.

Echoes merged the shots in the tunnel into a single hungry roar.

"Loot, the—" the sergeant began as he knelt beside the skirt, the jeep between him and the gunfire, his own weapon pointed back down the tunnel. He meant a teleporting warrior, of course, but the detector holograms had been within the driver's field of vision and they were calm with no yellow-violet flicker of warning.

Besides, the squad of Oltenians was coming back down the gallery talking excitedly, two of them supporting a third who hopped on one leg and gripped the calf of the other with both hands. But that was only a ricochet; you couldn't blaze away in a confined space and not expect to eat some of your own metal.

Bourne stood up and let his sling clutch the submachine gun back against his breastplate now that he knew there was no problem after all. Wisps of smoke eddied from the

barrels of the shotguns, residues of flash suppressant from
the propellant charges. The air in the nursery chamber must
be hazy with it. . . .

"What in the name of the *Lord* have you done?"
Lieutenant Hawker asked the captain in a tone that made
Profile Bourne realize that the trouble wasn't over yet after
all.

"It's not your planet, renter," the captain said. His face
was spattered with what Bourne decided was not his own
blood. "You don't capture Molts, you kill 'em. Every cursed
chance you get."

"C'mon, somebody get me a medic," the wounded man
whined. "This hurts like the very blazes!" The fabric of his
trousers was darkening around his squeezing hands, but the
damage didn't seem to Bourne anything to lose sleep over.

"I told you . . . ," the Loot said in a breathless voice,
as though he had been punched hard in the pit of the
stomach. The big mercenary was holding himself very
straight, the infant against his breastplate in the crook of
one arm, towering over the captain and the rest of the
poofs, but he had the look of a man being impaled.

A four-vehicle platoon of the combat cars which had
been firing in support now kicked themselves sedately from
the ridgeline and proceeded down the slope. Dust bloomed
neatly around the margin of the plenum chamber of each,
trailing and spreading behind the big, dazzle-painted iridium
forms. A powergun bolt hissed so high overhead that it
could scarcely be said to be aimed at the cars. Over a dozen
tribarrels replied in gorgeous fountains of light that merged
kilometers away like strands being spun into a single thread.

"When you've had as many of your buddies zapped as
we have," said a poof complacently to the Slammer who
had earned his commission on Emporion when he, as
ranking sergeant, had consolidated his company's position
on the landing zone, "then you'll understand."

"Blood and martyrs, Loot!" said Profile Bourne as he
squinted upslope. "That's Alpha Company—it's the White
Mice and Colonel Hammer!"

"The only good Molt," said the captain, raising overhead

the shotgun he held at the balance and eyeing the infant in Lieutenant Hawker's arms as if it were the nail he was about to hammer, "is a dead—"

And the Loot shot him through the bridge of the nose.

Bloody hell, thought Bourne as he sprayed first a poof whose gun was half-pointed, then the one who leaped toward the truck and the weapon mounted there. Had he reloaded after popping the round into the nursery chamber?

Bourne's first target was falling forward, tangled with the man the Loot had killed, and the second bounced from the side of the truck, the back of his uniform ablaze and all his muscles gone flaccid in mid-leap. A bolt that had gotten away from Bourne punched a divot of rock from the polished wall of the tunnel.

"Profile, that's *enough!*" the Loot screamed, but of course it wasn't.

The Oltenian with a bit of his own or a comrade's shot-charge in his calf was trying to unsling his shotgun. Everything in the sergeant's mind was as clear and perfect as gears meshing. The emotion that he felt, electric glee at the unity of the world centered on his gunsight, had no more effect on his functioning than would his fury if the submachine gun jammed. In that case, he would finish the job with the glowing iridium barrel as he had done twice in the past. . . .

The submachine gun functioned flawlessly. Bourne aimed low so that stray shots would clear the Loot, lunging to try to stop his subordinate; and as the trio of poofs doubled up, the second burst hacked into their spines.

This close, a firefight ended when nobody on one side or the other could pull a trigger anymore. The Loot knew that.

Combat cars whining like a pair of restive banshees slid to a dynamic halt to either side of the tunnel archway. The central tribarrel, directly behind the driver's hatch, and one wing gun of each bore on the detection team from close enough to piss if the wind were right. Despite the slope, the cars were not grounded; their drivers held them amazingly steady on thrust alone, their skirts hovering only millimeters above the rocky soil. The offside gunner from either car jumped out and walked around his vehicle with pistol drawn.

Lieutenant Hawker turned very slowly, raising his gunhand into the air. The infant Molt clutched in the crook of the other arm began to greet angrily, disturbed perhaps by the screams and the smell of men's bodies convulsing without conscious control.

A dead man's hand was thrashing at Profile's boot. He stepped back, noticing that the hair on the back of his left hand, clutching the foregrip of his weapon, had crinkled from the heat of the barrel.

"I want you both to unsnap the shoulder loop of your slings," said a voice, clear in Bourne's ears because it came through his commo helmet and not over the rush of the big fans supporting tonnes of combat car so close by.

There was no threat in the words, no emotion in the voice. The quartet of tribarrels was threat enough, and as for emotion—killing wasn't a matter of emotion for men like Profile Bourne and the troopers of Headquarters Company—the White Mice.

Lieutenant Hawker took a long look over his shoulder, past his sergeant and on to the Oltenian vehicles already disappearing over the far ridge—their path to Captain Henderson's infantry cleared by the risks the detection team had taken.

"Aye, aye, Colonel Hammer," Hawker said to the wing gunner in the right hand car, and he unsnapped his sling.

The hologram display began to flash between yellow and violet, warning that a Molt was about to appear.

"Nikki, I've been looking for you the past half hour," said General Radescu no louder than needful to be heard over the minuet that the orchestra had just struck up. His young aide nonetheless jumped as if goosed with a hot poker, bumping the urn that he had been peering around when Radescu came up behind him. "Alexi, I—" Major Nikki Tzigara said, his face flushed a darker red than the scarlet of his jacket bodice. There were white highlights on Nikki's cheekbones and brow ridge, and the boy's collar looked too tight. "Well it's a . . . ." He gestured toward the whirling tapestry of the dance. "I thought I ought to circulate, you know, since you were so busy with your uncle and *important* people."

The general blinked, taken aback by the unprovoked sharpness of his aide's tone. Nikki was counterattacking when there'd been no attack, Radescu had only said . . . "Ah, yes, there's no doubt something over a hundred people here I really ought to talk to for one reason or another," he said, filing Tzigara's tone in memory but ignoring it in his response because he hadn't the faintest notion of its cause. Nikki really ought to wear full makeup the way Radescu himself had done ever since he understood the effectiveness of Uncle Grigor's poker face. Antonescu might not have become Chief Tribune, despite all his gifts, had he not learned to rule his expression. Heavy makeup was the edge which concealed the tiny hints from blood and muscle that only the most accomplished politician could wholly control.

And Man, as Aristotle had said, was the political animal.

"Rather like being on the edge of a rhododendron thicket," Radescu continued, looking away from his aide to give Nikki room to compose himself, for pity's sake. Uncle Grigor had worked his way a few meters along the margin of the circular hall so that he was almost hidden by a trio of slender women whose beehive coiffures made them of a height with the tall Chief Tribune. "Very colorful, of course, but one can't *see* very much through it, can one?

"Which reminds me," he added, rising onto the toes of his gilded boots despite the indignity of it—and finding that he could see no farther across the ballroom anyway, "do you know where the mercenary adjutant is, Major Steuben?"

"Why would I know *that*? He could be anywhere!"

Makeup wouldn't keep Nikki's voice from being shrill as a powersaw when the boy got excited, Alexander Radescu thought; and thought other things, about the way Nikki's medals were now disarranged, rowels and wreathes and dangling chains caught and skewed among themselves. The back of Radescu's neck was prickling, and the hairs along his arms. He *hoped* it wasn't hormonal, hoped that he had better control of his emotions than that. But dear Lord! He didn't care about Nikki's sexual orientation, but *surely* he had better sense than to get involved with a killer like Steuben . . . didn't he?

Ignoring the whispers in his mind, Radescu eyed the gorgeous show on the ballroom floor and said, "This is *why* the war's being fought, you know, Nikki? The—all the men having to wear uniforms, all the women having to be *seen* with men in uniforms." Except for Uncle Grigor, who distanced himself and his fellow Tribunes from the war by starkly traditional robes. Everyone else—of the aristocracy—gained from the war the chance to cavort in splendid uniforms, while Grigor Antonescu settled for real control of the Oltenian State. . . .

"They don't fight the war—*we* don't fight the war, even the ones of us with regular commissions," Radescu continued, turning to face Nikki again and beginning to straighten the boy's medals, a task that kept his eyes from Tzigara's face. "But it couldn't be fought without our support."

The whole surface of his skin was feeling cold as if the nerves themselves had been chilled, though sweat from the hot, swirling atmosphere still tingled at his joints and the small of his back. The two blue john urns stood tall and aloof just as they had done for centuries, but between them—

"I think maybe the Molts would have something to say about ending the war," said Nikki Tzigara. "I mean, you have your *opinions*, Alexi, but we can't make peace—"

"*Nikki!*" Radescu shouted, for suddenly there was an ancient Molt warrior directly behind the young aide. The Molt's hide was the color of an algae-covered stone, soaked for decades in peat water, and his right brow horn was twisted in a way unique in the general's experience. The powergun he held was a full-sized weapon, too heavy for the Molt's stringy muscles to butt it against his shoulder the way one of the Slammers would have done.

The warrior had no need for technique at this range, of course.

Nikki had begun to turn, his mouth still open and saying "—the Molts don't—" when the warrior fired.

The first of his twenty-round magazine.

The human nearest to Ferad flew apart in an explosive cavitation effect, two-thirds of the mass of his thorax having been converted to super-hot steam by the bolt it absorbed from the powergun almost in contact with it. The remainder of the corpse was flung backward by the ball of vaporized matter which coated everything within a five-meter radius, Ferad and the urns included. The flailing yellow sleeves were still attached to the rest of the body, but the scarlet bodice which they had complemented was scooped away to the iridescent white of the membrane covering the inner surface of the victim's spine and ribs.

The taller human in pearl and gold who had been standing behind the first had locked eyes with Ferad. He was an easy target, fallen in a tangle of dancers and only partially covered by the corpse of the companion which had knocked him down . . . but the theme elder's finger paused and twitched only after the muzzle had swung to cover a paunchy man in green and brown and the silvery cape of an immature Molt. Ferad did not need to be fussy about his targets and could not afford the time it would take to pick and choose anyway; but in the case of the human screaming something on the floor, he chose *not* to kill. Perhaps it was the eyes, or something behind them.

The thickly-packed humans were trying to surge away from the gun like the waves of compression and rarefaction in a gas. Only those closest to Ferad knew what was happening—the bolts of energy hammered the air and struck with the sound of bombs underwater, but the sounds were not sharp enough to identify them to untrained ears in the noisy ballroom.

The orchestra on the far side of the hall continued to play some incomprehensible human melody, its members aware of the disturbance but stolidly unwilling to emphasize it by falling silent. Ferad shot into fleeing backs trapped by the press.

Sopasian had suggested a bomb in his calm voice that hid a cancer of emotions beneath—envy and scorn, but mostly envy. It was a reasonable suggestion, since a bomb would have killed more than the powergun could in targets as soft and frequent as these. The surface-absorbed two-centimeter bolts had no penetration, though the amount of energy they released could separate limbs from bodies—and the medals on the first victim's chest were still raining down all across the hall.

But Sopasian missed the point of this attack. They couldn't kill *all* the humans, not even if every Molt on the planet had Ferad's skill or Sopasian's. What Ferad brought to the gala was a personal death, not a sudden blast followed by dust and the screams of the injured. This attack went on and on in the safest place in the world, the victims would have said a moment before.

Cyan light spurted from a gunbarrel so hot that the scales on Ferad's left arm were lifting to trap a blanket of insulating air. The polished wood and stones inlaid into the groined ceiling reflected the shots as they echoed with the screams.

Ferad's peripheral vision was better than that of a human, an adaptation crucial to a Molt teleporting into the confusion of a battle or hunt who had to receive a great deal of data about his immediate surroundings in the first instant. The flash of white drew Ferad to the left, the powergun's barrel shimmering its own arc through the air before him.

None of them were armed. The ballroom was like a nursery tunnel, females and infants and all of them helpless as the veriest newborn—but it had to be done.

One of the Tribunes stood in glistening white, facing Ferad though the three shrieking females in between were scrabbling away. The theme elder fired, clearing a path for his next bolt by taking a female at the point where her bare skin met the ruffles at the base of her spine. Her corpse scissored backwards, its upper portion scarcely connected to the splaying legs, and the other two females—now in gowns only half pastel—were thrust from either side to close the gap.

The trio had been caught not by the general confusion but by the grip of the Tribune's arms, protective coloration and, in the event, a shield.

Ferad, wishing for the first time in decades that he had the muscles of a young adult, squeezed off another bolt that parted the white-gowned male from his females, only one of them screaming now and the gown covered with the residues from the flash-heated steam. Had Ferad been younger, he could have leaped on the Tribune, thrusting the heavy powergun against his target and finishing in an instant the business it had taken two shots to prepare. But a young, athletic warrior could never have gotten here, and the Tribune was now sprawled on the floor, his back against the wainscoting and only his palms and spread fingers between his face and the white iridium disk of the powergun muzzle.

The Molt's gun did not fire. Ferad had already spent the last round in his magazine.

The theme leader dropped his useless weapon on the floor, where wood and wax crackled away from the barrel. The hours he had spent in locating the urns here in Belvedere, in gripping them with his mind, were gone from memory. The antechamber of the tunnel system which had been the center of his existence for a hundred and forty years was a dazzling beacon though a thousand kilometers separated it from the theme elder.

For the instant only.

The ballroom and the carnage, almost as dreadful to Ferad as to the humans surviving, trembled for a moment, superimposed on the stone and lamps and shouting warriors of the nursery cave.

Two humans made a final impression on him: the male knocked down by the first bolt, now trying to rise; and another in the khaki of the mercenaries, so much more dangerous than the forces of the settlers themselves. This mercenary must have wedged his way through a counter-current of bodies in screaming panic. His hand was raised, a pistol in it, and there was a blue-green flash from the muzzle that Ferad did not quite see.

In his millisecond of limbo, the theme elder wondered
what success his rival, Sopasian, was having.

"There's a Molt—" said Lieutenant Hawker as the tone
in his left earpiece gave him a distance and vector, *bloody*
close, but the target designation was figured from the jeep
and not where he himself stood a couple paces away.

The trooper sent to collect Hawker's gun snatched the
weapon away, nervous to be reaching into the crossed cones
of fire of the tribarrels to either flank. "*Drop* it, he said,
cophead!" the headquarters trooper snarled, just as somebody shouted to Hammer from the other combat car, "Sir,
we've got'n incoming!"

For operations against the Molts, all the Slammers' line
armor—the tanks and combat cars—had been fitted with
ionization detectors similar to those on the team's jeep. For
reasons of space and the need for training to operate more
sophisticated gear, however, the detectors which equipped
the big blowers were relatively rudimentary. The troops of
A Company, Hammer's personal guard, were picked as
much for technical skills as they were for ruthlessness and
lethality—qualities which were not in short supply in the
line companies either. The man calling, "Thirty-five left,
eight meters—Colonel, he's coming right beside your car!"
was getting more precision from his hardware than Hawker
would have thought possible.

The big lieutenant stepped over the body of the Oltenian
officer, setting the limbs a-twitch again when the sole of
his boot brushed a thigh. The trooper with Hawker's gun
holstered his own pistol so that he could level the automatic
weapon as he turned toward Hammer and the combat car.

"Loot!" called Profile Bourne, familiar enough with
Hawker to know that the lieutenant's disquiet was not
simply because a warrior was about to attack. The White
Mice could handle *that*, the Lord knew, they weren't poofs
who needed a picture to figure which end to piss with.

The trooper who had advanced to take Bourne's gun as
his companion did Hawker's was now poised between the
sergeant and Hammer, impaled on the horns of a dilemma.

Bourne held his weapon muzzle-high, the barrel vertical and threatening to no one who had not seen how quickly he moved. The left hand, however, was thrust out like a traffic warden's—a barrier in defiance of the pistol which the man from A Company still pointed.

The fellow in the combat car had the vector right and the distance, but there was *something* wrong with what he'd said.

Hawker dropped into his seat in the jeep and laid the infant Molt beside him as Hammer's own combat car slid a few meters upslope, swinging so that the two manned guns still covered the expected target without threatening the dismounted troops besides. The flashing holograms of Hawker's display shifted simultaneously with a subtlety that no tone signal could have conveyed.

"Drop it or you're *dead*, trooper!" the man in front of Profile shouted, but even as he spoke, his pistol and his eyes were shifting to the danger behind him, the tribarrels that might be aligned with his spine.

"Colonel, it's right under you!" shouted the man on the combat car's detector.

Hammer's great car spurted sideways like fluff blown from a seed pod and the digits on Hawker's display shifted as quickly.

"Colonel!" the lieutenant bellowed, trying to make himself heard over the fans of the big blowers roaring in the machine equivalent of muscles bunched for flight. His unit link was to Henderson's infantry company, and tonguing Central wouldn't have given him the direct line to Hammer that he needed now.

"It's *in* your car!" Hawker shouted as he leaped out of the jeep, snatching for the submachine gun that had been taken from him.

The Molt was so old that wrinkles showed like dark striping on his face as the warrior appeared in the fighting compartment between Hammer and the other gunner, both of them craning their necks to scan the rocky ground beside the car. If their body hairs felt the sudden shift in electrostatic balance as the autochthon appeared behind them, that warning was buried in the subconscious of veterans faced with a known threat.

"Contact!" the A Company detection specialist shouted into the instruments on which his attention was focused, and his companion at the wing tribarrel triggered a shot into the empty soil by reflex. The Molt warrior's wiry arms held, raised, a blade of glittering blue steel; the junction between Hammer's helmet and body armor was bared as the Colonel stretched to find a target before him.

Hawker caught his gun, but the trooper holding it wouldn't have been in the White Mice if he were soft. He held the weapon with one hand and rabbit-punched the lieutenant with the other, an instinctive, pointless act since Hawker was wearing body armor; but the trooper *held* the gun as the Molt's sword swung downward, unseen by anyone but Hawker—

—and Sergeant Bourne. The Molt sword blade was a sandwich of malleable iron welded to either side of a core of high carbon steel, quick-quenched to a rich blue after forging. That razor sharp steel and the black iron which gave the blade resilience glowed momentarily cyan in reflecting the bolt flicking past them, brighter for that instant than the sun.

Hammer flattened behind the iridium bulkhead, his commo helmet howling with static induced by the bolt which had bubbled the plastic surface.

The trooper who should have disarmed Profile Bourne was one of those whose eyes were drawn by the bolt to the warrior in the combat car. The autochthon's sword sparked on the lip of the fighting compartment and bounced out. The Molt himself twisted. His face had two eyesockets but only one eye, and the wrinkles were bulged from his features when his head absorbed the energy of the single shot.

The driver of Hammer's car had no view of the scene behind him. He drew a pistol and presented it awkwardly through his hatch, trying to aim at Bourne while still holding the car steady with one hand.

"No!" cried the trooper who had tried to disarm Bourne,

windmilling his arms as he made sure he was between the sergeant and the guns threatening him.

Lieutenant Hawker and the trooper with whom he struggled now separated cautiously, Hawker releasing the submachine gun and the man from A Company licking the scraped knuckles of his left hand. There was a pop in the lieutenant's helmet, static from a message he did not himself receive, and the sound level dropped abruptly as both combat cars grounded and cut their fans.

The Molt's sword had stuck point first in the soil. It rang there, a nervous keening that complemented the cries of the infant Molt, dumped without ceremony on the driver's seat when Hawker had gotten into the jeep. The big lieutenant walked back toward his vehicle and lifted the Molt with both hands to hide the fact that they were both trembling.

Colonel Alois Hammer reappeared, standing up with deliberation rather than caution. He held something in his left hand which he looked at, then flipped like a coin to fall spinning onto the ground near the sword. It was the sapphire condensing plate from a combat car's navigation display, a thick fifty-millimeter disk whose internal cross-hatching made it a spot of fluid brilliance in the sunlight.

"He was holding that," said the Colonel, pointing to the disk with the pistol in his right hand. He fired, igniting grass and fusing a patch of soil without quite hitting his target. "I didn't know they could do that," and the condensing plate shattered like a bomb, the scored lines providing a myriad fracture sites.

Hammer fired twice more into the mass of glittering particles that carpeted the ground.

"Now, kid, it could be a lot worse," muttered Enzo Hawker as he patted the shivering infant's back and wondered if that were true for the little Molt, for any of them. The sounds of distant battle were like hogs rooting among the mast, shellfire and diesels and the mighty soughing of the Slammers' ground-effect vehicles.

"Hey!" called Sergeant Bourne, holding his weapon

vertical again and aloft at the length of its sling. "Still want
this, Colonel?" His voice was high and hectoring, a reaction
to having made a shot that he would never have dared
attempt had he paused to think about what he was doing.
A millimeter, two millimeters to the right, and the bolt
would have expended itself on Hammer's face an instant
before the sword finished the business.

"Disarm the man," Hammer ordered in a voice as far
away as the breeze moving wispy clouds in the high
stratosphere.

"Sure, all right," said Profile, and perhaps only Hawker
realized that the brittle edge in his voice was terror and
not a threat. The sergeant's left hand fumbled with the sling
catch while his right hand held clear the submachine gun,
though its barrel was by now cool enough to touch.

"Only one thing—" the enlisted man added.

"Profile, don't—" said Hawker, aware that three tribarrels
were again aimed at his partner's chest.

"Only you better keep the Loot on his console," Bourne
completed as he flung his weapon to the ground. "Until
you hunt up somebody else who knows how to use the
bloody gear, at least."

Three pistol bolts struck within a palm's scope, the first
shattering the urn of blue john. The other two sparkled
among the shivered fragments, reducing some of the
fluorspar to its ionized constituents. Other chips now ranged
in color from gray to brilliant amethyst, depending on how
close they had been to the momentary heat. Larger chunks,
the upper third of the urn, cascaded over the gun the Molt
had dropped and, dropping it, disappeared.

Ozone and nascent fluorine battled for ascendancy
between themselves, but neither could prevail over the
stench of death.

Someone had kicked Alexander Radescu in the temple
as he flopped backwards to the floor. His memory of the past
thirty seconds was a kaleidoscope rather than a connected
series, but he was not sure that the blow had anything to
do with his disorganization. The gun muzzle flickering like

a strobe light while the white glow of the iridium remained as a steady portent of further death . . .

Radescu's right hand lay across his gilded cap, so he could don it again without looking down. He stumbled on his first step toward Chief Tribune Antonescu, but he knew what was binding his right foot and knew also that he dared not actually view it.

Lifting his foot very carefully to clear what was no longer Nikki or anything human, the young general murmured, "I'm going to be fine if I don't think about it. I just don't want to think about it, that's all." His tone would have been suitable had he been refusing a glass of sherry or commenting on the hang of a uniform. He couldn't keep from remembering and imagining concrete realities, of course, but by acting very carefully he could keep them from being realities of *his* experience.

The screams had not stopped when the Molt warrior disappeared. Most of the crowd still did not know what had happened. Would the *Lord* that Alexander Radescu were as ignorant!

"I was afraid you'd been shot, my boy," said Grigor Antonescu, politic even at such a juncture, "by that—" he nodded toward the spilled crystals of blue john, cubic and octahedral, and the gun they lay across like a stone counterpane "—or the other."

Staring over his shoulder, Radescu saw Major Steuben picking his way toward them with a set expression and quick glances all around him, ready now for any target which presented itself. Hammer's bodyguard had been marginally too late for revenge, and not even *his* reflexes would have been quick enough to save Nikki. None of the rest mattered to Radescu, not the dead or the maimed, those catatonic with fear or the ones still screaming their throats raw.

But that was over, and the past could not be allowed to impede what the future required.

"This can't go on, Uncle Grigor," Radescu said with a twist of his neck, a dismissing gesture.

The Chief Tribune, whose face and robes were now as much red as white, said, "Security, you mean, Alexi? Yes, we should have had real guards, shouldn't we? Perhaps Hammer's men. . . ."

In his uncle's reasonable voice, Radescu heard himself—a mind that should have been in shock, but which had a core too tough to permit that in a crisis.

Members of the Honor Guard were running about, brilliant in their scarlet uniforms and almost as useless in a firefight as the unarmed militia 'officers' attending the ball. They were waving chrome and rhodium plated pistols as they spilled in through the doors at which they'd been posted to bar the uninvited. If they weren't lucky, there'd be more shots, more casualties. . . .

"Not security, not here at least," said General Radescu, gesturing curtly at one of the Honor Guards gagging at a tangle of bodies. "It's the war itself that has to be changed."

"We can't do that," Antonescu replied bitterly, "without changing the army."

"Changing its command, Uncle Grigor," said Alexander Radescu as his mind shuddered between Nikki's flailing body and the gunbarrel of the aged Molt. "Yes, that's exactly what we have to do first."

The young general flicked at spots on his jacket front, but he stopped when he saw they were smearing further across the pearl fabric.

"I need two gunmen who won't argue about orders," said Radescu to Colonel Hammer, standing where a granite pillar had been blasted to glittering gravel to prevent Molt warriors from materializing on top of them. The Oltenian general spoke loudly to be heard over the pervasive intake rush of the four command vehicles maneuvering themselves back to back to form the Field Operations Center. The verdigrised black head and cape of an ancient Molt were mounted on a stake welded to the bow of one of the cars.

The aide standing with Hammer smiled, but the mercenary colonel himself looked at Radescu with an expression soured both by the overall situation and specifically by the appearance of Alexander Radescu: young, dressed in a uniform whose gold and pearl fabrics were showing signs of blowing grit only minutes after the general disembarked from his aircraft—and full facial makeup, including lip tint and a butterfly-shaped beauty patch on his right cheekbone.

"There's a whole Oltenian army out there," said Hammer bitterly, waving in the direction of the local forces setting up in the near distance. "Maybe you can find two who know which end of a gun the bang comes out of. Maybe you can even find a couple willing to get off their butts and *move*. Curst if I've been able to find 'em, though."

Radescu had worn his reviewing uniform for its effect on the Oltenian command staff, but it was having the opposite result on the mercenaries. "The Tribunes are aware of that," he said with no outward sign of his anger at this stocky, worn, *deadly* man. Grime and battledress did not lower Hammer in the Oltenian's opinion, but the mercenary's deliberate sneering *coarseness* marked him as incurably common. "That's why they've sent me to the field: to take over and get the army moving again. My uncle—" he added, by no means inconsequently "—is Chief Tribune."

The Oltenian general reached into a breast pocket for his identification—a message tube which would project a hologram of Chief Tribune Antonescu with his arm around his nephew, announcing the appointment 'to all members of the armed forces of Oltenia and allied troops.' Hammer's aide forestalled him, however, by saying, "This is General Radescu, sir."

"Sure, I haven't forgotten," Colonel Hammer remarked with an even deeper scowl, "but he's not what *I* had in mind when I heard they were going to send somebody out to take charge."

He looked from his aide to Radescu and continued, "Oh, don't look so surprised, General. That's part of what you hired us for, wasn't it? Better communications and detection gear than you could supply on-planet?"

Radescu's tongue touched his vermilion lips and he said, "Yes, of course, Colonel," though it was not 'of course' and he was quite certain that Chief Tribune Antonescu would have been even more shocked at the way these outsiders had penetrated the inner councils of the State. Radescu had flown to the front without even an aide to accompany him because of the complete secrecy needed for the success of his mission. Though what the mercenaries knew of his plan was not important . . . so long as they had not communicated what they knew to the Oltenian planetary forces.

Which brought the young general back to the real point at issue. "This time the help I need involves another part of the reason we hired you, though."

"General," said Hammer coldly, "I've lost equipment and I've lost men because local forces didn't support my troops when they advanced. We're going to carry out basic contract commitments from here on . . . but I don't do any favors for Oltenian tarts. No, I don't have two men to spare."

"There's Hawker and Bourne," said the aide unexpectedly. He gave Radescu a sardonic smile as he continued. "Might be a way out of more problems than one."

A trio of Slammers were striding toward their leader from the assembled Operations Center, two men and a woman who looked too frail for her body armor and the equipment strapped over it. Hammer ignored them for the moment and said to his aide, "Look, Pritchard, we can't afford to lose our bond over something like this."

"Look, I have full—" Radescu interjected.

"We're turning them over to the local authority for processing," said Pritchard, as little impressed with the general in gold and pearl as his colonel was. "Via, Colonel, you don't want to call out a firing party for our own men, not for something like that."

Hammer nodded to the three officers who had halted a respectful two paces from him; then, to Radescu, he said as grimly as before, "General, I'm turning over to you Lieutenant Hawker and Sergeant-Commander Bourne, who have been sentenced to death for the murder of six members of the allied local forces. Whatever action you take regarding them will be regarded as appropriate."

He turned his head from Radescu to the waiting trio. "Captain?" he said on a note of query.

"Hammer to Radescu," the woman said with a nod.

"It's being transmitted to the Bonding Authority representative."

"All right, General Radescu," Hammer continued, "you'll find the men in the adjutant's charge, Car four-five-niner. I wish you well of them. They were good men before they got involved with what passes for an army here on Oltenia."

Hammer and his aide both faced toward the trio of other mercenaries as if Radescu had already left them.

"But—" the Oltenian general asked, as unprepared for this development as for the scorn with which the offer was made. "*Why* did they, did they commit these murders?"

Hammer was deep in conversation with one of the other officers, but Pritchard glanced back over his shoulder at Radescu and said, "Why don't you ask *them*, General?" He smiled again without warmth as he turned his head and his attention again.

General Alexander Radescu pursed his lips, but he sucked back the comment he had started to make and quenched even the anger that had spawned it. He had made a request, and it had been granted. He was in no position to object that certain conventions had been ignored by the mercenaries.

"Thank you for your cooperation, Colonel," he said to the commo helmets bent away from him above backs clamshelled in porcelain armor. The woman, the communications officer, cocked an eye at the general only briefly. "I assure you that from here on you will have no call to complain about the cooperation the Oltenian forces offer you."

He strode away briskly, looking for a vehicle with skirt number 459. The set of his jaw was reflected alternately in the gilded toe-caps of his shoes.

"One moment, sir," said a graying man who might have been the adjutant—none of the Slammers seemed to wear rank insignia in the field, and officers wore the same uniforms as enlisted men.

Another of the mercenaries had, without being asked, walked to a room-sized goods container and rapped on the bars closing the front of it. "Profile!" he called. "Lieutenant Hawker! He's here to pick you guys up."

"We were informed, of course, sir," said the probable adjutant who looked the Oltenian up and down with an inward smile that was obvious despite its lack of physical manifestations. "Did you get lost in the encampment?"

"Something like that," said Radescu bitterly. "Perhaps you could find a vehicle to carry me and, and my new aides, to, ah, my headquarters?"

"We'll see about that, of course, sir," said the graying man, and the smile did tug a corner of his mouth.

The Slammers had sprayed the area of their intended base camp with herbicide. Whatever they used collapsed the cell walls of all indigenous vegetation almost completely so that in the lower, wetter areas, the sludge of dissolved plant residue was as much as knee deep. That didn't seem to bother the mercenaries, all of whom rode if they had more than twenty meters to traverse—but it had created a pattern of swamps for Radescu which he finally crossed despite its effect on his uniform. He would look a *buffoon* when he called the command staff together!

Then he relaxed. He dared not hold the meeting without two gunmen behind him, and if the mercenaries' public scorn was the price of those gunmen—so be it. Alexander Radescu had thought a long time before he requested this duty from his uncle. He was not going to second-guess himself now.

"Got your gear over here, Profile," said the mercenary who had opened the crude cell and stepped inside the similar—unbarred—unit beside it. He came out again, carrying a heavy suit of body armor on either arm.

The men who had just been freed took their equipment, eying Radescu. The young general stared back at them, expecting the sneering dismissal he had received from other mercenaries. What he got instead was an appraisal that went beneath the muck and his uniform, went deeper into Alexander Radescu than an outsider had ever gone before.

It was insufferable presumption on the part of these hirelings.

Lieutenant Hawker was a large, soft-looking man. There were no sharp angles to his face or frame, and his torso would have been egg-shaped in garments which fit closer than the floppy Slammers battledress. He swung the porcelain clamshell armor around himself unaided, however, an action that demonstrated exceptional strength and timing.

His eyes were blue, and the look in them made Radescu wonder how many of the six Oltenians Hawker had killed himself.

Profile, presumably Sergeant Bourne, was no taller than Colonel Hammer and was built along the lines of Radescu's own whippy thinness rather than being stocky like the mercenary commander. His bold smile displayed his upper incisors with the bluish tinge characteristic of tooth buds grown *in vitro*.

There was a scar on the sergeant's head above his right temple, a bald patch of keloid that he had tried to train his remaining hair to cover, and a streak of fluorescent orange wrapping his bare right forearm. Radescu thought the last was a third scar until he saw that it terminated in a dragon's head laid into the skin of Bourne's palm, a hideous and hideously obtrusive decoration . . . and a sign of scarring as well, though not in the physical sense.

Bourne locked shut his body armor and said, "Well, this is the lot of it, Major?" to the graying adjutant.

That mercenary officer grimaced, but said, "Give them their guns, Luckens."

The Slammer who had brought the armor had already ducked back from the storage container with a submachine gun in either hand and ammunition satchels in the crooks of both elbows, grinning almost as broadly as Sergeant Bourne.

The lieutenant who had just been freed had no expression at all on his face as he started to load his own weapon. His left hand slid a fresh magazine into the handgrip of his powergun, a tube containing not only the disks which would liberate bolts of energy but the liquid nitrogen which worked the action and cooled the chamber between shots. As his hands moved, Hawker's eyes watched the Oltenian general.

"I'll need to brief you men in private," Radescu said, managing to override the unexpected catch in his throat. "I'm General Radescu, and the two of you are assigned at my discretion." How private the briefing could be when Hammer listened to discussions in the Tribunal Palace was an open question . . . but again, it didn't matter what the *mercenary* command knew.

"Major Stanlas," said Hawker to the adjutant, only now rotating his face from the Oltenian, "do you see any problem with me borrowing back my jeep for the, ah, duration of the assignment?"

"General," said the adjutant, thumbing a switch in the oral notepad he pointed toward Radescu, "do you accept on behalf of your government the loan of a jeep with detection gear in it?" That gave Hammer somebody to bill if something went wrong . . . and they must already have a record of the level to which the Tribunes had authorized Radescu's authorization.

"Yes, yes, of course," the general snapped, noticing that Bourne had anticipated the question and answer by striding toward a saucer-shaped air cushion vehicle. It had been designed to hold four people, but this one had seats for only two because the back was filled with electronics modules.

"You may not be real comfortable riding on the hardware that way," Hawker said, "but it beats having a Molt pop out of the air behind you." He turned his head slowly, taking in the arc of nondescript landscape he could not have seen through the barred front of his cell. "Not," he added, "that we'll see action around here."

Radescu gave the big mercenary a brief, tight smile. "You don't think so, Lieutenant? I wouldn't have come to Colonel Hammer for someone to drive me and—" he appraised Hawker in a different fashion, then made a moue which flapped the wings of his beauty patch before he concluded "—bring me tea at night."

Hawker spat on the ground. He would probably have dropped the conversation even without Sergeant Bourne spinning the jeep to an abrupt halt between the two officers and calling cheerfully, "Hop in, everybody." His

submachine gun was now carried across his chest on an
inertia-locked sling which gave him access to the weapon
the instant he took his right hand from the tiller by which
he now guided the jeep.

The general settled himself, finding that the modules
had been arranged as the back and sides of a rough
armchair, with room enough for his hips in the upper
cavity. The handles for carrying the modules made excellent grips for Radescu; but there was no cushion, only
slick, hard composite, and he hoped Bourne would not
play the sort of game with the outsider which he in fact
expected.

"Get us a short distance beyond this position and stop,"
the Oltenian said, bracing himself for an ejection-seat start.
He thought of ordering Hawker to trade places with him,
but he was sure such a demand would also turn into an
embarrassment for him. "I'll brief you there."

Instead of a jackrabbit start, the mercenary sergeant
powered up the jeep in an acceleration curve so smooth
that only the airstream was a problem to Radescu on his
perch. The Oltenian snatched off his glistening, metalized
cap and held it against his lap as he leaned forward into
the wind.

Bourne was driving fast, but with an economy of
movement on the tiller and such skill that the attitude of
the jeep did not change even when it shot up the sloping
inner face of the berm around the firebase and sailed above
the steep outer contour in momentary free flight. He wasn't
trying to dump Radescu off the back: Bourne took too
much pride in his skill to drive badly as a joke.

"Colonel won't like the way you're speeding in his
firebase," Lieutenant Hawker said mildly to the sergeant.

"What's he going to do?" Bourne demanded. "Sentence
me to death?" But he slacked off the trigger throttle built
into the grip of the tiller.

Between the encampments, Oltenian and mercenary, was
a wooded ridge high enough to block shots fired from either
position toward targets in the no man's land between.
Radescu had understood the forces were integrated, but

obviously the situation in the field had changed in a fashion which had not yet been reported to the Tribunes in Belvedere. Bourne threaded his way into a copse of broad-leafed trees on the ridge while Radescu held his seat firmly, aware that even at their present reduced speed he would be shot over the front of the vehicle if the driver clipped one of the boles around which he maneuvered so blithely.

It was without incident, however, that Bourne set the jeep down out of direct sight of either encampment. He turned and looked up at Radescu with a sardonic grin; and Hawker, still-faced, looked as well.

Radescu laughed harshly. "I was wondering," he said to the surprised expressions of the mercenaries, "whether I'm speaking to you from the height of a throne—or of a cross." He swung himself to the ground, a trifle awkwardly because the padding in his uniform trousers to exaggerate his buttocks had not been sufficient to prevent the hard ride from cutting blood circulation to his legs.

"That's fitting, in a way," the Oltenian said to the Slammers watching as his hands massaged his thighs, a thumb and forefinger still gripping the gilded brim of his hat, "because the Tribunes have granted me power of life and death over all members of the armed forces of the State—but they haven't taught me how to bring the dead to life."

Without speaking Lieutenant Hawker slipped from his own seat and stood with one heel back against the ground-effect mantle of the jeep. Bourne shifted only very slightly so that he faced Radescu directly; the head of the dragon on his palm rested on the grip of his submachine gun.

"I have been given *full* authority to take command and get the offensive against the Molts on track again," Radescu continued, "and I have the responsibility as well as authority to deal with the situation. But the present command staff is going to resent me, gentlemen, and I do not believe I can expect to do my job unless I go into my initial meeting with you present."

"You think," said Hawker as something small and nervous shrilled down at the men from a treetop, "that the present officers will arrest you if we aren't there to protect you."

"There's two of us, General," added Profile Bourne, whose index finger traced the trigger guard of his weapon, "and there's three divisions over there." He thumbed toward the encampment. "We can't handle that, friend. No matter how much we might like to."

"The army command, and the commander and chief of staff of each division will be present," said General Radescu, stretching his arms out behind his back because when the muscles were under tension they could not tremble visibly. "And they won't do anything overt, no, it's not what they'll say—"

The young Oltenian straightened abruptly, glaring at the Slammers. "But I don't care what they say, gentlemen, I didn't come here to preside over an army sinking into a morass of lethargy and failure. I will remove any officer who seems likely to give only lip service to my commands.

"And—" he paused, for effect but also because the next words proved unexpectedly hard to get out his throat "—and if I give the signal, gentlemen, I expect you to kill everyone else in the room without question or hesitation. I will give the signal—" he twirled the band of his hat on his index finger "—by dropping my hat."

Glittering like a fairy crown in a shaft of sunlight, Radescu's hat spun to the forest floor. The only sound in the copse for the next ten seconds was the shrieking of the animal in the foliage above them.

"Via," said Sergeant Bourne, in a voice too soft for its precise emotional loading to be certain.

"Sir," said Lieutenant Hawker, shifting his weight from the jeep so that both feet rested firmly on the ground, "does Colonel Hammer know what you intend? For us?"

Radescu nodded crisply, feeling much lighter now that he had stated what he had not, as it turned out, clearly articulated even in his own mind. He felt as though he were listening to the conversation from a vantage point outside his own body. "I have told no one of my specific plans," his mouth said, "not even Chief Tribune Antonescu, my uncle. But I believe Colonel Hammer did—would not be

surprised by anything that happened. The point that caused
him to grant my request was your, your special status,
gentlemen."

"Via," Sergeant Bourne repeated.

Hawker walked over to the gilded cap and picked it up
with his left hand, the hand which did not hold a submachine gun.

"Here, sir," he said as he handed the hat back to General
Radescu. "You may be needing it soon."

"Hoo, *Lordy*!" said Sergeant Bourne to the captain who
nervously ushered them into the staff room to wait.
"Where's the girls, good son?" He pinched the Oltenian's
cheek, greatly to the man's embarrassment. "Not that you're
not cute yourself, dearie."

"This the way you—gentlemen—normally operate in the
field?" Hawker asked as his palm caressed the smooth
surface of a nymph in a wall fountain.

"Well, the water's recycled, of course," Radescu said in
mild surprise as he considered the matter for the first time.

He looked around the big room, the tapestries—repro-
ductions, of course—and ornately carven furniture, the
statues in the wall niches set off by foliage and rivulets.
The Slammers lieutenant looked as incongruous here,
wearing his scarred armor and unadorned weapon, as a bear
would in a cathedral: but it was Hawker, not the fittings,
which struck Radescu as out of place. "This does no harm,
Lieutenant, beyond adding a little to our transport require-
ments. A modicum of comfort during staff meetings doesn't
prevent officers from performing in a responsible and, and,
courageous manner in action."

He was wondering whether there would be enough time
to requisition an orderly to clean the muck from his boots.
On balance, that was probably a bad idea since the pearl
trousers were irredeemably ruined. Better to leave the
ensemble as it was for the moment rather than to increase
its absurdity. . . .

"Just how do you expect to get bloody Oltenian officers
to act courageously, General-sir?" Bourne asked in a tone

much more soberly questioning than the sarcasm of the words suggested. The three men were alone in the room now that the poof captain had banged the door nervously behind him, and Bourne watched Radescu over the decorated palm of his right hand.

"I'm going to lead from the front, Sergeant Bourne," the young general said quietly, noticing that the expression on the mercenary's face was very similar to that on the dead Molt staked to the bow of Hammer's command vehicle.

Radescu had seen no trophies of that sort in their drive through the State encampment. That could be a matter of taste—but equally it might mean that Oltenian forces had failed to kill any of the aliens.

Of the autochthons. Oltenia was, after all, the Molts' world alone until the human settlement three centuries before.

"I . . . ," said Radescu, choosing to speak aloud on a subject different from that on which his mind would whisper to him if his mouth remained silent. "Ah. . . . Tell me, if you will, how the charges came to be leveled against you, the two of you."

"Why we blew away those heroes of the Oltenian state, Lieutenant," restated Bourne with a bitter smile.

The big Slammers lieutenant sat down on the coping of the fountain. The seat of his trousers must have been in the water, but he did not appear to notice. "Sure, General," he said in the accentless Oltenia-Rumanian which all the Slammers had been sleep-taught when their colonel took the present contract. "I'll tell you about what happened."

Hawker closed his eyes and rubbed his brow with the knuckles of his right hand. In a heart-stopping flash, Radescu realized that the mercenary was removing his fingers from the grip of his weapon before he called up memories of the past.

"We cleared a bottleneck for a battalion of locals," Hawker said.

"Your boys, General," Sergeant Bourne interjected.

"Killed a few ourselves, pointed some others out with

gunfire," the lieutenant continued. "No point in knowing where a Molt's going to appear a minute ahead of time if it took us ten to relay the data. These're a pretty good short-range data link." He patted the gray plastic receiver of his submachine gun.

"You were able to have that much effect yourselves?" Radescu said, seating himself at the head of the long conference table. The richly-grained wood hid the ruin of his boots and uniform; though when the time came, he really ought to rise to greet the officers he had summoned. "To clear a corridor, I mean?"

"Got our bag limit that day," said Bourne, wiping his lips with the dragon on his palm. "By the *Lord* we did."

"We took the Molts by surprise," Hawker explained. "There really aren't that many of them, the warriors, and we cleared out the ones who knew the territory before they figured things out."

Hawker's right thumb stripped something from a belt dispenser to give his hands something to play with as he talked. The gesture relaxed Radescu somewhat until he realized that the mercenary was now juggling an eyeball-sized minigrenade.

"We ducked into a nursery tunnel then, to get clear of the snipers," Hawker said. "Figured that warriors could come at us there, but before we were in danger Profile'd hand 'em one to keep."

"Where the chicken got the ax," said Bourne, running an index finger—his left—across his throat. Radescu thought the gesture was figurative. Then he noticed the knife blade, the length of the finger along which it lay and so sharp that light rippled on its edges as it did on the water dancing down the nymph's stone arms.

Bourne smiled and flicked his left hand close to some of the decorative foliage in the nearest wall niche. A leaf gave a startled quiver; half of it fluttered to the floor, severed cleanly. Satisfied, Bourne stropped both sides of the blade against his thigh to clean any trace of sap from the weapon.

"Thing about the Molts," he went on, leaning closer to

Radescu, "is that how far they can pop through the air depends on how old they are." It was the sort of lecture the sergeant would have given a man fresh to the field . . . as Radescu was, but he and his ancestors in unbroken line had been living with the Molts for three hundred years. The Oltenian general listened with an air of careful interest, however; the disquisition indicated a level of positive feeling toward him on the mercenary's part; and for more reasons than his plan for the meeting, Radescu wanted Bourne to like him.

"The old males," the sergeant said, "there's no telling how far they can hop if there's a big enough piece of hard rock for 'em to get a *grip* of, like. With their minds, you know? But the females—not bad looking some of 'em either, in the right light—"

"Profile . . . ?"

"Yessir." Bourne's right hand nodded a gobbling gesture in front of his mouth as if the dragon's head were swallowing the words he had just spoken. "But the females can hop only maybe ten kays and it takes 'em longer to psych into doing it, even the old ones. And the little babies, they can't jump the length of my prick when they're newborn. So the adults keep 'em in holes in the rock so their minds can get the feel of the rock, like; touch the electrical charge when the rock shifts. And there they were when we got in, maybe a dozen a' the babes."

"And that was about when it dropped in the pot, I s'pose, General," said Hawker as he stood up deliberately and faced the wall so that he would not have to look at the cosmetic-covered Oltenian face as he finished the story. "A, a local officer . . . I told him to get the little ones out of the tunnel; figured they'd be put in a holding tank somewhere. And he killed them."

Hawker's back muscles strained against his clamshell armor, hunching it. "There was one more I was holding, a little Molt I'd brought out myself."

He turned again, proceeding through stress to catharsis. "I blew that poof to Hell, General Radescu, before he could kill that baby too."

Alexander Radescu had seen the Slammers' powerguns demonstrated. The snap of their blue-green energy was too sudden to be fully appreciated by the senses, though the retinas danced for almost a minute thereafter with after-images of the discharge's red-orange complement. A shot would be dazzling in a cavern of dark rock lighted by Molt torches and the lamps of the vehicles driven headlong within. The blood and stench of the sudden corpse, that too Radescu could visualize—had to be able to visualize or he would not stay functionally sane if this meeting this morning proceeded as he feared it might, planned that it might. . . .

"And you, Bourne," Radescu said, "you were condemned simply for being present?" It was more or less what he had expected, though he had presumed that the sergeant was the principal in the event and Lieutenant Hawker was guilty of no more than failure to control his murderous subordinate. It was the sort of clean sweep Chief Tribune Antonescu would have made. . . .

"Oh, one a' the poofs threw down on the Loot," Bourne said. He was smiling because he had returned to an awareness of the fact that he was alive: when Radescu had first seen the sergeant, Bourne was dead in his own mind; waiting as much for burial as the shot in the back of his neck that would immediately precede interment. "I took him out and, Via, figured better safe'n sorry."

He looked at the mercenary officer, and the set of his jaw was as fierce for the moment as any expression he had thrown Radescu. "I still think so, Loot. There a couple of times, I figured I'd been crazy to hand this over and let them put us in that box." His index finger tapped the submachine gun's receiver, then slipped within the trigger guard as if of its own volition. "And you know, we aren't out of it yet, are we?"

Bourne shifted his torso to confront Hawker, and the muzzle of the slung weapon pointed as well.

"Anybody ever swear you'd get out of the Slammers alive, Sergeant?" Lieutenant Hawker asked in a voice as slick and cold as the iridium barrel of the gun thrusting toward him.

Radescu tensed, but there was no apparent fear in Hawker's grim visage—and no more of challenge, either than that of a man facing a storm cloud in the knowledge that the rain will come if it will.

"Ah, Via, Loot," Bourne said, the sling slapping the submachine gun back against his chest when he let it go, "I didn't want ta grease the Colonel, cop. After all, he gave this poor boy a job didn't he?"

Hawker laughed, and Bourne laughed; and the door beside the sergeant opened as the first of the command staff entered the meeting room, already three minutes after the deadline in Radescu's summons.

The Oltenian general looked from the newcomer to the wall clock and back to the newcomer, Iorga, the Second Division commander. When Radescu himself smiled, Sergeant Bourne was uneasily reminded of a ferret he had once kept as a pet—and Hawker caught a glimpse, too, beneath the beauty patch and lip tint, of a mind as ruthless as the blade of a scythe.

It took the command staff thirty-six minutes to assemble in the large trailer in the center of the Oltenian encampment, though none of the officers were more than a kilometer away at the summons and Radescu had clearly stated that anyone who did not arrive in fifteen minutes put his command in jeopardy for that fact alone. It was not, he thought, that they did not believe the threat: it was simply that the men involved would be *unable* to act that promptly even if it were their lives that depended on it.

Which indeed was the case.

The quarters of the Army Commander, Marshal Erzul, adjoined the conference trailer; but it was to no one's surprise that Erzul arrived last of the officers summoned . . . and it did not surprise Alexander Radescu that the marshal attempted to enter surrounded by his personal aides. The milling, disconsolate troop of underlings outside the doorway of the conference room was warning enough that Radescu hewed precisely to the language of the summons; but Erzul's action was not motivated by ignorance.

Radescu had motioned the six earlier arrivals to chairs while he himself sat on a corner of the conference table and chatted with them—recruiting figures, the Season's colors in the capital, the gala for the Widows of the War at which a Molt had appeared with a powergun, firing indiscriminately. "There were two stone urns, no more than that, and the Molt focused on them across over a thousand kays—" he was saying, when the door opened and the divisional officers leaped to their feet to salute Marshal Erzul.

Radescu cocked his head toward the marshal and his entourage, then turned away. He did not rise for Erzul who was not, despite his rank, Radescu's superior officer, and he twisted the gold-brimmed cap furiously in his hands. Around and back, like the glittering spirals of a fly jumped by a spider, both of them together buzzing on the end of the spider's anchor line; around and back.

The young general took a deep breath. By looking at the two officers closest to where he sat at the head of the table, he was able to avoid seeing either of the Slammers poised along the wall where they seemed muddy shadows against the opulence and glitter of the room's furnishings and other occupants. He could not avoid his own imagination, however, and the doubt as to whether there would be any safe place in the room when the guns began to spray. He closed his eyes momentarily, not a blink but part of the momentary tensioning of all his muscles . . . but he *had* to learn whose orders they would take, these men around him.

"Generals Oprescu and Iorga," Radescu said loudly, fixing the commanders of the First and Second Divisions with eyes as pure as the blue enamel on his shoulder boards, "will you kindly put out of the conference room all those who seem to have entered with the marshal? All save General Forsch, that is, since the Tribunes have ordered him to attend as well."

There was a frozen pause. Iorga looked at Oprescu, Oprescu at his manicure as a flush mounted from his throat to the cheeks which he had not had time to prepare with a proper base of white gel.

Erzul was a stocky, jowly bulldog to Radescu's cat. As his aides twitched and twittered, the marshal himself crashed a step forward. "This is *my* command," he thundered to the back of Radescu's head, his eyes drawn unwillingly to the flickering highlights of the cap in the general's hands, "and *I* decide where my aides will be!"

"The summons that brought you here, Marshal," Radescu announced in a voice which became increasingly thin in his own ears, though no one else in the room seemed to hear the difference, "informed you that the Tribunes had placed me in charge of all personnel of the First Army, yourself included."

"The Tribunes," sneered Erzul as everyone else in the room stayed frozen and Sergeant Bourne's eyes focused on something a thousand leagues away. "Your *uncle*."

"Yes," said the young general as he rose to his muddy feet, fanning himself gently with the cap in his hand, "my uncle."

General Iorga made a little gesture with the backs of his hands and fingers as if he were a house servant trying to frighten a wasp out of the room with a napkin. "Go on," he said to the captain closest to him in a voice with a tinge of hysteria and desperation. "Go *on* then, you shouldn't *be* here!"

All of the divisional officers, not just the pair to whom Radescu had directed his order, sprang forward as if to physically thrust their juniors out of the conference room. General Forsch, Erzul's lanky, nervous chief of staff, slid behind the marshal as if for concealment and in fear that the sudden onslaught would force him out the door with subordinate aides.

Neither of the mercenaries changed the expression— lack of expression—on his face. Lieutenant Hawker stretched his left arm to the side and began flexing the fingers of that hand like a man trying to work out a muscle cramp.

"Marshal Erzul," said Radescu as he suppressed a hysterical urge to pat the blood-suffused cheek of the former army commander, "your resignation on grounds of health is regretfully accepted. Your services to the State

will be noted in my report to Chief Tribune Antonescu."
He paused. "To my uncle."

Radescu expected the older man to hit him, but instead
Erzul's anger collapsed, leaving behind an expression that
justified the accusation of ill-health. The marshal's flush
drained away abruptly so that only the grimy sallowness
of pigment remained to color his skin. "I—" he said.
"General, don't—"

General Iorga stepped between the two officers, the
former army commander and the man who had replaced
him. "Go on!" he cried to the marshal. Iorga's hands
fluttered on the catches of his holster.

In a final burst of frustration, Marshal Erzul snatched
off his cap, formal with ropes of gold and silver, and hurled
it blindly across the room. It thudded into the wall near
Hawker, who neither smiled nor moved as the hat spun
end over end to the floor. Erzul turned and charged the
door like a soccer player driving for the goal regardless of
who might be in his way.

In this case, Erzul's own chief of staff was the only man
who could not step clear in time. General Forsch grunted
as his superior elbowed him in the pit of the stomach and
then thrust past him through the outside door.

Under other circumstances, Forsch might have followed.
Now, however, he watched the marshal's back and the door
banging hard against its jamb—the automatic opening and
closing mechanisms had been disconnected to permit aides
to perform those functions in due deference to their superiors. The divisional officers were scurrying for their places
around the table, and Radescu was finally preparing to discuss the main order of business—the war with the Molts.

"It's easy to bully old men who've spent their lives in
the service of Man and the Tribunate, isn't it, Master
Radescu?" said Forsch in a voice as clear and cutting as
a well-played violin. "Do you think the Molts will be so
obliging to your whim?"

Radescu slid into the chair at the head of the table,
looking back over his shoulder at Forsch. The chief of staff
stood with his chin thrust out and slightly lifted, rather as

though he were baring his long, angular throat to a slaughterer's knife. Radescu had not realized the man even *had* a personality of his own: everything Antonescu's nephew had been told suggested that Forsch was no more than Erzul's shadow—a gaunt, panicky avatar of the marshal.

"No, General," said Radescu in a voice that did not tremble the way his hands would have done save for the polished tabletop against which he pressed them. "I don't think the Molts are going to be obliging at all. Why don't you sit down and we'll discuss the problem like loyal officers of Oltenia?"

He tapped with the brim of his cap on the chair to his immediate right. Forsch held himself rigid for a moment, his body still awaiting death or humiliation while his brain with difficulty processed the information freeing him from that expected end. Moving like a marionette with a string or two broken, the chief of staff—now Radescu's chief of staff, much to the surprise of both men—seated himself as directed.

"Hawker," said General Radescu as if the mercenary were his batman, "take this until we're ready to leave. I won't need it inside here."

Lieutenant Hawker stepped obsequiously from his place at the wall and took the gilded cap Radescu held out without looking away from his fellow Oltenian generals. The Slammer even bowed as he backed away again . . . but when he reached the fountain in its niche, he flipped the cap deliberately from his hand. The Oltenians, focused on one another, did not or did not seem to notice.

Profile Bourne relaxed and began rubbing his right arm with his left forefinger, tracing the length of the glowing orange dragon. Not that it would have mattered, but Radescu's cap was not on the floor.

It lay atop the hat which Erzul had thrown in anger.

"This war can only be a war of attrition," said pudgy General Oprescu with a care that came naturally to a man who needed to avoid dislocating his makeup. Radescu, watching the divisional commander, understood very well how the preternatural calm of the other man's face could cloak thoughts as violent as any which had danced through Marshal Erzul's features moments before. Radescu's face had been that calm, and he was willing to go to lengths beyond anything the Marshal had suspected. Perhaps Oprescu also had a core of rigid capability within . . . but it was very well hidden if that were the case.

"We can only hurt the Molts when they attack *us*," Oprescu continued as he examined his manicure. "Naturally, they inflict more damage on such occasions than we do . . . but likewise, their population base is much lower than ours."

"I believe the estimate," said the pale-eyed General Vuco, who had been a reasonably effective intelligence officer before promotion to Second Division chief of staff, "is seventy-three to one. That is, we can ultimately wipe the Molts from the face of Oltenia so long as we suffer no more than seventy-three casualties for each of the scaly-headed demons that we bag."

"The *problem* is," Oprescu went on, "that the seventy-three casualties aren't limited to the bunion-heads in the lower ranks, not when a Molt can pop out of the air in the middle of an officers' barracks that chances to be too close to a lump of granite."

Radescu's heart stopped for an instant and his eyes, unbidden, flicked sideways to Sergeant Bourne. The mercenary noncom grinned back at him, as relaxed as the trigger spring of his submachine gun. It struck the young Oltenian that there was a flaw in his plan of engaging gunmen to do what he could not have accomplished with guns alone: you have control over a gun as you do not over a man . . . not over men like those, the soft-featured lieutenant who was willing to kill for a matter of principle, and the scarred sergeant who needed far less reason than that. In Radescu's mind echoed the sergeant's gibe in the jeep: "What's he going to do? Sentence me to death?"

But Bourne smiled now and the moment passed with General Forsch saying as he gripped his biceps with bony fingers, "Of course the Molts have a—feeling for the casualty ratio, too; and while they're not as formally—

organized as we—" he blinked around the conference table, finally fixing Radescu with a look like that of a small animal caught at night in the headlights. "Ahem. Not as structured as we are. Nonetheless, when they feel that the fighting is to their disadvantage, they stop fighting—save for random attacks far behind the 'lines,' attacks in which they almost never suffer losses."

"Then," said Alexander Radescu, wishing that his voice were deep and powerful—though surely it could not be as tinny as it sounded in his own hypercritical ears—"we have to shift our strategy. Instead of advancing slowly—" "ponderously" was the word his mind suppressed a moment before his tongue spoke it; the lavish interior of the conference room had taken on a somewhat different aspect for Radescu since the mercenary lieutenant sneered at it "—into areas which the Molts infest, we shall make quick thrusts to capture the areas which make them vulnerable: the nursery caves."

"We *cannot* advance quickly," said General Vuco, who was more able than the others to treat Radescu as a young interloper rather than as the man with demonstrated control over the career of everyone else in the room, "so long as everyone in the assault must expect attack from behind at every instant. To—" he made a gesture with his left hand as if flinging chaff to the wind "—charge forward regardless, well, that was attempted in the early days of the conflict. Panache did not protect the units involved from total destruction, from massacre.

"Of course," Vuco added, directing his eyes toward a corner of the ceiling, "I'm perfectly willing to die for the State, even by what amounts to an order of suicide."

He dropped his gaze, intending to focus on the play of water in the alcove across the table from him. Instead, the Oltenian's eyes met those of Lieutenant Hawker. Vuco snapped upright, out of his pose of bored indolence. His mouth opened to speak, but no words came out.

"The mercenaries we hire, Hammer's troops," said Radescu, suppressing an urge to nod toward Hawker in appreciation, "manage well enough—or did," he added, glaring at his elders and new subordinates "until our failure to support them led to what I and the Tribunate agreed were needless and excessive casualties, casualties not covered by the normal war risks of their hiring contract."

Now for the first time, most of the senior officers looked up as though Hawker and Bourne were specimens on display. Vuco instead rubbed his eyes fiercely as if he were trying to wipe an image from their surface. Hawker accepted the attention stolidly, but the sergeant reacted with an insouciance Radescu decided was typical, making a surprisingly graceful genuflection—a form of courtesy unfamiliar on Oltenia and shockingly inappropriate from a man as ruggedly lethal as Profile Bourne.

"All very well," said General Forsch in the direction of the Slammers but answering Radescu's implied question, "if we had the detection capability that the mercenaries do. *They* have time, a minute or more, to prepare for an attack, even when they're moving."

Radescu's eyes traversed the arc of the divisional officers and General Forsch. His mind was too busy with his present words and the action which would develop from those words in the immediate future, however, for him really to be seeing the men around him. "Nonetheless," he heard his voice say, "General Forsch will determine a target suitable for sudden assault by Oltenian forces."

It was the intention he had formed before he accepted his uncle's charge, an intention vocalized here in the conference room for the first time.

"Troops for the exercise will come from Second Division. Generals Iorga, Vuco, your staff will coordinate with mine to determine the precise number and composition of the units to be involved in the exercise."

Radescu blinked. It was almost as if he had just opened his eyes because the staring officers sprang suddenly back into his awareness. "Are there any questions, gentlemen?"

General Forsch leaned forward, almost close enough for his long neck to snake out to Radescu's hand like a weasel snapping. "Youth will be served, I suppose," he said. "But, my leader, you have no idea of what it is like to battle the Molts on their own ground."

"I will before long, though," said Alexander Radescu as he rose in dismissal. "I'll be accompanying the force in person."

The sound of his subordinates sucking in breath in surprise was lost in the roar of blood through the young general's ears.

The most brilliant strategy, the most courageous intent, come alike to naught if the troops are marshalled at one point and their transport at another. The command group had scuttled out of the conference room with orders to plan an assault which none of them believed could be carried through successfully.

Radescu waited until he heard the door bang shut behind the last of his generals, Forsch; then, elbows on the table, he cradled his chin in his palms while his fingers covered his eyes. He did not like failure and, as he came nearer to the problem, he did not see any other likely result to his attempts.

It occurred to the young general that his subconscious might have planned the whole operation as a means of achieving not victory but solely an honorable excuse for him not to explain defeat to his uncle. The chances were very slim indeed that Alexander Radescu would survive a total disaster.

His pants legs were not only filthy, they stank. How his generals must be laughing at him!

"Sir . . . ?" intruded a voice whose owner he had forgotten.

"Ah, Lieutenant Hawker," said the Oltenian general, his personality donning its public mien as he looked up at the big mercenary. "Forgive me for not dismissing you sooner. I'll contact your colonel with thanks and—"

"General," Sergeant Bourne interrupted as he strode to the nearest chair and reversed it so that its back was toward the conference table, "those birds're right so far: if you just bull straight in like you're talking, your ass is grass and the

Molts'll well and truly mow it. You need support—and that's what you hired us Slammers for, isn't it?"

Bourne sat down, the weight of his gear suddenly evident from the crash it made when it bumped the chair. The sergeant's legs splayed to either side of the seat back which rose like an outer, ornately-carven, breastplate in front of his porcelain armor. The mercenary's method of seating himself was not an affectation, Radescu realized: the man's belt gear and the bulges of electronics built into the shoulders of his backplate would prevent him from sitting in a chair in the normal fashion.

"I thank you for your concern, Sergeant," Radescu said— had he ever before known the name of an enlisted man? He really couldn't be sure. "Colonel Hammer is no longer willing to divide his own forces and trust the Oltenian army to carry out its own portion of the operation. When I have proved my troops are capable of—active endeavor—on their own, then I believe we can come to an accommodation, he and I.

"For now," Radescu added brusquely as he rose, "I have business that does not concern mercenaries. If you'll be so good—"

"Sir, the Colonel *has* offered you troops," said Lieutenant Hawker as loudly as necessary to silence Radescu's voice without shrillness. "Us. All Profile means is you ought to use us, the best curst detection team in the Slammers. And he's right—you *ought* to use us, instead of throwing yourself away."

Radescu sat down again, heavily. The Slammers lieutenant was so much larger than the general that only by tricking his mind could Radescu keep from being cowed physically. "He didn't send you to me for that," he said, "for detection. You—you know that."

Bourne snorted and said, "Bloody *cop* we do."

At his side, with a hand now on the noncom's shoulder, Hawker replied, "The Colonel doesn't talk to me, sir. But if you think he doesn't keep up with what's happening with the people who hired him, hired *us*, there you're curst well wrong. Don't ever figure a man like Colonel Hammer isn't one step ahead of you—though he may not be ready to commit openly."

"Not," Bourne completed grimly, "when he's ready to call in the Bonding Authority and void the contract for employer's nonperformance."

"My Lord," said Radescu. He looked at the pair of mercenaries without the personal emotion—hope or fear or even disgust—he had always felt before. The implications of what Hawker had just said stripped all emotional loadings from the general's immediate surroundings. Hawker and Bourne could have been a pair of trees, gnarled and gray-barked; hard-used and very, very hard themselves. . . .

"My Lord," the Oltenian repeated, the words scarcely moving his lips. Then his gaze sharpened and he demanded, "You mean it was, was a game? You wouldn't have . . . ?"

"Try me, General," said Profile Bourne. He did not look at Radescu but at his open palm; and the dragon there bore an expression similar to that of the mercenary.

"It's not a game, killing people," said the lieutenant. "We got into the box where you found us by doing just what we told you we did. And believe me, sir, nobody ever complained about the support Profile and me gave when it came down to cases." The fingers of his right hand smoothed the receiver of the submachine gun where the greenish wear on the plastic showed the owner's touch was familiar.

"It's just I guess we can figure one thing out, now," the sergeant remarked, looking up with the loose, friendly look of a man lifting himself out of a bath in drugs. "We'd heard our sentence four days ago, not that there was a whole lotta doubt. I mean, we'd done it. The colonel watched us."

He gave Radescu the grin of a little boy caught in a peccadillo, sure of a spanking but winkingly hopeful that it might still be avoided. "We don't stand much on ceremony in the Slammers," Bourne went on. "For sure not on something like a shot in the neck. So the Loot'n me couldn't figure what the colonel was waiting for."

"I guess," the sergeant concluded with a very different sort of smile again, "he was waiting for you."

Hawker pulled a chair well away from the table, lifting it off the floor so that it did not scrape. The mercenary handled the chair so lightly that Radescu could scarcely believe that it was made of the same dense, heavily-carven wood as the one in which the Oltenian sat.

"You see, sir," the lieutenant said as he lowered himself carefully onto the seat, hunching forward a little to be able to do so, "we can't cover more than a platoon, the two of us—but a platoon's enough, for what you need."

"Any more'n that, they get screwed up," added Bourne. "Even if *we* get the range and bearing right, they don't. Just gives the Molts more targets to shoot at. That's not what we're here for."

"What *are* you here for?" Radescu asked, reaching out to touch Bourne's right palm to the other's great surprise. The skin was dry and calloused, not at all unlike the scaly head of a reptile. "What your colonel may want, I can see. But the danger to you personally—it isn't as though you'd be protected by, by your own, the tanks and the organization that strikes down Molts when they appear."

He withdrew his hand, looking at both the Slammers and marvelling at how stolid they appeared. Surely their like could have no emotion? "I'm an Oltenian," Radescu continued. "This is my planet, my State. Even so, everybody in the room just now—" his fingers waggled toward the door through which his fellow generals had exited "—thinks I'm mad to put myself in such danger. You two aren't lumps like our own peasants. You made it clear that I couldn't even *order* you without your willingness to obey. Would Hammer punish you if you returned to him without having volunteered to accompany me?"

"Guess we're clear on that one, wouldn't you say, Loot?" remarked Sergeant Bourne as he glanced at Hawker. Though the noncom was physically even smaller than Radescu, he did not sink into the ambience of the big lieutenant the way the Oltenian felt he did himself. Profile Bourne was a knife, double-edged and wickedly sharp; size had nothing to do with the aura he projected.

For the first time, Radescu considered the faces of his

divisional officers as they watched him in the light of the emotions he tried to hide when he looked at the pair of mercenaries. It could be that the Oltenians saw in him a core of something which he knew in his heart of hearts was not really there.

Hawker's body armor shrugged massively. "Look, sir," he said without fully meeting the Oltenian's eyes, "if we liked to lose, then we wouldn't be in the Slammers. I don't apologize for anything that happened before—" now he did focus his gaze, glacial in a bovine face, on Radescu "—but it wasn't what we were hired to do. Help win a war against the Molts."

Bourne tilted forward to grasp Radescu's hand briefly before the sergeant levered himself back to his feet. "And you know, General," the mercenary said as he rose, "until I met you, I didn't think the poofs had a prayer a' doin' that."

The encampment should in theory have been safe enough, with no chunk of crystalline rock weighing more than a kilogram located within a meter of the ground surface. Nobody really believed that a three-divisional area had been swept so perfectly, however, especially without the help which Hammer had refused to give this time.

The center of the encampment, the combined Army and the Second Division Headquarters, had been set up in a marsh and was probably quite secure. The nervousness of the troops mustered both for the operation and for immediate security was due less to intellectual fear of the Molts than to the formless concern which any activity raised in troops used to being sniped at from point-blank ambush with no time to respond.

Alexander Radescu felt sticky and uncomfortable in his new battledress, though its fabric and cut should have been less stiff than the formal uniforms he ordinarily wore. He could not bring himself to don body armor, knowing that it would cramp and distract him through the next hours when his best hope of survival lay in keeping flexible and totally alert.

Hawker and Bourne wore their own back-and-breast armor, heavier but far more resistant than the Oltenian version which Radescu had refused. They were used to the constriction, after all, and would probably have been more subconsciously hindered by its absence than by the weight.

Radescu would have been even more comfortable without the automatic shotgun he now cradled, a short-barrelled weapon which sprayed tiny razor-edged airfoils that spread into a three-meter circle ten meters from the muzzle. The gun was perfectly effective within the ranges at which Molt warriors were likely to appear; but it was the general's dislike of *personal* involvement in something as ignoble as killing, rather than his doubts about how accurately he could shoot, which put him off the weapon.

Still, he had to carry the shotgun for protective coloration. The mercenaries' jeep would stand out from the Oltenian units anyway, and the sole unarmed member of a combat patrol would be an even more certain choice for a Molt with the leisure to pick his target.

"Cop!" snarled Lieutenant Hawker from the side-seat of the jeep as he surveyed the numbers his apparatus projected glowing into the air before him. The mercenary's commo helmet was linked to epaulette speakers issued to the entire Oltenian contingent for this operation. Radescu heard the words both on his own borrowed helmet and, marginally later, directly from the lieutenant's mouth. "Discard Beacon Eighty-Seven. Team Seven, that's three duds so far outa this lot, and you've had *all* of 'em. Are you sure you know how to switch the bloody things on?"

"The numbers of the beacons being tested appear—on your screen, then?" General Radescu asked the mercenary sergeant beside him, wiggling his fingers toward the floating yellow numbers. Obviously, there was no screen; but he was uncertain how to describe in any other way what he saw.

"Naw, that's the playback from Central," replied Profile Bourne. He nodded his head toward the distant ridge beyond which sheltered Colonel Hammer and his armored regiment. "Doesn't matter if *we* pick up the signal or not, but How Batt'ry can't bust up rocks for us if they don't get the beacon."

"Yes, well . . . ," said General Radescu as he looked at the men and equipment around him. The Oltenian contingent was forty men mounted on ten light trucks—each with a load of explosives and radio beacons, plus a pintle-mounted automatic weapon which, at the flip of a switch, fired either solid shot for long-range targets or beehives of airfoil flechettes like the hand weapons.

The trucks were somewhat larger than the Slammers' jeep on which Radescu himself would be mounted. More significantly, the Oltenian vehicles rode on wheels spun from spring-wire rather than on air cushions. Ground effect vehicles of sufficient ruggedness and payload for scouting through brush required drive-systems of a better power-to-weight ratio than Oltenia could supply. The mercenaries' jeeps and one-man skimmers had the benefit of cryogenic accumulators, recharged at need—every hundred kilometers or so—from the fusion powerplants of the heavier combat cars and tanks.

The jeep which Sergeant Bourne drove and the energy weapon slung against his chest were thus both of a higher technology level than their Oltenian equivalents—but in neither case was the difference significant to the present mission. The range and quickness of the electronics which detected Molts before they appeared physically, and the needle-threading accuracy which terminal guidance gave the Slammers' rocket howitzers, were absolute necessities if the present operation were to succeed, however; and Colonel Hammer was supplying both.

Despite his public dismissal of Radescu, Hammer was giving him and the State of Oltenia one chance to seize back the initiative in this *accursed* war with the planet's dominant autochthons.

"We're ready, sir," said Lieutenant Hawker with his helmet mike shut off to make the report more personal than a radio message to the general two meters away. "The hardware is."

Radescu nodded. Bourne had already slipped onto his

seat on the left side of the jeep. Radescu had eaten a light, perfectly bland, meal of protein supplement an hour earlier. The food now lay like an anvil in his belly while his digestive system writhed in an attempt to crush it.

"Captain Elejash," the young general said, his signal broadcast to every member of the assault party, "are your men ready?" He lifted himself carefully onto his electronic throne on the back of the jeep, pleased to note that the motion decreased his nausea instead of causing him to vomit in the sight of several thousand putative subordinates.

"Yes sir," replied the commander of the Oltenian platoon, a rancher before the war as were most of his men. They were a hardbitten crew, many of them as old as the general himself, and very different in appearance from the pasty-faced young factory workers who made up the ordinary rank and file of the army. Forsch and Iorga had gone at least that far toward making the operation a success.

"General Radescu, the support battalion is ready," said an unbidden voice over the wailing background which Radescu had learned to associate with recompressed ultra-low frequency transmissions from Army HQ.

Alexander Radescu looked imperiously around him at the faces and heavy equipment and distant, wooded hills, all of which blurred in his fear-frozen mind to gray shadows.

"All right," he said in his cool, aristocratic voice. "Then let's go."

And before the last word had reached the general's throat mike, Profile Bourne was easing the jeep forward at a rapidly accelerating pace.

How smoothly it rides, thought General Radescu as the ground effect jeep sailed up a hillside pocked by the burrows of small grazing animals and Lieutenant Hawker opened fire from the front seat with shocking unexpectedness.

The ionization detectors had given no warning because the Molt was already sited, a picket waiting near the Oltenian base on a likely course of advance. Hawker's face shield was locked in place, and through its electronic additions to the normal sensory spectrum—passive infrared or motion enhancement—the mercenary had spotted his target as it rose to attack.

Cyan flashes squirted from Hawker's gun at a cyclic rate so high that their afterimage combined to form a solid orange bar on Radescu's dazzled retinas. The vehicles were in line abreast at ten-meter intervals with the Slammers' jeep in the center. A multistemmed bush to the jeep's right front hissed and shrivelled as it drank the energy bolts; then it and recognizable portions of an adolescent Molt were blasted apart by a violent secondary explosion. The autochthon had carried either a satchel charge or an unusually-powerful shoulder-launched missile. The red flash of its detonation, though harmless to the assault platoon, caused the driver of the nearest truck to stall his engine. He knew that if Hawker had been seconds slower, the blast would have enveloped the Oltenian vehicle.

"Eight red thirty degrees," said Hawker as unemotionally as though his gun's barrel was not pinging and discoloring the finish of the forward transom on which he rested it to cool. Numbers and symbols, not the ones the mercenary was relaying to the assault force, hung as images of yellow and violet in the air before him. "Four yellow zero degrees."

Most of the pintle-mounted weapons snarled bursts toward the range and bearing each gunner had computed from the Slammer's rough direction. First Hawker gave the number of the truck he chose as a base for that deflection; then red, orange or yellow for fifty, seventy-five or hundred meter arcs around that truck; and finally the bearing itself. Molts beyond a hundred meters were rarely dangerous to a moving target, even with the most modern weapons. When possible, the mercenary would point out such warriors with a burst from his own gun or even call in artillery; but there was no need to complicate a system of directions which had to work fast if it were to work at all.

"Cease fire," Hawker ordered as the jeep slid through a line of palmate leaves springing from the hillcrest and Radescu covered his face with one hand. "*Cease* fire, Six, they were going away!"

More pickets, Radescu thought as the echoes of gunfire died away and the line of vehicles rocked down the next slope without immediate incident. The blips of plasma which the mercenaries' detection equipment had caught this time were those resulting from Molts disappearing, not coalescing to attack. The pickets would be returning to their council, their headquarters, with warning of the direction and nature of the attack.

There was the sharp crash of an explosion nearby. The crew of Truck Six had tossed a charge overboard, onto a patch of crystalline rock which their own sensors had identified. Dirt showered the jeep and Radescu, while dual blasts sounded from opposite ends of the patrol line, deadened somewhat by distance. The shaped-charge packets were weighted to land cavity-down—most of the time. Even so, they did not have enough stand-off for the pencil of super-heated gas to reach maximum velocity and effectiveness before it struck the rock it was to shatter.

The bombs which the patrol set off could not break up even surface outcrops so effectively that no Molt could home on them. However, the charges did, with luck, lessen and change the piezoelectrical signature by relieving stresses on the crystalline structure. The oldest, most experienced, Molts could still pick their way to the location, sorting through the sea of currents and electrical charges for bits of previous reality which their brains could process like those of paleontologists creating a species from bone fragments.

Even these older warriors were slowed and limited as to the range from which they could project themselves to such damaged homing points, however. Younger Molts, equally deadly with their guns and buzzbombs, were effectively debarred from popping into ambush directly behind the advancing patrol.

Powerguns—and the Molts carried them, though Oltenian regulars did not—had an effective anti-personnel range, even in atmosphere, of line of sight. There was no practical way to prevent Molt snipers from firing into distant human arrays, then skipping back to safety. No way at all, except by killing every male Molt on Oltenia.

Or by ending the war, which everyone high in the government thought was also impossible. Everyone but Alexander Radescu.

"Six red one-eighty!" shouted Lieutenant Hawker, emotionless no longer as his instruments warned him of the Molt blurring out of the air through which Truck Six had just driven. The attacker was in Hawker's own blind spot, even if he had dared take his eyes from the read-outs now that the attack had come in earnest. "Ten yellow ninety!"

The jeep dropped a hand's breadth on irregular ground as the general twisted to look over his shoulder. The sinking feeling in his guts was more pronounced than the actual drop when he realized that all the pintle-mounted guns in the patrol had been swung forward at the first contact. The guns on even-numbered trucks were to have covered the rear at all times, but nervousness and enthusiasm had combined to give the autochthons a perfect opening. Now gunners were tugging at the grips of their long-barreled weapons, more handicapped by cramped footing than by the guns' inertia.

Black smoke from the shaped charge dissipated above the scar in the sod and flattened grass. Squarely in the center of the blast circle—so much for the effectiveness of the charges—a shadow thickened to solid form.

The Molt's gray scales had a blue tinge and what Radescu would have called a metallic luster had not the iridium barrel of the creature's powergun showed what luster truly was. The general did not even realize he had fired until the butt of the shotgun slammed him in the ribs: he had loose-gripped the unfamiliar weapon, and its heavy recoil punished the error brutally.

Radescu's shot twinkled like a soap bubble as the cloud of airfoils caught the sunlight twenty meters above their target. The Molt's figure was perfectly clear for a moment as it hulked behind the reflection of its gun; then the autochthon began to shrink and dissolve in a manner that made Radescu think it had teleported itself to another location before firing.

No.

There was a scarlet cloud in the air beyond the Molt as the trucks and jeep bounded away, blood and flesh and chips of yellow bone. An Oltenian soldier with a weapon like Radescu's and a skill the general had never been expected to learn had fired three times. The autochthon crumpled before the machineguns could even be rotated back in its direction.

Half a dozen shaped charges went off almost simultaneously, and there was heavy firing from the right. A powergun bolt sizzled across the ragged line of vehicles, an event so sudden that Radescu, as he turned back, could not be certain from which end it had been fired. Hawker was calling out vectors in the tight, high voice of a sportscaster. The young general hoped his fellows could understand the mercenary's directions; he was baffled by the unfamiliar data himself.

Sergeant Bourne banked the jeep around a copse of trees in a turn so sharp that the left side of the skirt dragged, spilling air in its brief hesitation. "Five red zero!" Hawker was calling, and the blur that focused down into a Molt was directly in front of the Slammers' vehicle. Bourne spun the tiller with his left hand and crossed his chest with his right, firing a burst of cyan bolts which the vehicle's own motion slewed across the creature's torso. The Molt fell onto its missile launcher, dead before its psychic jump was complete enough for the creature to be aware of its new surroundings.

Radescu's gun tracked the Molt as the jeep skidded past. He did not fire—it was obviously dead—but his bruised side throbbed as if the butt were pounding him again.

There was a whistle from the sky behind, bird cries which expanded into a roar so overpowering that earth fountained in apparent silence behind nearby trucks as they dropped shaped charges at the same time. The sound was so intense that Radescu felt it as a pressure on the back of his neck, then on his forehead and eyeballs. He wanted very badly to jump to the ground and cower there: the universe was so large and hostile . . .

Instead, the young general gripped the handle of one

of the modules which formed his seat and stood up as straight as he could without losing his hold. He was bent like someone trying to ride a bucking animal but the defiance was real.

A craggy, wooded hilltop three hundred meters ahead of the vehicles dimpled, dirt and fragments of foliage lifting into the air. There were no explosions audible. Radescu, slammed back into his seat when the jeep rose to meet him, thought the shell blasts were lost in the waterfall rush from overhead. That blanket of sound cut off with the suddenness of a thrown switch, its echoes a whisper to ears stunned by the roar itself.

Only then did the sextet of shells explode, their blasts muffled by the depth to which they had penetrated the rocky core of the hill. The slope bulged, then collapsed like cake dough falling. Larger trees sagged sideways, their roots crushed when the substrate was pulverized beneath them. No stones or fragments of shell casing were spewed out by the deep explosions, but a pall of dust rose to hide the immediate landscape—including a pair of Molts, killed by concussion just as they started to aim at the oncoming vehicles.

"Via!" swore Alexander Radescu. He had arranged the fire order himself two days earlier, six penetrator shells to land on a major intrusion of volcanic rock identified by satellite on the patrol's path. The plan had worked perfectly in demolishing what would otherwise have been a bastion for the autochthons.

But it had frightened him into a broil of fury and terror, because he had no personal experience with the tools he was using. Planning the fire order had been much like a game of chess played on holographic maps in the rich comfort of Army HQ. It had never occurred to Radescu that a salvo of twenty-centimeter shells would be louder than thunder as they ripped overhead, or that the ground would ripple at the hammerblows of impact even before the bursting charges went off.

Commanding soldiers is not the same as leading them.

"General, we—" Sergeant Bourne started to say, turning

in his seat though it was through Radescu's commo helmet that the words came.

"Teams One through Five, break left," the general said, overriding his driver's voice by keying his own throat mike. "Six through Ten—and Command—" the last an afterthought "—break right, avoid the shelled area."

There was confusion in the patrol line as trucks turned and braked for the unanticipated obstacle—which Radescu knew he should have anticipated. The churned soil and toppled vegetation would have bogged the trucks inextricably; and, while the terrain itself might have been passable for the air-cushion jeep, the dust shrouding it would have concealed fallen trunks and boulders lifted from the shuddering earth.

Bourne's head turned again as he cramped the tiller. His face shield had become an opaque mirror, reflecting Radescu in convex perfection. The Oltenian had forgotten that the Slammers' array of night vision devices included personal sonar which would, when necessary, map a lightless area with the fidelity of eyesight—though without, of course, color vision. The sergeant had been perfectly willing to drive into the spreading cloud, despite the fact that it would have blinded the hologram display of Hawker's detectors. That wasn't the sort of problem Profile Bourne was paid to worry about.

"We're blowing Truck Two in place," said a voice which Radescu recognized with difficulty as that of Captain Elejash. Almost at once, there was a very loud explosion from the left side of the line.

Looking over his shoulder, Radescu could see a black column of smoke extending jaggedly skyward from a point hidden by the undergrowth and the curve of the land. The jeep slowed because the trucks which had been to its right and now led it turned more awkwardly than the ground effect vehicle, slowing and rocking on the uneven ground. The smell of their diesel exhaust mingled with the dry, cutting odor of the dust shaken from the hillside.

Hawker was silent, though the yellow digits hanging in

the air before him proved that his instruments were still working. They simply had no Molts to detect.

"Truck Two overturned," resumed Elejash breathlessly. "We've split up the crew and are proceeding."

After blowing up the disabled vehicle, thought Radescu approvingly, to prevent the Molts from turning the gun and particularly the explosives against their makers. The trucks had better cross-country performance than he had feared—wet weather might have been a different story—but it was inevitable that at least one of the heavily-laden vehicles would come to grief. Truck Two had been lost without enemy action. Its driver had simply tried to change direction at what was already the highest practical speed on broken ground.

"Sir," said Sergeant Bourne, keying his helmet mike with his tongue-tip as he goosed the throttle to leap a shallow ravine that the Oltenian vehicles had to wallow through, "how'd you convince 'em to pick up the truck's crew?"

It was the first time Bourne had called him 'sir' rather than the ironic 'general.'

"I said I'd shoot—order shot—anyone who abandoned his comrades," Radescu replied grimly, "and I hoped nobody thought I was joking."

He paused. "Speed is—important," he continued after a moment spent scanning the tree-studded horizon. The separated halves of the patrol line were in sight of one another again, cutting toward the center. Boulders shaken by shellfire from the reverse slope of the hill still quivered at the end of trails that wormed through the vegetation. They would need follow-up salvos, but for the moment the Molts seemed unable to use their opportunities. . . . "But we have a war to win, not just a mission to accomplish. And I won't win it with an army of men who know they'll be abandoned any time there's trouble."

Numbers on Hawker's hologram display flashed back and forth from yellow to the violet that was its complement, warning at last of a resumption of Molt attacks. The mercenary lieutenant said, "Purple One," on a command

channel which Radescu heard in his left ear and the other
Oltenians did not hear at all.

"What?" he demanded, thinking Hawker must have
made a mistake that would give a clear shot to the
teleporting autochthon.

"Mark," said Hawker, in response to an answer even the
general had not heard.

Bourne, fishtailing to avoid Truck Five—itself pressed
by Truck Four, the vehicles had lost their spacing as they
reformed in line abreast—said, "They're landing way behind
us, sir. Loot's just called artillery on 'em while they're still
confused." Then he added, "We told you this was the way.
Not a bloody battalion, not a division—one platoon and catch
'em with their pants down."

They were in a belt of broad-leafed vegetation, soft-
trunked trees sprouted in the rich, well-watered soil of a
valley floor. There was relatively little undergrowth because
the foliage ten meters overhead met in a nearly solid mat.
The other vehicles of the patrol were grunting impressions,
patterns occasionally glimpsed through random gaps in the
trees. Amazingly, Truck Two appeared to have been the
only vehicle lost in the operation thus far, though the flurry
of intense fighting had almost certainly caused human casualties.

But teleporting Molts were vulnerable before they were
dangerous, and Radescu had been impressed by the way
bursts of airfoils had swept patches of ground bare. He
had felt like a step-child, leading men armed with indigenous weapons against an enemy with powerguns bought
from traders whose view of the universe was structured
by profit, not fantasies of human destiny. Though the energy
weapons had advantages in range and effectiveness against
vehicles—plus the fact that the lightly built autochthons
could not easily have absorbed the heavy recoil of Oltenian
weapons—none of those factors handicapped the members
of the patrol in their present job.

As trees snapped by and Bourne lifted the jeep a
centimeter to keep his speed down but still have maximum
maneuvering thrust available, the right earpiece of Radescu's

helmet said in a machine voice, "Central to Party. Halt your forces." They were that close, then, thought the Oltenian general. Without bothering to acknowledge—the satellite net that was Hammer's basic commo system on Oltenia would pick up the relayed order—Radescu said, "All units halt at once. All units halt." If he had tried to key the command channel alone to acknowledge, he might have had trouble with the unfamiliar mercenary helmet. Better to save time and do what was necessary instead of slavishly trying to obey the forms. If only he could get his officers to realize that simple truth. . . .

Sergeant Bourne had the principle of lower-rank initiative well in mind. Without waiting for the general to relay the order from Central, Bourne angled his fans forward and lifted the bow of the jeep to increase its air resistance. The tail skirt dragged through the loam but only slightly, not enough to whip the vehicle to a bone-jarring halt the way a less expert driver might have done in his haste.

Hawker's display was alive with flashes of yellow and violet, but he still did not call vectors to the Oltenian troops. A branch high above the jeep parted with an electric crackle as a bolt from a powergun spent itself in converting pulpy wood into steam and charred fragments.

The leaf canopy had become more ragged as the ground started to rise, so that Radescu could now see the escarpment of the ridge whose further face held their goal. The tilted strata before them were marked with bare patches from which the thin soil had slumped with its vegetation, though the trucks could—General Forsch had assured his commander—negotiate a route to the crest.

If it were undefended.

The world-shaking vibration of shells overhead was Radescu's attempt to meet his chief of staff's proviso.

Somebody should have ordered the members of the patrol to get down, but there was no opportunity now given the all-pervasive racket that would have overwhelmed even the bone-conduction speakers set into the Slammers' mastoids. The hiss-*thump* of powerguns as overeager Molts fired without proper targets also was lost, but the rare flicker of bolts in the foliage was lightning to the sky's own thunder. The thick soil of the valley floor was a warranty that no warrior was going to appear at arm's length of the deafened, cowering patrol, and the Molts' disinclination to cover significant distances on foot made it unlikely that any of them would race into the forest to get at the humans they knew were lurking there.

The initial shellbursts were lost in the rush of later salvoes. The first fire order had been intended to destroy a beacon on which the Molts would otherwise have focused. The present shellfire was turning the escarpment ahead into a killing ground.

Profile Bourne tapped the general's knee for attention, then gestured with the open, savage cup of his tattooed right hand toward the images which now hung over the jeep's bow. The modules projected a three-dimensional monochrome of the escarpment, including the heavy forest at its foot and the more scattered vegetation of the gentle reverse slope.

The Oltenian wondered fleetingly where the imaging sensor could be: all of the patrol's vehicles hid behind the barrier of trees, which concealed the escarpment as surely as it did the trucks. The angle was too flat for satellite coverage, and aircraft reconnaissance was a waste of hardware—with the crews if the aircraft were manned—in a military landscape dominated by light-swift powerguns. Perhaps it was a computer model using current satellite photography enhanced from a data base—of Hammer's, since the State of Oltenia had nothing of its own comparable.

The image of the rock face shattered. Instead of crumbling into a slide of gravel and boulders the way the hillock had done earlier when struck by penetrators, the escarpment held its new, fluid form as does a constantly replenished waterfall.

The rain feeding this spray was of bomblets from the firecracker rounds being hurled by all eighteen tubes of the Slammers' artillery. It was a prodigiously expensive undertaking—mechanized warfare is far more sparing of men than of material—but it was the blow from which Radescu prayed the Molts in this region would be unable to recover.

Each shell split in the air into hundreds of bomblets which in turn burst on the next thing they touched—rock, leaf, or the face of a Molt sighting down the barrel of his powergun. The sea of miniature blasts created a mist of glass-fiber shrapnel devouring life in all its forms above the microscopic—but without significantly changing the piezo-electrical constant of the rock on which the autochthons homed.

Hawker's detectors continued to flash notice of further Molts springing into the cauldron from which none of them would return to warn the warriors who followed them to doom.

Lieutenant Hawker was as still as the jeep, though that trembled with the shell-spawned vibration of the earth on which it now rested. Sergeant Bourne watched not the image of the fire-rippled escarpment but the detector display. His grin was alive with understanding, and he tapped together the scarred knuckles of his hands. Every violet numeral was a Molt about to die.

Short bursts were an inevitable hazard, impinging on Radescu's senses not by their sound—even the wash of the main bombardment was lost in the ballistic roar of the shells themselves—but by the fact that shafts of sunlight began to illuminate the forest floor. Stray bomblets stripped away the foliage they touched, but the low-mass shrapnel was not dangerous more than a meter or two from the center of each blast.

The Oltenian was nonetheless startled to see that the backs of his hands glittered in the sudden sunlight with glass fibers scarcely thicker than the hairs from among which they sprang. He had been too lost in the image of shellfire devouring the Molts to notice that it had put its mark on him as well.

The ionization detectors had been quiescent for almost a minute when the face of the escarpment slumped, no longer awash with firecracker rounds. Through the pulsing silence as the shellfire ceased came the rumble of collapsing rock—the final salvo had been of penetrator shells, now that the Molts had either recognized the killing ground for what it was or had run out of victims to send into the useless slaughter.

Like a bright light, the thunder of shellfire left its own afterimage on the senses of the men who had been subjected to it. Radescu's voice was a shadow of itself in his own ears with all its high frequencies stripped away as he said, "Platoon, forward. Each crew find its own path to the crest and await further orders."

Lord who aids the needy! thought the general as the jeep rocked onto its air cushion again. He was alive, and he had apparently won this first round of his campaign to end the war.

The second round: the command group of the army had been his opponent in the first, and he had won that too. Both victories due to the pair of mercenaries before him; and to the harsh, unexpectedly complex, colonel who commanded them.

With no need to match his speed to that of the trucks, Bourne sent his jeep through the remaining half-kilometer of forest with a verve that frightened Radescu—who had thought the initial salvo of shells passing overhead had drained him of any such emotion for months.

A few trees had grown all the way up to the original face of harder rock, but for the most part hard-stemmed scrub with less need for water and nutrient had replaced the more substantial vegetation near the escarpment. Everything, including the thin soil, had been swept away by the salvoes of antipersonnel bomblets. The paths down which tons of rock shattered by the penetrators slid were scarcely distinguishable from the stretches to either side which were untouched by the heavy shells.

The surface of an airless planetoid could not have been more barren; and there, at least, Radescu's nostrils would not have wrinkled at the smell of death.

Bourne took his right hand off his gun butt long enough

to pull rearward a dashboard lever while his left squeezed the hand throttle on the tiller wide open. The lever must have affected the angle of the fans within the plenum chamber, because the vehicle began to slide straight up the slope, stern lifted almost to a level with the bow like that of a funicular car.

The original angle of the escarpment had been in the neighborhood of one to one. The salvo of penetrators had shaken portions of the overhang down into a ramp at the foot of the slope, easing the ascent at the same time it changed the electrical signature. The sergeant's bow-on assault was still a surprise, to the Oltenian and to the Slammers' lieutenant, judging from Hawker's quick glance toward his fellow. The rear fans, those directly beneath Radescu and the electronics modules, spun with the angry sound of bullets ricocheting as they drove the vehicle upward.

Both mercenaries had locked their face shields down, less for visibility than for protection against pebbles still skipping from the hill's crumbled facade. Dust and grit, though blanketed somewhat by the overburden of topsoil from the further slope, boiled in the vortices beneath the skirt of the jeep.

The trucks of the patrol's Oltenian element crawled rather than loped in their ascent, but they were managing adequately. Their tires were spun from a single-crystal alloy of iron and chrome, and they gripped projections almost as well as the fingers of a human climber. Such monocrystal filaments were, with beef, the main export props of the economy of human Oltenia.

The Molts provided traders with the lustrous, jewel-scaled pelts of indigenous herbivores and with opportunities to mine pockets of high-purity ores. The senses which permitted the autochthons to teleport were far more sensitive and exact than were the best mechanical geosurveying devices in the human universe. Even so, Molt trade off-planet was only a tiny fraction of that of members of the Oltenian state.

The needs of the autochthons were very simple, however. As the jeep topped the rise, bounced fully a meter in the air by its momentum, a bolt from a powergun burst the trunk of one of the nearby trees mutilated in the hammering by firecracker rounds.

Bourne swore savagely in a language Radescu did not know, then cried, "Loot?" as he whipped the jeep in a double-S that brought it to a halt, partly behind another of the stripped boles which were the closest approach to cover on the blasted landscape.

"Take him," said the lieutenant as he rolled out of his seat before the jeep had fully grounded. As an afterthought, while he cleared his own weapon in the vehicle's shelter, he added, "Via, General, get *down!*"

The shot had come from across a valley three kilometers wide and as sere as the forest behind the patrol was lush. When slabs of granite tilted to form shallow wrinkles, layers of porous aquifer had been dammed and rerouted with startling effects for the vegetation on opposite sides of the impermeable divide. This valley had nothing like the dense canopy which had sheltered the vehicles while they waited for the firecracker rounds to do their work. Direct rainfall, the sole source of water for the vegetation here, had paradoxically stripped away much of the soil which might otherwise have been available because there was no barrier of foliage and strong root systems to break the rush of periodic torrents.

The native grass which fattened terran beefalo as efficiently as imported fodder provided a straggly, russet background to the occasional spike-leafed tree. Hiding places in the knobs and notches of the valley's further slope offered interlocking fields of fire across the entire area, and frequent outcrops among the grass below warned that Molts had free access to the valley floor as well.

The present shot had come from the far escarpment, however: it chopped shorter the trunk it hit at a flat angle. As he tumbled off his seat, obedient to the mercenary lieutenant, Radescu took with him a memory of the terrain three thousand meters away—an undifferentiated blur of gray and pale ochre—a background which could conceal a thousand gunmen as easily as one.

"We can't possibly find him!" the Oltenian whispered

to Hawker as Sergeant Bourne scanned for potential targets with only his eyes and weapon above the jeep's front skirt. "We'll have to wait for the artillery to get him."

The shelling had resumed, but it was of a different scale and tenor. Black splotches like oil-soaked cotton bloomed around momentary red cores as Oltenian artillery pummeled the far side of the valley. Hammer's three fully automated batteries of rocket howitzers were not involved in this bombardment. Their accuracy was needless—even indigenous artillery couldn't miss by three kilometers. The greater effectiveness of the mercenaries' shells would not change the fact that no practicable volume of fire could really affect the vast area involved. The shellbursts, though violent, left no significant mark once the puff of combustion products dispersed in the light breeze.

The State could not *afford* to use Hammer's hogs needlessly: the shells were imported over long Transit distances. Quite apart from their high cost in money terms, the length of time for replenishment might be disastrous in an emergency if stocks on Oltenia had been needlessly squandered.

Even as he spoke, General Radescu realized the absurdity of waiting for the shells speckling an area of twenty square kilometers to silence a single marksman. He grimaced, wishing he wore the makeup which would ordinarily have covered his flush of embarrassment.

"We got pretty good at countersniper work here on Oltenia," the lieutenant said mildly. The shellfire was not passing directly overhead, and in any case the trajectories were much higher than when the patrol cowered just short of the impact area of the heavy salvoes. "If this one just tries once more, Profile'll spot the heat signature and nail 'im." Hawker scowled. "Wish those bloody poofs'd get up here before the bastard decides to blow our detection gear all to hell. That first shot was too *cursed* close."

Alexander Radescu got to his feet, feeling like a puppet-master guiding the cunningly structured marionette of his body. He walked away from the jeep and the slender tree trunk which was probably as much an aiming point as protection for the crucial electronics. He stumbled because his eyes were dilated with fear and everything seemed to have merged into a blur of glaucous yellow.

"Sir!" someone cried. Then, in his head phones, *"Sir! Get back here!"*

Poofs could only draw fire, could they? Well, perhaps not even that. Radescu's ribcage hurt where the gun had kicked him the only time he fired a shot. As he lifted the weapon again, his vision steadied to throw boulders and hummocks across the valley into a clear relief that Radescu thought was impossible for unaided vision at that distance. His muscles were still shuddering with adrenaline, though, and the shotgun's muzzle wobbled in an arc between bare sky and the valley floor.

That didn't matter. The short-range projectiles could not reach the far slope, much less hit a specific target there. Radescu squeezed off and the recoil rotated his torso twenty degrees. A bitch of a weapon, but it hadn't really *hurt* this time because he had nestled the stock into him properly before he fired. The Molts were not marksmen either; there was no real danger in what he was doing, no *reason* for fear, only physiological responses to instinct—

The muzzle blast of his second shot surprised him; his trigger finger was operating without conscious control. Earth, ten meters downslope, gouted and glazed in the cyan flash of the sniper's return bolt. As grit flung by the release of energy flicked across Radescu's cheeks and forehead, another powergun bolt splashed a pit in the soil so close to Radescu's boots that the leather of them turned white and crinkled.

The crackling snarl of the bolt reaching for his life almost deafened the Oltenian to the snap of Bourne's submachine gun returning fire with a single round. Radescu was still braced against a finishing shot from the heavy powergun across the valley so that he did not move even as the sergeant scrambled back into the jeep and shouted, "Come *on*, let's get this mother down a *hole!*"

The jeep shuddered off its skirts again before even Lieutenant Hawker managed to jump aboard. Radescu, awakening to find himself an unexpected ten meters away, ran back to the vehicle.

"D'ye get him?" Hawker was asking, neither Slammer using the radio. There were things Central didn't have to know.

"Did I shoot at him?" the sergeant boasted, pausing a moment for Radescu to clamber onto his seat again. "Cop, yeah, Loot—he's got a third hole in line with his eyeballs." As the jeep boosted downslope, gravity adding to the thrust of the fans, Bourne added "Spoiled the bloody trophy, didn't I?"

Radescu knew that even a light bolt could be lethal at line of sight, and he accepted that magnification through the helmet faceplate could have brought the warrior's image within the appearance of arm's length. Nonetheless, a micron's unsteadiness at the gun muzzle and the bolt would miss a man-sized target three kays away. The general could not believe that anyone, no matter how expert, could rightfully be as sure of his accuracy as the Slammers' gunman was.

But there were no further shots from across the valley as the jeep slid over earth harrowed by the barrage of firecracker rounds and tucked itself into the mouth of the nursery tunnel which was the patrol's objective.

The multiple channels of the commo helmets were filled with message traffic, none of it intended for Radescu. If he had been familiar with the Slammers' code names, he could have followed the progress of the support operation— an armored battalion reinforced by a company of combat engineers—which should have gotten under way as soon as the patrol first made contact with the enemy. For now, it was enough to know that Hammer would give direct warning if anything went badly wrong: not because Radescu commanded the indigenous forces, but because he accompanied Hawker and Bourne, two of Hammer's own.

"Duck," said the helmet with unexpected clarity, Bourne on the intercom, and the general obeyed just as the vehicle

switched direction and the arms of the tunnel entrance
embraced them.

Though the nursery tunnels were carved through living
rock—many of them with hand tools by Molts millennia
in the past—the entrances were always onto gentle slopes
so that no precocious infant projected himself over a sharp
drop. That meant the approach was normally through soil,
stabilized traditionally by arches of small ashlars, or (since
humans landed) concrete or glazed earth portals.

Here the tunnel was stone-arched and, though the
external portion of the structure had been sandblasted by
the firecracker rounds, blocks only a meter within the
opening bore the patina of great age. Radescu expected
the jeep's headlights to flood the tunnel, supplementing the
illumination which seeped in past them. Instead Profile
Bourne halted and flipped a toggle on the dashboard.

There was a *thud!* within the plenum chamber, and
opaque white smoke began to boil out around the skirts.
It had the heavy odor of night-blooming flowers, cloying
but not choking to the men who had to breathe it. Driven
by the fans, the smoke was rapidly filling the tunnel in both
directions by the time it rose so high that Radescu, his head
raised to the arched roof, was himself engulfed by it.

The last thing he saw were the flashing holograms of
Hawker's display, warning of Molt activity in the near
distance. Before or behind them in the tunnel in this case,
because the rock shielded evidence of ionization in any
other direction.

Something touched the side of Radescu's helmet. He
barely suppressed a scream before his faceplate slid down
like a knife carving a swath of visibility through the palpable
darkness. He could see again, though his surroundings were
all in shades of saffron and the depth of rounded objects was
somewhat more vague than normally was the case. Lieutenant
Hawker was lowering the hand with which he had just
manipulated the controls of the Oltenian's helmet for him.

"Molts can't see in the smoke," Hawker said. "Want to
come with me—" the muzzle of his gun gestured down
the tunnel— "or stay here with the sarge?"

"I ought—" Radescu began, intending to say "to join my men." But the Oltenian portion of the patrol under Captain Elejash had its orders—set up on the crest, await support, and let the vehicles draw fire if the Molts were foolish enough to provide data for the Slammers' gunnery computers. Each location from which a satellite registered a bolt being fired went into the data base as a point to be hit not now—the snipers would have teleported away—but at a future date when a Molt prepared to fire from the same known position. In fact, the casualties during the patrol's assault seemed to have left the surviving Molts terrified of shellfire, even the desultory bombardment by Oltenian guns. "Yes, I'm with you," the general added instead.

The nursery tunnel would normally have been wide enough to pass the jeep much deeper within it, but the shock of the penetrators detonating had spalled slabs of rock from the walls, nearly choking the tunnel a few meters ahead.

"Dunno if it's safe," the mercenary said, feeling a facet of the new surface between his left finger and thumb.

"It's bedrock," Radescu responded nonchalantly. He had a fear of heights but no touch of claustrophobia. "It may be blocked, but nothing further should fall."

Hawker shrugged and resumed his careful advance.

The tunnel was marked by several sharp changes of direction in its first twenty meters, natural since its whole purpose was to train immature Molts to sense and teleport to locations to which they had no physical access. There were glowstrips and some light trickling through the airshafts in the tunnel roof, but the angled walls prevented the infants from seeing any distance down the gallery.

Radescu's gun wavered between being pointed straight ahead in the instinctive fear that a Molt warrior would bolt around a corner at him, and being slanted up at 45° in the intellectual awareness that to do otherwise needlessly endangered Lieutenant Hawker, a step ahead and only partially to the side. Noticing that, the Oltenian pushed past the Slammer so as not to have that particular problem on his mind.

When Radescu brushed closer to the wall, he noticed

that its surface seemed to brighten. That was the only
evidence that he was "seeing" by means of high-frequency
sound, projected stereoscopically from either side of the
commo helmet and, after it was reflected back, converted
to visible light within microns-thick layers of the face shield.

It was the apparent normalcy of his vision that made so
amazing the blindness of the pair of Molts which Radescu
encountered in the large chamber around the fourth sharp
angle. One of them was crawling toward him on hands and
knees, while the other waddled in a half crouch with his arms
spread as though playing blindman's bluff.

The shotgun rose—Radescu had instincts that amazed
him in their *vulgarity*—but the general instead of firing
cried, "Wait! Both of you! I want to talk about peace!"

The crawling Molt leaped upright, an arm going back
to the hilt of a slung weapon, while the other adult caught
up an infant. Both adults were very aged males, wizened
though the yellowish tinge which was an artifact of the
helmet's mechanism disconcerted eyes expecting the
greenish-black scales of great age. The one who was
crouching had a brow horn twisted like that of the old
warrior in Belvedere. . . .

Hawker was a presence to his left but the Oltenian general concentrated wholly on the chamber before him, sweat
springing out on his neck and on the underside of his jaw.
There were not merely two Molts in the chamber but over
a score, the rest infants in their neat beds of woven grass
scattered across the floor of the room—where the adults,
their lamps useless, could find them now only by touch.

"Keir, *stop!*" shouted the Molt who had not reached for
a weapon. He was speaking in Rumanian, the only language
common among the varied autochthonal themes as well as
between Molts and humans. In this case, however, the
Molts almost certainly spoke the same dialect, so the choice
of language was almost certainly a plea for further for-
bearance on the part of the guns which, though unseen,
must be there. "If they shoot, the young—"

The other Molt lunged forward—but toward a sidewall,
not toward the humans. He held a stabbing spear, a

traditional weapon with two blades joined by a short wooden handgrip in the center. One blade slashed upward in a wicked disemboweling stroke that rang on the stone like a sack of coins falling.

"We won't hurt your infants—" Radescu said as the spearcarrier rotated toward the sound with his weapon raised. Hawker fired and the Molt sagged in on himself, spitted on a trio of amber tracks: smoke concealed the normal cyan flash of the powergun, but shockwaves from the superheated air made their own mark on the brush of high-frequency sound.

The adult with the twisted horn disappeared, holding the infant he had snatched up as Radescu first spoke.

Alexander Radescu tried to lean his gun against the wall. It fell to the floor instead, but he ignored it to step to the nearest of the infant Molts. The little creature was surprisingly dense: it seemed to weigh a good five kilos in Radescu's arms, twisting against the fabric of his jacket to find a nipple. Its scales were warm and flexible; only against pressure end-on did they have edges which Radescu could feel.

"We'll carry them outside," said the Oltenian. "I'll carry them. . . . We'll keep them in—" his face broke into a broad smile, hidden behind his face shield "—in the conference room; maybe they'll like the fountains."

"Hostages?" asked Hawker evenly, as faceless as the general, turning in a slow sweep of the chamber to ensure that no further Molts appeared to resume the rescue mission.

The infant Radescu held began to mew. He wondered how many of the females and prepubescent males had been fleeing from the ridge in short hops when the bomblets swept down across them. "No, Lieutenant," Radescu said, noting the ripples of saffron gauze in his vision, heat waves drifting from the iridium barrel of Hawker's powergun. "As proof of my good faith. I've proved other things today."

He strode back toward the exit from the tunnel, realizing that his burden would prevent any hostile action by the Molts.

"Now I'll prove that," he added, as much to himself as to the mercenary keeping watch behind him in the lightless chamber.

The image of Grigor Antonescu in the tank of the commo set was more faithful than face-to-face reality would have been. The colors of the Chief Tribune's skin and the muted pattern of his formal robes glowed with the purity of transmitted light instead of being overlaid by the white glaze of surface reflection as they would have been had General Radescu spoken to him across the desk in his office.

"Good evening, Uncle," Radescu said. "I appreciate your—discussing matters with me in this way." Relays clicked elsewhere in the command car, startling him because he had been told he would be alone in the vehicle. Not that Hammer would not be scowling over every word, every nuance. . . .

"I'm not sure," replied the Tribune carefully, "that facilities supplied by the mercenaries are a suitable avenue for a conversation about State policy, however."

His hand reached forward and appeared to touch the inner surface of the tank in which Radescu viewed him. In fact, the older man's fingers must have been running across the outside of the similar unit in which he viewed his nephew's image. "Impressive, though. I'll admit that," he added.

The Tribune had the slim good looks common to men on his side of Radescu's family. He no longer affected the full makeup his nephew used regularly, because decades of imperious calm had given him an expression almost as artful. The general aped that stillness as he went on. "The key to our present small success has been the mercenaries; similarly, they are the key to the great success I propose for the near future."

"Wiping out an entire theme?" asked Antonescu over fingers tented so that the tips formed a V-notch like the rear sight of a gun.

"Peace with all the themes, Uncle," Radescu said, and

no amount of concentration could keep a cheek muscle from twitching and making the wings of his butterfly beauty patch flutter. "An end to this war, a return to peaceful relations with the Molts—which off-planet traders have easily retained. There's no need for men and Molts to fight like this. Oltenia has three centuries of experience to prove there's no need."

Cooling fans began to whirr in a ceiling duct. Something similar must have happened near the console which Antonescu had been loaned by Hammer's supply contingent in Belvedere, because the Chief Tribune looked up in momentary startlement—the first emotion he had shown during the call. "There are those, Alexi," he said to the tank again, "who argue that with both populations expanding, there is no longer enough room on Oltenia for both races. The toll on human farm stock is too high, now that most Molts live to warrior age—thanks to improvements in health care misguidedly offered the autochthons by humans in the past."

"Molt attacks on livestock during puberty rites are inevitable," Radescu agreed, "as more land is devoted to ranching and the number of indigenous game animals is reduced." He felt genuinely calm, the way he had when he committed himself in the conference room with Marshal Erzul. There was only one route to real success, so he need have no regrets at what he was doing. "We can't stop the attacks. So we'll formalize them, treat them as a levy shared by the State and by the Molts collectively."

"They don't have the organization to accomplish that," Antonescu said with a contemptuous snap of his fingers. "Even if you think our citizens would stand for the cost themselves."

"What are the costs of having powerguns emptied into crowded ballrooms?" the younger man shot back with the passionless precision of a circuit breaker tripping. "What is the cost of this army—in *money* terms, never mind casualties?"

Antonescu shrugged. Surely he could not really be that calm. . . . He said, "Some things are easier in war, my boy.

Emotions can be directed more easily, centralized decision making doesn't arouse the—negative comment that it might under other circumstances."

"The Molts," said the young general in conscious return to an earlier subject, "have been forced by the war to organize in much the same way that we have rallied behind the Tribunate."

By an effort of will, he held his uncle's eyes as he spoke the words he had rehearsed a dozen times to a mirror. "There could be no long-term—no middle-term—solution to Molt-human relations without that, I agree. But with firm control by the leaders of both races over the actions of their more extreme members, there *can* be peace—and a chance on this planet to accomplish things which aren't within the capacity of *any* solely human settlement, even Earth herself."

The Chief Tribune smiled in the warm, genuinely affectionate, manner which had made him the only relative—parents included—for whom Alexander Radescu had cared in early childhood. Radescu relived a dual memory, himself in a crib looking at his Uncle Grigor—and the infant Molt squirming against him for sustenance and affection.

Antonescu said, "Your enthusiasm, my boy, was certainly one of the reasons we gave the army into your charge when traditional solutions had failed. And of course—" the smile lapsed into something with a harder edge, but only for a moment "—because you're my favorite nephew, yes.

"But primarily," the Chief Tribune continued, "because you are a very intelligent young man, Alexi, and you have a record of doing what you say you'll do . . . which will bring you far, one day, yes."

He leaned forward, just as he had in Radescu's infancy, his long jaw and flat features a stone caricature of a human face. "But how can you offer to end a war that the Molts began—however fortunate their act may have been for some human ends?"

"I'm going to kick them," the general said with a cool smile of his own, "until they ask *me* for terms. And the terms I'll offer them will be fair to both races." He blinked, shocked to realize that he had been speaking as if Chief Tribune Antonescu were one of the coterie of officers he had brought to heel in the conference room. "With your permission, of course, sir. And that of your colleagues."

Antonescu laughed and stood up. Radescu was surprised to see that the Chief Tribune remained focused in the center of the tank as he walked around the chair in which he had been sitting. "Enthusiasm, Alexi, yes, we expect that," he said. "Well, you do your part and leave the remainder to us. You've done very well so far.

"But I think you realize," the older man went on with his hands clasped on the back of a chair of off-planet pattern, "that I've stretched very far already to give you this opportunity." Antonescu's voice was calm, but his face held just a hint of human concern which shrank his nephew's soul down to infancy again. "If matters don't—succeed, according to your plans and the needs of the State, then there won't be further options for you. Not even for you, Alexi."

"I understand, Uncle," said Alexander Radescu, who understood very well what failure at this level would require him, as an Oltenian aristocrat, to do in expiation. "I have no use for failures either."

As he reached for the power switch at the base of the vision tank, he wondered who besides Hammer would be listening in on the discussion—and what *they* thought of his chances of success.

The bolt was a flicker in the air, scarcely visible until it struck an Oltenian armored car. The steel plating burned with a clang and a white fireball a moment before a fuel tank ruptured to add the sluggish red flames of kerosene to the spectacle. The vehicle had been hull down and invisible from the ridge toward which the next assault would be directed; but the shot had been fired from the rear, perhaps kilometers distant.

Three men in Oltenian fatigues jumped from the body of the vehicle while a fourth soldier screamed curses in a variety of languages and squirmed from the driver's hatch,

cramped by the Slammer body armor which he wore. The
turrets on several of the neighboring armored cars began
to crank around hastily, though the sniper was probably
beyond range of the machine guns even with solid shot.
There was no chance of hitting the Molt by randomly spraying the landscape anyway; Radescu's tongue poised to pass
an angry order down when some subordinate forestalled him
and the turrets reversed again.

"Nothing to be done about that," Radescu said to the
pair of men closest to him. He nodded in the direction
of a few of the hundred or so armored vehicles he could
see from where he stood. Had he wished for it, satellite
coverage through the hologram projector in the combat car
would have shown him thousands more. "With a target the
size of this one, the odd sniper's going to hit something
even if he's beyond range of any possible counterfire."

A second bolt slashed along the side of an armored
personnel carrier a hundred meters from the first victim.
There was no secondary explosion this time—in fact,
because of the angle at which it struck, the powergun might
not have penetrated the vehicle's fighting compartment. Its
infantrymen boiled out anyway, many of them leaving
behind the weapons they had already stuck through
gunports in the APC's sides. Bright sunlight glanced
incongruously from their bulky infrared goggles, passive
night vision equipment which was the closest thing in the
Oltenian arsenal to the wide assortment of active and
passive devices built into the Slammers' helmets.

Thank the Lord for small favors: in the years before
squabbling broke out in open war between men and
Molts, the autochthons had an unrestricted choice of
imports through off-planet traders. They had bought huge
stocks of powerguns and explosives, weapons which made
an individual warrior the bane of hundreds of his sluggish human opponents. Since theirs would be the decision of when and where to engage, however, they had
seen no need of equipment like the mercenaries' helmets—equipment which expanded the conditions under
which one could fight.

"Don't bet your ass there's no chance a' counterfire," growled Profile Bourne; and as he was speaking, the main gun of one of Hammer's tanks blasted back in the direction from which the sniper's bolts had come.

The flash and the *thump!* of air closing back along the trail blasted through it by a twenty-centimeter powergun startled more Oltenians than had the sniper fire itself.

General Forsch had started to walk toward Radescu from one of the command trailers with a message he did not care to entrust either to radio or to the lips of a subordinate. When the tank fired, the gangling chief of staff threw himself flat onto ground which the barrage of two days previous had combed into dust as fine as baby powder. Forsch looked up with the anger of a torture victim at his young commander.

Radescu, seeing the yellow-gray blotches on the uniform which had been spotless until that moment, hurried over to Forsch and offered a hand to help him rise. Radescu had deliberately donned the same stained battledress he had worn during the previous assault, but he could empathize nonetheless with how his subordinate was feeling.

"The meteorologists say there should be a period of still air," the chief of staff muttered, snatching his hand back from Radescu's offer of help when he saw how dirty his palms were.

"Our personnel say that it may last for only a few minutes," Forsch continued, dusting his hands together with intense chopping motions on which he focused his eyes. "The—*technician* from the mercenaries—" he glanced up at Hawker and Bourne, following Radescu to either side "—says go with it." His face twisted. "Just 'Go with it.'"

The sky was the flawless ultramarine of summer twilight. "Thank you, General Forsch," Radescu said as he looked upward, his back to the lowering sun. Profile had been right: whether or not the tank blast had killed the sniper, its suddenness had at least driven the Molt away from the narrow circuit of rocks through which he had intended to teleport and confuse counterfire. A single twenty centimeter bolt could shatter a boulder the size of a house, and the consequent rain of molten glass and rock fragments would panic anyone within a hundred meters of the impact area.

Radescu tongued the helmet's control wand up and to the left, the priority channel that would carry his next words to every man in the attacking force and log him into the fire control systems of the Oltenian and mercenary gun batteries. "Execute Phase One," he said, three words which subsumed hundreds of computer hours and even lengthier, though less efficient, calculations by battery commanders, supply officers, and scores of additional human specialties.

True darkness would have been a nice bonus, but the hour or so around twilight was the only real likelihood of still air—and that was more important than the cloak Nature herself would draw over activities.

"All right," Alexander Radescu said, seeing General Forsch but remembering his uncle. The trailers of the Oltenian operations center straggled behind Forsch because of the slope. A trio of Slammers' combat cars with detectors like those of the jeep guarded the trailers against Molt infiltrators. Hull down on the ridge line, the seventeen tanks of Hammer's H Company waited to support the assault with direct fire. A company of combat cars, vulnerable (as the tanks were not) to bolts from the autochthons' shoulder weapons, would move up as soon as the attack was joined.

Apart from the combat car in which the commander himself would ride, every vehicle in the actual assault would be Oltenian; but all the drivers were Hammer's men.

Forsch saluted, turned, and walked back toward the trailers with his spine as stiff as a ramrod. There was an angry crackle nearby as a three-barrelled powergun on one of the combat cars ripped a bubble of ionization before it could become a functioning Molt. There were more shots audible and those only a fraction of the encounters which distance muffled, Radescu knew. A satchel charge detonated—with luck when a bolt struck it, otherwise when a Molt hurled it into a vehicle of humans whose luck had run out.

The autochthons were stepping up their harassing

attacks, though their main effort was almost certainly reserved for the moment that humans crowded into the killing ground of the open, rock-floored valley. Bolts fired from positions kilometers to either side would enfilade the attacking vehicles, while satchel charges and buzzbombs launched point-blank ripped even Hammer's panzers. Human counterfire itself would be devastating to the vehicles as confusion and proximity caused members of the assault force to blast one another in an attempt to hit the fleeing Molts.

It might still happen that way.

"Might best be mounting up," said Lieutenant Hawker, whose level of concern was shown only by the pressure-mottled knuckles of the hand which gripped his submachine gun. Bourne was snapping his head around like a dog trying to catch flies. He knew the link from the combat car to the lieutenant's helmet would beep a warning if a Molt were teleporting to a point nearby, but he was too keyed up to accept the stress of inaction. "Three minutes isn't very long."

"Long enough to get your clock cleaned," the sergeant rejoined as he turned gratefully to the heavy vehicle he would drive in this assault.

The first shells were already screaming down on the barren valley and the slope across it. The salvo was time-on-target: calculated so that ideally every shell would burst simultaneously, despite being fired from different ranges and at varying velocities. It was a technique generally used to increase the shock effect of the opening salvo of a bombardment. This time its purpose was to give the Molts as little warning as possible between their realization of Radescu's plan and its accomplishment. The young general sprinted for the combat car, remembering that its electronics would give him a view from one of the tanks already overlooking the valley.

Colonel Hammer and his headquarters vehicles were twenty kilometers to the rear, part of the security detachment guarding the three batteries of rocket howitzers. The mercenary units had been severely depleted by providing drivers for so many Oltenian vehicles, and a single Molt with a powergun could wreak untold havoc among the belts of live ammunition being fed to the hogs.

There was in any case no short-term reason that high officers should risk themselves in what would be an enlisted man's fight. Radescu had positioned his own headquarters in a place of danger so that his generals could rightfully claim a part in the victory he prayed he would accomplish. He was joining the assault himself because he believed, as he had said to Hawker and Bourne when he met them, in the value of leading from the front.

And also because he *was* Alexander Radescu.

There were footpegs set into the flank of the combat car, but Hawker used only the midmost one as a brace from which to vault into the open fighting compartment. The big mercenary then reached down, grasped Radescu by the wrist rather than by the hand he had thought he was offering, and snatched him aboard as well. Hawker's athleticism, even hampered by the weight and restriction of his body armor, was phenomenal.

The detection gear which had been transferred to the combat car for this operation took up the space in which the forward of the three gunners would normally have stood. The pintle-mounted tribarrels were still in place, but they would not be used during the assault. The Slammers' submachine guns and the shotgun which the general again carried would suffice for close-in defense without endangering other vehicles.

The thick iridium sides of the mercenary vehicle made it usable in the expected environment, which would have swept the jeep and any men aboard it to instant destruction. Radescu touched his helmet as he settled himself in the corner of the fighting compartment opposite Hawker: firing from the combat car meant raising one's head above the sidewalls.

The big vehicle quivered as Bourne, hidden forward in the driver's compartment, fed more power to the idling fans. Hawker brought up an image of the valley over the crest, his hands brushing touchplates on the package of additional instruments even before Radescu requested it. Very possibly the lieutenant acted on his own hook, uninterested in Radescu's wishes pro or con. . . .

The hologram was of necessity monochrome, in this case a deep red-orange which fit well enough with what Radescu remembered of the contours of rock covered by sere grass. The shell-bursts hanging and spreading over the terrain were the same sullen, fiery color as the ground, however, and that was disconcerting. It made Radescu's chest tighten as he imagined plunging into a furnace to be consumed in his entirety.

The tanks began to shoot across the valley with a less startling effect than the single countersniper blast. These bolts were directed away from the assault force, and they added only marginally to the ambient sound. The bombardment did not seem too loud to Radescu after the baptism he had received from shells plunging down point-blank the previous day. The sky's constant thrum was fed by nearly a thousand guntubes, some of them even heavier—though slower firing—than the Slammers' howitzers, and the effect was all-pervasive even though it had not called itself to the general's attention.

Dazzling reflections from the 200mm bolts played across even the interior of the combat car, washing Hawker's grim smile with the blue-green cast of death. The bolts did not show up directly on the display, but air heated by their passage roiled the upper reaches of the smoke into horizontal vortices. Across the valley the shots hammered computer-memorized positions from which Molts had sniped in the past. Rock sprayed high in the release of enormous crystalline stresses, and bubbles of heated air expanded the covering of smoke into twisted images larger than the tanks which had caused them.

"Base to Command," said the helmet in the voice of General Forsch, overlaid by a fifty-cycle hum which resulted from its transmission through the mercenaries' commo system. There were spits of static as well, every time a tank main gun released its packet of energy across the spectrum. "Phase One coverage has reached planned levels."

"Terminate Phase One," said Radescu. Across from him, Lieutenant Hawker patted a switch and the image of the valley collapsed. He did not touch other controls, so presumably the detection apparatus had been live all the time. The smile he flashed at Radescu when he saw the general's eyes on him was brief and preoccupied, but genuine enough.

"Phase One terminated," Forsch crackled back almost at once.

There was no effect directly obvious to the assault force, but that was to be expected: the flight time of shells from some of the guns contributing to the barrage was upwards of thirty seconds. "Prepare to execute Phase Two," said Radescu on the command channel as clearly as the hormones jumping in his bloodstream would permit. Everything around him was a fragment of a montage, each existing on a timeline separate from the rest.

"Give 'em ten seconds more," Profile broke in on the intercom. "Some bastard always takes one last pull on the firing lanyard to keep from having to unload the chamber."

"Execute Phase Two," ordered Radescu, his tongue continuing its set course as surely as an avalanche staggers downhill, the driver's words no more than a wisp of snow fencing overwhelmed in the rush of fixed intent.

Whatever Bourne may have thought about the order, he executed it with a precision smoother than any machine. The combat car surged forward, lagging momentarily behind the Oltenian APCs to either flank because the traction of their tires gave them greater initial acceleration than could the air cushion. Seconds later, when the whole line crested the ridge, the Slammers vehicle had pulled ahead by the half length that Bourne thought was safest.

In the stillness that replaced the howl of shells, small arms sizzled audibly among the grumble of diesels as soldiers responded to teleporting Molts—or to their own nervousness. A full charge of shot clanged into the combat car's port side, although Hawker's instruments showed that the gunman in the personnel carrier could not have had a real target.

Radescu raised himself to look over the bulkhead, though the sensible part of his mind realized that the added risk was considerable and unnecessary. To function in a world gone mad, a man goes mad himself: to be ruled by a sensible appreciation of danger in a situation where danger was both enormous and unavoidable would drive the victim into cowering funk—countersurvival in a combat zone where his own action might be required to save him. Bracing himself against the receiver of the tribarrel locked in place beside him, Alexander Radescu caught a brief glimpse of the results of his plan—before he plunged into them.

The sweep of the broad valley the assault must cross boiled with the contents of the thousands of smoke shells poured over it by the massed batteries. The brilliant white of rounds from Hammer's guns lay flatter and could be seen still spreading, absorbing and underlying the gray-blue chemical haze gushing from Oltenian shells. The coverage was not—could not be—complete, even within the two-kilometer front of the attack. Nonetheless, its cumulative effect robbed snipers of their targets at any distance from the vehicles.

Molts teleporting to positions readied to meet the attack found that even on the flanking slopes where the warriors were not blanketed by smoke, their gunsights showed featureless shades of gray instead of Oltenian vehicles. The wisest immediately flickered back to cover on the reverse slope. Younger, less perceptive autochthons began firing into the haze—an exercise as vain as hunting birds while blindfolded.

A pillar of crimson flame stabbed upward through the smoke as the result of one such wild shot; but Hammer's tanks and the combat cars joining them on the ridge combed out the frustrated Molts like burrs from a dog's hide. Had the snipers picked a target, fired once, and shifted position as planned, they would have been almost invulnerable to countermeasures. Warriors who angrily tried to empty their guns into an amorphous blur lasted five shots or fewer before a tank gun or a burst of automatic fire turned them into a surge of organic gases in the midst of a fireball of liquid rock.

All colors narrowed to shades of yellow as the combat car drove into the thickening smoke and Radescu switched on the sonic vision apparatus of his borrowed helmet. What had been an opaque fog opened into a 60° wedge of the landscape, reaching back twenty or thirty meters. It would not have done for top speed running, but the visibility was more than adequate for an assault line rolling across open terrain at forty KPH.

A tree stump, ragged and waist high, coalesced from the fog as the helmet's ultrasonic generators neared it. Bourne edged left to avoid it, the combat car swaying like a leaf in the breeze, while the Slammer driving the Oltenian vehicle to the right swerved more awkwardly in the other direction.

Alexander Radescu had been loaned a helmet from mercenary stores, but there was no question of equipping enough local troops to drive all the vehicles in the assault. The alternative had been to scatter a large proportion of the Slammers among packets of Oltenian regulars. That Hammer had found the alternative acceptable was praise for Radescu which the Oltenian had only hoped to receive.

A Molt with a buzzbomb on his shoulder, ready to launch, appeared beside the treestump.

The smoke did nothing to prevent warriors from teleporting into the valley to attack. The autochthons had expected a barrage of high explosives and armor piercing rounds, which would have had some effect but only a limited one. This valley was the center of a theme's territory; in a jump of a kilometer or two over ground so familiar, a young adult could position himself on a chunk of granite no larger than his head.

What the smoke shells did do was to prevent the autochthons from seeing anything after they projected themselves into the fog. Radescu cried out, raising his shotgun. The Molt was turned half away from them, hunching forward, hearing the diesel engine of the nearest APC but unable to see even that.

The combat car's acceleration and slight change of

attitude threw the Oltenian general back against the hard angles of the gun mount beside him. Bourne had brought up power and changed fan aspect in a pair of perfectly matched curves which showed just how relatively abruptly an air cushion vehicle could accelerate on a downslope, when gravity was on its side and the rolling friction of wheels slowed the conventional vehicles to either flank.

The Molt must have heard the rush of air at the last, because he whirled like a dancer toward the combat car with a look of utter horror as the bow slope rushed down on him. Radescu fired past the car's forward tribarrel, his shot missing high and to the left, as the autochthon loosed his shoulder-launched missile at the vehicle.

The buzzbomb struck the combat car beside the driver's hatch and sprang skyward, its rocket motor a hot spot in the smoke to infrared goggles and a ghostly pattern of vortices in the Slammers' ultrasound. The combat car, which weighed thirty-two tonnes, quivered only minutely as it spread the Molt between the ground and the steel skirt of the plenum chamber.

There was a violent outbreak of firing from the vehicles just behind the combat car. Passive infrared was useless for a driver because terrain obstacles did not radiate enough heat to bring them out against the ambient background. For soldiers whose only duty was to cut down Molts before the warriors could find targets of their own in the smoke, passive infrared was perfect.

The gunners in the armored car turrets and the infantry-men huddled behind vision blocks in the sides of their armored personnel carriers could see nothing—until Molt warriors teleported into the valley.

The autochthons' body temperature made them stand out like flares blazing in a sea of neutral gray. The automatic fire of the turret guns was not very accurate; but the ranges were short, the shot-cones deadly, and there were over fifteen thousand twitching trigger fingers packed into a constricted area. Warriors shimmered out of the smoke, hesitated in their unexpected blindness, and were swept away in bloody tatters by the rattling crossfire.

Charges of miniature airfoils sang from one vehicle to another, scarring the light armor and chipping away paint like a desultory sandblasting. The projectiles could not seriously harm the vehicles, however, and the armor was sufficient to preserve the crews and infantry complements as well.

The Molt Profile had just driven over was a wide blotch to the goggles of the Oltenians in the flanking APCs. Their guns stormed from either side, stirring the slick warmth and ricocheting from the rocky ground.

Lieutenant Hawker touched Radescu with his left hand, the one which did not hold the submachine gun. The combat car yawed as Profile braked it from the murderous rush he had just achieved, but the veteran lieutenant held steady without need to cling to a support as the Oltenian did.

"Arming distance," Hawker said over the intercom now that he had Radescu's attention. "The buzzbomb didn't go off because it was fired too close in. It's a safety so you don't blow yourself up that's all. Profile wasn't taking any risks."

"Yee-*ha*!" shouted the driver, clearly audible over the windrush.

Alexander Radescu was later surprised at how little he remembered of the assault—and that in flashes as brief and abrupt as the powergun bolt that lanced past him from behind, close enough to heat the left earpiece of his commo helmet before it sprayed dirt from the ground rising in front of the combat car. Bypassed sniper or mercenary gunner forgetting his orders not to fire into the smoke? No way to tell and no matter: all fire is hostile fire when it snaps by your head.

The slope that was their objective on the other side of the valley had been shrouded as thickly as the rest of the ground which the assault needed to cross. The hogs had kicked in final salvoes of firecracker rounds to catch Molts who thought the fog protected them. That explosive whisking, added to the greater time that the curtain had been in place, meant that the smoke had begun to part and thin here where the ground rose.

A crag, faceted like the bow of a great sea vessel,

appeared so abruptly in Radescu's vision that the Oltenian instinctively flipped up his face shield. The wedge of granite had a definite purple cast noticeable through the smoke of sun-infused white and gray streaming slowly down into the valley basin, heavier than the air it displaced.

It had been inevitable that the assault lines would straggle. Perhaps it was inevitable also that Profile Bourne would use his experience with his vehicle and its better power-to-weight ratio to race to the objective alone—despite clear orders, from Hawker as well as Radescu, to keep it reined in. There was no other vehicle close to them as the sergeant climbed to the left of the slab with his fans howling out maximum thrust and the ionization detector began flashing its violet and yellow warning, visible as the rock was through a thin neutral mask.

Alexander Radescu looked up and to the right, guided by instinct in the direction that the electronic tocsin was causing Hawker to turn with his submachine gun. The air solidified into a Molt with scales of as rich a color as the rock he stood on—spitting distance from the car laboring uphill, an easy cast for a satchel charge or a burst of fire into the open-topped compartment.

The Molt did not carry a weapon, and his right horn was twisted.

"*No!*" Radescu shouted, forgetting his intercom link as he lunged across the fighting compartment to grasp his companion's gun. His fingers locked at the juncture of the barrel and receiver, cold iridium and plastic which insulated too well to have any temperature apart from that which the general's hand gave the outer layer of molecules. "Not this one!"

"Steady," said Enzo Hawker, bracing the Oltenian with the free hand which could have plucked the man away, just as Radescu's slight body would have been no sufficient hindrance had the gunner wished to carry through and fire at the Molt. "Watch your side of the car."

The broad ravine into which Bourne plunged them was a watercut ramp to the crest. It held smoke dense enough to be instantly blinding. The autochthon had already disappeared, teleporting away with a smile which was probably an accident of physiognomy.

"I'm sorry, I—" Radescu said as he straightened, remembering this time to use his intercom. Hawker was as solid as the iridium bulkheads themselves, while the general's own mind leaped with fear and embarrassment and a sense of victory which intellectually he knew he had not yet won. "Shouldn't have touched you, Lieutenant, I was—" He raised his eyes to meet the other man's and saw nothing, even a hand's length apart, because the mercenary's face shield was a perfect mirror from the outside. "I didn't think."

"Just steady," Hawker said quietly. "You've been thinking fine."

Shells were hitting the ground, a considerable distance away but heavily enough that pebbles slid in miniature avalanches as the ravine walls quivered. As soon as the vehicles rolled into the valley, the artillery had shifted its points of aim to rocky areas within a few kilometers of the target of the assault.

These would be staging points for the Molt refugees, the females and the prepubescent males driven from what should have been the inviolable core of the theme holdings. They could stay ahead of human pursuit and would in a matter of a few hops scatter beyond the area which shells could saturate. But since the starting point was known, there was a finite number of initial landing areas available to the Molt noncombatants. Those were the targets for as many fragmentation and high-explosive rounds as the army could pump out.

Alexander Radescu had his own reasons, eminently logical ones, to want peace. He had to give the autochthons a reason whose logic the most high-spirited, glory-longing warrior would accept as overwhelming.

Dead comrades would not achieve that alone: a warrior *could* not accept the chance of dying as a sufficient reason to modify his actions, any more than could a mercenary soldier like Hawker, like Bourne in the forward hatch. Maimed females and children howling as they tried to stuff intestines back into their body cavities were necessary, as surely as the Molt in the ballroom of the Tribunal Palace in Belvedere had been, stooping behind the weight of his powergun—every shot turning a gay costume into burning, bloody rags.

"It's not worth it," the young general said, sickened by the coolness with which he had deliberated slaughter.

Only when Hawker said, "Hey?" did the Oltenian realize he had spoken not only aloud but loudly. He shrugged to the mercenary and their vehicle, sideslipping down the reverse slope, would have put an end to the conversation even had Radescu wished to continue it.

The smoke blanket here was tattered into no more than a memory of what the assault force had first driven into, though it—like a sheet of glass viewed endwise—was still opaque to a sniper trying to draw a bead any distance through it. There was a body sprawled forty meters from the combat car, an adult male killed by one of the shrapnel rounds which interspersed the smoke shells covering the ridge.

"Red two-ninety!" cried Lieutenant Hawker, "*Radescu!* Red two seventy!" and the general whirled to fire over the bulkhead at the Molt appearing almost beside the combat car, too close for Hawker himself to shoot.

The muzzle blast of the shotgun was a surprise, but this time the properly shouldered stock thrust and did not slam the young general. Neither did the charge hit the autochthon, a male with a powergun, though a bush a meter from him was stripped in a sharp-edged scallop.

The Molt threw his arms up and ran as the car sailed past him. Radescu fired again, missing even worse because he had not figured the vehicle's speed into his attempt to lead the runner; and as the Slammer lieutenant aimed over the back deck, the autochthon dissolved away in a further teleport. Only then did Radescu realize that the Molt had not only been too frightened to shoot, he had dropped his powergun as he fled.

The cave entrance for which Bourne steered was much larger than the one they had captured on the other side of

the ridge—larger, in fact, than anything of the sort which
Radescu had previously seen. The size was accentuated by
the hasty attempts the Molts had made to build a physical
barrier across the huge, pillared archway. There was a layer
of stones ranging from head-sized down to pebbles in the
entrance, the foundation course of a crude wall. Around the
stones were more bodies, half a dozen of them—probably
adult males, but too close to the epicenter of the firecracker
round that burst overhead for the bomblets to have left
enough of the corpses for certain identification.

A puff of breeze opened a rent in the smoke through
which the evening sky streamed like a comet's violet hair.

"Hang on," said the sergeant on the intercom. He had
driven past the archway and now, as he spoke, spun the
combat car on its axis to approach from the downhill side.

Radescu, clinging to the gun mount awkwardly because
of the personal weapon in his hand, cried, "There's a barrier
there, Sergeant—rocks!"

"Hang the cop on!" Bourne replied gleefully, and the
combat car, brought to the end of the tether of its downhill
inertia, accelerated toward the entrance at a rate that sailed
it over the pitiable stones through which a less ebullient
driver would have plowed.

There was light in the cavernous chamber beyond, a
portable area lamp of Oltenian manufacture, held up at
arm's length by a Molt with a twisted horn.

As cool as he had been when he prepared to execute
his own command group within minutes of meeting them,
General Radescu said, "Neither of you shoot," on the intercom. Then, tonguing the command channel though he was
not sure of signal propagation from inside the crystalline
rock, he added, "Command to all units. Phase Two is complete. Terminate all offensive activity, shoot only in self-
defense."

Bourne had not expected to halt immediately within
the entrance, nor had the general specifically ordered him
to do so. The sergeant would not have been condemned
for murder, however, if he had felt the need to wait for
orders before he took action he considered sensible. Now

he used the steel skirts of the plenum chamber as physical brakes against the floor of polished rock, screeching and sparking in an orange-white storm instead of depending on the thrust of the fans to halt the heavy vehicle. The dazzling afterimages of saturated blue seemed for a moment brighter than the lamp which the autochthon had continued to hold steady while the car slewed around him in a semicircle.

When the skirts rested solidly on the pavement, Radescu realized that the ground itself was not firm. Earth shocks from the distant impact zones made dust motes dance around the globe of light, and the bulkhead quivered as Radescu dismounted.

Lag time, General Radescu hoped as he stepped toward the wizened Molt, shells fired before his order to desist. Behind him, the combat car pinged and sizzled as metal found a new stasis. There was also the clicking sound of Lieutenant Hawker releasing the transport lock of a tribarrel, freeing the weapon for immediate use.

"I hope you're here to talk of peace," said the Oltenian, reaching out to take the lamp which seemed too heavy for the frail autochthon.

"No," said Ferad who relinquished the lamp willingly, though he would have held it as long as need required— the way he had supported the powergun until he had emptied the magazine. "I am here this time to *make* peace."

The placid landscape had a slightly gritty texture, but Alexander Radescu was not sure whether that was a real residue from the smoke shells or if it was just another result of his own tiredness.

Losing would have taken just as much effort as the triumph he had in fact achieved.

Lieutenant Hawker murmured a reply to his commo helmet, then leaned toward Radescu and whispered, "Seven minutes."

The Oltenian general nodded, then turned to Forsch and the divisional generals assembled behind him, each with a small contingent of troops in dress uniforms. "The Tribunes are expected to arrive in seven minutes," Radescu called, loudly enough for even the enlisted men to hear him.

Radescu had gone to some lengths to give this event the look of a review, not an occupation. Weapons had been inspected for external gloss. Dress uniforms—blue with orange piping for the other ranks, scarlet for officers through field grade, and pearl with gold for the generals— would not remind the watching autochthons of the smoke- shrouded, shot-rippling assault by which the Oltenian Army had entered a theme stronghold.

The Molts would not forget, the survivors watching from distant hills with the representatives of the other themes. There was no need to rub their broad noses in it, that was all.

"General Radescu," said a voice. "Sir?"

Radescu turned, surprised but so much a man living on his nerves that no event seemed significantly more probable than did any other. "Yes?" he said. "General Forsch?"

Profile Bourne watched the chief of staff with the expression of disdain and despair which had summed up his attitude toward all the local forces—until the Oltenian line had made the assault beside him. Even those men were poofs again when they donned their carnival uniforms.

The sergeant's hands were linked on his breastplate, but that put them adequately near to his slung submachine gun. The reason the two Slammers had given for continuing to guard Radescu was a valid one: a single disaffected Molt could destroy all chances of peace by publicly assassinating Alexander Radescu. The general had not been impelled to ask whether or not that was the real reason.

Forsch was nervous, looking back at the divisional generals two paces behind him for support. Iorga nodded to him with tight-lipped enthusiasm.

"Sir," the lanky chief of staff continued, though he seemed to be examining his expression in the mirrors of Radescu's gilded boots, "I—we want to say that . . ."

The hills whispered with the rush of an oncoming aircraft. That, and perhaps the sculptured placidity of Radescu's face, brought Forsch back to full functioning.

"You may have sensed," he said, meeting his commander's eyes, "a certain hostility when you announced your appointment to us."

"I surprised you, of course," Radescu murmured to make Forsch easier about whatever he intended to say. The great cargo plane commandeered to bring the Tribunes to sign the accords was visible a kilometer away, its wing rotors already beginning to tilt into hover mode for the set-down. "All of you performed to the highest expectations of the State."

"Yes," the chief of staff said, less agreement than an acceptance of the gesture which Radescu had made. "Well. In any case, sir—and I speak for all of us—" more nods from the officers behind him "—we were wrong. You *were* the man to lead us. And we'll follow you, the whole army will follow you, wherever you choose to lead us if the peace talks break down."

Lord and his martyrs, thought Alexander Radescu, surveying the faces of men up to twice his age, they really would. They would follow him because he had gotten something done, even though some of the generals must have realized by now that he'd have shot them out of hand if they stood in the way of his intent. Lord and martyrs!

"I—" Radescu began; then he reached out and took Forsch's right hand in his and laid the other on the tall officer's shoulder. "General—men—the peace talks won't fail." It was hard to view the quick negotiations between Ferad and himself as anything so formal that they could have been 'broken off,' but it was the same implicit dependence on bureaucratic niceties which had turned the war into a morass on the human side. "But I appreciate your words as, as much as I appreciated the skill and courage, the *great* courage, the whole army displayed in making this moment possible."

The Molts' problem had been the reverse of the self-inflicted wound from which the Oltenian Army had bled. The autochthons were too independent ever to deal the crushing blows that their ability to concentrate suddenly would have permitted them. Each side slashed at one another but struggled with itself, too ineffective either to win or to cease. And the same solution would extricate both from the bloody swamp: leaders who could see a way clear and who were willing to drive all before them.

"She's coming in," said Profile Bourne, not himself part of the formalities but willing to remind those who were of their duties. General Forsch wrung his superior's hand and slipped back to his place a pace to the rear, while the aircraft settled with a whining roar that echoed between the hills.

Debris and bodies had been cleared from the broad archway, and for the occasion the flagstone pavement had even been polished by a crew which ordinarily cared for the living quarters of general officers. Radescu had toyed only briefly with the thought of resodding the shell-scars and wheel tracks. The valley's rocky barrenness was the reason it had become a Molt center, and nothing the human attack had done changed its appearance significantly. It was perhaps well to remind the Tribunate that this was not merely a human event, that the autochthons watching from vantage points kilometers distant were a part of it and of the system the treaty would put into effect for the remainder of the planet's history.

The aircraft's turbines thrummed in a rapidly-descending rhythm when the oleo struts flexed and rose again as the wheels accepted the load. Dust billowed from among the russet grassblades, bringing General Radescu a flashback of a hillside descending in a welter of Molt bodies as the penetrators lifted it from within. He had been so frightened during that bombardment. . . .

The rear hatchway of the big cargo plane was levering itself down into an exit ramp. "Attention!" Radescu called, hearing his order repeated down the brief ranks as he himself braced. Most of the army was encamped five kilometers away in a location through which the troops had staged to the final assault. There they nervously awaited the outcome of this ceremony, reassured more by the sections of Hammer's men with detection gear scattered among them than they were by Radescu's promises as he rode off.

He'd done that much, at least, built trust between the indigenous and mercenary portions of his army on the way to doing the same between the intelligent species which shared the planet. It occurred to Alexander Radescu as he watched a pair of light trucks drive down the ramp, the first one draped with bunting for the ceremony, that wars could not be won: they could only be ended without having been lost. The skirmishes his troops had won were important for the way they conduced to the ends of peace.

The chairs draped in cloth-of-gold made an imposing-enough background for the Tribunes, but no one seemed to have calculated what uneven ground and the truck's high center of gravity would do to men attempting to sit on such chairs formally. Radescu suppressed a smile, remembering the way he had jounced on the back of the jeep.

That experience and others of recent days did not prevent him from being able to don a dress uniform and the makeup which had always been part of the persona he showed the world; but a week of blood and terror had won him certain pieces of self-knowledge which were, in their way, as important to him as anything he had accomplished in a military sense.

The driver of the lead truck tried to make a sweeping turn in order to bring the rear of his vehicle level with the red carpet which had been cut in sections from the flooring of the living trailers of high officers. An overly abrupt steering correction brought an audible curse from one of the men in the back of the vehicle, men who looked amazingly frail to Alexander Radescu after a week of troops in battledress.

Hawker and Bourne had kept a settled silence thus far during the makeshift procession until the six guards in scarlet—none of them were below the rank of major—jumped from the second truck to help the Tribunes down the steps welded to the back of the first. At the Honor Guards' appearance, Enzo Hawker snorted audibly and Radescu felt an impulse to echo the Slammer's disdain.

And yet those men were very similar to Radescu himself in background; not quite so well connected, but officers of the Tribunal Honor Guard for the same reason that Alexander Radescu was a general. That he was a man who could lead an army while they, with their rhodium-plated pistols, could not have guarded a school crossing, was an individual matter.

Grigor Antonescu, First among Equals, wore a pure white robe of office, while the collars of his two companions were black. Radescu saluted.

Instead of returning the formality the Chief Tribune took his nephew's hand in his own and raised it high in a gesture of triumph and acclamation. "Well done, my boy," the older man said loudly. "*Well* done."

More surprised by his uncle's open praise than he was by the brief scowls with which the other members of the Tribunate, Wraslov and Deliu, responded to it, the young general said, "Ah, Excellency, we all had confidence in the abilities of our men." Nodding to the side, toward the still-faced Bourne, he added in afterthought, "And in our allies, of course, in Colonel Hammer."

The presence of the troops braced to attention behind him vibrated in Radescu's mind like a taut bowstring. "Excellencies," he said, guiding down his uncle's hand and releasing it, "the actual meeting will be within the, the cavern, actually a tunnel complex as extensive as any Molt artifact on the planet, as it chances. The antechamber seemed a particularly suitable location for the signing since it—reminds the representatives of other themes that our troops are here without Molt sufferance."

Chief Tribune Antonescu patted at the front of his robe, frowning minutely when he realized that the marks he left in the fine dust were more disfiguring than the smooth layer which the ride from the plane had deposited over him. "The Molts are inside then, already?" he asked in a voice which, like his static face, gave away nothing save the fact that something was hidden.

"No, Excellency," said Radescu, finding that his slight, ingenuous smile had become a mask which he knew he must maintain, "they're—in sight, I suppose, the representatives."

He gestured with his spread fingers toward a few of the crags where, if he had squinted, he might have been able to see male autochthons waiting as the Oltenian Army waited in camp. "The young and females whom we captured are still at the lower levels within, under parole so to speak, those who might be able to teleport away now that we've stopped shelling."

For a moment, the general lost control of the smile he had been keeping neutral, and the Tribunes were shocked by the face of a man who recalled tumbled bodies and who now grinned that he might not weep. "But the theme elders who'll be signing—they'll arrive in the chamber when we set off a smoke grenade to summon them." The grin flashed back like a spring-knife. "Red smoke, not gray."

The pair of mercenaries, near enough to overhear, smiled as well but the reference escaped the newcomers who had not been part of the assault.

"Then let's go within," said Antonescu, "and we *won't* have the Molts present until you and I—until we all—" taking his nephew's hand again, the Chief Tribune began to walk along the carefully-laid carpet "—have had a chance to discuss this among ourselves."

Radescu raised an eyebrow as he stepped into line beside his uncle, but the facial gesture was a restrained one, even slighter than necessary to avoid cracking his makeup. Antonescu, a master both of restraint and interpretation of minute signals, said, "Only for a moment, Alexi."

"I was afraid for a moment," the general said in a carefully modulated voice as he walked along, "a symptom of my youthful arrogance, I'm afraid—" echoing in nervousness his uncle's words and his own "—that you didn't realize that the agreement stands or falls as a piece—that it can't be modified."

He thought as he spoke that he was being overly blunt with the man who was both his protector and a necessary part of final success, but Tribune Antonescu only replied, "Yes, we were in no doubt of that, my boy. Not from the first."

The six Honor Guards fell in behind the Tribunes in what Radescu found himself thinking of as courtly, not military, precision. The two mercenaries drifted along to either side of the procession. The general risked a glance around to see that while Hawker walked to the left and eyed the head of the valley with its smatterings of autochthons, many of them picked out by iridium highlights, Profile Bourne glowered at the gaily-caparisoned troops on review to the right.

Radescu had heard the Slammers discussing whether or not they should wear dress uniforms of their own. He agreed with their final assessment: tailored khakis would only accentuate the scarred functionality of the helmets and body armor they would wear regardless.

"The whole army," Radescu said, hoping to direct his uncle's attention to the troops who had sweated as hard for this display as they had in preparation for the assault, "performed in a way to honor the State."

Surely, as the plane circled to land, the Tribunes had seen the burned-out vehicles littering the course of the assault—particularly near the crest of this ridge, up whose gentle reverse slope the entourage now walked. Radescu's plan had made the attack possible and a success: nothing could have made it easy. The general's eyes prickled with emotion as he thought of these men and their comrades plunging into darkness to meet their terrifyingly agile opponents.

"As written," muttered the Tribune, Deliu, who walked behind Radescu, "this treaty permits the Molts to import anything they want without State control—specifically including weapons. Hard to imagine anyone but the most arrant traitor suggesting that the Molts should be allowed powerguns after the way they used one in Belvedere last month."

"Not the place for that, Mikhail," Antonescu said over his shoulder, the very flatness of his remark more damning than an undertone of anger.

Radescu did not miss a step as he paced along in front of men picked not for their smartness on review but because of the way each had distinguished himself in the assault which made this ceremony possible. His mind, however, clicked into another mode at the paired statements which were neither a question nor an answer—yet were both.

Aloud, drowning the other voices in his mind, the general said, "Quite apart from the question of whether Ferad would have agreed to it, Excellency, the prohibition would have been useless—and the past few days have made me extremely intolerant of pointless behavior."

"I didn't care to discuss such matters here where the Molts may be listening through directional microphones," said Antonescu in a louder voice as he passed Captain Elejash and the platoon which had made the preliminary assault.

"Since I've told the leader of the Molts precisely what I'm going to tell you," Alexander Radescu continued with a cool hauteur which he was too fiercely angry to disguise, "you need not be concerned on that score. Oltenia has no effective means of preventing off-planet merchants from dealing directly with the Molts—even now, in the middle of open warfare. Since they, the theme elders as surely as the young bucks, couldn't feel secure in peace without the sort of equipment renewed fighting would require, then I saw no reason to make them even *more* insecure by pretending to embargo it."

Now at midday the threshold of the autochthons' cave complex was bathed in light, but that only emphasized the wall of darkness just within. The high-vaulted antechamber was ancient enough to be set with sconces for rushlights, though the battery-powered floods now secured in them to wash the ceiling were of an efficiency equal to anything on the planet. There was no need to match the brilliance outdoors, however, so it was only as their eyes adapted that the men took in the rich, vaguely-purple ambience which white light stroked from polished granite.

The table in the center of the room was of thin, stamped metal which the cloth drapery did little to disguise. Ferad had offered a lustrous pelt of an autochthonal herbivore, but on reflection it had seemed to both that the feathery scales would prove an impossible surface on which to sign the treaty.

"We couldn't be more pleased with the way you broke the Molts in so short a time, my boy," said Grigor Antonescu as the rock enclosed the party. There were three semi-circular doorways spaced about the inner face of the antechamber, barricaded now—not in a misguided attempt to keep the Molts hostage further within the cave system, but simply to prevent Oltenian soldiers from wandering into places where they might cause problems. "But there are some matters of judgment in which you are, in all deference to your abilities, too young to make the decisions."

He spoke, thought Alexander Radescu, as if the sharp exchange in the sunlight had not occurred. Deliu's interference was not to be allowed to affect the calm tenor of the tutorial the Chief Tribune had prepared to give his nephew.

Avoiding the real meat of the opening statement, Radescu replied, "I won a couple skirmishes against an unprepared enemy, Uncle. Scarcely a matter of breaking the Molts, or even the one theme primarily involved."

"There were sizable contingents from all across Oltenia," put in the eldest of the Tribunes, Constantin Wraslov, who even in Radescu's earliest recollection had looked too skeletal to be long for the world. His tone lacked the deliberate venom of Deliu's, but it had the querulousness common to even the most neutral of Wraslov's pronouncements. "We've seen the report on the examination of the corpses after the battle."

Radescu looked at the Tribune, surprised at the dispassion with which his mind pictured the old man as one of the victims being examined by the Intelligence Section: the body pulped by a sheet of rock giving way on top of it . . . flayed by microshrapnel from a dozen nearby bomblets . . . halved by a point-blank, chest-high burst from an armored car's gun. . . . "Yes," the general said with the dynamic calm of a fine blade flexing under the pressure of a thrust, "all the themes had representatives here. That made it possible for Ferad to inflate what was really a minor occurrence into enough of an event to panic the other themes into making peace. Ferad himself knows better—as, of course, do I."

"The infants are their weak point," said Tribune Deliu, adding with a grudging approval, "and you fingered that well enough, boy, I grant you." There was no affection in the look he gave Radescu, however; and when the gilt brim of the general's hat threw a band of light across Deliu's eyes, the Tribune's glare could have been that of a furious boar.

"Yes, you've shown us how to exterminate the autochthons," Wraslov agreed gleefully, rubbing his hands and looking around the big chamber with the enthusiasm of an archeologist who had just penetrated a tomb. "Before, we tried to clear areas so that they couldn't attack us, you know, because it seemed they could always escape."

From where he stood, Radescu could not see the aged Tribune's face. The Honor Guard had aligned itself as a short chord across the portion of the curving wall toward which Wraslov was turned. The worried looks that flashed across the bland expressions of the six red-clad officers were a suggestion of what those men thought they saw in the Tribune's eyes.

"Excellencies, we *can't* . . ." Radescu began, breaking off when he realized that he didn't know where to take the words from there. His body felt so dissociated from his mind that his knees started to tremble and he was not sure that he could continue to stand up.

He was not alone in feeling the tension in the chamber. Chief Tribune Antonescu, for all his outward calm, had an inner heat which might have been no more than a well-bred distaste for the scene which he saw developing.

In fact, the only men in the antechamber who did seem relaxed were the two Slammers, and theirs was the calm of soldiers carrying out a familiar task. Hawker and Bourne had their backs to the stone to one side of the entranceway, too close together for a Molt to attempt to teleport between them but still giving their gun hands adequate clearance. They scanned the room, their face shields transparent but already locked in place in case the lights went out and vision aids were required.

Hawker's hands were still. Profile Bourne rubbed the

grip of his submachine gun, not with his fingers but with the palm of his right hand. The orange dragon caressed the plastic in a fashion that gave Radescu a thrill of erotic horror before he snatched his eyes away.

His uncle had not pressed when a sense of the futility of words had choked the young general's first attempt at argument. Antonescu still waited with a placid exterior and a core of disdain for the emotional diatribe which he expected to hear. Wraslov was lost in his contemplation of corpses, past and future; but Tribune Deliu was watching the general with a grin of pleasant anticipation.

He would not, thought Alexander Radescu, embarrass Uncle Grigor and give that stupid *animal* Deliu a moment of triumph. For some reason, that seemed more important than the fact that the plan he'd expected to weld together the races of Oltenia had just disintegrated like a sand castle in the surf. Perhaps it was because he had control over himself; and now, as he tumbled from his pinnacle of arrogant certainty, he realized that he had no control over anything else after all.

"The arguments against exterminating the Molts," Radescu said in the tone of cool disinterest with which he would have enumerated to a friend the failings of an ex-lover, "the negative arguments that is—" He paused and raised an eyebrow in question. "Since I presume the positive argument of Oltenia leading the galaxy through its combination of human and autochthonal talents has already been discounted? Yes?"

"We don't *need* to hear your arguments," rasped Deliu, "since we've already decided on the basis of common sense."

"Thought is a beneficial process for human beings, Excellence," said Radescu in a voice as clear and hard as diamond windchimes. "You should try it yourself on occasion."

One of the Honor Guards ten meters across the chamber gasped, but Chief Tribune Antonescu waved the underling to panicked silence without even bothering to look at the man. "Deliu," said the Chief Tribune, "I promised my nephew a discussion, and that he shall have. His merits to the State alone have earned him that."

Antonescu's careful terminology and the edge in his voice were extraordinarily blunt reminders of the difference in the current government between Tribunes and the Chief Tribune. He nodded toward the general. "Alexi," he prompted.

Which left the real situation exactly where Radescu had feared it was, the dream of Man/Molt partnership dissolved in a welter of blood, but there is a pleasure to small triumphs in the midst of disaster. Was this happening to Ferad among *his* fellows as well . . . ?

Aloud, Radescu continued, "If we could destroy every nursery chamber, and if every infant Molt were within such a chamber, neither of which statements is true—" he did not bother to emphasize his disclaimer, knowing that rhetorical tricks would lessen at least in his own mind the icy purity of what he was saying "—then it would still be two, more realistically, three decades, before the operation would by itself deplete the ranks of effective Molt warriors. Prepubescents, even adolescents with a range of a few kays per hop, have been met on the battlefield only in cases like this one where we have gone to *them*."

"Yes, yes," said Tribune Wraslov, turning to nod at Radescu. The young general felt as if he stood at the shimmering interface between reality and expectation. On the side that was reality, the skeletal tribune agreed with what Radescu had said and gave his thin equivalent of a smile. But surely his assumption that Wraslov was being sarcastic must be correct? It was obvious that everything Radescu had said was a bitter attack on what the Tribunate seemed to have decided.

"And what conclusions do you draw from your analysis, Alexi?" asked Grigor Antonescu, very much the pleased uncle . . . though he beamed, like a moon, coolly.

"That at best, Uncle, we're talking about another generation of war," Radescu replied, walking toward the chintz-covered table because his legs worked normally again and he needed the opportunity to try them out. The whole conversation had the feel of something he might have overheard twenty years before—two aristocrats talking about a planned marriage of peripheral interest to both their households. It *couldn't* be a discussion which would determine the future of Oltenia for the foreseeable future!

And he, Alexander Radescu, wasn't really talking part in it. He could not have shut down his emotions so thoroughly and be proceeding dispassionately in his mind to end game, not if it were Alexi and Uncle Grigor talking here in a Molt cavern. . . .

"Another generation of ballrooms filled with bodies," Radescu continued as his index finger traced the chintz into hills and valleys like those outside, baptized already in blood.

"We've destroyed those urns, of course," snapped Tribune Deliu to the general's back.

"Buildings collapsing because the foundations were on bedrock and a Molt flitted in to set a bomb there," Radescu said calmly to the table. "There've been a few of those already and there'll be more."

His copy of the treaty document, hand-lettered on parchment, crinkled in his breast pocket when he straightened. Ferad would bring the other copy himself, on archival-quality paper imported from Earth—and how long would the Molt leader wait for the red smoke before he realized that there would be no peace after all, not in his lifetime or the lifetime of anyone now on the planet . . . ?

"Yes, but we'll be killing many of them, very many " said Tribune Wraslov, whose eyes had a glazed appearance that removed him as far from the present as Radescu felt he himself had been removed. The two of them were only reflections, their lips moving without stirring anything around them. Only Chief Tribune Antonescu was real. . . .

"A generation of men walking the streets of Belvedere, of every city and village on Oltenia," the general continued because he could not stop without having made every possible effort to prevent what would otherwise occur, "who have been trained to shoot infants—"

"Shoot Molts," Deliu interrupted.

"Shoot *infants* as harmless and helpless as anything human they're going to find when they go home on leave," Radescu said, feeling his voice tremble as his control began to break. Something terrible would happen if he ever lost control. "*That's* what we'll have if the war goes on!"

"We will have a Tribunate with complete control of the State," said Chief Tribune Antonescu in a voice that penetrated the ears of every listener like a sword blade being slammed home in its sheath. "That's what we'll continue to have for so long as the war goes on."

The six men of the Honor Guard were tense ciphers at the curving wall, nervously watching State policy being made in a scene like an argument over cards. But men were men when personal emotions ran high, thought Alexander Radescu, and nothing could have been more personal than what he had just been told.

How naive of him to assume that Uncle Grigor would divorce personal benefit from matters of State. A political appointee like General Radescu should have known better.

The Chief Tribune walked over to his nephew and put a hand on his shoulder. He no longer towered over little Alexi; they were eye to eye with any difference in height to the younger man. . . . "Do you understand what I'm telling you, my boy?" he asked with the real warmth which almost none of his closest associates had heard in Antonescu's voice. "Surely you understand?"

"I understand that it's wrong," said the general. Loudly, almost shouting as he pulled away from the Chief Tribune, he added, "I understand that it's *evil*, Uncle Grigor!"

"Then understand *this*," roared Antonescu, who had not raised his voice when informed of his son's suicide thirty years before. "You have the authority we choose to give you. To carry out decisions of the Tribunate—and no more!"

"Yes, yes," murmured Wraslov, and Deliu blinked avid, swine-bright eyes beside him.

"You will summon the Molt leader, as planned," the Chief Tribune said in frigid certainty. "We will stand to the side, so that the Molts can be killed as they appear. These mercenaries are capable of that, I presume?"

"Oh yes," General Radescu said with a nonchalance born of a question with an easy answer in the midst of so much that had no answer at all that he cared to accept. It was only after he spoke that he even bothered to look at Bourne and Hawker, gray figures who could so easily be dismissed as age-tattered statues . . . until the sergeant gave Radescu a wink almost veiled beneath the highlights on his face shield.

"I think we'd best leave it to the professionals, then," the Chief Tribune said, dismissing with a nod the motions the hands of the Honor Guard were making toward their gleaming, black-finished pistol holsters.

"Yes, of course" the general agreed, as his mind superimposed every image of Ferad that it held in memory—and one image more, the wizened Molt staggering backwards with his chest shot away and the treaty ablaze in his hand.

Antonescu was walking toward the great archway with his nephew, though of course he could not leave the antechamber without warning the Molts of what was prepared. The other Tribunes were drifting for safety toward the young officers of the Honor Guard, out of the line of fire through autochthons appearing beside the flimsy table. "The trouble with you, my boy," said the Chief Tribune, laying his hand again on his nephew's shoulder, "is that you're very clever, but you're young—and you don't understand the use of power."

"Sir?" said General Forsch, waiting just outside in the sunshine. Beside him was Captain Elejash, looking uncomfortable in his scarlet uniform and holding the smoke grenade in big, capable hands.

Radescu shook his head sharply, then turned to look at his uncle and the plea in the older man's eyes that his protégé accept reality without an unpleasant scene.

"Don't I understand power, Uncle Grigor?" the general said, raising his right hand to his brow. "Well, perhaps you're right." The only thing his eyes could see as he looked back into the antechamber was the gape of the dragon that Bourne's palm stroked across the grip of his weapon.

Alexander Radescu tossed his cap toward the table in a scintillating arc.

The Honor Guard was crumpling before the cyan flashes which killed them were more than a stroboscopic effect to the men in the chamber. One Guard managed to open his holster flap, but his chest was lit by smoky flames which seemed to spring from the scarlet dye rather than the black craters the powergun had punched in the uniform.

Radescu could forget that afterwards, could forget the way Deliu's bladder and bowels stained his white robes as the bolts hit him and the look of ecstasy on Wraslov's face as his eyeballs reflected the blue-green glare from the muzzle of Hawker's submachine gun.

What he would never forget, however, was the wetness on his face, his fingertips coming down from his cheek red with the splattered blood of his Uncle Grigor.

When the weapons detector chimed, the man behind the console shouted, "The little one's holding!" and three shotguns pointed instinctively at Hawker and Bourne in the anteroom of the Chief Executive's Residence.

"Hey, it's Profile," said one of the quartet of guards, lifting the muzzle of his weapon in embarrassment. Down the hall, the bell responder in the guard commander's office shut off when that worthy bolted toward the anteroom.

"What's this cop?" Bourne snapped in outrage, not so angry, however, as to take a blustering step toward the leveled shotguns. "We offloaded our bloody hardware 'fore we came over!"

"Don't care if he's the Lord himself come to take me to heaven," rejoined a guard with his gun still centered. He was dressed in issue battledress, but the yellow bandana worn as a head covering and the paired pistols in crossdraw holsters gave him a piratical air. "If he's packin' he stays where he is."

"Excuse me, Sergeant Bourne," said the guard at the detector console as the guard commander—Elejash, now Colonel Elejash—burst into the anteroom with yet another shotgun, "but if you'd check your left forearm, the underside . . . ?"

"That's all right, Culcer," said Elejash, lifting his own

weapon and stepping across the line of fire from his men
to their targets "You did right, but we're to admit this pair
as is."

"Via," said Profile Bourne, blushing for the first time
in his partner's memory.

He twitched his left hand, and the spring clip on his
wrist flipped the knife into his waiting grip. "Lord and
martyrs, man, you're right," the sergeant said to the shimmering blade in a voice of wonder. "I forgot it."

Enzo Hawker laughed, both in amusement and from a
need to release the rigid lock into which he had set his
muscles at the unexpected challenge. The Oltenian guards,
all of them men he and Bourne had helped train, joined
with various levels of heartiness.

"That's all right, Sergeant," Elejash said as Bourne strode
over to the console and offered his knife pommel-first to
the guard seated there.

"Like hell it is," Bourne muttered, laying the little
weapon on the console when the guard refused to take it.
"I couldn't even bitch if they'd blown me away, could I?"

Elejash looked at Hawker and the big mercenary,
shrugging, said, "Well, we weren't expecting any special
treatment, but I think I'd have been disappointed in you
fellows if you'd shot us now, yeah."

"Briefly disappointed," said the guard at the console.

"Well," muttered Profile Bourne, starting to regain his
composure—mistakes about weapons weren't the sort of
thing the sergeant accepted in anyone, least of all himself,
"it wouldn't be the first time I'd missed Embarkation
Muster—but usually I was drunk'r in jail."

"You can go on in," said the guard commander. "The
Chief Executive told me to expect you."

"Or both," Bourne added to the nearer pair of guards.
All the Oltenians wore personal touches on their uniforms,
and the fatigues of the man at the console were patterned
with a loose gray mesh in which he could have passed at
a distance for a Molt warrior.

"Hey, how in blazes did he know that?" Bourne asked
Colonel Elejash. "We didn't—you know, want to intrude

when things were still settling out. This was pretty much spur a' the moment, with us gonna lift ship in a couple hours."

The guard commander shrugged, a gesture similar enough to that of the mercenary lieutenant earlier to be an unconscious copy. Others of the Slammers had helped to train the new Executive Guard, but Hawker and Bourne had had a particular impact because of their earlier association. "Why don't you ask him?" the Oltenian said, making a gesture that began as a wave toward the inner door and ended by opening it.

"The Slammers are here, sir," Elejash called through the doorway.

"Two of us, anyhow," said Bourne as he squared his shoulders and, swaggering to cover his nervousness—it wasn't the sort of thing he was used to, but the Loot was right to say they *had* to do it—he led the way into the circular Reception Chamber.

Across from the door, against the wall behind the desk and Chief Executive Radescu rising from his seat, was an urn of large blue and indigo crystals in a white matrix.

"Enzo, Profile," Radescu said, holding out his hands to either man. He was wearing trousers and a loose tunic, both of civilian cut and only in their color—pearl gray, with gold piping on the pants legs—suggestive of anything else. "I'd— well, I didn't want to order you in here, but I was really hoping to see you again before lift-off."

"Well, you were busy," the lieutenant said uncomfortably as he shook the hand offered him, "and we, we had training duties ourselves." Funny; they'd *made* him what he was, but Radescu was fully a planetary ruler now in Hawker's mind . . . while he and Profile were better'n fair soldiers in the best outfit in the galaxy.

"What do you think of them?" Radescu asked brightly, drawing the mercenaries to the trio of chairs beside his desk—prepared for them, apparently, for the Oltenian leader seated himself in the middle one and guided the others down to either side. "What do you think of them, then? The new Guards?"

"They'll do," said Profile Bourne, wriggling his back

against a chair he found uncomfortable because it was more deeply upholstered than he was used to.

"We told a couple of them," Hawker amplified, "that the Slammers were always hiring if they felt like getting off-planet."

"Via, though, they still don't *look* like soldiers," the sergeant said, miming with his left hand the bandana of the guard with the evident willingness to have blown him away.

"Conversely," said Alexander Radescu, "you know that there's a job here for you if you decide to stay. I'll clear it with Colonel Ham—"

"Sure, Profile," interrupted the big lieutenant, "and when's the last time you wore a fatigue shirt with a right sleeve on it? *Talk* to me about issue uniforms!"

Sometimes the best way to give a negative answer to a question, an offer, was to talk about something else instead. Well, Radescu thought, he could appreciate the courtesy, though he would much have preferred the other response.

To the Slammers, the Chief Executive said, "There's been a tradition here on Oltenia that officers could modify their outfits according to personal taste—when they weren't on field service, that is. I decided that the same standards should apply to the Exec—to my personal guard. A—" he spread and closed his fingers as his mind sorted words and found some that were close enough "—mark of the honor in which I hold them."

He laughed aloud, knowing as he heard the sound that there was very little humor in it. "After all," he said, "they keep me alive."

Sergeant Bourne had been eyeing the room, spacious and looking the more so for its almost complete lack of furnishings: the trio of chairs which seemed out of place; the large desk with an integral seat; and the blue john urn toward which Profile now nodded and asked, "That there what I think it is?"

"Yes, the surviving one of the pair," agreed the Chief Executive, following the sergeant's eyes. Neither mercenary had ever been in this building when it was the Tribunal Palace, but that story would have gotten around. "I'd been told it was destroyed also, but it appears that my uncle had instead removed it to storage in a warehouse. It permits Ferad to visit me at need." He smiled. "Or at whim. We've gotten to be friends, in a way, in the month since the shooting stopped."

Radescu got up and stepped toward the circular wall, his arm describing a 90° arc of the plain surface. "That's going to be covered with a twenty-centimeter sheet of black granite," the leader—the dictator—of Oltenia said. "It's been quarried by machinery, but the polish is being put to it by Molts—by hand. From every theme, and all of them who want to help. Ferad tells me that mothers are bringing infants as small—"

He coughed, clearing away the constriction of memory from his throat "—as small as the one I took out of the nursery chamber myself. They're putting the little ones' hands on the stone and sliding them along it, so that in the future, they'll be able to find this room as they can anything on the planet."

Sergeant Bourne guffawed, but anything he might have intended to say was swallowed when Radescu continued bitterly, "That means, I suppose, that my human enemies will find a way to hire a Molt warrior to assassinate me. No doubt my spirit will lie more easily for having helped achieve that degree of cooperation between the two intelligent races on the planet."

"Problems, General?" Bourne asked, levering himself out of the chair with an expression which did not seem so much changed from what he had worn a moment before but rather was a refinement of it. As when a fresh casting is struck to remove the sand clinging to its surface, thus the lines of the sergeant's face sprang into full relief when the thought of action rang in the little man's mind.

"I meant it about the job," replied the young Oltenian evenly, meeting the mercenary's eyes.

"We've been moving around a lot," said Hawker, with the same calm and the same underlying determination as had been in Radescu's voice when he repeated the offer. "Being with the Regiment, it more or less keeps an edge on without it getting—you know, outa control."

Profile Bourne looked quizzically at his lieutenant, not at all unwilling himself, at this point, to have heard more about what Radescu wanted—and needed. Hawker, knowing that and determined to forestall the discussion, went on, "If we left Hammer and tried to settle down here, either we'd dump it all, all we'd been—doing, you know, you aren't talking about a couple detection specialists now, are you?"

He took a deep breath, raising his hand to hold the floor for the moment he had to pause before continuing, "We'd lose it, or we'd—" his eyes flicked toward Sergeant Bourne in a gesture so minute that Radescu could not be certain that it had been intentional "—go the other way, turn into something you couldn't have around anyplace you'd—be wearing civilian clothes, put it that way."

Alexander Radescu nodded brusquely and turned again to face the wall that would be replaced by a surface of polished granite. He did not speak.

To his back, Lieutenant Hawker said in a tone that reminded Bourne of the way the Loot had stroked the little Molt, "You're having trouble with the Chief Tribune's relatives, then? Sort of thought you might. . . ."

"Them?" said Alexander Radescu with sardonic brightness as he turned again to the Slammers. "Oh, no, not at all. For one thing, they're my relatives too, you know. They think they're sitting well—which they are, since they're the only pool of people I can trust, besides the army. And anyway, nobody on either side of the family was close enough to Uncle Grigor to think of, of avenging him.

"Nobody but me."

Radescu began to pace, his left hand swinging to touch the wall at intervals as he circled it. Bourne rotated to watch him, but Lieutenant Hawker remained seated, his eyes apparently on the backs of his hands. "Things are settling in quite well, people forgetting the war—and the Molts putting it behind them as well, from what Ferad says and the other reports, the *lack* of incidents."

"There's been shooting," Sergeant Bourne interjected. He talked to Oltenians, now, to members of the Guard and to the soldiers *they* talked to. It gave him more awareness of the planet on which he served than he could ever before remember having. Planets, to one of Hammer's Slammers, were generally a circumscribed round of fellows, "recreation establishments," and gunsight pictures. For the past month, Profile Bourne had found fellows among the local forces.

"There's always *been* incidents," Radescu snapped. His cheeks were puffier than they had been in the field, thought Lieutenant Hawker as he glanced sidelong. . . . "There's going to be shootings in mining camp bars and ranch dormitories as long as there's men, much less men and Molts. But it's no worse than, oh, ten years ago—I can get the exact figures. Having the Slammers around for an additional month to settle what *anybody* started, that was useful; but basically, three years of war haven't undone three centuries of peace, or as close to peace as Nature seems ready to allow anyone."

"Well," said Bourne, still standing, figuring that they'd done what, Via, courtesy demanded in making the call. He didn't look real great, the general didn't, but at least he wasn't a tarted-up clown the way he had been that first day, through the bars of the holding cell. . . . "Glad things are workin' out, and you know that if you need the Slammers again—"

"It's the Tzigara family," said Radescu, speaking through the sergeant's leave-taking as if oblivious to it. "Isn't that amusing?"

Lieutenant Hawker met the Chief Executive's painted smile with calm eyes and no expression of his own, waiting to hear what would be dragged out by the fact that when he and Bourne upped ship there would be no one for Radescu to speak to. That was what they had come for, though Profile didn't know it. That, and the one thing Hawker needed to say to pay their debt to the man who, after all, had saved their lives. . . .

"You never met Nikki, did you?" Radescu continued in

a bantering tone. "He was my aide, k-killed at the, in the ballroom . . . that night."

He cleared his throat, forced unwillingly to pause, but neither of the Slammers showed any sign of wanting to break in on the monologue. "He had a cousin, and I don't think I even knew that, in the, you know, in the Honor Guard. And it couldn't have made any difference, I don't mean *that*, but the family blames me now for both deaths."

"He was one a' the ones we blew away in the cave, you mean?" the sergeant asked, not particularly concerned but hoping that if the question were clarified he would be able to understand what in blazes the general was driving at.

"You did what I ordered you to do, what *had* to be done!" Alexander Radescu replied in a tone more fitting for condemnation than approval. But it was the world which he wanted to condemn, not the pair of mercenaries . . . and not even himself, though that was increasingly easy to do, when he lay awake at three in the morning. "There's been one attempt to kill me already, poison, and I've had word of others planned. . . ."

Radescu tented his fingers in front of him and seemed to carry out a brief series of isometrics, pressing the hands together and letting them spring back. "Sometimes I think that I won't be safe so long as there's a single one of the Tzigaras alive," he said. Then, with his eyes still determinedly focused on his fingertips, he added, "I'd be—very pleased if you gentlemen changed your minds, you know."

Lieutenant Hawker rose from the chair without using his arms to lift him, despite the depth and give of the upholstery. The lack of body armor made him feel lighter; and, though most of his waking hours were spent as he was now, without the heavy porcelain clamshell latched to him, being around Radescu made the Slammers lieutenant feel that he *ought* to be in armor. Habituated response, he supposed.

"I think we'd best be getting back to the regiment, sir," said Enzo Hawker, stretching out his hand to shake Radescu's.

"Of course," agreed the Chief Executive, clasping the

mercenary's firmly. "Colonel Hammer performed to the perfect satisfaction of his contract. What you two did was more."

"Don't worry 'bout missing us, general," said Profile as he took the hand offered him in turn. "You got boys out there—" he nodded to the anteroom "—can handle anything we would."

He laughed, pleasantly in intention, though the harshness of the sound made Radescu think of the fluorescent dragon on the palm wringing his. "Dudn't take a world a' smarts, dudn't even take a lotta training. Just to be willing, that's all." He laughed again and stepped toward the door.

Hawker touched the sergeant on the shoulder, halting and turning him. "Sir," the big lieutenant said as his subordinate watched and waited with a frown of confusion, "you're where you are now because you were willing to do what had to be done. Everybody else wanted an easy way out. Wanted to kill Molts instead of ending a war."

"Where I am now," Alexander Radescu repeated, quirking his lips into a smile of sorts.

"If you didn't have the balls to handle a tough job," said Hawker sharply, "you'd have seen the last of me 'n the sarge a long while back, mister."

Hawker and Radescu locked eyes while Bourne looked from one man to the other, puzzled but not worried; there was nothing here to worry about.

"I appreciate the vote of confidence," said the Oltenian as he broke into a grin and reached out to shake the lieutenant's hand again.

"Oh, there's one thing more," Hawker added in a gentle voice as he willingly accepted the handclasp. "Profile, I'll bet the Chief Executive thinks we were firing long bursts there when we cleared the cave."

"What?" said Radescu in amazement, pausing with the mercenary's hand still in his.

"Oh, Via, no," Profile Bourne blurted, *his* surprise directed at the suggestion rather than the fact that the Loot had voiced it. "Blood 'n martyrs, General, single shots only. Lord, the polish that stone had, the ricochets'd fry us all like pork rinds if we'd just tried to hose things down." He stared at Radescu in the hopeful horror of a specialist who prays that he's been able to prevent a friend from doing something lethally dangerous through ignorance.

"That's right sir," said Enzo Hawker as he met the Chief Executive's wondering eyes. "You have to know exactly what you're doing before you decide to use guns."

Radescu nodded very slowly as the two guns for hire walked out of his office.

THE BUTCHER'S BILL

"You can go a thousand kays any direction there and there's nothing to see but the wheat," said the brown man to the other tankers and the woman. His hair was deep chestnut, his face and hands burnt umber from the sun of Emporion the month before and the suns of seven other worlds in past years. He was twenty-five but looked several years older. The sleeves of his khaki coveralls were slipped down over his wrists against the chill of the breeze that had begun at twilight to feather the hillcrest. "We fed four planets from Dunstan—Hagener, Weststar, Mirage, and Jackson's Glade. And out of it we made enough to replace the tractors when they wore out, maybe something left over for a bit of pretty. A necklace of fireballs to set off a Lord's Day dress, till the charge drained six, eight months later. A static cleaner from Hagener, it was one year, never quite worked off our powerplant however much we tinkered with it. . . .

"My mother, she wore out too. Dad just kept grinding on, guess he still does."

The girl asked a question from the shelter of the tank's scarred curtain. Her voice was too mild for the wind's tumbling, her accent that of Thrush and strange to the tanker's ears. But Danny answered, "Hate them? Oh, I know about the Combine, now, that the four of them kept other merchants off Dunstan to freeze the price at what they thought to pay. But Via, wheat's a high bulk cargo,

175

there's no way at all we'd have gotten rich on what it could bring over ninety minutes' transit. And why shouldn't I thank Weststar? If ever a world did me well, it was that one."

He spat, turning his head with the wind and lofting the gobbet invisibly into the darkness. The lamp trembled on its base, an overturned ration box. The glare skipped across the rusted steel skirts of the tank, the iridium armor of hull and turret; the faces of the men and the woman listening to the blower chief. The main gun, half shadowed by the curve of the hull, poked out into the night like a ghost of itself. Even with no human in the tank, at the whisper of a relay in Command Central the fat weapon would light the world cyan and smash to lava anything within line of sight of its muzzle.

"We sold our wheat to a Weststar agent, a Hindi named Sarim who'd lived, Via, twenty years at least on Dunstan but he still smelled funny. Sweetish, sort of; you know? But his people were all back in Ongole on Weststar. When the fighting started between the Scots and the Hindi settlers, he raised a battalion of farm boys like me and shipped us over in the hold of a freighter. Hoo Lordy, that was a transit!

"And I never looked back. Colonel Hammer docked in on the same day with the Regiment, and he took us all on spec. Six years, now, that's seven standard . . . and not all of us could stand the gaff, and not all who could wanted to. But I never looked back, and I never will."

From the mast of Command Central, a flag popped unseen in the wind. It bore a red lion rampant on a field of gold, the emblem of Hammer's Slammers, the banner of the toughest regiment that ever killed for a dollar.

"Hotel, Kitchen, Lariat, Michael, move to the front in company columns and advance."

The tiny adamantine glitter winking on the hilltop ten kays distant was the first break in the landscape since the Regiment had entered the hypothetical war zone, the Star Plain of Thrush. It warmed Pritchard in the bubble at the same time it tightened his muscles. "Goose it, Kowie," he ordered his driver in turn, "they want us panzers up front. Bet it's about to drop in the pot?"

Kowie said nothing, but the big blower responded with a howl and a billow of friable soil that seethed from under the ground effect curtain. Two Star in the lead, H Company threaded its way in line ahead through the grounded combat cars and a company from Infantry Section. The pongoes crouched on their one-man skimmers, watching the tanks. One blew an ironic kiss to Danny in Two Star's bubble. Moving parallel to Hotel, the other companies of Tank Section, K, L, and M, advanced through the center and right of the skirmish line.

The four man crew of a combat car nodded unsmilingly from their open-topped vehicle as Two Star boomed past. A trio of swivel-mounted powerguns, 2cm hoses like the one on Danny's bubble, gave them respectable firepower; and their armor, a sandwich of ceramics and iridium, was in fact adequate against most hand weapons. Buzzbombs aside, and tankers didn't like to think about those either. But Danny would have fought reassignment to combat cars if anybody had suggested it—Lord, you may as well dance in your skin for all the good that hull does you in a firefight! And few car crewmen would be caught dead on a panzer— or rather, were sure that was how they would be caught if they crewed one of those sluggish, clumsy, blind-sided behemoths. Infantry Section scorned both, knowing how the blowers drew fire but couldn't flatten in the dirt when it dropped in on them.

One thing wouldn't get you an argument, though: when it was ready to drop in the pot, you sent in the heavies. And nothing on the Way would stop the Tank Section of Hammer's Slammers when it got cranked up to move.

Even its 170 tonnes could not fully dampen the vibration of Two Star's fans at max load. The oval hull, all silvery-smooth above but of gouged and rusty steel below where the skirts fell sheer almost to the ground, slid its way through the grass like a boat through yellow seas. They were dropping into a swale before they reached the upgrade. From the increasing rankness of the vegetation that flattened before and beside the tank, Pritchard suspected they would find a meandering stream at the bottom. The brow of the hill cut off sight of the unnatural glitter visible from a distance. In silhouette against the pale bronze sky writhed instead a grove of gnarled trees.

"Incoming, fourteen seconds to impact," Command Central blatted. A siren in the near distance underscored the words. "Three rounds only."

The watercourse was there. Two Star's fans blasted its surface into a fine mist as the tank bellowed over it. Danny cocked his powergun, throwing a cylinder of glossy black plastic into the lowest of the three rotating barrels. There was shrieking overhead.

WHAM

A poplar shape of dirt and black vapor spouted a kay to the rear, among the grounded infantry.

WHAM WHAM

They were detonating underground. Thrush didn't have much of an industrial base, the rebel portions least of all. Either they hadn't the plant to build proximity fuses at all, or they were substituting interference coils for miniature radar sets, and there was too little metal in the infantry's gear to set off the charges. With the main director out, Central wasn't even bothering to explode the shells in flight.

"Tank Section, hose down the ridge as you advance, they got an OP there somewhere."

"Incoming, three more in fourteen." The satellite net could pick up a golf ball in flight, much less a two hundred kilo shell.

Pritchard grinned like a death's head, laying his 2cm automatic on the rim of the hill and squeezing off. The motor whirred, spinning the barrels as rock and vegetation burst in the blue-green sleet. Spent cases, gray and porous, spun out of the mechanism in a jet of coolant gas. They bounced on the turret slope, some clinging to the iridium to cool there, ugly dark excrescences on the metal.

"Outgoing."

Simultaneously with Central's laconic warning, giants tore

a strip off the sky. The rebel shells dropped but their bursts were smothered in the roar of the Regiment's own rocket howitzers boosting charges to titanic velocity for the several seconds before their motors burned out. Ten meters from the muzzles the rockets went supersonic, punctuating the ripping sound with thunderous slaps. Danny swung his hose toward the grove of trees, the only landmark visible on the hilltop. His burst laced it cyan. Water, flash-heated within the boles by the gunfire, blew the dense wood apart in blasts of steam and splinters. A dozen other guns joined Pritchard's, clawing at rock, air, and the remaining scraps of vegetation.

"Dead on," Central snapped to the artillery. "Now give it battery five and we'll show those freaks how they should've done it."

Kowie hadn't buttoned up. His head stuck up from the driver's hatch, trusting his eyes rather than the vision blocks built into his compartment. The tanks themselves were creations of the highest technical competence, built on Terra itself; but the crews were generally from frontier worlds, claustrophobic in an armored coffin no matter how good its electronic receptors were. Danny knew the feeling. His hatch, too, was open, and his hand gripped the rounded metal of the powergun itself rather than the selsyn unit inside. They were climbing sharply now, the back end hopping and skittering as the driver fed more juice to the rear fans in trying to level the vehicle. The bow skirts grounded briefly, the blades spitting out a section of hillside as pebbles.

For nearly a minute the sky slammed and raved. Slender, clipped-off vapor trails of counter-battery fire streamed from the defiladed artillery. Half a minute after they ceased fire, the drumbeat of shells bursting on the rebels continued. No further incoming rounds fell.

Two Star lurched over the rim of the hill. Seconds later the lead blowers of K and M bucked in turn onto the flatter area. Smoke and ash from the gun-lit brushfire shoomped out in their downdrafts. There was no sign of the enemy, either Densonite rebels or Foster's crew—though if the mercenaries were involved, they would be bunkered beyond probable notice until they popped the cork themselves. "Tank Section, ground! Ground in place and prepare for director control."

Danny hunched, bracing his palms against the hatch coaming. Inside the turret the movement and firing controls of the main gun glowed red, indicating that they had been locked out of Pritchard's command. Kowie lifted the bow to kill the tank's immense inertia. There was always something spooky about feeling the turret purr beneath you, watching the big gun snuffle the air with deadly precision on its own. Danny gripped his tribarrel, scanning the horizon nervously. It was worst when you didn't know what Central had on its mind . . . and you did know that the primary fire control computer was on the fritz—they always picked the damnedest times!

"Six aircraft approaching from two-eight-three degrees," Central mumbled. "Distance seven point ought four kays, closing at one one ought ought."

Pritchard risked a quick look away from where the gun pointed toward a ridgeline northwest of them, an undistinguished swelling half-obscured by the heat-wavering pall of smoke. Thirteen other tanks had crested the hill before Central froze them, all aiming in the same direction. Danny dropped below his hatch rim, counting seconds.

The sky roared cyan. The tank's vision blocks blanked momentarily, but the dazzle reflected through the open hatch was enough to make Pritchard's skin tingle. The smoke waved and rippled about the superheated tracks of gunfire. The horizon to the northwest was an expanding orange dome that silently dominated the sky.

"Resume advance." Then, "Spectroanalysis indicates five hostiles were loaded with chemical explosives, one was carrying fissionables."

Danny was trembling worse than before the botched attack. The briefing cubes had said the Densonites were religious nuts, sure. But to use unsupported artillery against a force whose satellite spotters would finger the guns before the first salvo landed; aircraft—probably converted cargo haulers—thrown against director-controlled powerguns that shot light swift and line straight; and then nukes, against a regiment more likely to advance stark naked than without a nuclear damper up! They weren't just nuts—Thrush central government was that, unwilling to have any of its own people join the fighting—they were as crazy as if they thought they could breathe vacuum and live. You didn't play that sort of game with the Regiment.

They'd laager for the night on the hilltop, the rest of the outfit rumbling in through the afternoon and early evening hours. At daybreak they'd leapfrog forward again, deeper into the Star Plain, closer to whatever it was the Densonites wanted to hold. Sooner or later, the rebels and Foster's Infantry—a good outfit but not good enough for this job—were going to have to make a stand. And then the Regiment would go out for contact again, because they'd have run out of work on Thrush.

"She'll be in looking for you pretty soon, won't she, handsome?"

"Two bits to stay."

"Check. Sure, Danny-boy, you Romeos from Dunstan, you can pick up a slot anywhere, huh?"

A troop of combat cars whined past, headed for their position in the laager. Pritchard's hole card, a jack, flipped over. He swore, pushed in his hand. "I was folding anyway. And cut it out, will you? I didn't go looking for her. I didn't tell her to come back. And she may as well be the colonel for all my chance of putting her flat."

Wanatamba, the lean, black Terran who drove Fourteen, laughed and pointed. A gold-spangled skimmer was dropping from the east, tracked by the guns of two of the blowers on that side. Everybody knew what it was, though. Pritchard grimaced and stood. "Seems that's the game for me," he said.

"Hey, Danny," one of the men behind him called as he walked away. "Get a little extra for us, hey?"

The skimmer had landed in front of Command Central, at rest an earth-blended geodesic housing the staff and much of the commo hardware. Wearing a wrist-to-ankle sunsuit, yellow where it had tone, she was leaning on the plex windscreen. An officer in fatigues with unlatched body armor stepped out of the dome and did a double take. He must have recollected, though, because he trotted off toward a bunker before Danny reached the skimmer.

"Hey!" the girl called brightly. She looked about seventeen, her hair an unreal cascade of beryl copper over one shoulder. "We're going on a trip."

"Uh?"

The dome section flipped open again. Pritchard stiffened to attention when he saw the short, mustached figure who exited. "Peace, Colonel," the girl said.

"Peace, Sonna. You're such an ornament to a firebase that I'm thinking of putting you on requisition for our next contract."

Laughing cheerfully, the girl gestured toward the rigid sergeant. "I'm taking Danny to the Hamper Shrine this afternoon."

Pritchard reddened. "Sir, Sergeant-Commander Daniel Pritchard—"

"I know you, trooper," the colonel said with a friendly smile. "I've watched Two Star in action often enough, you know." His eyes were blue.

"Sir, I didn't request—that is . . ."

"And I also know there's small point in arguing with our girl here, hey, Sonna? Go see your shrine, soldier, and worse comes to worst, just throw your hands up and yell 'Exchange.' You can try Colonel Foster's rations for a week or two until we get this little business straightened out." The colonel winked, bowed low to Sonna, and reentered the dome.

"I don't figure it," Danny said as he settled into the passenger seat. The skimmer was built low and sleek as if a racer, though its top speed was probably under a hundred kays. Any more would have put too rapid a drain of the rechargables packed into the decimeter-thick floor—a fusion unit would have doubled the flyer's bulk and added four hundred kilos right off the bat. At that, the speed and an operating altitude of thirty meters were more than enough for the tanker. You judge things by what you're used to, and the blower chief who found himself that far above the cold, hard ground—it could happen on a narrow switchback—had seen his last action.

While the wind whipped noisily about the open cockpit, the girl tended to her flying and ignored Danny's curiosity. It was a hop rather than a real flight, keeping over the same hill at all times and circling down to land scarcely a minute after takeoff. On a field of grass untouched by the recent fire rose the multi-tinted crystalline structure Pritchard had glimpsed during the assault. With a neat spin and a brief whine from the fans, the skimmer settled down.

Sonna grinned. Her sunsuit, opaquing completely in the direct light, blurred her outline in a dazzle of fluorescent saffron. "What don't you figure?"

"Well, ah . . . ." Danny stumbled, his curiosity drawn between the girl and the building. "Well, the colonel isn't that, ah, easy to deal with usually. I mean . . ."

Her laugh bubbled in the sunshine. "Oh, it's because I'm an Advisor, I'm sure."

"Excuse?"

"An Advisor. You know, the . . . well, a representative. Of the government, if you want to put it that way."

"My Lord!" the soldier gasped. "But you're so young."

She frowned. "You really don't know much about us, do you?" she reflected.

"Umm, well, the briefing cubes mostly didn't deal with the friendlies this time because we'd be operating without support. . . . Anything was going to look good after Emporion, that was for sure. All desert there—you should've heard the cheers when the colonel said that we'd lift."

She combed a hand back absently through her hair. It flowed like molten bronze. "You won on Emporion?" she asked.

"We could've," Danny explained, "even though it was really a Lord-stricken place, dust and fortified plateaus and lousy recce besides because the government had two

operating spacers. But the Monarchists ran out of money
after six months and that's one sure rule for Hammer's
Slammers—no pay, no play. Colonel yanked their bond so
fast their ears rang. And we hadn't orbited before offers
started coming in."

"And you took ours and came to a place you didn't know
much about," the girl mused. "Well, we didn't know much
about you either."

"What do you need to know except we can bust anybody
else in this business?" the soldier said with amusement.
"Anybody, public or planet-tied. If you're worried about
Foster, don't; he wouldn't back the freaks today, but when
he has to, we'll eat him for breakfast."

"Has to?" the girl repeated in puzzlement. "But he
always has to—the Densonites hired him, didn't they?"

Strategy was a long way from Danny's training, but the
girl seemed not to know that. And besides, you couldn't
spend seven years with the Slammers and not pick up some
basics. "OK," he began, "Foster's boys'll fight, but they're
not crazy. Trying to block our advance in open land like
this'd be pure suicide—as those coppy freaks—pardon,
didn't mean that— must've found out today. Foster likely
got orders to support the civvies but refused. I know for
a fact that his arty's better'n what we wiped up today, and
those *planes* . . ."

"But his contract . . . ?" Sonna queried.

"Sets out the objectives and says the outfit'll obey civvie
orders where it won't screw things up too bad," Danny said.
"Standard form. The legal of it's different, but that's what
it means."

The girl was nodding, eyes slitted, and in a low voice
she quoted, ". . . 'except in circumstances where such
directions would significantly increase the risks to be
undergone by the party of the second part without cor-
responding military advantage." She looked full at Danny.
"Very . . . interesting. When we hired your colonel, I don't
think any of us understood that clause."

Danny blinked, out of his depth and aware of it. "Well,
it doesn't matter really. I mean, the colonel didn't get his

rep from ducking fights. It's just, well . . . say we're supposed to clear the Densonites off the, the Star Plain? Right?"

The girl shrugged.

"So that's what we'll do." Danny wiped his palms before gesturing with both hands. "But if your Advisors—"

"We Advisors," the girl corrected, smiling.

"Anyway," the tanker concluded, his enthusiasm chilled, "if you tell the colonel to fly the whole Regiment up to ten thousand and jump it out, he'll tell you to go piss up a rope. Sorry, he wouldn't say that. But you know what I mean. We know our job, don't worry."

"Yes, that's true," she said agreeably. "And we don't, and we can't understand it. We thought that—one to one, you know?—perhaps if I got to know you, one of you . . . They thought we might understand all of you a little."

The soldier frowned uncertainly.

"What we don't see," she finally said, "is how you—"

She caught herself. Touching her cold fingertips to the backs of the tanker's wrists, the girl continued, "Danny, you're a nice . . . you're not a, a sort of monster like we thought you all must be. If you'd been born of Thrush you'd have had a—different—education, you'd be more, forgive me, I don't mean it as an insult, sophisticated in some ways. That's all.

"But how can a nice person like you go out and kill?"

He rubbed his eyes, then laced together his long, brown fingers. "You . . . well, it's not like that. What I said the other night—look, the Slammers're a good outfit, the best, and I'm damned lucky to be with them. I do my job the best way I know. I'll keep on doing that. And if somebody gets killed, OK. My brother Jig stayed home and he's two years dead now. Tractor rolled on a wet field but Via, coulda been a tow-chain snapped or old age; doesn't matter. He wasn't going to live forever and neither is anybody else. And I haven't got any friends on the far end of the muzzle."

Her voice was very soft as she said, "Perhaps if I keep trying . . ."

Danny smiled. "Well, I don't mind," he lied, looking at the structure. "What is this place, anyhow?"

Close up, it had unsuspected detail. The sides were a hedge of glassy rods curving together to a series of peaks ten meters high. No finger-slim member was quite the thickness or color of any other, although the delicacy was subliminal in impact. In ground plan it was a complex oval thirty meters by ten, pierced by scores of doorways which were not closed off but were foggy to look at.

"What do you think of it?" the girl asked.

"Well, it's . . ." Danny temporized. A fragment of the briefing cubes returned to him. "It's one of the alien, the Gedel, artifacts, isn't it?"

"Of course," the girl agreed. "Seven hundred thousand years old, as far as we can judge. Only a world in stasis, like Thrush, would have let it survive the way it has. The walls are far tougher than they look, but seven hundred millennia of earthquakes and volcanoes . . ."

Danny stepped out of the skimmer and let his hand run across the building's cool surface. "Yeah, if they'd picked some place with a hotter core there wouldn't be much left but sand by now, would there?"

"Pick it? Thrush was their home," Sonna's voice rang smoothly behind him. "The Gedel chilled it themselves to make it suitable, to leave a signpost for the next races following the Way. We can't even imagine how they did it, but there's no question but that Thrush was normally tectonic up until the last million years or so."

"Via!" Danny breathed, turning his shocked face toward the girl. "No wonder those coppy fanatics wanted to control this place. Why, if they could figure out just a few of the Gedel tricks they'd . . . Lord, they wouldn't stop with Thrush, that's for sure."

"You still don't understand," the girl said. She took Danny by the hand and drew him toward the nearest of the misty doorways. "The Densonites have well, quirks that make them hard for the rest of us on Thrush to understand. But they would no more pervert Gedel wisdom to warfare than you would, oh, spit on your colonel. Come here."

She stepped into the fuzziness and disappeared. The tanker had no choice but to follow or break her grip; though, oddly, she was no longer clinging to him on the other side of the barrier. She was not even beside him in the large room. He was alone at the first of a line of tableaux, staring at a group of horribly inhuman creatures at play. Their sharp-edged faces, scale-dusted but more avian than reptile, stared enraptured at one of their number who hung in the air. The acrobat's bare, claw-tipped legs pointed 180 degrees apart, straight toward ground and sky.

Pritchard blinked and moved on. The next scene was only a dazzle of sunlight in a glade whose foliage was redder than that of Thrush or Dunstan. There was something else, something wrong or strange about the tableau. Danny felt it, but his eyes could not explain.

Step by step, cautiously, Pritchard worked his way down the line of exhibits. Each was different, centered on a group of the alien bipeds or a ruddy, seemingly empty landscape that hinted unintelligibly. At first, Danny had noticed the eerie silence inside the hall. As he approached the far end he realized he was conscious of music of some sort, very crisp and distant. He laid his bare palm on the floor and found, as he had feared, that it did not vibrate in the least. He ran the last twenty steps to plunge out into the sunlight. Sonna still gripped his hand, and they stood outside the doorway they had entered.

The girl released him. "Isn't it incredible?" she asked, her expression bright. "And every one of the doorways leads to a different corridor—recreation there, agriculture in another, history—everything. A whole planet in that little building."

"That's what the Gedel looked like, huh?" Danny said. He shook his head to clear the strangeness from it.

"The Gedel? Oh, no," the girl replied, surprised again at his ignorance. "These were the folk we call the Hampers. No way to pronounce their own language, a man named Hamper found this site is all. But their homeworld was Kalinga IV, almost three days transit from Thrush. The shrine is here, we think, in the same relation to Starhome as Kalinga was to Thrush.

"You still don't understand," she concluded aloud, watching Danny's expression. She sat on the edge of the flyer, crossing her hands on the lap of her sunsuit. In the glitter thrown by the structure the fabric patterned oddly across her lithe torso. "The Gedel association—it wasn't an empire, couldn't have been. But to merge, a group ultimately needs a center, physical and intellectual. And Thrush and the Gedel were that for twenty races.

"And they achieved genuine unity, not just within one race but among all of them, each as strange to the others as any one of them would have been to man, to us. The . . . power that gave them, over themselves as well as the universe, was incredible. This—even Starhome itself— is such a tiny part of what could be achieved by perfect peace and empathy."

Danny looked at the crystal dome and shivered at what it had done to him. "Look," he said, "peace is just great if the universe cooperates. I don't mean just my line of work, but it doesn't happen that way in the real world. There's no peace spending your life beating wheat out of Dunstan, not like I'd call peace. And what's happened to the Gedel and their buddies for the last half million years or so if things were so great?"

"We can't even imagine what happened to them," Sonna explained gently, "but it wasn't the disaster you imagine. When they reached what they wanted, they set up this, Starhome, the other eighteen shrines as . . . monuments. And then they went away, all together. But they're not wholly gone, even from here, you know. Didn't you feel them in the background inside, laughing with you?"

"I . . ." Danny attempted. He moved, less toward the skimmer than away from the massive crystal behind him. "Yeah, there was something. That's what you're fighting for?"

You couldn't see the laager from where the skimmer rested, but Danny could imagine the silvery glitter of tanks and combat cars between the sky and the raw yellow grass. Her eyes fixed on the same stretch of horizon, the girl said, "Someday men will be able to walk through Starhome and understand. You can't live on Thrush without feeling the impact of the Gedel. That impact has . . . warped, perhaps, the Densonites. They have some beliefs about the Gedel that most of us don't agree with. And they're actually willing to use force to prevent the artifacts from being defiled by anyone who doesn't believe as they do."

"Well, you people do a better job of using force," Danny said. His mind braced itself on its memory of the Regiment's prickly hedgehog.

"Oh, not us!" the girl gasped.

Suddenly angry, the tanker gestured toward the unseen firebase. "Not you? The Densonites don't pay us. And if force isn't what happened to those silly bastards today when our counter-battery hit them, I'd like to know what is."

She looked at him in a way that, despite her previous curiosity, was new to him. "There's much that I'll have to discuss with the other Advisors," she said after a long pause. "And I don't know that it will stop with us, we'll have to put out the call to everyone, the Densonites as well if they will come." Her eyes caught Danny's squarely again. "We acted with little time for deliberation when the Densonites hired Colonel Foster and turned all the other pilgrims out of the Star Plain. And we acted in an area beyond our practice—thank the Lord! The key to understanding the Gedel and joining them, Lord willing and the Way being short, is Starhome. And nothing that blocks any man, all men, from Starhome can be . . . tolerated. But with what we've learned since . . . well, we have other things to take into account."

She broke off, tossed her stunning hair. In the flat evening sunlight her garment had paled to translucence. The late rays licked her body red and orange. "But now I'd better get you back to your colonel." She slipped into the skimmer.

Danny boarded without hesitation. After the Gedel building, the transparent skimmer felt almost comfortable. "Back to my tank," he corrected lightly. "Colonel may not care where I am, but he damn well cares if Two Star is combat ready." The sudden rush of air cut off thought of further conversation, and though Sonna smiled as she landed Danny beside his blower, there was a blankness in her expression that indicated her thoughts were far away.

Hell with her, Danny thought. His last night in the Rec Center on Emporion seemed a long time in the past.

At three in the morning the Regiment was almost two hundred kilometers from the camp they had abandoned at midnight. There had been no warning, only the low hoot of the siren followed by the colonel's voice rasping from every man's lapel speaker, "Mount up and move, boys. Order seven, and your guides are set." It might have loomed before another outfit as a sudden catastrophe. After docking one trip with the Slammers, though, a greenie learned that everything not secured to his blower had better be secured to him. Colonel Hammer thought an armored regiment's firepower was less of an asset than its mobility. He used the latter to the full with ten preset orders of march and in-motion recharging for the infantry skimmers, juicing from the tanks and combat cars.

Four pongoes were jumpered to Two Star when Foster's outpost sprang its ambush.

The lead combat car, half a kay ahead, bloomed in a huge white ball that flooded the photon amplifiers of Danny's goggles. The buzzbomb's hollow detonation followed a moment later while the tanker, cursing, simultaneously switched to infra-red and swung his turret left at max advance. He ignored the head of the column, where the heated-air thump of powerguns merged with the crackle of mines blasted to either side by the combat cars; that was somebody else's responsibility. He ignored the two infantrymen wired to his tank's port side as well. If they knew their business, they'd drop the jumpers and flit for Two Star's blind side as swiftly as Danny could spin his heavy turret. If not, well, you don't have time for niceness when somebody's firing shaped charges at you.

"Damp that ground-sender!" Central snapped to the lead elements. Too quickly to be a response to the command, the grass trembled under the impact of a delay-fused rocket punching down toward the computed location of the enemy's subsurface signaling. The Regiment must have rolled directly over an outpost, either through horrendously bad luck or because Foster had sewn his vedettes very thickly.

The firing stopped. The column had never slowed and Michael, first of the heavy companies behind the screen of combat cars, fanned the grass fires set by the hoses. Pritchard scanned the area of the firefight as Two Star rumbled through it in turn. The antipersonnel charges had dimpled the ground with shrapnel, easily identifiable among the glassy scars left by the powerguns. In the center of a great vitrified blotch lay a left arm and a few scraps of gray coverall. Nearby was the plastic hilt of a buzzbomb launcher. The other vedette had presumably stayed on the commo in his covered foxhole until the penetrator had scattered it and him over the landscape. If there had been a third bunker, it escaped notice by Two Star's echo sounders.

"Move it out, up front," Central demanded. "This cuts our margin."

The burned-out combat car swept back into obscurity as Kowie put on speed. The frontal surfaces had collapsed inward from the heat, leaving the driver and blower chief as husks of carbon. There was no sign of the wing gunners. Perhaps they had been far enough back and clear of the spurt of directed radiance to escape. The ammo canister of the port tribarrel had flash-ignited, though, and it was more likely that the men were wasted on the floor of the vehicle.

Another hundred and fifty kays to go, and now Foster and the Densonites knew they were coming.

There were no further ambushes to break the lightless monotony of gently rolling grassland. Pritchard took occasional sips of water and ate half a tube of protein ration. He started to fling the tube aside, then thought of the metal detectors on following units. He dropped it between his feet instead.

The metal-pale sun was thrusting the Regiment's shadow in long fingers up the final hillside when Central spoke again. You could tell it was the colonel himself sending. "Everybody freeze but Beta-First, Beta-First proceed in column up the rise and in. Keep your intervals, boys, and don't try to bite off too much. Last data we got was Foster had his antiaircraft company with infantry support holding the target. Maybe they pulled out when we knocked on the door tonight, maybe they got reinforced. So take it easy—and don't bust up anything you don't have to."

Pritchard dropped his seat back inside the turret. There was nothing to be seen from the hatch but the monochrome sunrise and armored vehicles grounded on the yellow background. Inside, the three vision blocks gave greater variety. One was the constant 360 degrees display, better than normal eyesight according to the designers because the blower chief could see all around the tank without turning his head. Danny didn't care for it. Images were squeezed a good deal horizontally. Shapes weren't quite what you expected, so you didn't react quite as fast; and that was a good recipe for a dead trooper. The screen above the three-sixty was variable in light sensitivity and in magnification, useful for special illumination and first-shot hits.

The bottom screen was the remote rig; Pritchard dialed it for the forward receptors of Beta-First-Three. It was strange to watch the images of the two leading combat cars trembling as they crested the hill, yet feel Two Star as stable as 170 tonnes can be when grounded.

"Nothing moving," the platoon leader reported unnecessarily. Central had remote circuits too, as well as the satellite net to depend on.

The screen lurched as the blower Danny was slaved to boosted its fans to level the downgrade. Dust plumed from the leading cars, weaving across a sky that was almost fully light. At an unheard command, the platoon turned up the wick in unison and let the cars hurtle straight toward the target's central corridor. It must have helped, because Foster's gunners caught only one car when they loosed the first blast through their camouflage.

The second car blurred in a mist of vaporized armor plate. Incredibly, the right wing gunner shot back. The deadly flame-lash of his hose was pale against the richer color of the hostile fire. Foster had sited his calliopes, massive 3cm guns whose nine fixed barrels fired extra-length charges. Danny had never seen a combat car turned into Swiss cheese faster than the one now spiked on the muzzles of a pair of the heavy guns.

Gray-suited figures were darting from cover as if the cars' automatics were harmless for being outclassed. The damaged blower nosed into the ground. Its driver leaped out, running for the lead car which had spun on its axis and was hosing blue-green fire in three directions. One of Foster's troops raised upright, loosing a buzzbomb at the wreckage of the grounded car. The left side of the vehicle flapped like a batwing as it sailed across Danny's field of view. The concussion knocked down the running man. He rose to his knees, jumped for a handhold as the lead car accelerated past him. As he swung himself aboard, two buzzbombs hit the blower simultaneously. It bloomed with joined skullcaps of pearl and bone.

Pritchard was swearing softly. He had switched to a stern pickup already, and the tumbled wreckage in it was bouncing, fading swiftly. Shots twinkled briefly as the four escaping blowers dropped over the ridge.

"In column ahead," said the colonel grimly, "Hotel, Kitchen, Michael. Button up and hose 'em out, you know the drill."

And then something went wrong. "Are you insane?" the radio marveled, and Danny recognized that voice too. "I forbid you!"

"You can't. Somebody get her out of here."

"Your contract is over, finished, do you hear? Heavenly Way, we'll all become Densonites if we must. This horror must end!"

"Not yet. You don't see—"

"I've seen too—" The shouted words cut off.

"So we let Foster give us a bloody nose and back off? That's what you want? But it's bigger than what you want now, sister, it's the whole Regiment. It's never bidding another contract without somebody saying, 'Hey, they got sandbagged on Thrush, didn't they?' And nobody remembering that Foster figured the civvies would chill us—and he was right. Don't you see? They killed my boys, and now they're going to pay the bill.

"Tank Section, execute! Dig 'em out, panzers!"

Danny palmed the panic bar, dropping the seat and locking the hatch over it. The rushing-air snarl of the fans was deadened by the armor, but a hot bearing somewhere filled the compartment with its high keening. Two Star hurdled the ridge. Its whole horizon flared with crystal dancing and scattering in sunlight and the reflected glory of automatic weapons firing from its shelter. Starhome was immensely larger than Danny had expected.

A boulevard twenty meters wide divided two ranks of glassy buildings, any one of which, towers and pavillions, stood larger than the shrine Danny had seen the previous day. At a kilometer's distance it was a coruscating unity of parts as similar as the strands of a silken rope. Danny rapped up the magnification and saw the details spring out; rods woven into columns that streaked skyward a hundred meters; translucent sheets formed of myriads of pinhead beads, each one glowing a color as different from the rest as one star is from the remainder of those seen on a moonless night; a spiral column, free-standing and the thickness of a woman's wrist, that pulsed slowly through the spectrum as it climbed almost out of sight. All the structures seemed to front on the central corridor, with the buildings on either side welded together by tracery mazes, porticoes, arcades—a thousand different plates and poles of glass.

A dashed cyan line joined the base of an upswept web of color to the tank. Two Star's hull thudded to the shock of vaporizing metal. The stabilizer locked the blower's pitching out of Danny's sight picture. He swung the glowing orange bead onto the source of fire and kicked the pedal. The air rang like a carillon as the whole glassy facade sagged, then avalanched into the street. There was a shock of heat in the closed battle compartment as the breech flicked open and belched out the spent case. The plastic hissed on the floor, outgassing horribly while the air-conditioning strained to clear the chamber. Danny ignored the stench, nudged his sights onto the onrushing splendor of the second structure on the right of the corridor. The breech of the big powergun slapped again and again, recharging instantly as the tanker worked the foot trip.

Blue-green lightning scattered between the walls as if the full power of each bolt was flashing the length of the corridor. Two Star bellowed in on the wake of its fire, and crystal flurried under the fans. Kowie leveled their stroke slightly, cutting speed by a fraction but lifting the tank higher above the abrasive litter. The draft hurled glittering shards across the corridor, arcs of cold fire in the light of Two Star's gun and those of the blowers following. Men in gray were running from their hiding places to avoid the sliding crystal masses, the iridescent rain that pattered on the upper surfaces of the tanks but smashed jaggedly through the infantry's body armor.

Danny set his left thumb to rotate the turret counter-clockwise, held the gun-switch down with his foot. The remaining sixteen rounds of his basic load blasted down the right half of Starhome, spread by the blower's forward motion and the turret swing. The compartment was gray with fumes. Danny slammed the hatch open and leaned out. His hands went to the 2cm as naturally as a calf turns to milk. The wind was cold on his face. Kowie slewed the blower left to avoid the glassy wave that slashed into the corridor from one of the blasted structures. The scintillance halted, then ground a little further as something gave way inside the pile.

A soldier in gray stepped from an untouched archway to the left. The buzzbomb on his shoulder was the size of a landing vessel as it swung directly at Danny. The tribarrel seemed to traverse with glacial slowness. It was too slow. Danny saw the brief flash as the rocket leaped from the shoulder of the other mercenary. It whirred over Two Star and the sergeant, exploded cataclysmically against a spike of Starhome still rising on the other side.

The infantryman tossed the launcher tube aside. He froze, his arms spread wide, and shouted, "Exchange!"

"Exchange yourself, mother!" Danny screamed back white-faced. He triggered his hose. The gray torso exploded. The body fell backward in a mist of blood, chest and body armor torn open by four hits that shriveled bones and turned fluids to steam.

"Hard left and goose it, Kowie," the sergeant demanded. He slapped the panic bar again. As the hatch clanged shut over his head, Danny caught a momentary glimpse of the vision blocks, three soldiers with powerguns leaping out of the same towering structure from which the rocketeer had come. Their faces were blankly incredulous as they saw the huge blower swinging toward them at full power. The walls flexed briefly under the impact of the tank's frontal slope, but the filigree was eggshell thin. The structure disintegrated, lurching toward the corridor while Two Star plowed forward within it. A thousand images kaleidoscoped in Danny's skull, sparkling within the windchime dissonance of the falling tower.

The fans screamed as part of the structure's mass collapsed onto Two Star. Kowie rocked the tank, raising it like a submarine through a sea of ravaged glass. The gentle, green-furred humanoids faded from Danny's mind. He threw the hatch open. Kowie gunned the fans, reversing the blower in a polychrome shower. Several tanks had moved ahead of Two Star, nearing the far end of the corridor. Gray-uniformed soldiers straggled from the remaining structures, hands empty, eyes fixed on the ground. There was very little firing. Kowie edged into the column and followed the third tank into the laager forming on the other side of Starhome. Pritchard was drained. His throat was dry, but he knew from past experience that he would vomit if he swallowed even a mouthful of water before his muscles stopped trembling. The blower rested with its skirts on the ground, its fans purring gently as they idled to a halt.

Kowie climbed out of the driver's hatch, moving stiffly. He had a powergun in his hand, a pistol he always carried for moral support. Two Star's bow compartment was frequently nearer the enemy than anything else in Hammer's Slammers.

Several towers still stood in the wreckage of Starhome. The nearest one wavered from orange to red and back in the full blaze of sunlight. Danny watched it in the iridium mirror of his tank's deck, the outline muted by the hatchwork of crystal etching on the metal.

Kowie shot off-hand. Danny looked up in irritation. The driver shot again, his light charge having no discernible effect on the structure.

"Shut it off," Danny croaked. "These're shrines."

The ground where Starhome had stood blazed like the floor of Hell.

HANGMAN

The light in the kitchen alcove glittered on Lieutenant Schilling's blond curls; glittered also on the frost-spangled window beside her and from the armor of the tank parked outside. All the highlights looked cold to Captain Danny Pritchard as he stepped closer to the infantry lieutenant.

"Sal—" Pritchard began. From the orderly room behind them came the babble of the radios ranked against one wall and, less muted, the laughter of soldiers waiting for action. "You can't think like a Dutchman any more. We're Hammer's Slammers, all of us. We're mercs. Not Dutch, not Frisians—"

"You're not," Lieutenant Schilling snapped, looking up from the cup of bitter chocolate she had just drawn from the urn. She was a short woman and lightly built, but she had the unerring instinct of a bully who is willing to make a scene for a victim who is not willing to be part of one. "You're a farmer from Dunstan, what d'you care about Dutch miners, whatever these bleeding French do to them. But a lot of us do care, Danny, and if you had a little compassion—"

"But Sal—" Pritchard repeated, only his right arm moving as he touched the blond girl's shoulder.

"Get your hands off me, Captain!" she shouted. "That's over!" She shifted the mug of steaming chocolate in her hand. The voices in the orderly room stilled. Then, simultaneously, someone turned up the volume of the radio

198

and at least three people began to talk loudly on unconnected subjects.

Pritchard studied the back of his hand, turned it over to examine the calloused palm as well. He smiled. "Sorry, I'll remember that," he said in a normal voice. He turned and stepped back into the orderly room, a brown-haired man of thirty-four with a good set of muscles to cover his moderate frame and nothing at all to cover his heart. Those who knew Danny Pritchard slightly thought him a relaxed man, and he looked relaxed even now. But waiting around the electric grate were three troopers who knew Danny very well indeed: the crew of the Plow, Pritchard's command tank.

Kowie drove the beast: a rabbit-eyed man whose fingers now flipped cards in another game of privy solitaire. His deck was so dirty that only familiarity allowed him to read the pips. Kowie's hands and eyes were just as quick at the controls of the tank, sliding its bulbous hundred and fifty metric tons through spaces that were only big enough to pass it. When he had to, he drove nervelessly through objects instead of going around. Kowie would never be more than a tank driver; but he was the best tank driver in the Regiment.

Rob Jenne was big and as blond as Lieutenant Schilling. He grinned up at Pritchard, his expression changing from embarrassment to relief as he saw that his captain was able to smile also. Jenne had transferred from combat cars to tanks three years back, after the Slammers had pulled out of Squire's World. He was sharp-eyed and calm in a crisis. Twice after his transfer Jenne had been offered a blower of his own to command if he would return to combat cars. He had refused both promotions, saying he would stay with tanks or buy back his contract, that there was no way he was going back to those open-topped coffins again. When a tank commander's slot came open, Jenne got it; and Pritchard had made the blond sergeant his own blower chief when a directional mine had retired the previous man. Now Jenne straddled a chair backwards, his hands flexing a collapsible torsion device that kept his muscles as dense and hard as they had been the day he was recruited from a quarry on Burlage.

Line tanks carry only a driver and the blower chief who directs the tank and its guns when they are not under the direct charge of the Regiment's computer. In addition to those two and a captain, command tanks have a Communications Technician to handle the multiplex burden of radio traffic focused on the vehicle. Pritchard's commo tech was Margritte DiManzo, a slender widow who cropped her lustrous hair short so that it would not interfere with the radio helmet she wore most of her waking hours. She was off duty now, but she had not removed the bulky headgear which linked her to the six radios in the tank parked outside. Their simultaneous sound would have been unintelligible babbling to most listeners. The black-haired woman's training, both conscious and hypnotic, broke that babbling into a set of discrete conversations. When Pritchard reentered the room, Margritte was speaking to Jenne. She did not look up at her commander until Jenne's brightening expression showed her it was safe to do so.

Two commo people and a sergeant with Intelligence tabs were at consoles in the orderly room. They were from the Regiment's HQ Battalion, assigned to Sector Two here on Kobold but in no sense a part of the sector's combat companies: Captain Riis' S Company—infantry—and Pritchard's own tanks.

Riis was the senior captain and in charge of the sector, a matter which neither he nor Pritchard ever forgot. Sally Schilling led his first platoon. Her aide, a black-haired corporal, sat with his huge boots up, humming as he polished the pieces of his field-stripped powergun. Its barrel gleamed orange in the light of the electric grate. Electricity was more general on Kobold than on some wealthier worlds, since mining and copper smelting made fusion units a practical necessity. But though the copper in the transmission cable might well have been processed on Kobold, the wire had probably been drawn offworld and shipped back here. Aurore and Friesland had refused to allow even such simple manufactures here on their joint colony. They had kept Kobold a market and a supplier of raw materials, but never a rival.

"Going to snow tonight?" Jenne asked.

"Umm, too cold," Pritchard said, walking over to the grate. He pretended he did not hear Lieutenant Schilling stepping out of the alcove. "I figure—"

"Hold it," said Margritte, her index finger curling out for a volume control before the duty man had time to react. One of the wall radios boomed loudly to the whole room. Prodding another switch, Margritte patched the signal separately through the link implanted in Pritchard's right mastoid. "—guns and looks like satchel charges. There's only one man in each truck, but they've been on the horn too and we can figure on more Frenchies here any—"

"Red Alert," Pritchard ordered, facing his commo tech so that she could read his lips. "Where is this?"

The headquarters radiomen stood nervously, afraid to interfere but unwilling to let an outsider run their equipment, however ably. "Red Alert," Margritte was repeating over all bands. Then, through Pritchard's implant, she said, "It's Patrol Sigma three-nine, near Haacin. Dutch civilians've stopped three outbound provisions trucks from Barthe's Company."

"Scramble First Platoon," Pritchard said, "but tell 'em to hold for us to arrive." As Margritte coolly passed on the order, Pritchard picked up the commo helmet he had laid on his chair when he followed Lieutenant Schilling into the kitchen. The helmet gave him automatic switching and greater range than the bioelectric unit behind his ear.

The wall radio was saying, "—need some big friendlies fast or it'll drop in the pot for sure."

"Sigma three-niner," Pritchard said, "this is Michael One."

"Go ahead, Michael One," replied the distant squad leader. Pritchard's commo helmet added an airy boundlessness to his surroundings without really deadening the ambient noise.

"Hold what you've got, boys," the tank captain said. "There's help on the way."

The door of the orderly room stood•ajar the way
Pritchard's crewmen had left it. The captain slammed it
shut as he too ran for his tank. Behind in the orderly room,
Lieutenant Schilling was snapping out quick directions to
her own platoon and to her awakened commander.

The Plow was already floating when Danny reached it.
Ice crystals, spewed from beneath the skirts by the lift fans,
made a blue-white dazzle in the vehicle's running lights.
Frost whitened the ladder up the high side of the tank's
plenum chamber and hull. Pritchard paused to pull on his
gloves before mounting. Sergeant Jenne, anchoring himself
with his left hand on the turret's storage rack, reached down
and lifted his captain aboard without noticeable effort. Side
by side, the two men slid through the hatches to their battle
stations.

"Ready," Pritchard said over the intercom.

"Movin' on," replied Kowie, and with his words the tank
slid forward over the frozen ground like grease on a hot
griddle.

The command post had been a district road-maintenance
center before all semblance of central government on
Kobold had collapsed. The orderly room and officers'
quarters were in the supervisor's house, a comfortable
structure with shutters and mottoes embroidered in French
on the walls. Some of the hangings had been defaced by
short-range gunfire. The crew barracks across the road now
served the troopers on headquarters duty. Many of the
Slammers could read the Dutch periodicals abandoned
there in the break-up. The equipment shed beside the
barracks garaged the infantry skimmers because the battery-
powered platforms could not shrug off the weather like the
huge panzers of M Company. The shed doors were open,
pluming the night with heated air as the duty platoon ran
for its mounts. Some of the troopers had not yet donned
their helmets and body armor. Jenne waved as the tank
swept on by; then the road curved and the infantry was
lost in the night.

Kobold was a joint colony of Aurore and Friesland.
When eighty years of French oppression had driven the

Dutch settlers to rebellion, their first act was to hire Hammer's Slammers. The break between Hammer and Friesland had been sharp, but time has a way of blunting anger and letting old habits resume. The Regimental language was Dutch, and many of the Slammers' officers were Frisians seconded from their own service. Friesland gained from the men's experience when they returned home; Hammer gained company officers with excellent training from the Gröningen Academy.

To counter the Slammers, the settlers of Auroran descent had hired three Francophone regiments. If either group of colonists could have afforded to pay its mercenaries unaided, the fighting would have been immediate and brief. Kobold had been kept deliberately poor by its homeworlds, however; so in their necessities the settlers turned to those homeworlds for financial help.

And neither Aurore nor Friesland wanted a war on Kobold.

Friesland had let its settlers swing almost from the beginning, sloughing their interests for a half share of the copper produced and concessions elsewhere in its sphere of influence. The arrangement was still satisfactory to the Council of State, if Frisian public opinion could be mollified by apparent activity. Aurore was on the brink of war in the Zemla System. Her Parliament feared another proxy war which could in a moment explode full-fledged, even though Friesland had been weakened by a decade of severe internal troubles. So Aurore and Friesland reached a compromise. Then, under threat of abandonment, the warring parties were forced to transfer their mercenaries' contracts to the home worlds. Finally, Aurore and Friesland mutually hired the four regiments: the Slammers; Compagnie de Barthe; the Alaudae; and Phenix Moirots. Mercs from either side were mixed and divided among eight sectors imposed on a map of inhabited Kobold. There the contract ordered them to keep peace between the factions; prevent the importation of modern weapons to either side; and—wait.

But Colonel Barthe and the Auroran leaders had come to a further, secret agreement; and although Hammer had

learned of it, he had informed only two men—Major
Steuben, his aide and bodyguard; and Captain Daniel
Pritchard.

Pritchard scowled at the memory. Even without the
details a traitor had sold Hammer, it would have been
obvious that Barthe had his own plans. In the other sectors,
Hammer's men and their French counterparts ran joint
patrols. Both sides scattered their camps throughout the
sectors, just as the villages of either nationality were
scattered. Barthe had split his sectors in halves, brusquely
ordering the Slammers to keep to the west of the River
Aillet because his own troops were mining the east of the
basin heavily. Barthe's Company was noted for its minefields. That skill was one of the reasons they had been hired
by the French. Since most of Kobold was covered either
by forests or by rugged hills, armor was limited to roads
where well-placed mines could stack tanks like crushed
boxes.

Hammer listened to Barthe's pronouncement and laughed,
despite the anger of most of his staff officers. Beside him,
Joachim Steuben had grinned and traced the line of his cut-
away holster. When Danny Pritchard was informed, he had
only shivered a little and called a vehicle inspection for the
next morning. That had been three months ago. . . .

The night streamed by like smoke around the tank.
Pritchard lowered his face shield, but he did not drop his
seat into the belly of the tank. Vision blocks within gave
a 360 degree view of the tank's surroundings, but the
farmer in Danny could not avoid the feeling of blindness
within the impenetrable walls. Jenne sat beside his captain
in a cupola fitted with a three-barrelled automatic weapon.
He too rode with his head out of the hatch, but that was
only for comradeship. The sergeant much preferred to be
inside. He would button up at the first sign of hostile
action. Jenne was in no sense a coward; it was just that
he had quirks. Most combat veterans do.

Pritchard liked the whistle of the black wind past his
helmet. Warm air from the tank's resistance heaters jetted
up through the hatch and kept his body quite comfortable.

The vehicle's huge mass required the power of a fusion plant to drive its lift motors, and the additional burden of climate control was inconsequential.

The tankers' face shields automatically augmented the light of the moon, dim and red because the sun it reflected was dim and red as well. The boosted light level displayed the walls of forest, the boles snaking densely to either side of the road. At Kobold's perihelion, the thin stems grew in days to their full six-meter height and spread a ceiling of red-brown leaves the size of blankets. Now, at aphelion, the chilled, sapless trees burned with almost explosive intensity. The wood was too dangerous to use for heating, even if electricity had not been common, but it fueled the gasogene engines of most vehicles on the planet.

Jenne gestured ahead. "Blowers," he muttered on the intercom. His head rested on the gun switch though he knew the vehicles must be friendly. The Plow slowed.

Pritchard nodded agreement. "Michael First, this is Michael One," he said. "Flash your running lights so we can be sure it's you."

"Roger," replied the radio. Blue light flickered from the shapes hulking at the edge of the forest ahead. Kowie throttled the fans up to cruise, then chopped them and swung expertly into the midst of the four tanks of the outlying platoon.

"Michael One, this is Sigma One," Captain Riis' angry voice demanded in the helmet.

"Go ahead."

"Barthe's sent a battalion across the river. I'm moving Lieutenant Schilling into position to block 'em and called Central for artillery support. You hold your first platoon at Haacin for reserve and any partisans up from Portela. I'll take direct command of the rest of—"

"Negative, negative, Sigma One!" Pritchard snapped. The Plow was accelerating again, second in the line of five tanks. They were beasts of prey sliding across the landscape of snow and black trees at eighty kph and climbing. "Let the French through, Captain. There won't be fighting, repeat, negative fighting."

"There damned well *will* be fighting, Michael One, if Barthe tries to shove a battalion into my sector!" Riis thundered back. "Remember, this isn't your command or a joint command. *I'm* in charge here."

"Margritte, patch me through to Battalion," Pritchard hissed on intercom. The Plow's turret was cocked thirty degrees to the right. It covered the forest sweeping by to that side and anything which might be hiding there. Pritchard's mind was on Sally Schilling, riding a skimmer through forest like that flanking the tanks, hurrying with her fifty men to try to stop a battalion's hasty advance.

The commo helmet popped quietly to itself. Pritchard tensed, groping for the words he would need to convince Lieutenant Colonel Miezierk. Miezierk, under whom command of Sectors One and Two was grouped, had been a Frisian regular until five years ago. He was supposed to think like a merc, now, not like a Frisian; but . . .

The voice that suddenly rasped, "Override, override!" was not Miezierk's. "Sigma One, Michael One, this is Regiment."

"Go ahead," Pritchard blurted. Captain Riis, equally rattled, said, "Yes, *sir*!" on the three-way link.

"Sigma, your fire order is cancelled. Keep your troops on alert, but keep 'em the hell out of Barthe's way."

"But Colonel Hammer—"

"Riis, you're not going to start a war tonight. Michael One, can your panzers handle whatever's going on at Haacin without violating the contract?"

"Yes, sir." Pritchard flashed a map briefly on his face shield to check his position. "We're almost there now."

"If you can't handle it, Captain, you'd better hope you're killed in action," Colonel Hammer said bluntly. "I haven't nursed this regiment for twenty-three years to lose it because somebody forgets what his job is." Then, more softly—Pritchard could imagine the colonel flicking his eyes side to side to gauge bystanders' reactions—he added, "There's support if you need it, Captain—if they're the ones who breach the contract."

"Affirmative."

"Keep the lid on, boy. Regiment out."

The trees had drunk the whine of the fans. Now the road curved and the tanks banked greasily to join the main highway from Dimo to Portela. The tailings pile of the Haacin Mine loomed to the right and hurled the drive noise back redoubled at the vehicles. The steel skirts of the lead tank touched the road metal momentarily, showering the night with orange sparks. Beyond the mine were the now-empty wheat fields and then the village itself.

Haacin, the largest Dutch settlement in Sector Two, sprawled to either side of the highway. Its houses were two- and three-story lumps of cemented mine tailings. They were roofed with tile or plastic rather than shakes of native timber, because of the wood's lethal flammability. The highway was straight and broad. It gave Pritchard a good view of the three cargo vehicles pulled to one side. Men in local dress swarmed about them. Across the road were ten of Hammer's khaki-clad infantry, patrol S-39, whose ported weapons half-threatened, half-protected the trio of drivers in their midst. Occasionally a civilian turned to hurl a curse at Barthe's men, but mostly the Dutch busied themselves with off-loading cartons from the trucks.

Pritchard gave a brief series of commands. The four line tanks grounded in a hedgehog at the edge of the village. Their main guns and automatics faced outward in all directions. Kowie swung the command vehicle around the tank which had been leading it. He cut the fans' angle of attack, slowing the Plow without losing the ability to accelerate quickly. The command vehicle eased past the squad of infantry, then grounded behind the rearmost truck. Pritchard felt the fans' hum through the metal of the hull.

"Who's in charge here?" the captain demanded, his voice booming through the command vehicle's public address system.

The Dutch unloading the trucks halted silently. A squat man in a parka of feathery native fur stepped forward. Unlike many of the other civilians, he was not armed. He

did not flinch when Pritchard pinned him with the spotlight
of the tank. "I am Paul van Oosten," the man announced
in the heavy Dutch of Kobold. "I am Mayor of Haacin.
But if you mean who leads us in what we are doing here,
well . . . perhaps Justice herself does. Klaus, show them
what these trucks were carrying to Portela."

Another civilian stepped forward, ripping the top off the
box he carried. Flat plastic wafers spilled from it, glittering
in the cold light: powergun ammunition, intended for
shoulder weapons like those the infantry carried.

"They were taking powerguns to the beasts of Portela
to use against us," van Oosten said. He used the slang term,
"skepsels" to name the Francophone settlers. The Mayor's
shaven jaw was jutting out in anger.

"Captain!" called one of Barthe's truck drivers, brushing
forward through the ring of Hammer's men. "Let me
explain."

One of the civilians growled and lifted his heavy musket.
Rob Jenne rang his knuckles twice on the receiver of his
tribarrel, calling attention to the muzzles as he swept them
down across the crowd. The Dutchman froze. Jenne smiled
without speaking.

"We were sent to pick up wheat the regiment had
purchased," Barthe's man began. Pritchard was not familiar
with Barthe's insignia, but from the merc's age and bearing
he was a senior sergeant. An unlikely choice to be driving
a provisions truck. "One of the vehicles happened to be
partly loaded. We didn't take the time to empty it because
we were in a hurry to finish the run and go off duty—
there was enough room and lift to handle that little bit
of gear and the grain besides.

"In any case—" and here the sergeant began pressing,
because the tank captain had not cut him off at the first
sentence as expected "—you do not, and these fools *surely*
do not, have the right to stop Colonel Barthe's transport.
If you have questions about the way we pick up wheat,
that's between your CO and ours. Sir."

Pritchard ran his gloved index finger back and forth
below his right eyesocket. He was ice inside, bubbling

ice that tore and chilled him and had nothing to do with the weather. He turned back to Mayor van Oosten. "Reload the trucks," he said, hoping that his voice did not break.

"You can't!" van Oosten cried. "These powerguns are the only chance my village, my *people* have to survive when you leave. You know what'll happen, don't you? Friesland and Aurore, they'll come to an agreement, a *trade-off*, they'll call it, and all the troops will leave. It's our lives they're trading! The beasts in Dimo, in Portela if you let these go through, they'll have powerguns that *their* mercenaries gave them. And we—"

Pritchard whispered a prepared order into his helmet mike. The rearmost of the four tanks at the edge of the village fired a single round from its main gun. The night flared cyan as the 200mm bolt struck the middle of the tailings pile a kilometer away. Stone, decomposed by the enormous energy of the shot, recombined in a huge gout of flame. Vapor, lava, and cinders spewed in every direction. After a moment, bits of high-flung rock began pattering down on the roofs of Haacin.

The bolt caused a double thunderclap, that of the heated air followed by the explosive release of energy at the point of impact. When the reverberations died away there was utter silence in Haacin. On the distant jumble of rock, a dying red glow marked where the charge had hit. The shot had also ignited some saplings rooted among the stones. They had blazed as white torches for a few moments but they were already collapsing as cinders.

"The Slammers are playing this by rules," Pritchard said. Loudspeakers flung his quiet words about the village like the echoes of the shot; but he was really speaking for the recorder in the belly of the tank, preserving his words for a later Bonding Authority hearing. "There'll be no powerguns in civilian hands. Load every bit of this gear back in the truck. Remember, there's satellites up there—" Pritchard waved generally at the sky "—that see everything that happens on Kobold. If one powergun is fired by a civilian in this sector, I'll come for him. I promise you."

The mayor sagged within his furs. Turning to the crowd behind him, he said, "Put the guns back on the truck. So that the Portelans can kill us more easily."

"Are you mad, van Oosten?" demanded the gunman who had earlier threatened Barthe's sergeant.

"Are *you* mad, Kruse?" the mayor shouted back without trying to hide his fury. "D'ye doubt what those tanks would do to Haacin? And do you doubt this butcher—" his back was to Pritchard but there was no doubt as to whom the mayor meant "—would use them on us? Perhaps tomorrow we could have . . ."

There was motion at the far edge of the crowd, near the corner of a building. Margritte, watching the vision blocks within, called a warning. Pritchard reached for his panic bar—Rob Jenne was traversing the tribarrel. All three of them were too late. The muzzle flash was red and it expanded in Pritchard's eyes as a hammer blow smashed him in the middle of the forehead.

The bullet's impact heaved the tanker up and backwards. His shattered helmet flew off into the night. The unyielding hatch coaming caught him in the small of the back, arching his torso over it as if he were being broken on the wheel. Pritchard's eyes flared with sheets of light. As reaction flung him forward again, he realized he was hearing the reports of Jenne's powergun and that some of the hellish flashes were real.

If the tribarrel's discharges were less brilliant than that of the main gun, then they were more than a hundred times as close to the civilians. The burst snapped within a meter of one bystander, an old man who stumbled backward into a wall. His mouth and staring eyes were three circles of empty terror. Jenne fired seven rounds. Every charge but one struck the sniper or the building he sheltered against. Powdered concrete sprayed from the wall. The sniper's body spun backwards, chest gobbled away by the bolts. His right arm still gripped the musket he had fired at Pritchard. The arm had been flung alone onto the snowy pavement. The electric bite of ozone hung in the air with the ghostly afterimages of the shots. The dead

man's clothes were burning, tiny orange flames that rippled
into smoke an inch from their bases.

Jenne's big left hand was wrapped in the fabric of
Pritchard's jacket, holding the dazed officer upright. "There's
another rule you play by," the sergeant roared to the crowd.
"You shoot at Hammer's Slammers and you get your balls
kicked between your ears. Sure as god, boys; sure as death."
Jenne's right hand swung the muzzles of his weapon across
the faces of the civilians. "Now, load the bleeding trucks
like the captain said, heroes."

For a brief moment, nothing moved but the threatening
powergun. Then a civilian turned and hefted a heavy crate
back aboard the truck from which he had just taken it.
Empty-handed, the colonist began to sidle away from the
vehicle—and from the deadly tribarrel. One by one the
other villagers reloaded the hijacked cargo, the guns and
ammunition they had hoped would save them in the cata-
clysm they awaited. One by one they took the blower chief's
unspoken leave to return to their houses. One who did not
leave was sobbing out her grief over the mangled body of
the sniper. None of her neighbors had gone to her side.
They could all appreciate—now—what it would have meant
if that first shot had led to a general firefight instead of
Jenne's selective response.

"Rob, help me get him inside," Pritchard heard Margritte
say.

Pritchard braced himself with both hands and leaned
away from his sergeant's supporting arm. "No, I'm all right,"
he croaked. His vision was clear enough, but the landscape
was flashing bright and dim with varicolored light.

The side hatch of the turret clanked. Margritte was
beside her captain. She had stripped off her cold weather
gear in the belly of the tank and wore only her khaki
uniform. "Get back inside there," Pritchard muttered. "It's
not safe." He was afraid of falling if he raised a hand to
fend her away. He felt an injector prick the swelling flesh
over his cheekbones. The flashing colors died away though
Pritchard's ears began to ring.

"They carried some into the nearest building," the

noncom from Barthe's Company was saying. He spoke in Dutch, having sleep-trained in the language during the transit to Kobold just as Hammer's men had in French.

"Get it," Jenne ordered the civilians still near the trucks. Three of them were already scurrying toward the house the merc had indicated. They were back in moments, carrying the last of the arms chests.

Pritchard surveyed the scene. The cargo had been reloaded, except for the few spilled rounds winking from the pavement. Van Oosten and the furious Kruse were the only villagers still in sight. "All right," Pritchard said to the truck drivers, "get aboard and get moving. And come back by way of Bitzen, not here. I'll arrange an escort for you."

The French noncom winked, grinned, and shouted a quick order to his men. The infantrymen stepped aside silently to pass the truckers. The French mercenaries mounted their vehicles and kicked them to life. Their fans whined and the trucks lifted, sending snow crystals dancing. With gathering speed, they slid westward along the forest-rimmed highway.

Jenne shook his head at the departing trucks, then stiffened as his helmet spat a message. "Captain," he said, "we got company coming."

Pritchard grunted. His own radio helmet had been smashed by the bullet, and his implant would only relay messages on the band to which it had been verbally keyed most recently. "Margritte, start switching for me," he said. His slender commo tech was already slipping back inside through the side hatch. Pritchard's blood raced with the chemicals Margritte had shot into it. His eyes and mind worked perfectly, though all his thoughts seemed to have razor edges on them.

"Use mine," Jenne said, trying to hand the captain his helmet.

"I've got the implant," Pritchard said. He started to shake his head and regretted the motion instantly. "That and Margritte's worth a helmet any day."

"It's a whole battalion," Jenne explained quietly, his eyes scanning the Bever Road down which Command Central had warned that Barthe's troops were coming. "All but the artillery—that's back in Dimo, but it'll range here easy enough. Brought in the antitank battery and a couple calliopes, though."

"Slide us up ahead of Michael First," Pritchard ordered his driver. As the Plow shuddered, then spun on its axis, the captain dropped his seat into the turret to use the vision blocks. He heard Jenne's seat whirr down beside him and the cupola hatch snick closed. In front of Pritchard's knees, pale in the instrument lights, Margritte DiManzo sat still and open-eyed at her communications console.

"Little friendlies," Pritchard called through his loud-speakers to the ten infantrymen, "find yourselves a quiet alley and hope nothing happens. The Lord help you if you fire a shot without me ordering it." The Lord help us all, Pritchard added to himself.

Ahead of the command vehicle, the beetle shapes of First Platoon began to shift position. "Michael First," Pritchard ordered sharply, "get back as you were. We're not going to engage Barthe, we're going to meet him." Maybe.

Kowie slid them alongside, then a little forward of the point vehicle of the defensive lozenge. They set down. All of the tanks were buttoned up, save for the hatch over Pritchard's head. The central vision block was a meter by 30-cm panel. It could be set for anything from a 360 degree view of the tank's surroundings to a one-to-one image of an object a kilometer away. Pritchard focused and ran the gain to ten magnifications, then thirty. At the higher power, motion curling along the snow-smoothed grainfields between Haacin and its mine resolved into men. Barthe's troops were clad in sooty-white coveralls and battle armor. The leading elements were hunched low on the meager platforms of their skimmers. Magnification and the augmented light made the skittering images grainy, but the tanker's practiced eye caught the tubes of rocket launchers clipped to every one of the skimmers. The skirmish line swelled at two points where self-propelled guns were strung like beads on the cord of men: antitank weapons, 50mm powerguns firing high-intensity

Butcher's Bill

charges. They were supposed to be able to burn through the heaviest armor. Barthe's boys had come loaded for bear; oh yes. They thought they knew just what they were going up against. Well, the Slammers weren't going to show them they were wrong. Tonight.

"Running lights, everybody," Pritchard ordered. Then, taking a deep breath, he touched the lift on his seat and raised himself head and shoulders back into the chill night air. There was a hand light clipped to Pritchard's jacket. He snapped it on, aiming the beam down onto the turret top so that the burnished metal splashed diffused radiance up over him. It bathed his torso and face plainly for the oncoming infantry. Through the open hatch, Pritchard could hear Rob cursing. Just possibly Margritte was mumbling a prayer.

"Batteries at Dimo and Harfleur in Sector One have received fire orders and are waiting for a signal to execute," the implant grated. "If Barthe opens fire, Command Central will not, repeat, negative, use Michael First or Michael One to knock down the shells. Your guns will be clear for action, Michael One."

Pritchard grinned starkly. His face would not have been pleasant even if livid bruises were not covering almost all of it. The Slammers' central fire direction computer used radar and satellite reconnaissance to track shells in flight. Then the computer took control of any of the Regiment's vehicle-mounted powerguns and swung them onto the target. Central's message notified Pritchard that he would have full control of his weapons at all times, while guns tens or hundreds of kilometers away kept his force clear of artillery fire.

Margritte had blocked most of the commo traffic, Pritchard realized. She had let through only this message that was crucial to what they were about to do. A good commo tech; a very good person indeed.

The skirmish line grounded. The nearest infantrymen were within fifty meters of the tanks and their fellows spread off into the night like lethal wings. Barthe's men rolled off their skimmers and lay prone. Pritchard began to relax when he noticed that their rocket launchers were still aboard the skimmers. The antitank weapons were in instant reach, but at least they were not being leveled for an immediate salvo. Barthe didn't want to fight the Slammers. His targets were the Dutch civilians, just as Mayor van Oosten had suggested.

An air cushion jeep with a driver and two officers aboard drew close. It hissed slowly through the line of infantry, then stopped nearly touching the command vehicle's bow armor. One of the officers dismounted. He was a tall man who was probably very thin when he was not wearing insulated coveralls and battle armor. He raised his face to Pritchard atop the high curve of the blower, sweeping up his reflective face shield as he did so. He was Lieutenant Colonel Benoit, commander of the French mercenaries in Sector Two, a clean-shaven man with sharp features and a splash of gray hair displaced across his forehead by his helmet. Benoit grinned and waved at the muzzle of the 200mm powergun pointed at him. Nobody had ever said Barthe's chief subordinate was a coward.

Pritchard climbed out of the turret to the deck, then slid down the bow slope to the ground. Benoit was several inches taller than the tanker, with a force of personality which was daunting in a way that height alone could never be. It didn't matter to Pritchard. He worked with tanks and with Colonel Hammer; nothing else was going to face down a man who was accustomed to those.

"Sergeant Major Oberlie reported how well and . . . firmly you handled their little affair, Captain," Benoit said, extending his hand to Pritchard. "I'll admit that I was a little concerned that I would have to rescue my men myself."

"Hammer's Slammers can be depended on to keep their contracts," the tanker replied, smiling with false warmth. "I told these squareheads that any civilian caught with a powergun was going to have to answer to me for it. Then we made sure nobody thinks we were kidding."

Benoit chuckled. Little puffs of vapor spurted from his mouth with the sounds. "You've been sent to the Gröningen

Academy, have you not, Captain Pritchard?" the older man asked. "You understand that I take an interest in my opposite numbers in this sector."

Pritchard nodded. "The Old Man picked me for the two-year crash course on Friesland, yeah. Now and again he sends noncoms he wants to promote."

"But you're not a Frisian, though you have Frisian military training," the other mercenary continued, nodding to himself. "As you know, Captain, promotion in some infantry regiments comes much faster than it does in the . . . Slammers. If you feel a desire to speak to Colonel Barthe some time in the future, I assure you this evening's business will not be forgotten."

"Just doing my job, Colonel," Pritchard simpered. Did Benoit think a job offer would make a traitor of him? Perhaps. Hammer had bought Barthe's plans for very little, considering their military worth. "Enforcing the contract, just like you'd have done if things were the other way around."

Benoit chuckled again and stepped back aboard his jeep. "Until we meet again, Captain Pritchard," he said. "For the moment I think we'll just proceed on into Portela. That's permissible under the contract, of course."

"Swing wide around Haacin, will you?" Pritchard called back. "The folks there're pretty worked up. Nobody wants more trouble, do we?"

Benoit nodded. As his jeep lifted, he spoke into his helmet communicator. The skirmish company rose awkwardly and set off in a counter-clockwise circuit of Haacin. Behind them, in a column reformed from their support positions at the base of the tailings heap, came the truck-mounted men of the other three companies. Pritchard stood and watched until the last of them whined past.

Air stirred by the tank's idling fans leaked out under the skirts. The jets formed tiny deltas of the snow which winked as Pritchard's feet caused eddy currents. In their cold precision the tanker recalled Colonel Benoit's grin.

"Command Central," Pritchard said as he climbed his blower, "Michael One. Everything's smooth here. Over." Then, "Sigma One, this is Michael One. I'll be back as quick as fans'll move me, so if you have anything to say we can discuss it then." Pritchard knew that Captain Riis must have been burning the net up, trying to raise him for a report or to make demands. It wasn't fair to make Margritte hold the bag now that Pritchard himself was free to respond to the sector chief; but neither did the Dunstan tanker have the energy to argue with Riis just at the moment. Already this night he'd faced death and Colonel Benoit. Riis could wait another ten minutes.

The Plow's armor was a tight fit for its crew, the radios, and the central bulk of the main gun with its feed mechanism. The command vehicle rode glass-smooth over the frozen roadway, with none of the jouncing that a rougher surface might bring even through the air cushion. Margritte faced Pritchard over her console, her seat a meter lower than his so that she appeared a suppliant. Her short hair was the lustrous purple-black of a grackle's throat in sunlight. Hidden illumination from the instruments brought her face to life.

"Gee, Captain," Jenne was saying at Pritchard's side, "I wish you'd a let me pick up that squarehead's rifle. I know those groundpounders. They're just as apt as not to claim the kill credit themselves, and if I can't prove I stepped on the body they might get away with it. I remember on Paradise, me and Piet de Hagen—he was left wing gunner, I was right—both shot at a partisan. And then damned if Central didn't decide the slope had blown herself up with a hand grenade after we'd wounded her. So *neither* of us got the credit. You'd think—"

"Lord's *blood*, Sergeant," Pritchard snarled, "are you so damned proud of killing one of the poor bastards who hired us to protect them?"

Jenne said nothing. Pritchard shrank up inside, realizing what he had said and unable to take the words back. "Oh, Lord, Rob," he said without looking up, "I'm sorry. It . . . I'm shook, that's all."

After a brief silence, the blond sergeant laughed. "Never been shot in the head myself, Captain, but I can see it might

shake a fellow, yeah." Jenne let the whine of the fans stand
for a moment as the only further comment while he decided
whether he would go on. Then he said, "Captain, for a week
after I first saw action I meant to get out of the Slammers,
even if I had to sweep floors on Curwin for the rest of my
life. Finally I decided I'd stick it. I didn't like the . . . rules
of the game, but I could learn to play by them.

"And I did. And one rule is, that you get to be as good
as you can at killing the people Colonel Hammer wants
killed. Yeah, I'm proud about that one just now. It was a
tough snap shot and I made it. I don't care why we're on
Kobold or who brought us here. But I know I'm supposed
to kill anybody who shoots at us, and I will."

"Well, I'm glad you did," Pritchard said evenly as he
looked the sergeant in the eyes. "You pretty well saved
things from getting out of hand by the way you reacted."

As if he had not heard his captain, Jenne went on, "I
was afraid if I stayed in the Slammers I'd turn into an
animal, like the dogs we trained back home to kill rats in
the quarries. And I was right. But it's the way I am now,
so I don't seem to mind."

"You do care about those villagers, don't you?" Margritte
asked Pritchard unexpectedly.

The captain looked down and found her eyes on him.
They were the rich powder-blue of chicory flowers. "You're
probably the only person in the Regiment who thinks that,"
he said bitterly. "Except for me. And maybe Colonel
Hammer. . . ."

Margritte smiled, a quick flash and as quickly gone.
"There're rule-book soldiers in the Slammers," she said,
"captains who'd never believe Barthe was passing arms to
the Auroran settlements since he'd signed a contract that
said he wouldn't. You aren't that kind. And the Lord knows
Colonel Hammer isn't, and he's backing you. I've been
around you too long, Danny, to believe you like what you
see the French doing."

Pritchard shrugged. His whole face was stiff with bruises
and the drugs Margritte had injected to control them. If
he'd locked the helmet's chin strap, the bullet's impact

would have broken his neck even though the lead itself did not penetrate. "No, I don't like it," the brown-haired captain said. "It reminds me too much of the way the Combine kept us so poor on Dunstan that a thousand of us signed on for birdseed to fight off-planet. Just because it *was* off-planet. And if Kobold only gets cop from the worlds who settled her, then the French skim the best of that. Sure, I'll tell the Lord I feel sorry for the Dutch here."

Pritchard held the commo tech's eyes with his own as he continued, "But it's just like Rob said, Margritte: I'll do my job, no matter who gets hurt. We can't do a thing to Barthe or the French until they step over the line in a really obvious way. That'll mean a lot of people get hurt too. But that's what I'm waiting for."

Margritte reached up and touched Pritchard's hand where it rested on his knee. "You'll do something when you can," she said quietly.

He turned his palm up so that he could grasp the woman's fingers. What if she knew he was planning an incident, not just waiting for one? "I'll do something, yeah," he said. "But it's going to be too late for an awful lot of people."

Kowie kept the Plow at cruising speed until they were actually in the yard of the command post. Then he cocked the fan shafts forward, lifting the bow and bringing the tank's mass around in a curve that killed its velocity and blasted an arc of snow against the building. Someone inside had started to unlatch the door as they heard the vehicle approach. The air spilling from the tank's skirts flung the panel against the inner wall and skidded the man within on his back.

The man was Captain Riis, Pritchard noted without surprise. Well, the incident wouldn't make the infantry captain any angrier than the rest of the evening had made him already.

Riis had regained his feet by the time Pritchard could jump from the deck of his blower to the fan-cleared ground in front of the building. The Frisian's normally pale face was livid now with rage. He was of the same somatotype as Lieutenant Colonel Benoit, his French counterpart in the sector: tall, thin, and proudly erect. Despite the fact that Riis was only twenty-seven, he was Pritchard's senior in grade by two years. He had kept the rank he held in Friesland's regular army when Colonel Hammer recruited him. Many of the Slammers were like Riis, Frisian soldiers who had transferred for the action and pay of a fighting regiment in which their training would be appreciated.

"You cowardly filth!" the infantryman hissed as Pritchard approached. A squad in battle gear stood within the orderly room beyond Riis. He pursed his fine lips to spit.

"Hey, Captain!" Rob Jenne called. Riis looked up. Pritchard turned, surprised that the big tank commander was not right on his heels. Jenne still smiled from the Plow's cupola. He waved at the officers with his left hand. His right was on the butterfly trigger of the tribarrel.

The threat, unspoken as it was, made a professional of Riis again. "Come on into my office," he muttered to the tank captain, turning his back on the armored vehicle as if it were only a part of the landscape.

The infantrymen inside parted to pass the captains. Sally Schilling was there. Her eyes were as hard as her porcelain armor as they raked over Pritchard. That didn't matter, he lied to himself tiredly.

Riis' office was at the top of the stairs, a narrow cubicle which had once been a child's bedroom. The sloping roof pressed in on the occupants, though a dormer window brightened the room during daylight. One wall was decorated with a regimental battle flag—not Hammer's rampant lion but a pattern of seven stars on a white field. It had probably come from the unit in which Riis had served on Friesland. Over the door hung another souvenir, a big-bore musket of local manufacture. Riis threw himself into the padded chair behind his desk. "Those bastards were carrying powerguns to Portela!" he snarled at Pritchard.

The tanker nodded. He was leaning with his right shoulder against the door jamb. "That's what the folks at

Haacin thought," he agreed. "If they'll put in a complaint with the Bonding Authority, I'll testify to what I saw."

"Testify, *testify!*" Riis shouted. "We're not lawyers, we're soldiers! You should've seized the trucks right then and—"

"No, I should *not* have, Captain!" Pritchard shouted back, holding up a mirror to Riis' anger. "Because if I had, Barthe would've complained to the Authority himself, and we'd at least've been fined. At least! The contract says the Slammers'll cooperate with the other three units in keeping peace on Kobold. Just because we suspect Barthe is violating the contract doesn't give us a right to violate it ourselves. Especially in a way any *simpleton* can see is a violation."

"If Barthe can get away with it, we can," Riis insisted, but he settled back in his chair. He was physically bigger than Pritchard, but the tanker had spent half his life with the Slammers. Years like those mark men; death is never very far behind their eyes.

"I don't think Barthe can get away with it," Pritchard lied quietly, remembering Hammer's advice on how to handle Riis and calm the Frisian without telling him the truth. Barthe's officers had been in on his plans; and one of them had talked. Any regiment might have one traitor.

The tanker lifted down the musket on the wall behind him and began turning it in his fingers. "If the Dutch settlers can prove to the Authority that Barthe's been passing out powerguns to the French," the tanker mused aloud, "well, they're responsible for half Barthe's pay, remember. It's about as bad a violation as you'll find. The Authority'll forfeit his whole bond and pay it over to whoever they decide the injured parties are. That's about three years' gross earnings for Barthe, I'd judge—he won't be able to replace it. And without a bond posted, well, he may get jobs, but they'll be the kind nobody else'd touch for the risk and the pay. His best troops'll sign on with other people. In a year or so, Barthe won't have a regiment any more."

"He's willing to take the chance," said Riis.

"Colonel Hammer isn't!" Pritchard blazed back.

"You don't know that. It isn't the sort of thing the colonel could say—"

"Say?" Pritchard shouted. He waved the musket at Riis. Its breech was triple-strapped to take the shock of the industrial explosive it used for propellant. Clumsy and large, it was the best that could be produced on a mining colony whose home worlds had forbidden local manufacturing. "Say? I bet my life against one of these tonight that the colonel wanted us to obey the contract. Do you have the guts to ask him flat out if he wants us to run guns to the Dutch?"

"I don't think that would be proper, Captain," said Riis coldly as he stood up again.

"Then try not to 'think it proper' to go do some bloody stupid stunt on your own—sir," Pritchard retorted. So much for good intentions. Hammer—and Pritchard—had expected Riis' support of the Dutch civilians. They had even planned on it. But the man seemed to have lost all his common sense. Pritchard laid the musket on the desk because his hands were trembling too badly to hang it back on the hooks.

"If it weren't for you, Captain," Riis said, "there's not a Slammer in this sector who'd object to our helping the only decent people on this planet the way we ought to. You've made your decision, and it sickens me. But I've made decisions too."

Pritchard went out without being dismissed. He blundered into the jamb, but he did not try to slam the door. That would have been petty, and there was nothing petty in the tanker's rage.

Blank-faced, he clumped down the stairs. His bunk was in a parlor which had its own door to the outside. Pritchard's crew was still in the Plow. There they had listened intently to his half of the argument with Riis, transmitted by the implant. If Pritchard had called for help, Kowie would have sent the command vehicle through the front wall buttoned up, with Jenne ready to shoot if he had to, to rescue his CO. A tank looks huge when seen close up. It is all howling steel and iridium, with black muzzles ready to spew death across a planet. On a battlefield, when the sky is a thousand shrieking colors no god ever made and the earth beneath trembles and gouts in sudden mountains, a tank is a small world indeed for its crew. Their loyalties are to nearer things than an abstraction like "The Regiment."

Besides, tankers and infantrymen have never gotten along well together.

No one was in the orderly room except two radiomen. They kept their backs to the stairs. Pritchard glanced at them, then unlatched his door. The room was dark, as he had left it, but there was a presence. Pritchard said, "Sal—" as he stepped within and the club knocked him forward into the arms of the man waiting to catch his body.

The first thing Pritchard thought as his mind slipped toward oblivion was that the cloth rubbing his face was homespun, not the hard synthetic from which uniforms were made. The last thing Pritchard thought was that there could have been no civilians within the headquarters perimeter unless the guards had allowed them; and that Lieutenant Schilling was officer of the guard tonight.

Pritchard could not be quite certain when he regained consciousness. A heavy felt rug covered and hid his trussed body on the floor of a clattering surface vehicle. He had no memory of being carried to the truck, though presumably it had been parked some distance from the command post. Riis and his confederates would not have been so open as to have civilians drive to the door to take a kidnapped officer, even if Pritchard's crew could have been expected to ignore the breach of security.

Kidnapped. Not for later murder, or he would already be dead instead of smothering under the musty rug. Thick as it was, the rug was still inadequate to keep the cold from his shivering body. The only lights Pritchard could see were the washings of icy color from the night's doubled shock to his skull.

That bone-deep ache reminded Pritchard of the transceiver implanted in his mastoid. He said in a husky whisper which he hoped would not penetrate the rug, "Michael One to any unit, any unit at all. Come in please, any Slammer."

Nothing. Well, no surprise. The implant had an effective range of less than twenty meters, enough for relaying to and from a base unit, but unlikely to be useful in Kobold's empty darkness. Of course, if the truck happened to be passing one of M Company's night defensive positions. . . . "Michael One to any unit," the tanker repeated more urgently.

A boot slammed him in the ribs. A voice in guttural Dutch snarled, "Shut up, you, or you get what you gave Henrik."

So he'd been shopped to the Dutch, not that there had been much question about it. And not that he might not have been safer in French hands, the way everybody on this cursed planet thought he was a traitor to his real employers. Well, it wasn't fair; but Danny Pritchard had grown up a farmer, and no farmer is ever tricked into believing that life is fair.

The truck finally jolted to a stop. Gloved hands jerked the cover from Pritchard's eyes. He was not surprised to recognize the concrete angles of Haacin as men passed him hand to hand into a cellar. The attempt to hijack Barthe's powerguns had been an accident, an opportunity seized; but the crew which had kidnapped Pritchard must have been in position before the call from S-39 had intervened.

"Is this wise?" Pritchard heard someone demand from the background. "If they begin searching, surely they'll begin in Haacin."

The two men at the bottom of the cellar stairs took Pritchard's shoulders and ankles to carry him to a spring cot. It had no mattress. The man at his feet called, "There won't be a search, they don't have enough men. Besides, the beasts'll be blamed—as they should be for so many things. If Pauli won't let us kill the turncoat, then we'll all have to stand the extra risk of him living."

"You talk too much," Mayor van Oosten muttered as he dropped Pritchard's shoulders on the bunk. Many civilians had followed the captive into the cellar. The last of them swung the door closed. It lay almost horizontal to the ground. When it slammed, dust sprang from the ceiling. Someone switched on a dim incandescent light. The scores of men and women in the storage room were as hard and fell as the bare walls. There were three windows at street level, high on the wall. Slotted shutters blocked most of their dusty glass.

"Get some heat in this hole or you may as well cut my throat," Pritchard grumbled.

A woman with a musket cursed and spat in his face. The man behind her took her arm before the gun butt could smear the spittle. Almost in apology, the man said to Pritchard, "It was her husband you killed."

"You're being kept out of the way," said a husky man—Kruse, the hothead from the hijack scene. His facial hair was pale and long, merging indistinguishably with the silky fringe of his parka. Like most of the others in the cellar, he carried a musket. "Without your meddling, there'll be a chance for us to . . . get ready to protect ourselves, after the tanks leave and the beasts come to finish us with their powerguns."

"Does Riis think I won't talk when this is over?" Pritchard asked.

"I told you—" one of the men shouted at van Oosten. The heavy-set mayor silenced him with a tap on the chest and a bellowed, "Quiet!" The rising babble hushed long enough for van Oosten to say, "Captain, you will be released in a very few days. If you—cause trouble, then, it will only be an embarrassment to yourself. Even if your colonel believes you were doing right, he won't be the one to bring to light a violation which was committed with—so you will claim—the connivance of his own officers."

The mayor paused to clear his throat and glower around the room. "Though in fact we had no help from any of your fellows, either in seizing you or in arming ourselves for our own protection."

"Are you all blind?" Pritchard demanded. He struggled with his elbows and back to raise himself against the wall. "Do you think a few lies will cover it all up? The only ships that've touched on Kobold in three months are the ones supplying us and the other mercs. Barthe maybe's smuggled in enough guns in cans of lube oil and the like

to arm some civilians. He won't be able to keep that a
secret, but maybe he can keep the Authority from proving
who's responsible.

"That's with three months and preplanning. If Riis tries
to do anything on his own, that many of his own men are
going to be short sidearms—they're all issued by serial
number, Lord take it!—and a blind Mongoloid could get
enough proof to sink the Regiment."

"You think we don't understand," said Kruse in a quiet
voice. He transferred his musket to his left hand, then slapped
Pritchard across the side of the head. "We understand very
well," the civilian said. "All the mercenaries will leave in a
few days or weeks. If the French have powerguns and we
do not, they will kill us, our wives, our children. . . . There's
a hundred and fifty villages on Kobold like this one, Dutch,
and as many French ones scattered between. It was bad
before, with no one but the beasts allowed any real say in
the government; but now if they win, there'll be French
villages and French mines—and slave pens. Forever."

"You think a few guns'll save you?" Pritchard asked.
Kruse's blow left no visible mark in the tanker's livid flesh,
though a better judge than Kruse might have noted that
Pritchard's eyes were as hard as his voice was mild.

"They'll help us save ourselves when the time comes,"
Kruse retorted.

"If you'd gotten powerguns from French civilians
instead of the mercs directly, you might have been all
right," the captain said. He was coldly aware that the lie
he was telling was more likely to be believed in this
situation than it would have been in any setting he might
deliberately have contrived. There had to be an incident,
the French civilians *had* to think they were safe in using
their illegal weapons. . . . "The Portelans, say, couldn't
admit to having guns to lose. But anything you take from
mercs—us or Barthe, it doesn't matter—we'll take back
the hard way. You don't know what you're buying into."

Kruse's face did not change, but his fist drew back for
another blow. The mayor caught the younger man's arm
and snapped, "Franz, we're here to show him that it's not

a few of us, it's every family in the village behind . . . our holding him." Van Oosten nodded around the room. "More of us than your colonel could dream of trying to punish," he added naively to Pritchard. Then he flashed back at Kruse, "If you act like a fool, he'll want revenge anyway."

"You may never believe this," Pritchard interjected wearily, "but I just want to do my job. If you let me go now, it—may be easier in the long run."

"Fool," Kruse spat and turned his back on the tanker.

A trap door opened in the ceiling, spilling more light into the cellar. "Pauli!" a woman shouted down the opening, "Hals is on the radio. There's tanks coming down the road, just like before!"

"The Lord's wounds!" van Oosten gasped. "We must—"

"They can't know!" Kruse insisted. "But we've got to get everybody out of here and back to their own houses. Everybody but me and him—" a nod at Pritchard "—and this." The musket lowered so that its round black eye pointed straight into the bound man's face.

"No, by the side door!" van Oosten called to the press of conspirators clumping up toward the street. "Don't run right out in front of them." Cursing and jostling, the villagers climbed the ladder to the ground floor, there presumably to exit on an alley.

Able only to twist his head and legs, Pritchard watched Kruse and the trembling muzzle of his weapon. The village must have watchmen with radios at either approach through the forests. If Hals was atop the heap of mine tailings— where Pritchard would have placed his outpost if he were in charge, certainly—then he'd gotten a nasty surprise when the main gun splashed the rocks with Hell. The captain grinned at the thought. Kruse misunderstood and snarled, "If they *are* coming for you, you're dead, you treacherous bastard!" To the backs of his departing fellows, the young Dutchman called, "Turn out the light here, but leave the trap door open. That won't show on the street, but it'll give me enough light to shoot by."

The tanks weren't coming for him, Pritchard knew, because they couldn't have any idea where he was. Perhaps his disappearance had stirred up some patrolling, for want of more directed action; perhaps a platoon was just changing ground because of its commander's whim. Pritchard had encouraged random motion. Tanks that freeze in one place are sitting targets, albeit hard ones. But whatever the reason tanks were approaching Haacin, if they whined by in the street outside they would be well within range of his implanted transmitter.

The big blowers were audible now, nearing with an arrogant lack of haste as if bears headed for a beehive. They were moving at about thirty kph, more slowly than Pritchard would have expected even for a contact patrol. From the sound there were four or more of them, smooth and gray and deadly.

"Kruse, I'm serious," the Slammer captain said. Light from the trap door back-lit the civilian into a hulking beast with a musket. "If you—"

"Shut up!" Kruse snarled, prodding his prisoner's bruised forehead with the gun muzzle. "One more word, any word, and—"

Kruse's right hand was so tense and white that the musket might fire even without his deliberate intent.

The first of the tanks slid by outside. Its cushion of air was so dense that the ground trembled even though none of the blower's 170 tonnes was in direct contact with it. Squeezed between the pavement and the steel curtain of the plenum chamber, the air spurted sideways and rattled the cellar windows. The rattling was inaudible against the howling of the fans themselves, but the trembling shutters chopped facets in the play of the tank's running lights. Kruse's face and the far wall flickered in blotched abstraction.

The tank moved on without pausing. Pritchard had not tried to summon it.

"That power," Kruse was mumbling to himself, "that should be for us to use to sweep the beasts—" The rest of his words were lost in the growing wail of the second tank in the column.

Pritchard tensed within. Even if a passing tank picked up his implant's transmission, its crew would probably ignore the message. Unless Pritchard identified himself, the tankers would assume it was babbling thrown by the ionosphere. And if he did identify himself, Kruse—

Kruse thrust his musket against Pritchard's skull again, banging the tanker's head back against the cellar wall. The Dutchman's voice was lost in the blower's howling, but his blue-lit lips clearly were repeating, "One word . . ."

The tank moved on down the highway toward Portela. ". . . and maybe I'll shoot you anyway," Kruse was saying. "That's the way to serve traitors, isn't it? *Mercenary!*"

The third blower was approaching. Its note seemed slightly different, though that might be the after-effect of the preceding vehicles' echoing din. Pritchard was cold all the way to his heart, because in a moment he was going to call for help. He knew that Kruse would shoot him, knew also that he would rather die now than live after hope had come so near but passed on, passed on. . . .

The third tank smashed through the wall of the house. The Plow's skirts were not a bulldozer blade, but they were thick steel and backed with the mass of a 150 tonne command tank. The slag wall repowdered at the impact. Ceiling joists buckled into pretzel shape and ripped the cellar open to the floor above. Kruse flung his musket up and fired through the cascading rubble. The boom and red flash were lost in the chaos, but the blue-green fire stabbing back across the cellar laid the Dutchman on his back with his parka aflame. Pritchard rolled to the floor at the first shock. He thrust himself with corded legs and arms back under the feeble protection of the bunk. When the sound of falling objects had died away, the captain slitted his eyelids against the rock dust and risked a look upward.

The collision had torn a gap ten feet long in the house wall, crushing it from street level to the beams supporting the second story. The tank blocked the hole with its gray bulk. Fresh scars brightened the patina of corrosion etched onto its skirts by the atmospheres of a dozen planets. Through the buckled flooring and the dust whipped into arabesques by the idling fans, Pritchard glimpsed a slight figure clinging left-handed to the turret. Her right hand still threatened the

wreckage with a submachine gun. Carpeting burned on the
floor above, ignited by the burst that killed Kruse. Somewhere a woman was screaming in Dutch.

"Margritte!" Pritchard shouted. "Margritte! Down here!"

The helmeted woman swung up her face shield and tried
to pierce the cellar gloom with her unaided eyes. The tank-
battered opening had sufficed for the exchange of shots,
but the tangle of structural members and splintered flooring
was too tight to pass a man—or even a small woman. Sooty
flames were beginning to shroud the gap. Margritte jumped
to the ground and struggled for a moment before she was
able to heave open the door. The Plow's turret swung to
cover her, though neither the main gun nor the tribarrel
in the cupola could depress enough to rake the cellar.
Margritte ran down the steps to Pritchard. Coughing in
the rock dust, he rolled out over the rubble to meet her.
Much of the smashed sidewall had collapsed onto the street
when the tank backed after the initial impact. Still, the
crumpled beams of the ground floor sagged further with
the additional weight of the slag on them. Head-sized pieces
had splanged on the cot above Pritchard.

Margritte switched the submachine gun to her left hand
and began using a clasp knife on her captain's bonds. The
cord with which he was tied bit momentarily deeper at the
blade's pressure.

Pritchard winced, then began flexing his freed hands.
"You know, Margi," he said, "I don't think I've ever seen
you with a gun before."

The commo tech's face hardened as if the polarized
helmet shield had slipped down over it again. "You hadn't,"
she said. The ankle bindings parted and she stood, the dust
graying her helmet and her foam-filled coveralls. "Captain,
Kowie had to drive and we needed Rob in the cupola at
the gun. That left me to—do anything else that had to be
done. I did what had to be done."

Pritchard tried to stand, using the technician as a post
on which to draw himself upright. Margritte looked frail,
but with her legs braced she stood like a rock. Her arm
around Pritchard's back was as firm as a man's.

"You didn't ask Captain Riis for help, I guess," Pritchard said, pain making his breath catch. The line tanks had two-man crews with no one to spare for outrider, of course.

"We didn't report you missing," Margritte said, "even to First Platoon. They just went along like before, thinking you were in the Plow giving orders." Together, captain and technician shuffled across the floor to the stairs. As they passed Kruse's body, Margritte muttered cryptically, "That's four."

Pritchard assumed the tremors beginning to shake the woman's body were from physical strain. He took as much weight off her as he could and found his numbed feet were beginning to function reasonably well. He would never have been able to board the Plow without Sergeant Jenne's grip on his arm, however.

The battered officer settled in the turret with a groan of comfort. The seat cradled his body with gentle firmness, and the warm air blown across him was just the near side of heaven.

"Captain," Jenne said, "what d'we do about the slopes who grabbed you? Shall we call in an interrogation team and—"

"We don't do anything," Pritchard interrupted. "We just pretend none of this happened and head back to . . ." He paused. His flesh wavered both hot and cold as Margritte sprayed his ankles with some of the apparatus from the medical kit. "Say, how did you find me, anyway?"

"We shut off coverage when you—went into your room," Jenne said, seeing that the commo tech herself did not intend to speak. He meant, Pritchard knew, they had shut off the sound when their captain had said, "Sal." None of the three of them were looking either of the other two in the eyes. "After a bit, though, Margi noticed the carrier line from your implant had dropped off her oscilloscope. I checked your room, didn't find you. Didn't see much point talking it over with the remfs on duty, either.

"So we got satellite recce and found two trucks'd left the area since we got back. One was Riis', and the other was a civvie junker before that. It'd been parked in the woods out of sight, half a kay up the road from the buildings. Both trucks unloaded in Haacin. We couldn't tell which load was you, but Margi said if we got close, she'd home on your carrier even though you weren't calling us on the implant. Some girl we got here, hey?"

Pritchard bent forward and squeezed the commo tech's shoulder. She did not look up, but she smiled. "Yeah, always knew she was something," he agreed, "but I don't think I realized quite what a person she was until just now."

Margritte lifted her smile. "Rob ordered First Platoon to fall in with us," she said. "He set up the whole rescue." Her fine-fingered hands caressed Pritchard's calves.

But there was other business in Haacin, now. Riis had been quicker to act than Pritchard had hoped. He asked, "You say one of the infantry's trucks took a load here a little bit ago?"

"Yeah, you want the off-print?" Jenne agreed, searching for the flimsy copy of the satellite picture. "What the Hell would they be doing, anyhow?"

"I got a suspicion," his captain said grimly, "and I suppose it's one we've got to check out."

"Michael First-Three to Michael One," the radio broke in. "Vehicles approaching from the east on the hardball."

"Michael One to Michael First," Pritchard said, letting the search for contraband arms wait for this new development. "Reverse and form a line abreast beyond the village. Twenty meter intervals. The Plow'll take the road." More weapons from Riis? More of Barthe's troops when half his sector command was already in Portela? Pritchard touched switches beneath the vision blocks as Kowie slid the tank into position. He split the screen between satellite coverage and a ground-level view at top magnification. Six vehicles, combat cars, coming fast. Pritchard swore. Friendly, because only the Slammers had armored vehicles on Kobold, not that cars were a threat to tanks anyway. But no combat cars were assigned to this sector; and the unexpected is always bad news to a company commander juggling too many variables already.

"Platoon nearing Tango Sigma four-two, three-two, please

identify to Michael One," Pritchard requested, giving Haacin's map coordinates.

Margritte turned up the volume of the main radio while she continued to bandage the captain's rope cuts. The set crackled, "Michael One, this is Alpha One and Alpha First. Stand by."

"God's bleeding cunt!" Rob Jenne swore under his breath. Pritchard was nodding in equal agitation. Alpha was the Regiment's special duty company. Its four combat car platoons were Colonel Hammer's bodyguards and police. The troopers of A Company were nicknamed the White Mice, and they were viewed askance even by the Slammers of other companies—men who prided themselves on being harder than any other combat force in the galaxy. The White Mice in turn feared their commander, Major Joachim Steuben; and if that slightly-built killer feared anyone, it was the man who was probably travelling with him this night. Pritchard sighed and asked the question. "Alpha One, this is Michael One. Are you flying a pennant, sir?"

"Affirmative, Michael One."

Well, he'd figured Colonel Hammer was along as soon as he heard what the unit was. What the Old Man was doing here was another question, and one whose answer Pritchard did not look forward to learning.

The combat cars glided to a halt under the guns of their bigger brethren. The tremble of their fans gave the appearance of heat ripples despite the snow. From his higher vantage point, Pritchard watched the second car slide out of line and fall alongside the Plow. The men at the nose and right wing guns were both short, garbed in nondescript battle gear. They differed from the other troopers only in that their helmet shields were raised and that the faces visible beneath were older than those of most Slammers: Colonel Alois Hammer and his hatchetman.

"No need for radio, Captain," Hammer called in a husky voice. "What are you doing here?"

Pritchard's tongue quivered between the truth and a lie. His crew had been covering for him, and he wasn't about to leave them holding the bag. All the breaches of regulations they had committed were for their captain's sake. "Sir, I brought First Platoon back to Haacin to check whether any of the powerguns they'd hijacked from Barthe were still in civvie hands." Pritchard could feel eyes behind the cracked shutters of every east-facing window in the village.

"And have you completed your check?" the colonel pressed, his voice mild but his eyes as hard as those of Major Steuben beside him; as hard as the iridium plates of the gun shields.

Pritchard swallowed. He owed nothing to Captain Riis, but the young fool was his superior—and at least he hadn't wanted the Dutch to kill Pritchard. He wouldn't put Riis' ass in the bucket if there were neutral ways to explain the contraband. Besides, they were going to need Riis and his Dutch contacts for the rest of the plan. "Sir, when you approached I was about to search a building where I suspect some illegal weapons are stored."

"And instead you'll provide backup for the major here," said Hammer, the false humor gone from his face. His words rattled like shrapnel. "He'll retrieve the twenty-four powerguns which Captain Riis saw fit to turn over to civilians tonight. If Joachim hadn't chanced, *chanced* onto that requisition . . ." Hammer's left glove shuddered with the strength of his grip on the forward tribarrel. Then the colonel lowered his eyes and voice, adding, "The quartermaster who filled a requisition for twenty-four pistols from Central Supply is in the infantry again tonight. And Captain Riis is no longer with the Regiment."

Steuben tittered, loose despite the tension of everyone around him. The cold was bitter, but Joachim's right hand was bare. With it he traced the baroque intaglios of his holstered pistol. "Mr. Riis is lucky to be alive," the slight Newlander said pleasantly. "Luckier than some would have wished. But, Colonel, I think we'd best go pick up the merchandise before anybody nerves themself to use it on us."

Hammer nodded, calm again. "Interfile your blowers with ours, Captain," he ordered. "Your panzers watch street level while the cars take care of upper floors and roofs."

Pritchard saluted and slid down into the tank, relaying the order to the rest of his platoon. Kowie blipped the Plow's throttles, swinging the turreted mass in its own length and sending it back into the village behind the lead combat car. The tank felt light as a dancer, despite the constricting sidestreet Kowie followed the car into. Pritchard scanned the full circuit of the vision blocks. Nothing save the wind and armored vehicles moved in Haacin. When Steuben had learned a line company was requisitioning two dozen extra sidearms, the major had made the same deductions as Pritchard had and had inspected the same satellite tape of a truck unloading. Either Riis was insane or he really thought Colonel Hammer was willing to throw away his life's work to arm a village—inadequately. Lord and Martyrs! Riis would have *had* to be insane to believe that!

Their objective was a nondescript two-story building, separated from its neighbors by narrow alleys. Hammer directed the four rearmost blowers down a parallel street to block the rear. The searchlights of the vehicles chilled the flat concrete and glared back from the windows of the building. A battered surface truck was parked in the street outside. It was empty. Nothing stirred in the house.

Hammer and Steuben dismounted without haste. The major's helmet was slaved to a loudspeaker in the car. The speaker boomed, "Everyone out of the building. You have thirty seconds. Anyone found inside after that'll be shot. Thirty seconds!"

Though the residents had not shown themselves earlier, the way they boiled out of the doors proved they had expected the summons. All told there were eleven of them. From the front door came a well-dressed man and woman with their three children: a sexless infant carried by its mother in a zippered cocoon; a girl of eight with her hood down and her hair coiled in braids about her forehead; and a twelve-year-old boy who looked nearly as husky as his father. Outside staircases disgorged an aged couple on the one hand and four tough-looking men on the other.

Pritchard looked at his blower chief. The sergeant's right

hand was near the gun switch and he mumbled an old ballad under his breath. Chest tightening, Pritchard climbed out of his hatch. He jumped to the ground and paced quietly over to Hammer and his aide.

"There's twenty-four pistols in this building," Joachim's amplified voice roared, "or at least you people know where they are. I want somebody to save trouble and tell me."

The civilians tensed. The mother half-turned to swing her body between her baby and the officers.

Joachim's pistol was in his hand, though Pritchard had not seen him draw it. "Nobody to speak?" Joachim queried. He shot the eight-year-old in the right knee. The spray of blood was momentary as the flesh exploded. The girl's mouth pursed as her buckling leg dropped her face-down in the street. The pain would come later. Her parents screamed, the father falling to his knees to snatch up the child as the mother pressed her forehead against the door jamb in blind panic.

Pritchard shouted, "You son of a bitch!" and clawed for his own sidearm. Steuben turned with the precision of a turret lathe. His pistol's muzzle was a white-hot ring from its previous discharge. Pritchard knew only that and the fact that his own weapon was not clear of its holster. Then he realized that Colonel Hammer was shouting, "No!" and that his open hand had rocked Joachim's head back.

Joachim's face went pale except for the handprint burning on his cheek. His eyes were empty. After a moment, he holstered his weapon and turned back to the civilians. "Now, who'll tell us where the guns are?" he asked in a voice like breaking glassware.

The tear-blind woman, still holding her infant, gurgled, "Here! In the basement!" as she threw open the door. Two troopers followed her within at a nod from Hammer. The father was trying to close the girl's wounded leg with his hands, but his palms were not broad enough.

Pritchard vomited on the snowy street.

Margritte was out of the tank with a medikit in her hand. She flicked the civilian's hands aside and began freezing the wound with a spray. The front door banged open again. The two White Mice were back with their submachine guns slung under their arms and a heavy steel weapons chest between them. Hammer nodded and walked to them.

"You could have brought in an interrogation team!" Pritchard shouted at the backs of his superiors. "You don't shoot children!"

"Machine interrogation takes time, Captain," Steuben said mildly. He did not turn to acknowledge the tanker. "This was just as effective."

"That's a little girl!" Pritchard insisted with his hands clenched. The child was beginning to cry, though the local anesthetic in the skin-sealer had probably blocked the physical pain. The psychic shock of a body that would soon end at the right knee would be worse, though. The child was old enough to know that no local doctor could save the limb. "This isn't something that human beings *do*!"

"Captain," Steuben said, "they're lucky I haven't shot all of them."

Hammer closed the arms chest. "We've got what we came for," he said. "Let's go."

"Stealing guns from my colonel," the Newlander continued as if Hammer had not spoken. The handprint had faded to a dull blotch. "I really ought to—"

"Joachim, shut it off!" Hammer shouted. "We're going to talk about what happened tonight, you and I. I'd rather do it when we were alone but I'll tell you now if I have to. Or in front of a court-martial."

Steuben squeezed his forehead with the fingers of his left hand. He said nothing.

"Let's go," the colonel repeated.

Pritchard caught Hammer's arm. "Take the kid back to Central's medics," he demanded.

Hammer blinked. "I should have thought of that," he said simply. "Some times I lose track of . . . things that aren't going to shoot at me. But we don't need this sort of reputation."

"I don't care cop for public relations," Pritchard snapped. "Just save that little girl's leg."

Steuben reached for the child, now lying limp. Margritte had used a shot of general anesthetic. The girl's father went wild-eyed and swung at Joachim from his crouch. Margritte jabbed with the injector from behind the civilian. He gasped as the drug took hold, then sagged as if his bones had dissolved. Steuben picked up the girl.

Hammer vaulted aboard the combat car and took the child from his subordinate's arms. Cutting himself into the loudspeaker system, the stocky colonel thundered to the street, "Listen you people. If you take guns from mercs— either Barthe's men or my own—we'll grind you to dust. Take 'em from civilians if you think you can. You may have a chance, then. If you rob mercs, you just get a chance to die."

Hammer nodded to the civilians, nodded again to the brooding buildings to either side. He gave an unheard command to his driver. The combat cars began to rev their fans.

Pritchard gave Margritte a hand up and followed her. "Michael One to Michael First," he said. "Head back with Alpha First."

Pritchard rode inside the turret after they left Haacin, glad for once of the armor and the cabin lights. In the writhing tree limbs he had seen the Dutch mother's face as the shot maimed her daughter.

Margritte passed only one call to her commander. It came shortly after the combat cars had separated to return to their base camp near Midi, the planetary capital. The colonel's voice was as smooth as it ever got. It held no hint of the rage which had blazed out in Haacin. "Captain Pritchard," Hammer said, "I've transferred command of Sigma Company to the leader of its First Platoon. The sector, of course, is in your hands now. I expect you to carry out your duties with the ability you've already shown."

"Michael One to Regiment," Pritchard replied curtly. "Acknowledged."

Kowie drew up in front of the command post without the furious caracole which had marked their most recent approach. Pritchard slid his hatch open. His crewmen did not move. "I've got to worry about being sector chief for a while," he said, "but you three can sack out in the barracks now. You've put in a full tour in my book."

"Think I'll sleep here," Rob said. He touched a stud, rotating his seat into a couch alongside the receiver and loading tube of the main gun.

Pritchard frowned. "Margritte?" he asked.

She shrugged. "No, I'll stay by my set for a while." Her eyes were blue and calm.

On the intercom, Kowie chimed in with, "Yeah, you worry about the sector, we'll worry about ourselves. Say, don't you think a tank platoon'd be better for base security than these pongoes?"

"Shut up, Kowie," Jenne snapped. The blond Burlager glanced at his captain. "Everything'll be fine, so long as we're here," he said from one elbow. He patted the breech of the 200mm gun.

Pritchard shrugged and climbed out into the cold night. He heard the hatch grind shut behind him.

Until Pritchard walked in the door of the building, it had not occurred to him that Riis' replacement was Sally Schilling. The words "First Platoon leader" had not been a name to the tanker, not in the midst of the furor of his mind. The little blonde glanced up at Pritchard from the map display she was studying. She spat cracklingly on the electric stove and faced around again. Her aide, the big corporal, blinked in some embarrassment. None of the headquarters staff spoke.

"I need the display console from my room," Pritchard said to the corporal.

The infantryman nodded and got up. Before he had taken three steps, Lieutenant Schilling's voice cracked like pressure-heaved ice, "Corporal Webbert!"

"Sir?" The big man's face went tight as he found himself a pawn in a game whose stakes went beyond his interest.

"Go get the display console for our new commander. It's in his room."

Licking his lips with relief, the corporal obeyed. He carried the heavy four-legged console back without effort.

Sally was making it easier for him, Pritchard thought. But how he wished that Riis hadn't made so complete a fool of himself that he had to be removed. Using Riis to set up a double massacre would have been a lot easier to justify when Danny awoke in the middle of the night and found himself remembering. . . .

Pritchard positioned the console so that he sat with his back to the heater. It separated him from Schilling. The top of the instrument was a slanted, 40 cm screen which glowed when Pritchard switched it on. "Sector Two display," he directed. In response to his words the screen sharpened into a relief map. "Population centers," he said. They flashed on as well, several dozen of them ranging from a few hundred souls to the several thousand of Haacin and Dimo. Portela, the largest Francophone settlement west of the Aillet, was about twenty kilometers west of Haacin.

And there were now French mercenaries on both sides of that division line. Sally had turned from her own console and stood up to see what Pritchard was doing. The tanker said, "All mercenary positions, confirmed and calculated."

The board spangled itself with red and green symbols, each of them marked in small letters with a unit designation. The reconnaissance satellites gave unit strengths very accurately and computer analysis of radio traffic could generally name the forces. In the eastern half of the sector, Lieutenant Colonel Benoit had spread out one battalion in platoon-strength billets. The guardposts were close enough to most points to put down trouble immediately. A full company near Dimo guarded the headquarters and two batteries of rocket howitzers.

The remaining battalion in the sector, Benoit's own, was concentrated in positions blasted into the rocky highlands ten kays west of Portela. It was not a deployment that would allow the mercs to effectively police the west half of the sector, but it was a very good defensive arrangement. The forest that covered the center of the sector was ideal for hit-and-run sniping by small units of infantry. The tree boles were too densely woven for tanks to plow through them. Because the forest was so flammable at this season, however, it would be equally dangerous to ambushers. Benoit was wise to concentrate in the barren high ground.

Besides the highlands, the fields cleared around every settlement were the only safe locations for a modern firefight. The fields, and the broad swathes cleared for roads through the forest. . . .

"Incoming traffic for Sector Chief," announced a radioman. "Its from the skepsel colonel, sir." He threw his words into the air, afraid to direct them at either of the officers in the orderly room.

"Voice only, or is there visual?" Pritchard asked. Schilling held her silence.

"Visual component, sir."

"Patch him through to my console," the tanker decided. "And son—watch your language. Otherwise, you say 'beast' when you shouldn't."

The map blurred from the display screen and was replaced by the hawk features of Lieutenant Colonel Benoit. A pick-up on the screen's surface threw Pritchard's own image onto Benoit's similar console.

The Frenchman blinked. "Captain Pritchard? I'm very pleased to see you, but my words must be with Captain Riis directly. Could you wake him?"

"There've been some changes," the tanker said. In the back of his mind, he wondered what had happened to Riis. Pulled back under arrest, probably. "I'm in charge of Sector Two, now. Co-charge with you, that is."

Benoit's face steadied as he absorbed the information without betraying an opinion about it. Then he beamed like a feasting wolf and said, "Congratulations, Captain. Some day you and I will have to discuss the . . . events of the past few days. But what I was calling about is far less pleasant, I'm afraid."

Benoit's image wavered on the screen as he paused. Pritchard touched his tongue to the corner of his mouth. "Go ahead, Colonel," he said. "I've gotten enough bad news today that a little more won't signify."

Benoit quirked his brow in what might or might not have been humor. "When we were proceeding to Portela," he said, "some of my troops mistook the situation and set up passive tank interdiction points. Mines, all over the sector. They're booby-trapped, of course. The only safe way to remove them is for the troops responsible to do it. They will of course be punished later."

Pritchard chuckled. "How long do you estimate it'll take to clear the roads, Colonel?" he asked.

The Frenchman spread his hands, palms up. "Weeks, perhaps. It's much harder to clear mines safely than to lay them, of course."

"But there wouldn't be anything between *here* and Haacin, would there?" the tanker prodded. It was all happening just as Hammer's informant had said Barthe planned it. First, hem the tanks in with nets of forest and minefields; then, break the most important Dutch stronghold while your mercs were still around to back you up. . . . "The spur road to our HQ here wasn't on your route; and besides, we just drove tanks over it a few minutes ago."

Behind Pritchard, Sally Schilling was cursing in a sharp, carrying voice. Benoit could probably hear her, but the colonel kept his voice as smooth as milk as he said, "Actually, I'm afraid there *is* a field—gas, shaped charges, and glass-shard antipersonnel mines—somewhere on that road, yes. Fortunately, the field was signal activated. It wasn't primed until after you had passed through. I assure you, Captain Pritchard, that all the roads west of the Aillet may be too dangerous to traverse until I have cleared them. I warn you both as a friend and so that we will not be charged with damage to any of your vehicles—and men. You have been fully warned of the danger; anything that happens now is your responsibility."

Pritchard leaned back in the console's integral seat, chuckling again. "You know, Colonel," the tank captain said, "I'm not sure that the Bonding Authority wouldn't find those mines were a hostile act justifying our retaliation." Benoit stiffened, more an internal hardness than anything that showed in his muscles. Pritchard continued to speak

through a smile. "We won't, of course. Mistakes happen.
But one thing, Colonel Benoit—"

The Frenchman nodded, waiting for the edge to bite.
He knew as well as Pritchard did that, at best, if there
were an Authority investigation, Barthe would have to throw
a scapegoat out. A high-ranking scapegoat.

"Mistakes happen," Pritchard repeated, "but they can't
be allowed to happen twice. You've got my permission to
send out a ten-man team by daylight—only by daylight—
to clear the road from Portela to Bever. That'll give you
a route back to your side of the sector. If any other troops
leave their present position, for any reason, I'll treat it as
an attack."

"Captain, this demarcation within the sector was not a
part of the contract—"

"It was at the demand of Colonel Barthe," Pritchard
snapped, "and agreed to by the demonstrable practice of
both regiments over the past three months." Hammer had
briefed Pritchard very carefully on the words to use here,
to be recorded for the benefit of the Bonding Authority.
"You've heard the terms, Colonel. You can either take them
or we'll put the whole thing—the minefields and some other
matters that've come up recently—before the Authority
right now. Your choice."

Benoit stared at Pritchard, apparently calm but tugging
at his upper lip with thumb and forefinger. "I think you
are unwise, Captain, in taking full responsibility for an area
in which your tanks cannot move; but that is your affair,
of course. I will obey your mandate. We should have the
Portela-Haacin segment cleared by evening; tomorrow we'll
proceed to Bever. Good day."

The screen segued back to the map display. Pritchard
stood up. A spare helmet rested beside one of the radiomen. The tank captain donned it—he had forgotten to
requisition a replacement from stores—and said, "Michael
One to all Michael units." He paused for the acknowledgment lights from his four platoons and the command
vehicle. Then, "Hold your present positions. Don't attempt
to move by road, any road, until further notice. The roads

have been mined. There are probably safe areas, and we'll get you a map of them as soon as Command Central works it up. For the time being, just stay where you are. Michael One, out."

"Are you really going to take that?" Lieutenant Schilling demanded in a low, harsh voice.

"Pass the same orders to your troops, Sally," Pritchard said. "I know they can move through the woods where my tanks can't, but I don't want any friendlies in the forest right now either." To the intelligence sergeant on watch, Pritchard added, "Samuels, get Central to run a plot of all activity by any of Benoit's men. That won't tell us where they've laid mines, but it'll let us know where they can't have."

"What happens if the bleeding skepsels ignore you?" Sally blazed. "You've bloody taught them to ignore you, haven't you? Knuckling under every time somebody whispers 'contract'? You can't move a tank to stop them if they do leave their base, and I've got 198 effectives. A battalion'd laugh at me, *laugh!*"

Schilling's arms were akimbo, her face as pale with rage as the snow outside. Speaking with deliberate calm, Pritchard said, "I'll call in artillery if I need to. Benoit only brought two calliopes with him, and they can't stop all the shells from three firebases at the same time. The road between his position and Portela's just a snake-track cut between rocks. A couple firecracker rounds going off above infantry strung out there—Via, it'll be a butcher shop."

Schilling's eyes brightened. "Then for tonight, the sector's just like it was before we came," she thought out loud. "Well, I suppose you know best," she added in false agreement, with false nonchalance. "I'm going back to the barracks. I'll brief First Platoon in person and radio the others from there. Come along, Webbert."

The corporal slammed the door behind himself and his lieutenant. The gust of air that licked about the walls was cold, but Pritchard was already shivering at what he had just done to a woman he loved.

It was daylight by now, and the frosted windows turned to flame in the ruddy sun. Speaking to no one but his

console's memory, Pritchard began to plot tracks from each
tank platoon. He used a topographic display, ignoring the
existence of the impenetrable forest which covered the
ground.

Margritte's resonant voice twanged in the implant,
"Captain, would you come to the blower for half a sec?"

"On the way," Pritchard said, shrugging into his coat.
The orderly room staff glanced up at him.

Margritte poked her head out of the side hatch. Pritchard
climbed onto the deck to avoid some of the generator whine.
The skirts sang even when the fans were cut off completely.
Rob Jenne, curious but at ease, was visible at his battle station beyond the commo tech. "Sir," Margritte said, "we've
been picking up signals from—there." The blue-eyed woman
thumbed briefly at the infantry barracks without letting her
pupils follow the gesture.

Pritchard nodded. "Lieutenant Schilling's passing on my
orders to her company."

"Danny, the transmission's in code, and it's not a code of
ours." Margritte hesitated, then touched the back of the
officer's gloved left hand. "There's answering signals, too.
I can't triangulate without moving the blower, of course, but
the source is in line with the tailings pile at Haacin."

It was what he had planned, after all. Someone the
villagers could trust had to get word of the situation to
them. Otherwise they wouldn't draw the Portelans and their
mercenary backers into a fatal mistake. Hard luck for the
villagers who were acting as bait, but very good luck for
every other Dutchman on Kobold. . . . Pritchard had no
reason to feel anything but relief that it had happened. He
tried to relax the muscles which were crushing all the
breath out of his lungs. Margritte's fingers closed over his
hand and squeezed it.

"Ignore the signals," the captain said at last. "We've
known all along they were talking to the civilians, haven't
we?" Neither of his crewmen spoke. Pritchard's eyes closed
tightly. He said, "We've known for months, Hammer and
I, every damned thing that Barthe's been plotting with the
skepsels. They want a chance to break Haacin now, while

they're around to cover for the Portelans. We'll give them
their chance and ram it up their ass crosswise. The Old
Man hasn't spread the word for fear the story'd get out,
the same way Barthe's plans did. We're all mercenaries,
after all. But I want you three to know. And I'll be glad
when the only thing I have to worry about is the direction
the shots are coming from."

Abruptly, the captain dropped back to the ground. "Get
some sleep," he called. "I'll be needing you sharp tonight."

Back at his console, Pritchard resumed plotting courses
and distances. After he figured each line, he called in a
series of map coordinates to Command Central. He knew
his radio traffic was being monitored and probably
unscrambled by Barthe's intelligence staff; knew also that
even if he had read the coordinates out in clear, the
French would have assumed it was a code. The locations
made no sense unless one knew they were ground zero
for incendiary shells.

As Pritchard worked, he kept close watch on the French
battalions. Benoit's own troops held their position, as
Pritchard had ordered. They used the time to dig in. At
first they had blasted slit trenches in the rock. Now they
dug covered bunkers with the help of mining machinery
trucked from Portela by civilians. Five of the six antitank
guns were sited atop the eastern ridge of the position. They
could rake the highway as it snaked and switched back
among the foothills west of Portela.

Pritchard chuckled grimly again when Sergeant Samuels
handed him high-magnification off-prints from the satellites.
Benoit's two squat, bulky calliopes were sited in defilade
behind the humps of the eastern ridge line. There the
eight-barrelled powerguns were safe from the smashing fire
of M Company's tanks, but their ability to sweep artillery
shells from the sky was degraded by the closer horizon.
The Slammers did not bother with calliopes themselves.
Their central fire director did a far better job by working
through the hundreds of vehicle-mounted weapons. How
much better, Benoit might learn very shortly.

The mine-sweeping team cleared the Portela-Haacin road, as directed. The men returned to Benoit's encampment an hour before dusk. The French did not come within five kilometers of the Dutch village.

Pritchard watched the retiring minesweepers, then snapped off the console. He stood. "I'm going out to my blower," he said.

His crew had been watching for him. A hatch shot open, spouting condensate, as soon as Pritchard came out the door. The smooth bulk of the tank blew like a restive whale. On the horizon, the sun was so low that the treetops stood out in silhouette like a line of bayonets.

Wearily, the captain dropped through the hatch into his seat. Jenne and Margritte murmured greeting and waited, noticeably tense. "I'm going to get a couple hours' sleep," Pritchard said. He swung his seat out and up, so that he lay horizontal in the turret. His legs hid Margritte's oval face from him. "Punch up coverage of the road west of Haacin would you?" he asked. "I'm going to take a tab of Glirine. Slap me with the antidote when something moves there."

"If something moves," Jenne amended.

"When." Pritchard sucked down the pill. "The square-heads think they've got one last chance to smack Portela and hijack the powerguns again. Thing is, the Portelans'll have already distributed the guns and be waiting for the Dutch to come through. It'll be a damn short fight, that one. . . ." The drug took hold and Pritchard's consciousness began to flow away like a sugar cube in water. "Damn short. . . ."

At first Pritchard felt only the sting on the inside of his wrist. Then the narcotic haze ripped away and he was fully conscious again.

"There's a line of trucks, looks like twenty, moving west out of Haacin, sir. They're blacked out, but the satellite has 'em on infrared."

"Red Alert," Pritchard ordered. He locked his seat upright into its combat position. Margritte's soft voice sounded the general alarm. Pritchard slipped on his radio helmet. "Michael One to all Michael units. Check off." Five green lights flashed their silent acknowledgments across the top of the captain's face-shield display. "Michael One to Sigma One," Pritchard continued.

"Go ahead, Michael One." Sally's voice held a note of triumph.

"Sigma One, pull all your troops into large, clear areas—the fields around the towns are fine, but stay the hell away from Portela and Haacin. Get ready to slow down anybody coming this way from across the Aillet. Over."

"Affirmative, Danny, affirmative!" Sally replied. Couldn't she use the satellite reconnaissance herself and see the five blurred dots halfway between the villages? They were clearly the trucks which had brought the Portelans into their ambush positions. What would she say when she realized how she had set up the villagers she was trying to protect? Lambs to the slaughter. . . .

The vision block showed the Dutch trucks more clearly than the camouflaged Portelans. The crushed stone of the roadway was dark on the screen, cooler than the surrounding trees and the vehicles upon it. Pritchard patted the breech of the main gun and looked across it to his blower chief. "We got a basic load for this aboard?" he asked.

"Do bears cop in the woods?" Jenne grinned. "We gonna get a chance to bust caps tonight, Captain?"

Pritchard nodded. "For three months we've been here, doing nothing but selling rope to the French. Tonight they've bought enough that we can hang 'em with it." He looked at the vision block again. "You alive, Kowie?" he asked on intercom.

"Ready to slide any time you give me a course," said the driver from his closed cockpit.

The vision block sizzled with bright streaks that seemed to hang on the screen though they had passed in microseconds. The leading blobs expanded and brightened as trucks blew up.

"Michael One to Fire Central," Pritchard said.

"Go ahead, Michael One," replied the machine voice.

"Prepare Fire Order Alpha."

"Roger, Michael One."

"Margritte, get me Benoit."

"Go ahead, Captain."

"Slammers to Benoit. Pritchard to Benoit. Come in please, Colonel."

"Captain Pritchard, Michel Benoit here." The colonel's voice was smooth but too hurried to disguise the concern underlying it. "I assure you that none of my men are involved in the present fighting. I have a company ready to go out and control the disturbance immediately, however."

The tanker ignored him. The shooting had already stopped for lack of targets. "Colonel, I've got some artillery aimed to drop various places in the forest. It's coming nowhere near your troops or any other human beings. If you interfere with this necessary shelling, the Slammers'll treat it as an act of war. I speak with my colonel's authority."

"Captain, I don't—"

Pritchard switched manually. "Michael One to Fire Central. Execute Fire Order Alpha."

"On the way, Michael One."

"Michael One to Michael First, Second, Fourth. Command Central has fed movement orders into your map displays. Incendiary clusters are going to burst over marked locations to ignite the forest. Use your own main guns to set the trees burning in front of your immediate positions. One round ought to do it. Button up and you can move through the fire—the trees just fall to pieces when they've burned."

The turret whined as it slid under Rob's control. "Michael Third, I'm attaching you to the infantry. More Frenchmen're apt to be coming this way from the east. It's up to you to see they don't slam a door on us."

The main gun fired, its discharge so sudden that the air rang like a solid thing. Seepage from the ejection system filled the hull with the reek of superheated polyurethane. The side vision blocks flashed cyan, then began to flood with the mounting white hell-light of the blazing trees. In the central block, still set on remote, all the Dutch trucks were burning as were patches of forest which the ambush had ignited. The Portelans had left the concealment of the trees and swept across the road, mopping up the Dutch.

"Kowie, let's move," Jenne was saying on intercom, syncopated by the mild echo of his voice in the turret. Margritte's face was calm, her lips moving subtly as she handled some traffic that she did not pass on to her captain. The tank slid forward like oil on a lake. From the far distance came the thumps of incendiary rounds scattering their hundreds of separate fireballs high over the trees.

Pritchard slapped the central vision block back on direct; the tank's interior shone white with transmitted fire. The Plow's bow slope sheared into a thicket of blazing trees. The wood tangled and sagged, then gave in a splash of fiery splinters whipped aloft by the blower's fans. The tank was in Hell on all sides, Kowie steering by instinct and his inertial compass. Even with his screens filtered all the way down, the driver would not be able to use his eyes effectively until more of the labyrinth had burned away.

Benoit's calliopes had not tried to stop the shelling. Well, there were other ways to get the French mercs to take the first step over the line. For instance—

"Punch up Benoit again," Pritchard ordered. Even through the dense iridium plating, the roar of the fire was a subaural presence in the tank.

"Go ahead," Margritte said, flipping a switch on her console. She had somehow been holding the French officer in conversation all the time Pritchard was on other frequencies.

"Colonel," Pritchard said, "we've got clear running through this fire. We're going to chase down everybody who used a powergun tonight; then we'll shoot them. We'll shoot everybody in their families, everybody with them in this ambush, and we'll blow up every house that anybody involved lived in. That's likely to be every house in Portela, isn't it?"

More than the heat and ions of the blazing forest distorted Benoit's face. He shouted, "Are you mad? You can't think of such a thing, Pritchard!"

The tanker's lips parted like a wolf's. He could think of mass murder, and there were plenty of men in the Slammers who would really be willing to carry out the threat. But Pritchard wouldn't have to, because Benoit was like Riis and Schilling: too much of a nationalist to remember his first duty as a merc. . . . "Colonel Benoit, the contract demands we keep the peace and stay impartial. The record shows how we treated people in Haacin for *having* powerguns. For what the Portelans did tonight—don't worry, we'll be impartial. And they'll never break the peace again."

"Captain, I will not allow you to massacre French civilians," Benoit stated flatly.

"Move a man out of your present positions and I'll shoot him dead," Pritchard said. "It's your choice, Colonel. Michael One out."

The Plow bucked and rolled as it pulverized fire-shattered trunks, but the vehicle was meeting nothing solid enough to slam it to a halt. Pritchard used a side block on remote to examine Benoit's encampment. The satellite's enhanced infrared showed a stream of sparks flowing from the defensive positions toward the Portela road: infantry on skimmers. The pair of larger, more diffuse blobs were probably antitank guns. Benoit wasn't moving his whole battalion, only a reinforced company in a show of force to make Pritchard back off.

The fool. Nobody was going to back off now.

"Michael One to all Michael and Sigma units," Pritchard said in a voice as clear as the white flames around his tank. "We're now in a state of war with Barthe's Company and its civilian auxiliaries. Michael First, Second and Fourth, we'll rendezvous at the ambush site as plotted on your displays. Anybody between there and Portela is fair game. If we take any fire from Portela, we go down the main drag in line and blow the cop out of it. If any of Barthe's people are in the way, we keep on sliding west. Sigma One, mount a fluid defense, don't push, and wait for help. It's coming. If this works, it's Barthe against Hammer—and that's wheat against the scythe. Acknowledged?"

As Pritchard's call board lit green, a raspy new voice

broke into the sector frequency. "Wish I was with you, panzers. We'll cover your butts and the other sectors—if anybody's dumb enough to move. Good hunting!"

"I wish you *were* here and not me, Colonel," Pritchard whispered, but that was to himself . . . and perhaps it was not true even in his heart. Danny's guts were very cold, and his face was as cold as death.

To Pritchard's left, a lighted display segregated the area of operations. It was a computer analog, not direct satellite coverage. Doubtful images were brightened and labeled—green for the Slammers, red for Barthe; blue for civilians unless they were fighting on one side or the other. The green dot of the Plow converged on the ambush site at the same time as the columns of First and Fourth Platoons. Second was a minute or two farther off. Pritchard's breath caught. A sheaf of narrow red lines was streaking across the display toward his tanks. Barthe had ordered his Company's artillery to support Benoit's threatened battalion.

The salvo frayed and vanished more suddenly than it had appeared. Other Slammers' vehicles had ripped the threat from the sky. Green lines darted from Hammer's own three firebases, off-screen at the analog's present scale. The fighting was no longer limited to Sector Two. If Pritchard and Hammer had played their hand right, though, it would stay limited to only the Slammers and Compagnie de Barthe. The other Francophone regiments would fear to join an unexpected battle which certainly resulted from someone's contract violation. If the breach were Hammer's, the Dutch would not be allowed to profit by the fighting. If the breach were Barthe's, anybody who joined him would be punished as sternly by the Bonding Authority.

So violent was the forest's combustion that the flames were already dying down into sparks and black ashes. The command tank growled out into the broad avenue of the road west of Haacin. Dutch trucks were still burning— fabric, lubricants, and the very paint of their frames had been ignited by the powerguns. Many of the bodies sprawled beside the vehicles were smoldering also. Some corpses still clutched their useless muskets. The dead were victims of six centuries of progress which had come to Kobold prepackaged, just in time to kill them. Barthe had given the Portelans only shoulder weapons, but even that meant the world here. The powerguns were repeaters with awesome destruction in every bolt. Without answering fire to rattle them, even untrained gunmen could be effective with weapons which shot line-straight and had no recoil. Certainly the Portelans had been effective.

Throwing ash and fire like sharks in the surf, the four behemoths of First Platoon slewed onto the road from the south. Almost simultaneously, Fourth joined through the dying hellstorm to the other side. The right of way was fifty meters wide and there was no reason to keep to the center of it. The forest, ablaze or glowing embers, held no ambushes any more.

The Plow lurched as Kowie guided it through the bodies. Some of them were still moving. Pritchard wondered if any of the Dutch had lived through the night, but that was with the back of his mind. The Slammers were at war, and nothing else really mattered. "Triple line ahead," he ordered. "First to the left, Fourth to the right; the Plow'll take the center alone till Second joins. Second, wick up when you hit the hardball and fall in behind us. If it moves, shoot it."

At one hundred kph, the leading tanks caught the Portelans three kilometers east of their village. The settlers were in the trucks that had been hidden in the forest fringe until the fires had been started. The ambushers may not have known they were being pursued until the rearmost truck exploded. Rob Jenne had shredded it with his tribarrel at five kilometers' distance. The cyan flicker and its answering orange blast signaled the flanking tanks to fire. They had just enough parallax to be able to rake the four remaining trucks without being blocked by the one which had blown up. A few snapping discharges proved that some Portelans survived to use their new powerguns on tougher meat than before. Hits streaked ashes on the tanks' armor. No one inside noticed.

From Portela's eastern windows, children watched their parents burn.

A hose of cyan light played from a distant roof top. It touched the command tank as Kowie slewed to avoid a Portelan truck. The burst was perfectly aimed, an automatic weapon served by professionals. Professionals should have known how useless it would be against heavy armor. A vision block dulled as a few receptors fused. Jenne cursed and trod the foot-switch of the main gun. A building leaped into dazzling prominence in the microsecond flash. Then it and most of the block behind collapsed into internal fires, burying the machine gun and everything else in the neighborhood. A moment later, a salvo of Hammer's high explosive got through the calliopes' inadequate screen. The village began to spew skyward in white flashes.

The Portelans had wanted to play soldier, Pritchard thought. He had dammed up all pity for the villagers of Haacin; he would not spend it now on these folk.

"Line ahead—First, Fourth, and Second," Pritchard ordered. The triple column slowed and reformed with the Plow the second vehicle in the new line. The shelling lifted from Portela as the tanks plunged into the village. Green trails on the analog terminated over the road crowded with Benoit's men and over the main French position, despite anything the calliopes could do. The sky over Benoit's bunkers rippled and flared as firecracker rounds sleeted down their thousands of individual bomblets. The defensive fire cut off entirely. Pritchard could imagine the carnage among the unprotected calliope crews when the shrapnel whirred through them.

The tanks were firing into the houses on either side, using tribarrels and occasional wallops from their main guns. The blue-green flashes were so intense they colored even the flames they lit among the wreckage. At fifty kph the thirteen tanks swept through the center of town, hindered only by the rubble of houses spilled across the street. Barthe's men were skittering white shadows who burst when powerguns hit them point blank.

The copper mine was just west of the village and three

hundred meters north of the highway. As the lead tank bellowed out around the last houses, a dozen infantrymen rose from where they had sheltered in the pit head and loosed a salvo of buzzbombs. The tank's automatic defense system was live. White fire rippled from just above the skirts as the charges there flailed pellets outward to intersect the rockets. Most of the buzzbombs exploded ten meters distant against the steel hail. One missile soared harmlessly over its target, its motor a tiny flare against the flickering sky. Only one of the shaped charges burst alongside the turret, forming a bell of light momentarily bigger than the tank. Even that was only a near miss. It gouged the iridium armor like a misthrust rapier which tears skin but does not pierce the skull.

Main guns and tribarrels answered the rockets instantly. Men dropped, some dead, some reloading. "Second Platoon, go put some HE down the shaft and rejoin," Pritchard ordered. The lead tank now had expended half its defensive charges. "Michael First-Three, fall in behind First-One. Michael One leads," he went on.

Kowie grunted acknowledgment. The Plow revved up to full honk. Benoit's men were on the road, those who had not reached Portela when the shooting started or who had fled when the artillery churned the houses to froth. The infantry skimmers were trapped between sheer rocks and sheer drop-offs, between their own slow speed and the onrushing frontal slope of the Plow. There were trees where the rocks had given them purchase. Scattered incendiaries had made them blazing cressets lighting a charnel procession.

Jenne's tribarrel scythed through body armor and dismembered men in short bursts. One of the antitank guns—was the other buried in Portela?—lay skewed against a rock wall, its driver killed by a shell fragment. Rob put a round from the main gun into it. So did each of the next two tanks. At the third shot, the ammunition ignited in a blinding secondary explosion.

The antitank guns still emplaced on the ridge line had not fired, though they swept several stretches of the road. Perhaps the crews had been rattled by the shelling, perhaps

Benoit had held his fire for fear of hitting his own men. A narrow defile notched the final ridge. The Plow heaved itself up the rise, and at the top three bolts slapped it from different angles.

Because the bow was lifted, two of the shots vaporized portions of the skirt and the front fans. The tank nosed down and sprayed sparks with half its length. The third bolt grazed the left top of the turret, making the iridium ring as it expanded. The interior of the armor streaked white though it was not pierced. The temperature inside the tank rose thirty degrees. Even as the Plow skidded, Sergeant Jenne was laying his main gun on the hot spot that was the barrel of the leftmost antitank weapon. The Plow's shot did what heavy top cover had prevented Hammer's rocket howitzers from accomplishing with shrapnel. The antitank gun blew up in a distance-muffled flash. One of its crewmen was silhouetted high in the air by the vaporizing metal of his gun.

Then the two remaining weapons ripped the night and the command blower with their charges.

The bolt that touched the right side of the turret spewed droplets of iridium across the interior of the hull. Air pistoned Pritchard's eardrums. Rob Jenne lurched in his harness, right arm burned away by the shot. His left hand blackened where it touched bare metal that sparked and sang as circuits shorted. Margritte's radios were exploding one by one under the overloads. The vision blocks worked and the turret hummed placidly as Pritchard rotated it to the right with his duplicate controls.

"Cut the power! Rob's burning!" Margritte was shrieking. She had torn off her helmet. Her thick hair stood out like tendrils of bread mold in the gathering charge. Then Pritchard had the main gun bearing and it lit the ridge line with another secondary explosion.

"Danny, our ammunition! It'll—"

Benoit's remaining gun blew the tribarrel and the cupola away deafeningly. The automatic's loading tube began to gang-fire down into the bowels of the tank. It reached a bright column up into the sky, but the turret still rolled.

Electricity crackled around Pritchard's boot and the foot trip as he fired again. The bolt stabbed the night. There was no answering blast. Pritchard held down the switch, his nostrils thick with ozone and superheated plastic and the sizzling flesh of his friend. There was still no explosion from the target bunker. The rock turned white between the cyan flashes. It cracked and flowed away like sun-melted snow, and the antitank gun never fired again.

The loading tube emptied. Pritchard slapped the main switch and cut off the current. The interior light and the dancing arcs died, leaving only the dying glow of the bolt-heated iridium. Tank after tank edged by the silent command vehicle and roared on toward the ridge. Benoit's demoralized men were already beginning to throw down their weapons and surrender.

Pritchard manually unlatched Jenne's harness and swung it horizontal. The blower chief was breathing but unconscious. Pritchard switched on a battery-powered handlight. He held it steady as Margritte began to spray sealant on the burns. Occasionally she paused to separate clothing from flesh with a stylus.

"It had to be done," Pritchard whispered. By sacrificing Haacin, he had mousetrapped Benoit into starting a war the infantry could not win. Hammer was now crushing Barthe's Company one on one, in an iridium vise. Friesland's Council of State would not have let Hammer act had they known his intentions, but in the face of a stunning victory they simply could not avoid dictating terms to the French.

"It had to be done. But I look at *what* I did—" Pritchard swung his right hand in a gesture that would have included both the fuming wreck of Portela and the raiders from Haacin, dead on the road beyond. He struck the breech of the main gun instead. Clenching his fist, he slammed it again into the metal in self-punishment. Margritte cried out and blocked his arm with her own.

"Margi," Pritchard repeated in anguish, "it isn't something that human beings *do* to each other."

But soldiers do.

And hangmen.

THE IRRESISTIBLE FORCE

Lamartiere sat in the driver's compartment of the supertank *Hoodoo*, which he'd stolen from Hammer's Slammers as the mercenaries left Ambiorix for Beresford and another contract. The tank's 20cm main gun could smash mountains; the fully automatic 2cm tribarrel in the cupola defended her against incoming artillery as well as packing a sizable punch in its own right. She was the most powerful weapon within twenty light-years.

In theory, at least. *Hoodoo*'s practical value to the sputtering remnants of the Mosite Rebellion would have to wait until Lamartiere and Dr. Clargue figured out how to transfer ammunition from the tank's storage magazines in the hull to the ready magazines in the turret.

"The reconnaissance drone has turned east," Clargue said over the intercom. "The AI predicts it's completed its search pattern, but I suppose we should wait a short time to be sure."

"Right," Lamartiere said, wondering if he'd fall asleep if he closed his eyes for a moment. "We'll wait."

Even with *Hoodoo* at rest in a narrow gorge, her internal systems and the hum of the idling drive fans made her noisy. It would have been difficult to shout directly through the narrow passage between the fighting compartment and the driver's position in the bow. The Slammers would have used commo helmets to cut off the ambient noise, but Lamartiere hadn't bothered with frills the night he drove *Hoodoo* out of the spaceport at Brione.

The Government of Ambiorix had decided the Mosite Rebellion was broken, so they'd terminated the mercenaries' contract to save the cost of paying for such sophisticated troops and equipment. *Hoodoo* was the last piece of Slammers' hardware on the planet. An electrical fault had held it and its two-man crew back when the rest of the regiment lifted for Beresford, 300 light-years away.

Those planning the operation on behalf of the Mosite Council in Goncourt had claimed that *Hoodoo* would win the war. With a single supertank the Council could force the Carcassone government to grant autonomy to the Western District where the Mosite faith predominated.

Lamartiere had been at the sharp end, infiltrating Brione as one of the mercenaries' Local Service Personnel—cheap local labor who did fetch and carry for the Slammers' skilled service technicians. He hadn't thought beyond completion of the operation, and even that only in the moments when he had enough leisure to think more than half a second ahead. If asked, though, he'd have said that *Hoodoo*'s enormous power would restore military parity between Mosite forces and the government.

Maybe, just maybe, that would have been true—if he and Clargue could use *Hoodoo*'s armament properly. As it was, with luck and fewer than a hundred rounds of 2cm ammunition gleaned from the local militia, they'd been able to smash a government mechanized battalion at the Lystra River.

It wouldn't work that way again, though. By now the government would have analyzed the wreckage of the previous battle and realized that *Hoodoo*'s main gun wasn't working, though they might not guess why. A powerful force would attack *Hoodoo* again as soon as Carcassone learned where she had fled. This time Lamartiere's trickery wouldn't be enough to win.

In addition to the government, the tank's mercenary crew, Sergeant Heth and Trooper Stegner, had stayed on Ambiorix instead of rejoining the regiment. They might or might not be actively helping the government forces, but in any case they contributed to the aura of overhanging doom Lamartiere had felt ever since his triumph at stealing *Hoodoo* had worn off.

"The drone hasn't returned," Clargue said in his usual mild tone. The doctor was as tired and frustrated as Lamartiere, but you never heard that in his voice.

"Sorry," Lamartiere said. "I was daydreaming."

Daydreaming in the middle of the night, with the stars above jewels in the desert air. It was thirty-six hours since Lamartiere had last slept.

He raised the drive fans from idle speed to full power, then broadened the angle of the blades so that they pushed the atmosphere instead of simply cutting it. *Hoodoo* rose on the bubble of air trapped within her steel-skirted plenum chamber, then slid out of the gully in which Lamartiere had hidden her when the government drone came over the horizon. With the nacelles tilted forward to retard the tank's rush down the slope, *Hoodoo* entered the Boukasset.

Most of Ambiorix' single large continent was organized in districts under administrators appointed by Carcassone. The sparsely settled Boukasset, the rocky wasteland in the rain shadow of the mountains forming the Western District, had always been ignored as a poor relation. Since the Western District had rebelled when the Synod of the Established Church attempted to put down what it described as the Mosite Heresy, the Boukasset's connection to Carcassone had become even more tenuous.

Hoodoo squirmed out of the mountains and into a broad riverbasin, dry now but a gushing, foaming torrent once every decade or so when cloudbursts drenched the Boukasset. The bottom was carpeted with vegetation that survived on groundwater dribbling beneath the sand. The coarse brush flattened beneath a 170-tonne tank with the power of a fusion bottle to drive it, then sprang up again to conceal all traces of *Hoodoo*'s passage.

Lamartiere pulled his control yoke back, increasing speed gradually. The AI overlaid a recommended course on the terrain display and steered the tank along it as long as Lamartiere permitted it to do so.

Their intended destination was the Shrine of the Blessed Catherine. If Lamartiere fell asleep now, *Hoodoo* would roar past the site in three hours and forty-nine minutes according to the countdown clock at the top of the display.

Giggling and aware that he wasn't safe to drive, Lamartiere pulled the yoke back a hair farther. The Estimated Time of Arrival dropped to three hours and twenty-four minutes.

Nowhere on Ambiorix was safe for Lamartiere until he and Clargue got *Hoodoo*'s guns working. He wouldn't be safe then either, but at least he could fight back.

Maury, the rebel commander in the Boukasset, dealt with off-planet smugglers who slipped down in small vessels. *Hoodoo*'s tribarrel used the same ammunition as the 2cm shoulder weapons of the Slammers' infantry and others who could afford those smashingly effective weapons. Maury had some of the guns, so he could supply the tank if he chose to.

If . . .

"What do you know about Maury, doctor?" Lamartiere asked, partly to keep himself awake. "He seems to have held the government out of his region, which we couldn't do in the mountains."

Great trees overhung the riverbed. The pinlike leaves of their branches shivered as the tank slid past. The trees' taproots penetrated the buried aquifer, but their trunks were clear of the flash floods that periodically scoured the channel.

"There's nothing in the Boukasset that the government wanted badly enough to commit Hammer's mercenaries to get it," Clargue said. "Nomadic herdsmen and small-scale farmers using terraces and deep wells. Our mines in the Western District were Ambiorix' main source of foreign exchange before the rebellion."

Clargue was a small, precise man in his sixties; a doctor who'd left the most advanced hospital in Carcassone to serve the sick of his home village of Pamiers in the mountains. Because of his experience with medical computers as complex as the systems of this tank, the Council had chosen him to help Lamartiere make *Hoodoo* operational. He'd tried despite his distaste for the war that had wrecked his home and Ambiorix as a whole, but he hadn't been able to find a way to access the ammunition Lamartiere *knew* was stored in *Hoodoo*'s hull.

"As for what I know of Maury," Clargue continued, "nothing to his credit. At the best of times leaders in the Boukasset have been one step removed from posturing thugs. 'Posturing thug' would be a kind description of Maury if half the rumors one hears are true."

"Beggars can't be choosers, I suppose," Lamartiere muttered. The yoke twitched in his hands as the AI guided *Hoodoo*.

He had a bad feeling about this, but he'd had a bad feeling about the operation almost from the beginning. He'd bloodied the government badly both when he escaped from Brione with the tank and at the Lystra River. But Pamiers had received a hammering by artillery and perhaps worse because *Hoodoo* had hidden there, and at Brione Lamartiere's sister Celine had died while driving a truckload of explosive into the main gate of the base.

So long as the war went on, everybody lost. If *Hoodoo* became fully operational, she could extend the war for years and maybe decades.

"Beggars have no power," Clargue said. He sniffed. "A man like Maury understands no language but that of power. The Council must be fools to send us into the Boukasset with that message."

Lamartiere sighed. "Yeah," he said. "But we already knew that, and we're here anyway. We'll see what we can work out."

The dry riverbed lost itself among the plains. The skirts began to ring on rocks, the heavy debris dumped here at the last spate and not yet covered by sand. Lamartiere edged *Hoodoo* northward to where the ground was smoother. The AI reconfigured the course slightly; the ETA changed again.

Hoodoo roared through the starlit night, heading at speed toward the next way-station on a road to nowhere.

✧ ✧ ✧

It was an hour past dawn. The low sun deepened the color of the red cliffs and the red sand into which those cliffs decayed. By midday the sun would turn the sky brassy and bleach every hue to a ghost of itself.

The shrine was in the Boukasset where four generations ago Catherine had given birth to the child who became Bishop Moses, to whom God revealed the foundations of the Mosite faith. The site had been a pilgrimage center during peacetime, but Lamartiere hadn't been religious in that fashion.

Since Lamartiere learned what had happened to his sister Celine, he hadn't been religious in any way at all; but now there was no way out of the course he'd chosen in the days when he could believe in a future.

The first sign of habitation was the line of conical shelters, two or three abreast, which wound across the plain. Low hills lay in the distance to east and west, and a jagged sandstone slope rose immediately north of the site.

The shrine itself was a fortress walled in the russet stone of the overlooking cliff. It was built on a lower slope where the rise could be accommodated by a single terrace, but the gullied rock behind it rose at 1:2 or even 1:1.

The spire of a church showed above the enclosure's ten-meter sidewalls. A bell there rang when *Hoodoo* appeared out of the east, trailing a great plume of dust.

Lamartiere disengaged the AI and began slowing the tank by turning the fan nacelles vertical instead of tilting them to the rear. *Hoodoo*'s enormous inertia meant control inputs had to be added well in advance.

"They grow lemon trees in those shelters," Dr Clargue said. He sounded puzzled at something. "The plantings are laid out over an underground aquifer, but without protection the wind would scour the leaves and even bark off the trees."

He paused, then added, "There weren't nearly as many trees when I came here twelve years ago. Only a handful of Brothers tended to the shrine then."

Lamartiere guided the tank past the cones straggling as

they followed a seam in the bedrock. Overlying sand kept
the water from evaporating. He knew that lemons from the
Boukasset had a reputation for flavor, but because he'd
never visited the region he hadn't wondered how terrain
so barren could grow citrus fruit.

Hoodoo had slowed to a crawl when she was still a hundred meters from the high walls of the shrine. Lamartiere
cut his fan speed but angled the nacelles sternward again.
The tank slid the remainder of the way forward under perfect control.

Lamartiere ruefully congratulated himself on his skill. He
was probably the only person in the Boukasset who knew
how difficult it was to drive a 170-tonne air-cushion vehicle.

He slid open his hatch. What looked from a distance
like the shrine's entrance had been closed by sandstone
blocks many years in the past. A woman leaned over the
battlements. Beside her, a basket hung on a crane extending
from the wall. A great geared wheel within raised and
lowered it. The basket was apparently the only way in and
out of the shrine.

"Tell your leader that we need help to spread the
camouflage cover over this tank," Lamartiere called to the
woman. "Otherwise we'll be spotted if the government
overflies us."

Men and women were approaching from the lemon
orchard, though the sprawled extent of the plantings meant
it would be half an hour before the more distant folk
reached the shrine. There were hundreds of people, far
more than Lamartiere had expected.

"The Brothers have been sheltering refugees," Clargue
realized aloud. He sat on the edge of his hatch, his legs
dangling down the turret's smooth iridium armor.

Lamartiere looked up at his companion and hid a
frown. The doctor had always seemed frail. Now he was
skeletal, worn to the bone by strain and the frustration
of not being able to find the command that would transfer
ammunition and permit *Hoodoo* to use her devastating
weaponry.

"Go away!" the woman shouted. Her left hand was

bandaged. "Go back to the hell you came from and leave us alone!"

An old man in black robes and a pillbox hat appeared on the battlements beside her. He and the woman held a brief discussion while Lamartiere kept silent.

The woman unpinned the gearwheel, letting the basket wobble down. The man held his hat on with one hand as he bent forward. "Please," he said. "If you gentlemen will come up, it will be easier for us to discuss your presence."

Lamartiere looked at Clargue. "One of us should stay with . . ." he said.

The doctor smiled. "Yes, of course," he said, "but you should carry out the negotiations. I wouldn't know what to say to them."

"And you think I do?" Lamartiere said; but he knew Clargue was right. The doctor was smarter and older and better educated; but this was war, and Clargue was utterly a man of peace.

Denis Lamartiere was . . . not a man of peace. He and Clargue were operating in a world at war, now, however much both of them might hate it.

Lamartiere got into the basket. He let the sway of it ratcheting upward soothe his tension.

The basket was still several feet below the stone coping when the pulley touched the fiber cage connecting the rim to the draw rope. The old man helped Lamartiere onto the battlements. Normally Lamartiere would have scrambled over easily by himself, but his head was swaying with fatigue even though the basket was steady again.

The old man wore a clean white tunic with a red sash under the black robe. Though his beard was gray, not white, his face bore the lines of someone much older than Lamartiere would have guessed from a distance.

"Sorry, ah, father?" Lamartiere said. "You're in charge of the shrine?"

"I'm Father Blenis," the old man said. "We try to work cooperatively here in the presence of the Blessed

Catherine, but because of my age the others let me speak for us all."

"It's not your age!" the woman said. She'd pinned the ratchet, locking the wheel so that a breeze didn't send the basket hurtling down uncontrolled. She looked at Lamartiere and continued, "Father Blenis is a saint. He's taken us in after your kind would have let us all die—once you'd stolen everything we had."

"Marie," Father Blenis said. "This gentleman—"

He looked at Lamartiere and raised an eyebrow.

"Lamartiere, Denis Lamartiere," Lamartiere said. "Dr. Clargue and I won't stay any longer than we need to, ah, do some work on *Hoodoo*. On our tank."

Three of the people coming in from the field were nearing the base of the walls. A thin younger man was pushing ahead of a woman while a much larger fellow clumped along close behind.

"It's the job of whoever last comes up the walls to lift the next person," Marie said with a challenging glare at Lamartiere. He first guessed she was well into middle age, but she might be considerably younger. Hunger and hard use could have carved the lines in her face.

And anger. Anger was as damaging to a woman's appearance as a spray of acid.

"Yes, all right," Lamartiere said. He was a little steadier now. Just getting out of the tank and its omnipresent vibration had helped, though he knew he was both weak and desperately tired.

He removed the pin and lifted the ratchet pawl, controlling the basket with his other hand on the crank. "Don't you have any power equipment here?"

"You should ask!" Marie spat. Pus had seeped through the bandage on her left hand; it needed to be changed again. "When it's your kind who stole it!"

"Marie," Father Blenis murmured. He put his own frail hands on the crank beside Lamartiere's, silently rebuking the woman for her lack of charity.

"We'd ordered a winch and solar power unit for it, Mr. Lamartiere," he explained, "but it didn't arrive. In general the parties who rule the region allow us to trade unhindered so long as we pay taxes to them—"

"I'll handle it, father," Marie said contritely. She patted both Blenis and Lamartiere away from the winch. The process of moving hundreds of people in and out of the fortress must be a very time-consuming one, though having each person lift the next one kept it from being an unbearable physical burden.

Blenis stepped aside, gesturing Lamartiere with him. Lamartiere would have protested, but he was suddenly so dizzy that he sat down in order not to fall.

"When we order something that looks particularly enticing, though," Blenis went on, "it may not arrive. By living simply here we avoid such problems for the most part."

He grinned. "Another example of how those who follow God's tenets avoid temporal concerns," he said. It took Lamartiere a moment to realize that he was joking.

There was angry shouting at the base of the walls. Concern wiped the smile from the Father's face. He leaned over to see what was happening.

"It's not taxes," Marie muttered to Lamartiere. "It's pure theft, and by both sides. But what can *we* do since you have the guns, eh?"

"Rasile, Louise," Father Blenis called. His voice had penetrating volume when he chose to use it. Living in this windswept wasteland would teach a man to speak with authority. "Let Pietro come up first, then he can lift both of you together. Let us leave struggle outside our community."

"I haven't robbed anybody," Lamartiere said. He'd killed. Some of those he'd killed had probably been civilians as innocent as the refugees here at the shrine, but even in his present exhausted state it made him angry to be accused of things he hadn't done.

He shook his head, trying to clear it of the hot white fuzz that clogged his thoughts. "You pay taxes to the government, then?" he said. "I didn't know Carcassone had officials in the Boukasset nowadays."

Marie grunted with the effort of hauling up the first of the civilians below. Before she could catch her breath to speak, Father Blenis said, "There aren't regular officials, or regular troops either. The government sent a group of former rebels, Ralliers, into the Boukasset under a Captain de Laburat."

He smiled again. The Father's consistent good-humor was a shock to Lamartiere. For years most of the people he'd been around were soured by war and fury.

"I'm not sure whether the government was trying to impose its will or merely hoping to prevent Maury from having things all his own way." Blenis continued. "In any case, Maury's band and the Ralliers under de Laburat decided to cooperate rather than fight. A model for the whole planet, wouldn't you say?"

The heavyset man got out of the basket. Lamartiere had seen more obvious signs of intelligence on the faces of sheep. Marie stepped away from the crank.

"Pietro," Father Blenis said, "bring up Rasile and your sister, please."

To Lamartiere he went on, "Pietro's strength has been a great help to our community since he and Louise arrived last month."

Marie turned and sniffed. Her good hand played with the stained dressings of the other.

"Look, father," Lamartiere said. He spoke toward his hands in his lap because he was too tired to raise his eyes as he knew he should. The rhythmic squeals of the winch were starting to put him to sleep. "I don't mean to disturb your peace, but we have to stay here until we get in touch with Maury."

He shook his head again. It didn't help him think. "Or with the Council in Goncourt if they've got a better idea," he said. "We're going to need food and water, and if you don't help us get *Hoodoo* under cover you're going to learn how much the government cares for your neutrality as soon as the first drone comes over."

With Pietro's strength on the crank, the basket had already reached the battlements. The slim man and the woman, Louise, got out on opposite sides with the tense hostility of rival dogs. They looked remarkably fit in contrast to Marie, but neither was a person Lamartiere would have chosen to know in peacetime. He supposed that pimps and hard-faced whores sometimes became refugees also.

"Carcassone doesn't fly anything over the Boukasset," Rasile said. Lamartiere blinked in surprise to hear so throaty and pleasant a voice coming from the rat-faced civilian. "If they do, Maury shoots them down. Or de Laburat does it himself."

Marie stepped forward. "Look, you don't belong here!" she said harshly to Lamartiere. "We'll give you water, and you can have food too. I suppose you'll like the taste even better because you're snatching it out of the mouths of widows and orphans, won't you? But take your tank and your war away from us—or die, that would be fine. That would be even better!"

"Marie," Father Blenis said. His tone was sharper than Lamartiere had heard from him previously, though it was still mild after the rasping anger of the others who'd been speaking. "Mr. Lamartiere has come as a distressed traveller. You can see how tired he is. The Blessed Catherine has never turned such folk away in the past, as you well know."

"He's a soldier!" she said. "He came in a tank!"

"We won't let him bring weapons within the walls," Blenis replied. With the gentle humor Lamartiere was learning to recognize he added, "Especially his tank. But he and his companion are welcome to the hospitality we offer to anyone passing by."

Houses two and three stories high were built around the interior of the shrine. The rooms had external staircases and windows opening onto the central courtyard where an herb garden grew. Lamartiere could see two well copings and, at the upper end of the courtyard, a stone trough into which water trickled from an ancient bronze pipe.

Several younger women holding infants stood in the doorways, watching the group around the winch. All of them had the same worn look that Lamartiere had noticed in Marie. A woman alone—and worse, a woman with small children—would have had a tough time crossing a wasteland ruled by rival gangs. There were, quite literally, fates worse than death, because the dead didn't wake from a screaming nightmare before every dawn.

The basket was tight against the pulley. Pietro still held the crank, possibly because nobody'd told him to do otherwise. Someone shouted from below. Pietro looked at Louise, who snapped, "Yes, yes, bring the next one up. For God's sake!"

"Louise?" Blenis said.

The woman grimaced. She might have been attractive once, but the glint of her eyes was a worse disfigurement than the old scar on her right cheek. "Sorry, father," she said. "I'll watch my language."

Lamartiere tried to stand. He didn't belong in a place where people worried about taking the name of God in vain.

"Look, the hell with you," he said. He was furious because of frustration at his inability to accomplish anything he could feel good about. "We'll go, just get us water."

The world went white. Lamartiere was lying on the stone battlements. He didn't remember how he got there. "We'll leave you alone," he tried to whisper.

"Marie, make a bed for Mr. Lamartiere here," Father Blenis murmured through the buzzing white blur. "Later on we can consider the future."

Lamartiere awoke to see Father Blenis rearranging a slatted screen so that the lowering sun didn't fall on the sleeper's face. The rattle and flickering light had brought Lamartiere up from the depths to which exhaustion had plunged him. Near the winch a young woman nursed her infant while an older child played at her feet.

"Oh God, help me," Lamartiere groaned. There was nothing blasphemous in the words. His every muscle ached and his head throbbed in tune with his heartbeat, though the haloes of light framing objects settled back to normal vision after a few moments.

"I'm sorry, I didn't mean to wake you," Blenis said. "Can you drink something, or . . . ?"

"Please," Lamartiere said. He sat up, ignoring the pain because he *had* to get moving. He had no traumatic injury, just the cumulative effects of a day and a half spent as a component of a tank.

Hoodoo's metal, seals and insulation became worn in the course of service. A bearing in Number 7 drive fan would be repacked if the vehicle were in Brione for depot maintenance, and the lip of the skirts needed recontouring if not replacement.

The crew needed down-time also, but they wouldn't have gotten it in the field any more than the tank itself would. Heth and Stegner would have gone on until the mission was accomplished or something irretrievably broke.

Lamartiere was in the same situation, except that by now he was quite certain his mission—defeat of the Carcassone government—could never be accomplished. The only question was whether he or *Hoodoo* fell to ruin first.

Father Blenis held out a gourd cup. Lamartiere took it from the old man and drank unaided. The contents were milk, not water; goat's milk, he supposed, since he'd seen goats scrambling about the hillsides nearby. It was hard to imagine that the Boukasset had enough vegetation even for goats. No doubt they, like the shrine's human residents, had simple tastes.

Lamartiere looked over the wall coping. The camouflage tarp was stretched between poles and hooks hammered into wall crevices, so from this angle only *Hoodoo*'s bow was visible. The fabric provided a radar barrier and a sophisticated matrix which mimicked the thermal signature of the materials to either side. Aerial reconnaissance would show only a blotch of rock against the wall of the shrine.

Most of the residents were at work again in the orchard, either picking ripe lemons or building additional drystone shelters. The latter work was performed by gangs of refugees, but a black-robed Brother oversaw each group.

A few civilians sat or stood near *Hoodoo*'s bow. Dr. Clargue was in the driver's hatch, draining the sore on a child's shin while the mother looked on. A slightly older girl stood on a headlight bracket and, with a self-important expression, held the exiguous medical kit Clargue had brought with him from Pamiers. The equipment would have slipped down the bow slope if the doctor had laid it directly on the armor.

"I've got to go down and spell Clargue," Lamartiere said. "Has he been awake all the time?"

"In a moment," Father Blenis said. He smiled. "Your companion has been a godsend. We've never had a doctor in residence here, and some of the distressed folk coming for shelter recently have needed help beyond what I and the other Brothers are trained to provide. Regrettably, medical supplies don't reach us here."

Lamartiere scowled. He got carefully to his feet by bracing himself on the stone. As he slept the residents had slid a blanket-wrapped mattress of springy brush beneath him. It was the best bed than Lamartiere had had since he thundered out of Brione in the stolen tank.

Lamartiere's discomfort came from being shaken for over a day in the strait confines of *Hoodoo*'s driving compartment. Dr. Clargue understood the tank's software better than Lamartiere could ever hope to do, but driving a tank was a specialized skill that Clargue had never learned. They couldn't switch positions during the high-speed run into the Boukasset.

Lamartiere paused; he'd intended to climb into the basket, but his body wasn't quite ready. "You're in regular touch with the rest of Ambiorix, then?" he asked.

"A truck comes every week to pick up our lemons and bring us the things we've ordered with the proceeds," Blenis explained. "An aircraft would be better but as Rasile said, no one flies in the Boukasset. Maury and de Laburat both import very sophisticated weaponry, much of it by starship. Not medical supplies, though; at least not to share with us."

He shook his head. "I'm not complaining," he said. "God has poured her bounty over us with great generosity. We give thanks daily that She allows us to help so many of Her afflicted."

"I'll go down now and send the doctor up," Lamartiere said. "He needs sleep at least as much as I did."

He stepped into the basket. The woman moved the slung infant to her right hip so that she could grip the crank.

"You know, all people really need is peace," Father Blenis said. "I regret that this isn't understood more widely. Ambiorix would be a better place."

Lamartiere walked to *Hoodoo*'s bow, feeling stronger with each step. He wasn't looking forward to getting inside again, but perhaps he wouldn't have to if he stayed close to the hatch.

Dr. Clargue was rebandaging Marie's hand. "The dry air is an advantage," he said, pitching his voice to greet Lamartiere as well as speaking to his patient. "Germs don't find it any more attractive than I do. Though I'd prefer to have a greater supply of antibiotic cream as well."

Rasile, Louise, and the woman's dimwitted brother—if Pietro really was her brother—loitered near the tank. Unlike Marie, none of them had any obvious medical problems.

"You three," Lamartiere ordered harshly. Whatever they were doing, it wasn't together: Louise and Rasile liked each other as little as Lamartiere liked either one of them. "Get out of here. Either out in the orchard or inside the shrine, I don't care which."

Pietro was in a different category. You couldn't dislike him any more than you could dislike a rock, though a rock could be dangerous enough in the wrong circumstances.

"Who do you think you are, giving me orders?" Rasile said.

"The guy who's going to be testing *Hoodoo*'s drive fans in a moment," Lamartiere said as he hopped onto the bow slope. "If you're within a hundred meters when I crank up, there won't be anything left of you but a smear by the time I shut down again. Just a friendly warning."

If trouble started, Lamartiere needed to be in the driver's seat. He wished Clargue weren't there now, but the doctor wouldn't have been able to work on his patients from the cupola.

The refugees drifted toward the orchard instead of pushing matters. Louise and Pietro walked together, while

Rasile stayed twenty meters distant in space and a lot farther away in spirit.

Lamartiere supposed they'd been hoping to steal equipment. Tanks in the field were generally festooned with gear, but Heth and Stegner had stripped *Hoodoo* to be loaded on a starship before Lamartiere drove her out of the base. He and Clargue had only the clothes they stood in, but Lamartiere still didn't want the likes of those three rummaging around inside the tank.

Clargue got out of the compartment very stiffly. "I'm sorry, Denis," he said. "I should have been working on the software, but I found I was a doctor before I was a tank crewman."

"Go get a bath and some sleep, doctor," Lamartiere said. "There's plenty of water here, for our purposes anyway."

He gripped Clargue's hand to permit him to negotiate the iridium slope under control. "You did just what you should've done. I wish I could say the same."

Clargue trudged toward the basket, carrying his medical kit. Marie still stood close to the tank. "I'll leave in a moment," she said. "I wanted to apologize for what I said when you arrived. Dr. Clargue is a good man, and he tells me that you are too."

Lamartiere snorted. "Then he knows something I don't," he said. He squatted on the edge of the hatch instead of lowering his body inside. The driver's seat had almost infinite possible adjustments, but at the end of the long run there was no part of Lamartiere's body that hadn't been rubbed or pounded.

"Look," he said, "I'm sorry we're here. I'm sorry about a lot of things, though I know that doesn't make them any better. If Maury can get us ammo, then we'll go back across the mountains to where we can maybe do something about the war. Or whatever the Council decides it wants."

"Maury won't give you anything unless there's advantage in it for him," the woman said. "The last thing he wants is for the war to end. He and de Laburat are making too good a thing about being the only authorities in the Boukasset."

Despite Marie's initial comment, she didn't show any sign of wanting to leave. Lamartiere was glad of her company.

"They manufacture drugs, you know," Marie said. She glared at Lamartiere as though he was responsible for the situation. "Most of the output goes off-planet, but I suppose there's enough left over for Ambiorix as well."

"I wasn't aware of that, no," Lamartiere said evenly. It made sense, though. He should have wondered what Maury traded to the smugglers in exchange for his gang's weaponry. Goat-hair textiles or even the subtly flavored lemons of the Boukasset didn't buy many powerguns and antiaircraft missiles.

"I was at one of the factories for three months," Marie said. Her tone was harsh, but Lamartiere now saw the misery in her eyes. "Not as staff—they have off-planet technicians for that. As entertainment. Until they raided some other family of refugees and replaced me with someone who was in better shape. I came to the shrine instead of dying in the desert."

"I'm responsible for the things I've done," Lamartiere said. He deliberately met the woman's fierce glare. "I won't apologize for things other people have done. However much I may regret them."

Marie nodded. Her expression relaxed slightly. "I just wanted you to know the sort of people you'll be dealing with," she said. "And don't misunderstand me: de Laburat's gang ran the factory where I was held. But they're both the same. They and all their men are demons."

The sun was almost on the rim of the western hills. The shrine's residents were coming back from the lemon orchard, carrying their tools. Some of them were even singing.

Over the southern horizon roared a score of vehicles, both wheeled and air-cushion. They bristled with weapons. Dust mounted in a pall that turned blood red in the light of the lowering sun.

The rulers of the Boukasset were paying a call on *Hoodoo*.

✦   ✦   ✦

Lamartiere slid into the driver's hatch. His body no longer ached. He switched on the fans and checked the readouts. All were within parameters except Number 7, and that bearing wasn't of immediate concern. He blipped the throttle once, then let the blades drop to a humming idle.

A blast of fine grit sprayed beneath the skirt at the pressure spike in the plenum chamber. It staggered Marie as she backed away from the vehicle. Lamartiere was sorry, but he didn't have a lot of time. Worse things were likely to happen soon anyway.

The vehicles approaching in line abreast were already within a klick of the shrine. Even without magnification Lamartiere could tell that they were overloaded, wallowing over irregularities in the desert's surface.

He brought up the gunnery controls on the lower of the compartment's two displays. It was impossible for one person to drive and handle *Hoodoo*'s armament simultaneously, but though he was prepared to move the tank Lamartiere didn't expect to need to.

He hoped he wouldn't be shooting either, not when he had only seven 2cm rounds in the tribarrel's ready magazine and no ammunition at all for the main gun.

In the middle of the oncoming vehicles was a three-axle truck which flew a pennant of some sort. The windshield was covered with metal plates; the driver could only see through a slit in his armor. That was just barely better than driving blindfolded. If Lamartiere had been in either of the adjacent vehicles, he'd have given the truck at least fifty meters clearance to avoid a collision.

The truck's bed was armored with flat slabs of concrete, a makeshift that would stop small arms but not much more. Three launching tubes were bracketed to either side; Lamartiere couldn't tell whether they held antitank missiles or unguided bombardment rockets. On top was a turret that must have come from a light military vehicle: it mounted an automatic cannon and a coaxial machine gun, both of them electromotive weapons.

The remainder of the vehicles were similar though

smaller: four- and six-wheeled trucks, massively overloaded with men, weapons, and armor, as well as half a dozen air-cushion vehicles of moderate capacity. The latter weren't armored or they wouldn't have been able to move. The wheeled vehicles' panoply of mild steel and concrete was next to valueless anyway.

Lamartiere had fought among the guerrillas of the Western District before the Council picked him to steal a tank for the rebellion. The rebels had tried to convert civilian trucks into armored fighting vehicles, but they'd immediately given up the practice as a suicidal waste. In combat against purpose-built military equipment, makeshifts were merely tombs for their crews. They were good for nothing but to threaten civilians and rival groups of undisciplined thugs.

Which was obviously what these were being used for.

Well, Denis Lamartiere was neither of those things. He rested his hands on the control yoke. His index finger was a centimeter away from the firing control on the screen in front of him. To his surprise, he was smiling.

The vehicles halted near the base of the shrine, disgorging men and a few women. Their clothing was a mixture of military uniforms, the loose robes of the Boukasset, and tawdry accents of Carcassone finery. A band of pirates, Lamartiere thought; about two hundred of them all told.

The residents still at a distance either stopped where they were or returned to the orchard which provided concealment if not shelter. Civilians who'd already reached the shrine squeezed against the walls, their eyes on the armed gang.

The basket was descending; Dr. Clargue was in it, doing what he saw as his duty. Lamartiere wished the doctor had stayed safe in the fortress, but there was no help for it now.

The big truck pulled up twenty meters from *Hoodoo*. Grit sprayed up from the tires, but the breeze carried it back away from the tank.

A man nearly two meters tall and broad in proportion got

out of the door set in the concrete armor of the bed. He
wore a blue and gold uniform—a military uniform, Lamartiere supposed, though he couldn't imagine what military
force wore something so absurdly ornate. There was even
a saber in a gilded sheath dangling from a shoulder belt.

"My name's Maury!" he called to Lamartiere. He put
his hands on his hips. "I own everything in the Boukasset,
so I guess I own you too."

"No," said Lamartiere. He spoke through the conformal
speakers in *Hoodoo's* hull. His voice boomed across the
desert, echoing from the cliffs and tall stone walls of the
shrine. "You don't own us."

Maury laughed cheerfully. Lamartiere's amplified voice
had made some members of the gang flinch or even hit
the ground, but their leader seemed unafraid. "I like a
boy with spirit," he said. "Come down out of that thing
and we'll talk about how we can all win this one."

"We can discuss anything we need just like we are,"
Lamartiere replied. "You might say I've gotten used to
being in the driver's seat."

The big man chuckled again. He sauntered toward
Hoodoo.

"I said we're fine like we are!" Lamartiere repeated. "I
can hear anything you've got to say from where you're
standing."

Maury had fair hair and the pale complexion that goes
with it. His expression didn't change, but a flush climbed
his cheeks like fluid in a thermometer on a hot day.

"I got a message from the Council that they'd like me to
give you a hand, boy," he said. "I don't take orders from
Goncourt but I'm willing to be neighborly. Thing is, the way
you're acting don't put me in a very neighborly frame of
mind."

The rest of the gang didn't know how to take what was
going on. The thugs seemed more nervous than angry. A
hundred-and-seventy-tonne tank was impressive even if it
were shut down. When purring and under the control of
someone who sounded unfriendly, it was enough to frighten
most people.

"I was told you might help me with supplies," Lamartiere said. He kept the emotion out of his voice, but the tank's speakers threw his words like the judgment of God. "Now that I'm here, I get the impression that any help you gave me would come at a price I wouldn't be willing to pay. Why don't you go back where you came from before there's an accident?"

Maury laughed again. His heart wasn't in it, but even as bravado it took courage. Most of his gang was festooned with weapons—there were at least a dozen 2cm powerguns whose ammo would have filled *Hoodoo*'s ready magazine if Lamartiere had dared ask for it—but Maury himself wore only the saber.

"We haven't even talked price," the big man said, almost cajoling. "Believe me, you'll do fine with your share. The Boukasset may not look like much—"

He gestured broadly. The gold braid on his cuff glowed in the sun's last ruddy light.

"—but my friends don't lack for anything. Anything at all!"

There was a commotion near the wall of the shrine. Lamartiere risked a quick glance sideward. He could drop his seat into the driver's compartment and button the hatch up over himself, but that would give Maury the psychological edge.

One of Maury's men had backed a woman against the stone. She shouted and tried to move sideways. The man caught her arm and lifted it, drawing her closer to him.

"Let go of her!" Dr. Clargue said as he stepped toward the pair. The gangster shoved the woman violently toward Clargue, then stepped back and unslung a submachine gun.

"Freeze!" Lamartiere said. His shout made dust in the air quiver.

"Let her go, Schwitzer," Maury said. His bellow was dwarfed by the echoes of Lamartiere's amplified voice. "For now at least. This is just a neighborly visit."

He turned to Lamartiere again and continued, "But let's say for the sake of discussion that you *did* want to make something out of this, kid—just how did you plan to do that? Because I know from Goncourt that you don't have any ammo for those pretty guns of yours."

Cursing under his breath the *idiots* on the Council who'd given this man a hold over him, Lamartiere slid the targeting pipper onto Maury's face in the gunnery display. The turret whined, bringing the 20cm main gun squarely in line with the self-styled chief of the Boukasset.

"I can't swear on my sister's grave," Lamartiere said, "because she doesn't have one. But by her soul in the arms of God, I swear to you that *Hoodoo* carries ten thousand rounds for the tribarrel and two hundred for the main gun. Shall I demonstrate for the rest of your men?"

The main gun's barrel was a polished iridium tunnel. Maury was no coward, but what he saw staring at him was not merely death but annihilation. After a frozen moment's indecision he turned his back. He took off his stiff cap and slammed it into the ground.

"Mount up!" Maury snarled. "We're moving out!"

He stalked to the armored truck. His men obeyed with the disorganized certainty of pebbles rolling downhill. One of them scuttled over to retrieve the cap, then dropped it again and ran off when he made the mistake of looking up at the 20cm bore.

Maury halted at the door. Drivers were starting their engines: turbines, diesels, and even a pair of whining electrics. Maury pointed an arm the size of a bridge truss at Lamartiere and said, "Maybe you'll come to talk to me when you've thought about things. And maybe we'll come to you again first!"

He got in and his motley squadron started to pull away from the shrine. The air-cushion vehicles merely swapped ends, but those with wheels turned awkwardly or even backed and filled. The bolted-on armor interfered both with visibility and their turning circles.

Dr. Clargue walked over to the tank's bow. He looked wobbly. Lamartiere himself felt as though he'd been bathed in ice water. He was shivering with reaction and had to take his hands away from the controls to keep from accidentally doing something he'd regret.

The gang vehicles headed south in a ragged line, looking like survivors from a rout. The leaders continued to draw farther ahead of the others. Maury's own overloaded truck wobbled in the rear of the procession.

"Doctor," Lamartiere said. He'd switched off the speakers, so he had to raise his voice to be heard over *Hoodoo's* idling fans. "There's self-defense strips just above the skirts. They're supposed to blast pellets into incoming missiles, but I don't know if they're live. Can you check that for me?"

"Yes," Clargue said. "I'll do that now."

Lamartiere reached out a hand to help the doctor clamber up the bow slope. Before he got into the turret Clargue paused and said, "I worried when I stood watch alone, Denis, because I wasn't sure I'd be able to use a weapon. I was trained to save lives, as you know. But I think I can do that too, if I must."

"I know what you mean," Lamartiere said. "Look, keep looking for the transfer command so we can use the ammo in the storage magazines if we have to. *When* we have to. Maury'll decide to call my bluff before long."

"Yes, I'll keep looking," the doctor said in a weary tone.

"I wish to God I was in a different place," Lamartiere whispered. "I wish to God I was in a different *life*."

The stars shone through the dry air in brilliant profusion. *Hoodoo's* displays careted movement, but Lamartiere had already heard the winch squeal. He focused the upper screen on the descending basket, using light enhancement at 40:1 magnification.

"It's Marie," he said to Clargue. "She's carrying a couple buckets on a pole across her shoulders."

"Ah," said the doctor without noticeable interest. The turret's yellow, low-intensity lighting was on as Clargue searched the database for the command that would turn *Hoodoo* from a vehicle into a *fighting* vehicle.

Lamartiere was letting the screens' own dim ambiance provide the only illumination for the driver's station. He could have slept beside the tank if he'd wanted to, setting an audible alarm to warn him of motion; but so long as Clargue was working, Lamartiere preferred to be alert also.

He got out of the hatch and slid to the ground. The smooth iridium hull reflected starlight well enough to show him in silhouette. Marie stepped from the basket and said, "I brought you some food and water. Bread and vegetable stew—we're vegetarians here. But it's fresh and hot."

Lamartiere took the pole from her. He'd eaten as much as he wanted earlier in the evening. The pounding drive had left him too run down to be really hungry, and it was even an effort to drink though he knew his body needed the fluids.

"Hot food, doctor," he called. "Want to come out, or shall I bring it in to you?"

"Perhaps in a while, Denis," replied Clargue's voice with a hint of irritation. "I will run this sequence before I stop, if God and the world permit me."

Lamartiere set the buckets on the ground and squatted beside them; the tank's armor slanted too sharply to use it as a ledge. "Thanks," he said to Marie as he took one of the pair of bottles from the left-hand basket. The loaf in the other one smelled surprisingly good.

"Government radio says they're launching an attack on Goncourt," Marie said as she sat across from him. "I don't know whether that's true or not."

The bottle contained water with just enough lemon juice to give it flavor. Lamartiere drank, let his stomach settle, and drank more.

"The other is goat's milk," Marie said. "I've come to like the taste."

"I didn't know about Goncourt," Lamartiere said as he lowered the bottle. "I didn't think to listen to the commercial bands. That would explain why nobody's contacted us the way they were supposed to. To tell us what the fuck we're supposed to do!"

"What *are* you going to do?" the woman asked quietly.

Lamartiere shrugged. He broke off a piece of bread and dipped it into the stew. "We won't stay here much longer," he said. He wished he had a real answer to the question, but he wished a lot of things.

"We have our own garden inside the walls," Marie said. "We buy the grain for the bread, though. It's the main thing we do buy."

"We're just making things worse," Lamartiere said. He was glad for someone to talk to, to talk *at*. "The government was wrong and *stupid* to say that unless you did what the Synod said you weren't a citizen, you were only a taxpayer. But this war has made things so much worse. Me stealing *Hoodoo* has . . . got a lot of people killed that didn't have to be. Including my sister."

Marie shrugged. "I don't know who's right," she said. "I never did. It's easier to see who's wrong, and in the Boukasset that's pretty much everybody with a gun. Pretty much."

She stood. "I'll take back the containers in the morning," she said. "People like you and me can't change anything."

To her back Lamartiere said, "I changed things when I stole this tank, Marie. I changed things when I drove it here and put you all in danger. I want to start changing things for the better!"

Hoodoo's warning chime sounded. Lamartiere was climbing the bow slope before he was really aware of his movement. Consciously he viewed the tank more as Purgatory than as shelter, but he'd dived into the driver's compartment so often recently that reflex sent him there at the first hint of danger.

He brought up the fans before he checked to see what movement the sensors had found; he brought up the gunnery screen also, even though the weapons were more easily controlled from the fighting compartment where Dr. Clargue was. Clargue was the rebellion's best hope to decipher *Hoodoo*'s coded systems, but Denis Lamartiere was far the better choice to use the tank's weaponry.

An air-cushion jeep carrying a single person was coming out of the hills three kilometers west of the shrine. Its headlights were on.

So far as Lamartiere could tell, neither the vehicle nor the driver carried a weapon. He was using 100:1

magnification, as much as he trusted when coupled with light enhancement. Anything higher was a guess by the AI, and Lamartiere preferred his own instincts to machine intelligence when his life depended on it.

"What do you want me to do?" Clargue asked over the intercom.

"Close your hatch and warn me if anything happens," Lamartiere said. "This guy is too harmless to be out at night if he didn't have a hell of a lot lined up behind him."

"There's no one else in the direction he came from," Clargue reported. "I'll continue to monitor the sensors, but otherwise I'll not interfere with your business."

After a brief mental debate, Lamartiere raised his seat to await the visitor with his head out of the hatch. Clargue would warn him if *Hoodoo's* electronics showed a danger that unaided eyes would miss.

After hesitating again, he cut the drive fans back to their minimum speed. A normal idle sent ringing harmonics through the surrounding air. To talk over that level of background noise, the parties would have had to shout. Shouting triggered anger and hostility deep in people's subbrains, even if consciously they would have preferred to avoid it.

If there'd been two figures in the jeep, Lamartiere would have guessed they were Heth and Stegner, *Hoodoo's* original crew. He'd seen the mercenaries at the Lystra River, observing the battle from a similar vehicle. He supposed they were hoping to steal back their tank.

At this point he'd have rather that they'd driven *Hoodoo* aboard a starship and lifted for Beresford, 300 light-years distant, the way they'd planned to do. Then Lamartiere wouldn't have had to make decisions when all the alternatives seemed equally bad. It was too late to go back, though.

The jeep halted ten meters from *Hoodoo's* bow. The driver shut off his turbine and stood. "May I approach you, Mr. Lamartiere?" he asked. His voice was cultured but a little too high-pitched. "Or is it Dr. Clargue?"

"I'm Lamartiere," Lamartiere said. "And you can come closer, yeah."

The man walked to the tank, moving with an easy grace. Lamartiere heard the winch squeal once more, then stop. Marie must have reached the battlements, but he didn't look up to be sure.

"My name is Alexis de Laburat," the man said. He was a slim, pantherlike fellow with a strikingly handsome face. His left cheek bore a serpentine scar and there was a patch over that eye. "I've come alone and unarmed to offer you a business proposition."

"I've heard about your business," Lamartiere said, more harshly than he'd intended. He was remembering what Marie had told him. "No thanks. And I think you'd better go now."

"I was born a Mosite and fought in the rebellion," de Laburat said. "I rallied to the government and fought for it when I saw the rebellion was doomed to fail; so did the other men under my command. But what I'm offering now, Mr. Lamartiere, is peace."

De Laburat's fingers toyed with the tip of his neat moustache. "As well as enough money to keep you and the doctor comfortably on any world to which you choose to emigrate. Obviously you can't stay on Ambiorix unless you join me, which I don't suppose you'd care to do."

"I told you, we have no business with you!" Lamartiere said.

The Rallier shook his head. "Think clearly," he said. "I know you're a clever man or you'd never have gotten this far. The Council wouldn't be able to use this tank, even if you were able to get ammunition for it. The rebellion is *over*. Goncourt will fall within the week. Though the Council will probably relocate to some cave in the hills, they'll control nothing at all."

De Laburat smiled. "You're the cause of that, you know," he said. He was trying to be pleasant, but his voice scraped Lamartiere's nerves to hear. "The attack on Goncourt has been very expensive. The government probably wouldn't have had the courage to attempt it except that they were afraid to let the embers of the rebellion smolder on when the Mosites had this superweapon. As they thought."

"You're not part of this war," Lamartiere said. "You've made that clear, you and Maury both. I am. You came unarmed so I won't hurt you—but you'd better leave now or you'll have to walk back, because I'll have driven *Hoodoo* over your jeep."

"Listen to me!" de Laburat said. He had to look up because Lamartiere was in the vehicle. He still gave the impression of a panther, but a caged one.

"*I'll* protect the Boukasset," de Laburat said. "The government knows I'm no threat to it. They won't come here to chase me, and the Synod won't try to impose its definition of heresy here while I have this tank!"

"Protect the Boukasset under yourself," Lamartiere said.

De Laburat chuckled. "You've met Maury," he said. "He has a strong back and about enough intellect to pull on his boots in the morning. Would you entrust the Shrine of the Blessed Catherine to him? And even if you did, one of his own men will shoot him in the back in a few weeks or months, as surely as the sun rises tomorrow."

"Go away," Lamartiere said. In sudden fury he repeated, "Go away, or by God I'll kill you now so that I can say there's one good deed to balance against all the harm I've done in this life!"

De Laburat nodded with stiff propriety. "Good day, Mr. Lamartiere," he said. "I hope you'll reconsider while there's still time."

Lamartiere watched the Rallier drive back across the desert the way he'd come. The jeep's headlights cut a wedge across the rocks and scrub, disappearing at last through a cleft in the low hills.

"What do we do now?" Dr. Clargue asked quietly.

"I wish I knew," Lamartiere said. "I wish to God I knew."

He slept curled up on the floor of the driver's compartment. He continued to hear the purr of *Hoodoo*'s computers late into the night as Clargue worked on a problem that neither he nor Lamartiere now believed they would ever solve.

❖   ❖   ❖

The warning chime awakened Lamartiere. After a moment of blurred confusion—he was too tired and uncomfortable for panic—he realized what the problem was.

"It's all right, doctor," he said. "I left the audible alarm on, and it's registering the locals leaving to go to the orchard."

It wasn't dawn yet, but the sky over the eastern mountains was noticeably lighter than in the west. Two hundred kilometers into those mountains was Goncourt, where Lamartiere supposed shellbursts had been glaring all night.

"Ah," said Clargue. They'd seen very little of one another despite having been no more that a meter or two apart during most of the past week. Crewing *Hoodoo* was like being imprisoned in adjacent cells.

"Go get a bath and some breakfast," Lamartiere said. He cleared his throat and added, "I think we may as well move out today, even if we don't hear anything from the Council. Otherwise we're going to bring something down on these people that they don't deserve."

"Yes," said Clargue. "I'm afraid you're right."

He didn't ask Lamartiere where he intended to go. The only possible answer was *away*. They needed to go some place where there wasn't anybody else around to be harmed by what *Hoodoo* attracted.

Residents were coming down by pairs in the basket. Even so the process would take at least an hour. The Shrine of the Blessed Catherine hadn't been intended for its present population, at least not in the years since the ground-level gate had been blocked. The walls were little defense against heavy weapons, but they protected the handful of Brothers from the small arms and banditry of the Boukasset during normal times.

Hoodoo could turn the shrine into a pile of rubble in a matter of seconds. Not that anyone would bother to do so . . . except, perhaps, as a whim along the lines of pulling the wings off flies.

Clargue slid clumsily down the bow and walked toward the basket. Civilians coming in the other direction murmured greetings to the doctor. Everyone here was glad of his presence.

Indeed, most of them probably thought of *Hoodoo*
herself as protection for the shrine and themselves. They
were wrong. Even if Lamartiere could have used the
ammunition he *knew* was in the storage magazines, the tank
was sure to summon increasing levels of violence until
everything in its vicinity was shattered to dust and vapor.

Lamartiere supposed he was dozing in the hatch, though
his eyes were open. He wasn't consciously aware of his
surroundings until Dr. Clargue said, "I will watch now,
Denis," and Lamartiere realized direct sunlight stabbed
across the plain through the notch in the hills by which
Hoodoo had entered.

"Right," Lamartiere said, trying to clear his brain. He
crawled out of the hatch, bitterly aware that he was in
terrible shape. He supposed it didn't matter. The best
option he could see now was to drive *Hoodoo* fifty kilometers out into the desert, and the AI could handle that
once he got her under way.

De Laburat had been right about one thing. Dr. Clargue
might be able to return to helping the sick in a village lost
in the mountains, but there was no longer any place on
Ambiorix for Denis Lamartiere. Like *Hoodoo* herself, he
was a valuable resource: a tank crewman, to be captured
if possible but otherwise killed to prevent another faction
from gaining his expertise.

He stepped into the basket as a mother and her twins
got out. The woman nodded while the children whispered
excitedly to one another. They'd been close enough to the
soldier to *touch* him!

The basket jogged its way up the wall of the shrine. His
shadow sprawled across the hard sandstone blocks.

Below Lamartiere, most of the residents were trudging
toward the orchard. Parties of the healthiest refugees were
loading two-man cradles with blocks crumbled from the
cliff face. Ordinary wheelbarrows would be useless on this
terrain of sand and irregular stone. Human beings were
more adaptable than even the simplest of machines.

Rasile was on the winch, somewhat to Lamartiere's
surprise, but Marie sat nearby. She was embellishing a piece

of canvas with a Maltese cross in needlepoint, holding the frame against her thighs with her left wrist and using her good right hand to direct the needle. The pattern of tight, small stitches was flawless so far as Lamartiere could tell.

"Will you lower Mr. Rasile to the ground?" Marie said to Lamartiere. "Or are you still—"

"I'm healthy enough," Lamartiere said. "Tired, is all."

And so frustrated that he felt like kicking a hole in the battlements, but neither fact would prevent him from turning a crank.

Children played within the courtyard, their voices shrilly cheerful. Lamartiere saw a pair of them momentarily, chasing one another among the rows of pole beans. The shrine wasn't really the Garden of Eden; but it was closer to that, and to Paradise, than most of the refugees could have hoped to find.

"I'm not going down," Rasile said. "I have permission from Father Blenis to read my scriptures here today."

He reached into the knapsack at his feet and brought out a fabric-bound volume. It was probably the *Revelations of Moses*, though Lamartiere couldn't see the title. Despite the book in his hand, Rasile looked even more like a pimp—or a rat—than usual.

"What?" Marie said, both angry and amazed.

"I have permission!" Rasile said. "I'm not shirking. It's hard work to bring people up in the basket!"

"I wouldn't know that?" said the woman. "Father Blenis's so gentle he'd give you permission to carry off all the communion dishes, but we're not all of us such innocent saints here, Rasile!"

Lamartiere turned his head away as he would have done if he'd stumbled into someone else's family quarrel. Only then did he see the six-wheeled truck driving up from the south. It had an open cab and cargo of some sort in the bed under a reflective tarp, but there were no signs of weapons. The driver was alone.

"What's that?" Lamartiere said sharply. Marie and Rasile instantly stopped bickering to stare over the battlements. Fear made the woman look drawn and a decade older than she'd been a moment before; Rasile's expression was harder to judge, but fear was a large part of it also.

"It's just the provisions truck," Marie said. She sighed in relief. "It's a day early, but it seems . . ."

The driver parked near the wall and pulled the tarp back to uncover his cargo. He was carrying several hundred-kilo burlap grain sacks and a number of less-definable bags and boxes. It all looked perfectly innocent.

The residents who were still close to the shrine gathered around the truck. Others, including a pair of black-robed Brothers, were on their way back from the orchard.

Lamartiere noticed with approval that Dr. Clargue had closed the tank's hatches and was even aiming his tribarrel at the truck. Some of the shrines' residents sprawled away in panic when the weapon moved, but the driver didn't seem to care. If the fellow made this trip across the Boukasset regularly, he must be used to having guns pointed at him.

Rasile said, "Ah!" with a shudder. He'd dropped the book in his haste, but he'd grabbed the knapsack itself and was holding it in front of him. It was a sturdy piece of equipment and apparently quite new.

"I was hoping to wash up before we go," Lamartiere said quietly to the woman. "We'll be leaving soon. And I'd like to thank Father Blenis for his hospitality."

"He's usually in the chapel till midday," Marie said with a nod. "I'll get you some breakfast. You can draw the water yourself now, can't you?"

"Yes, I—" Lamartiere said.

Hoodoo's siren began to wind. Lamartiere looked down. The tank's turret gimballed southward, pointing the guns at the line of vehicles racing toward the shrine.

Maury was returning.

"Let me down!" Lamartiere said. He stepped toward the basket, wondering if he could reach the tank before the armed band arrived.

Rasile backed away, fumbling inside his knapsack. His right hand came out holding a bell-mouthed mob gun. The weapon fired sheafs of aerofoils that spread enough to hit everyone in a normal-sized room with a single shot. As close as Lamartiere was to the muzzle, the charge would cut him in half.

"Don't either of you try to move!" Rasile screamed.

An oncoming vehicle fired its automatic cannon. Lamartiere suspected that the gunner had intended to shoot over the heads of the people streaming back from the orchard, but it was hard to aim accurately from a bouncing vehicle. Several shells exploded near the civilians. A woman remained standing after those around her had flung themselves to the ground. She finally toppled, her blood soaking the sand around her black.

The truck firing had dual rear wheels and an enclosure of steel plates welded onto the bed. The gun projected through a slot in the armor over the cab. *Hoodoo's* tribarrel hit the vehicle dead center. The bolts of cyan plasma turned the steel into white fire an instant before the truck's fuel tank boomed upward in an orange geyser.

One round would have been enough for the job. Dr. Clargue fired all seven, emptying the loading tube. Lamartiere supposed that was a waste, but he saw where the woman sprawled on a flag of her own blood and he couldn't feel too unhappy. At least the short-term result was good.

Maury's surviving vehicles bounced and wallowed toward the shrine. None of them shot at *Hoodoo*, demonstrating a level of discipline Lamartiere wouldn't have expected of the gang. Several of the band were firing in the air, though. Their muzzle flashes flickered in the sunlight.

"Don't move or I'll kill you!" Rasile said, squeaking two octaves up from his normal voice. He waggled the mob gun.

Maury's agent in the shrine was as high as a kite either from drugs he'd taken to nerve himself up, or from simple adrenaline. Lamartiere guessed there was a radio in Rasile's knapsack. He'd signaled his master when Lamartiere was out of the tank. Dr. Clargue was the better of the two men in *Hoodoo's* crew, but he wasn't a danger to Maury's plans.

Maury's vehicles pulled up in a ragged semicircle around the shrine's southern wall. *Hoodoo* and the provisions truck were within the arc, but the gang had cut most of the residents off from the structure.

If Lamartiere had been in *Hoodoo*, he'd have driven straight through one or more of the gang's vehicles: not even the heavy truck was a real barrier to a tank's weight and power. Clargue didn't think in those terms; and anyway, he couldn't drive the tank.

Most of the gangsters got out of their vehicles. Today Maury wore expensive battledress of chameleon fabric which took on the hues of its surroundings. He carried a submachine gun, but that was no more his real weapon than the saber of the previous day had been. Maury may have been a thug to begin with, but now he'd risen to a level that he ordered people killed instead of having to kill them himself.

"I'll be his chief man after this," Rasile said. A line of drool hung from the corner of his mouth. "I'll have all the women I want. Any woman at all."

Maury glanced up to make sure Lamartiere was out of the way. He waved the submachine gun cheerfully, then spoke to two henchmen. They grabbed an old man who'd been standing nearby. One gangster twisted the victim's hands behind his back while the other put a pistol to his temple.

The driver of the provisions truck got up from where he'd lain beside his vehicle while the shooting was going on. He also looked toward Lamartiere, lifting his cap in a casual salute.

The driver was Sergeant Heth, *Hoodoo*'s commander until Lamartiere stole the tank from Brione.

"Come on out, doctor!" Maury said in a voice loud enough for those on the battlements to hear. "We're going to start killing these people. We'll kill every one of them unless you give us the tank!"

Lamartiere opened his mouth but remained silent because he didn't know what advice to give Clargue. He didn't doubt that Maury would carry out his threat, and since the doctor couldn't drive *Hoodoo*—

The gangster fired. Ionized plasma from the projectile's driving skirt ignited a lock of the hair it blew from the victim's scalp. Hydrostatic shock fractured the cranial vault, deforming the skull into softer lines.

The shooter laughed. His partner flung the body down with a curse and wiped spattered blood from his face.

Hoodoo's hatches opened. Dr. Clargue climbed out of the cupola, bent and dejected. He might have been planning to surrender the tank anyway. Maury's men had acted before he'd really had a chance to make up his mind.

Rasile cackled in triumph. "Any woman—" he said.

Lamartiere caught a flicker of movement in the corner of his eye. An antitank missile hit the side of Maury's big armored truck. The warhead blew the slab of concrete into pebbles and a worm of reinforcing mesh twisted away.

The blast threw everyone within twenty meters to the ground. Dr. Clargue lost his grip and bounced down *Hoodoo*'s flank. He lay still on the ground. Ammunition inside the stricken vehicle went off in a series of red secondary explosions like a string of firecrackers, reducing to blazing junk whatever the warhead had left.

Rasile stared disbelievingly at the destruction. Lamartiere twisted the mob gun's broad muzzle skyward, then punched the smaller man at the corner of the jaw.

Rasile toppled over the battlements. For a moment he kept his grip on the butt of the pistol whose barrel Lamartiere held. Marie leaned forward and jabbed her needle into the back of Rasile's hand. His screams as he fell were lost in the sudden ripping destruction below.

Two more missiles hit, each destroying its target with a blast intended to gut purpose-built armored vehicles. A shockwave flipped the provisions truck onto its back; Lamartiere didn't see what had happened to Sergeant Heth.

Even before the third warhead exploded, automatic cannons firing from the hills west of the shrine began to rake Maury's other vehicles. Three kilometers was well within their accurate range.

Maury's air-cushion vehicles disintegrated like tissue paper in a storm. The steel armor of some wheeled trucks wasn't thick enough to stop the shells, and the concrete slabs protecting the others fractured at the first impact. Following shells passed through unhindered, igniting cataclysms of fuel and stored ammunition.

"Let me down!" Lamartiere said as he jumped into the basket. He should have waited. Marie had to struggle with the locking pin because Lamartiere's weight was already on the winch, but she jerked it loose before he realized the problem. The basket wobbled downward.

Still shooting, the attacking vehicles drove out of the hills where they'd waited in ambush. There were three of them, air-cushion armored personnel carriers of the type used by government forces.

Each thirty-tonne APC could carry a platoon of troops behind armor thick enough to stop small arms projectiles. The small turret near the bow carried a light electromotive cannon as well as a launching rail on the left side for an antitank missile. The hatches on the APCs' back decks opened. Troops leaned out, aiming rifles and submachine guns.

The men in the APCs wore government uniforms, though with cut-off sleeves and flourishes of metal and bright fabrics. Maury had played his card; now de Laburat's Ralliers were trumping the hand.

The gangs' alliance of convenience had broken down under the weight of loot that couldn't be shared and which gave the party owning it an overwhelming advantage over the other. In this at least, *Hoodoo*'s presence had benefitted the other inhabitants of the Boukasset.

Most of Maury's men had thrown themselves to the ground or were running toward the rocks behind the shrine, the only available cover. Their leader stood and emptied his submachine gun at the oncoming vehicles.

The APCs' turrets were stabilized to fire accurately on the move. Two of the automatic cannon shot back simultaneously. Maury's head and torso disintegrated in white flashes. An arm flew skyward; the legs below the knees remained upright for an instant before toppling onto the sand.

Lamartiere was halfway to the ground when a Rallier noticed the mob gun and took him for one of Maury's gang. Chips of sandstone flew from the wall close enough to cut Lamartiere's arm: the shooter was either lucky or better than any man had a right to be when firing from a moving platform.

Lamartiere saw a cannon tracking toward him. The ground was still five meters below but there was no choice. Cradling the mob gun to his belly and hoping it wouldn't go off when he hit, he jumped. A burst of shells devoured the basket as he left it, stinging his back with fragments of casing and stone.

He knew to flex his knees as he hit, but his feet flew backward and he slapped the ground hard enough to knock his breath out and bloody his chin. He'd dropped the mob gun. He snatched it up again, then staggered toward *Hoodoo* with knifeblade pains jetting from two lower ribs.

The APCs closed to within thirty meters of the burning vehicles and flared broadside to a halt. The Ralliers wanted to stay beyond range of a hand-thrown bomb as they finished off the survivors of Maury's band. Bullets sparkled on the APCs' sides; a Rallier sprawled, bleeding down the sloping armor. Gunfire from the vehicles was twenty to one compared to what they received.

Lamartiere grabbed a headlight bracket with his left hand. Behind him a woman's voice shrilled, "Stop him, Pietro!" through the roar of gunfire.

Lamartiere swung his right leg up. Pietro closed a hand like a bear trap on his ankle and jerked him back. With the muzzle of the mob gun tight against the giant's body, Lamartiere pulled the trigger.

Recoil bashed the gun butt hard against Lamartiere's ribs. He doubled up. Pietro stepped back with a look of blank incomprehension on his face. There was a hole two centimeters in diameter just above his navel. His tunic was smoldering.

Pietro pivoted and fell on his face. The cavity in his back was bigger than a man's head. Sections of purple-veined intestine squirmed out of the general red mass.

Louise stood behind her brother's body. "You bastard!" she cried and drew a small pistol from the bosom of her blouse.

Lamartiere hesitated a heartbeat, but there was no

choice. Louise and her brother were combatants, agents
working for de Laburat just as Rasile had worked for
Maury—and she was about to kill him.

He pulled the trigger. Nothing happened. Excessive
chamber pressure when he'd fired with the muzzle against
Pietro's chest had ruptured the cartridge case. The mob
gun was jammed.

Sergeant Heth grabbed the woman's wrist from behind,
spun her, and broke her elbow neatly over his knee. The
mercenary had lost the loose robe he'd worn for a disguise, and his left arm and shoulder were black with oil
or soot.

"You drive, kid!" he shouted. He used *Hoodoo's* toolbox
as a handhold and a patch welded on the side skirt for a
step to lift himself up the tank's side. "I'll take care of the
rest!"

Lamartiere climbed the bow slope and dropped into the
driver's compartment. He switched the fans on and closed
the hatch above him.

De Laburat must have ordered his troops not to fire
at the tank since its capture undamaged was the whole
purpose of the attack, but now a dozen shells exploded
against the side of the turret. They were as harmless as
so many raindrops.

Fan speed built smoothly; only the ragged line of
Number 7's readout reminded Lamartiere that there was
a problem. *Hoodoo's* systems were coming alive all around
him. There were hums and purrs and the demanding whine
of a hydraulic accumulator building pressure.

Some of the sounds were unfamiliar. With a sudden leap
of his heart, Lamartiere realized that the rhythmic *shoop-
shoop-shoop* from deep in the hull must be ammunition
rising from the storage magazines.

Out of nervousness he coarsened blade pitch too fast.
The fans threatened to bog, but Lamartiere rolled back on
the adjustment in time. Adding power with his right
handgrip and pitch with the left, he brought *Hoodoo* to
hover in place.

The driver's compartment felt more comfortable to him

without a gunnery display in the center of the lower screen. He'd regularly driven tanks during the months he'd worked as one of the Slammers' Local Service Personnel, but he'd never *seen* a gunnery display until Dr. Clargue went over *Hoodoo's* systems in Pamiers.

Dozens of Ralliers were blazing away at *Hoodoo* with rifles and submachine guns, a dangerous waste of ammunition. Somebody with a better notion of utility jumped down from his APC and ran forward, swinging a satchel charge for a side-armed throw. A bullet ricocheting from the tank tore his face away as he released the satchel.

The bomb flew toward *Hoodoo* in a high arc. A section of self-defense strip fired, making the tank ring. Tungsten pellets shredded the satchel into tatters of cloth and explosive, flinging it back the way it had come. It didn't detonate.

Lamartiere eased his control yoke forward and twisted left to move the tank away from the shrine. There were too many civilians nearby. Shots that couldn't damage *Hoodoo* would kill and maim people who'd only looked for peace.

The APCs were driving away. Ralliers who'd gotten out to finish off Maury's men on foot ran along behind the vehicles, shouting and waving their arms. One of the gunners depressed his cannon as his APC turned, intending to rake *Hoodoo's* skirts. If the plenum chamber was holed badly enough, the tank's fans couldn't build enough pressure to lift her off the ground.

Blue-green light sparkled on the APC's turret as a dozen bolts from *Hoodoo's* 2cm weapon hit it. The tribarrel's rotation was an additional whirr in the symphony of the tank at work. In the driver's compartment, the plasma discharges were scarcely louder than peanuts cracking.

The turret flew apart like steam puffed into a stiff breeze. The APC's armor was a sandwich of ceramic within high-maraging steel: the steel burned white while glassy knives of the core ripped in all directions. The torso of a Rallier trying to climb back aboard the vehicle vanished in bloody spray.

Lamartiere crawled through the chaos. The ground in front of the shrine was littered with bodies and debris. Residents who'd been caught in the fighting lay intermixed with Maury's gang. Some of them might still be alive.

Above Lamartiere the tribarrel spat short bursts. Sergeant Heth was picking off dismounted Ralliers instead of firing at the fleeing vehicles. Some of de Laburat's men turned to run for shelter in the rocks when they saw the APCs weren't going to stop for them. None of them made it, and the ones who threw themselves down to feign death didn't survive either.

It was easy to tell dead Ralliers from those shamming. At short range a 2cm bolt tore a human body apart. When several hit the same target, the result was indistinguishable from a bomb blast.

Lamartiere drove over the wreckage of a truck that had been hit by an antitank missile. Lubricant and the synthetic rubber tires burned with low, smokey flames. *Hoodoo*'s skirt plowed a path through the skeletal frame, whipping the blaze higher with the downdraft from the plenum chamber.

The main gun fired.

The tribarrel had so little effect inside the tank that Lamartiere was merely aware that Heth was shooting. The 20cm weapon's discharge rocked *Hoodoo* backward despite the inertia of her 170 tonnes. Air clapped to fill the vacuum which the jolt of plasma had burned through its heart. Lamartiere shouted in surprise.

The leading APC, by now nearly a kilometer distant, burst as though a volcano had erupted beneath it. The bolt transferred its megajoules of energy to the vehicle, vaporizing even the ceramic armor. A fireball forty meters in diameter bloomed where the APC had been; bits of solid matter sprayed out of it, none of them bigger than a man's thumbnail.

The gun cycled, ejecting the spent round into the fighting compartment. Heat and stinking fumes flooded *Hoodoo*'s interior even though the ventilation fans switched to high speed. Lamartiere's eyes were watering and the back of his throat burned.

"Thought I'd wait till we were clear of the civilians," Sergeant Heth explained over the intercom in a conversational voice. "Sidescatter from the big gun can blister bare skin if you're anywhere nearby."

He fired the 20cm weapon again. This time the *clang* and the way the tank bucked weren't a surprise to Lamartiere, though his head wobbled back and forth in response to the hull's motion.

The second APC was making a skidding turn to avoid running through the flaming ruin that had exploded before it. The cyan bolt hit the vehicle at a slant, perfectly centered, and devoured it as completely as its fellow. The fireball dimmed to a ghost of its initial fury, but brush ignited by debris ignited hundreds of meters away.

The last Rallier vehicle fled at over 100 kph despite the broken terrain. It was drawing away because *Hoodoo*'s mass took so long to accelerate despite the tank's higher top speed. Lamartiere concentrated on driving, avoiding knobs of rock too heavy to smash through and crevices that would spill air from the plenum chamber and ground *Hoodoo* shriekingly.

He heard the turret gimbal onto its target. A Rallier stood on the deck of the APC and jumped. The man hit the ground and bounced high, limbs flailing in rubbery curves. He'd broken every bone in his body and was obviously dead.

But then, so were his fellows.

The main gun slammed. The third APC vanished in a smear of fire across the desert floor. The sun was high enough to pale the flames, but the pall of black smoke drifted west with the breeze.

"Go back to the fort, kid," Heth ordered. "Stegner's heading there in our jeep."

The mercenary chuckled, then started coughing. The ozone and matrix residue from the main gun burned his throat also. "We planned that Steg'd set off some fireworks on the hills. While everybody was looking that way I'd hop into *Hoodoo*. The locals made a better job of fireworks than we ever thought of, didn't they? Bloody near did for me, I'll tell the world!"

Lamartiere braked the tank with the caution its mass

demanded. Unlike the driver of a wheeled vehicle, he didn't have the friction of tires against the ground to slow him unless he dumped air from the plenum chamber and deliberately skidded the skirt.

There was no need now for haste. Lamartiere wasn't in a hurry to face what came next.

He opened his hatch, thinking the draft would clear fumes from the tank's interior faster than the filtered ventilation system. The hatch rolled shut again an instant later; Sergeant Heth had used the commander's override.

"Not just yet, kid," he said. "The guy in charge of this lot, de Laburat . . . Did you ever meet him?"

"Yes," Lamartiere said. "I'd sooner trust a weasel."

"Yeah, that's the guy," the mercenary said. "But he's a smart sonuvabitch. He saw the way things were going before any of his people did. He bailed out and ran into the rocks right away. I didn't have the ready magazines charged yet, so I couldn't do anything about it."

"You mean de Laburat got away?" Lamartiere said in horror.

The main gun fired. The unexpected *CLANG/jerk!* whipsawed Lamartiere's head again. Fumes seeped through the narrow passage from the fighting compartment, but both hatches opened before he had time to sneeze. The wind of *Hoodoo*'s forward motion scoured Lamartiere's station.

This time the bolt had struck at the base of the cliff a hundred meters west of the shrine. Rock shattered in a blue-green flash.

The slope bulged, then slid downward with a roar. A plume of pulverized rock settled slowly, displaying an enormous cavity in the cliff. Below the crater was a pile of irregular blocks which in some cases were larger than a man. The mass was still shifting internally, giving it the look of organic life.

Civilians who'd been returning from the orchard, some of them running to check on loved ones, flattened again to the ground. They had no way of telling what had just happened.

"He got away for a while," Heth said with satisfaction.

"But then he stuck his head up outa the crevice where he was hiding to see what was going on. He didn't get a very long view, did he?"

Heth's laughter changed again to coughing, though with a cheerful undercurrent. Because the fumes escaped via the cupola, the turret took longer to clear than the driver's compartment.

Father Blenis was on the battlements, standing as straight in his robes as age would permit him. He was alone. He hadn't flinched when the 20cm gun fired, even though he was closer to the bolt's crashing impact than any of the other civilians.

A jeep was racing across the desert from the foothills to the east, trailing a pennant of ruddy dust. Lamartiere wondered if Heth was armed. Probably not. The gangs searched the provisions truck, so one or the other of them would have confiscated any weapon the mercenary had tried to bring with him.

It didn't matter. Lamartiere had run as far as he was going to. The tank he'd stolen with such high hopes had brought disaster to everyone around him.

Hoodoo was nearing Maury's vehicles. Black smoke still poured out of the carcasses. Lamartiere swung his fan nacelles vertical, lifting the tank for an instant to spill air from the plenum chamber. *Hoodoo* pogoed, touching several times as she slowed. The impacts were too gentle to damage the skirts.

They nosed through the gap they'd plowed in pursuit of the Ralliers. Lamartiere drove carefully; there were civilians moving behind the smoke. He didn't see anyone holding a weapon, though there were plenty of guns strewn across the ground. Dr. Clargue squatted near the walls, bandaging a child's leg.

"Sir?" Lamartiere asked.

"I'm no fucking officer, kid," Heth said, at least half serious. "Anyway, 'sarge' was good enough when you were an LSP at the base, wasn't it?"

"That was a long time ago, sarge," Lamartiere said. Five calendar days, and a lifetime. "Anyway, I was wondering what the command was to transfer ammo to the ready magazines. Dr. Clargue's searched the data banks up, down and crosswise and he can't find it. Couldn't find it."

Heth laughed himself into another fit of coughing. "Oh, blood and martyrs, was *that* the problem? Steg and me knew there must be something going on why you didn't use the main gun, but we couldn't on our lives figure out what it was!"

Lamartiere nestled the tank against the shrine. He shut down the fans. The jeep with Trooper Stegner was still a minute or two distant. "Well, what was it then?" he said sharply. There were worse things happening than Heth laughing at him, but it was still irritating.

The sergeant had cocked the turret to the side; the 20cm barrel was no longer glowing, but heat waves still distorted the air above the iridium. He climbed out of the cupola and slid down beside the driver's hatch. Lamartiere raised his seat, but for the moment he was too exhausted to get out of the vehicle.

"Hey, simmer down," Heth said. "I'm just laughing because of how lucky we were. Not that I'm not going to have some explaining to do about why *Hoodoo*'s late joining the regiment on Beresford, but at least you didn't turn Carcassone inside out with the main gun."

The jeep wound between a pair of truck chassis. The open flames had died down, though the wreckage still smoldered. Stegner, a tall man with wispy hair and a face like a rabbit's, waved to them.

"Transfer isn't a software process," Heth went on. "It's hardwired. There's a thumb switch on the firing lever. To recharge the ready magazines you roll it up for the tribarrel and down for the main gun."

"Oh," Lamartiere said. "Yeah, that explains why the doctor couldn't find the command."

He put a boot on the seat and lifted himself out of the compartment. Heth steadied him till he'd settled on the open hatch.

"Kid," the sergeant said. "There's maybe three million parts in one of these suckers. How were you supposed to know what every one of them is, and you not even through proper training?"

He patted *Hoodoo* with an affectionate hand. "You did plenty good enough with what you had. I watched you chew up that mechanized battalion at the Lystra, remember? I'll tell the world!"

The sergeant's torso was badly scraped besides being half covered in oil, but apart from occasionally rubbing his elbow he showed no signs of discomfort. Lamartiere's chest hurt badly, particularly where the mob gun had recoiled into his ribs when he fired, but he thought the damage was probably limited to bruising.

"Did you see the holes in the skirt, sarge?" Stegner called as he stood scowling at *Hoodoo's* flank. "Must be about a hundred of 'em. Nothing very big but I don't want to drive back to Brione with her mushing like a pig."

"She sagged left," Lamartiere said. "I had to tilt the nacelles to keep her straight, but it wasn't as bad as the damage we took at the Lystra."

"Probably the warhead that flipped my truck over on me," Heth said judiciously. "Well, we can use the truck's bed for patching. Do they have a welder here, kid?"

Half the residents had returned to the shrine. They were crying in amazement and horror at the carnage. Many others still hid among the stone shelters of the orchard, waiting to be sure that it was safe to show themselves. Lamartiere couldn't blame them for their fear.

"I doubt it," he said. He thought for a moment. "There's mastic, though. I saw some where they're tiling the chapel entryway. It'll work for a patch on the inside of the skirts, since air pressure tightens the seal."

"Yeah, that'll work," said Stegner approvingly. He walked to the overturned truck and kicked it, judging the thickness of the body metal by the sound.

"Sergeant Heth," Lamartiere said, looking at the stone wall of the shrine. "Are you going to hand me over to the government, or . . . ?"

He turned and gestured toward the body of the old man Maury's thugs had shot as a warning to Dr.

Clargue—a few moments before they and all their fellows died also.

"Hey, we don't work for the government of Ambiorix any more, kid," Heth said. "The only reason Steg and me are still on the planet is we *really* didn't want to explain to Colonel Hammer how we managed to lose one of his tanks. Do you have any idea what one of these costs?"

He patted *Hoodoo* again.

Marie's body lay at the foot of the wall. Her upturned face was peaceful and unmarked, but there was a splotch of blood on her upper chest. Lamartiere supposed a stray bullet had hit her. There'd been enough of them flying around.

"I know what it costs," he said. "I know what it cost these people."

"Yeah, that's so," Heth agreed. "And I'm not arguing with you. But you might remind yourself that things may be a little better for the folks here now that the gangs are out of the way. I don't say it will, mind you; but it may be."

He spat accurately onto the corpse of one of Maury's men; the one who'd held the hostage for his partner to shoot, Lamartiere thought.

"I don't work for the government, like I told you," Heth said quietly. "But sometimes I do things on my own personal account. War isn't a business where there's a lot of obvious good guys, but sometimes the bad guys are pretty easy to spot."

Lamartiere put a hand on Heth's shoulder so that the mercenary would look him straight in the eye. "Sergeant," Lamartiere said, "am I free to go? Is that what you're telling me?"

Heth shrugged. "Sure, if you want to," he said. "But Steg and me was hoping you might like to join the Slammers. The Colonel's always looking for recruits."

Stegner morosely rubbed a dimple in the hull surrounded by a halo of bright radial scratches. A high-explosive shell had burst there against the armor. "If we bring you along," he said, "maybe we can get a few of these extra dings passed off as training accidents, you know?"

"And you might like to be someplace there wasn't a price on your head," Heth said, rubbing the armor with his thumb. "Nobody at the port's going to think twice if there's three of us boarding a ship for Beresford along with *Hoodoo*, here."

Lamartiere looked toward the battlements. Father Blenis knelt in prayer. A pair of young women, one of them holding an infant, were with him. At the base of the wall three laymen and a Brother worked with focused desperation to jury-rig a platform in place of the shattered basket.

"I guess I don't have a choice," Lamartiere said.

Trooper Stegner looked up from the side of the tank. "Sure you got a choice," he said in a hard, angry voice. Lamartiere had thought of the trooper as a little slow, but invariably good-humored. "There's always a choice. I coulda stayed on Spruill sniping at Macauleys till one of the Macauleys nailed me!"

"For me," said Sergeant Heth, "the problem was her father and brothers. I decided that joining the Slammers was better that the rest of my life married to Anna Carausio."

He smiled faintly in reminiscence. "I still think I was right, but who knows, hey?"

Lamartiere nodded. "Yeah, who knows?" he said.

He looked at Marie's silent body. Maybe she was in the arms of God; maybe Celine was there too, and all the others who'd died since Denis Lamartiere stole a tank. It would be nice to believe that.

Lamartiere didn't believe in much of anything nowadays; certainly not in the Mosite Rebellion as a cause to get other people killed in. But one thing he did believe.

"Ambiorix'll be a better place if I'm off-planet," he said to the mercenaries. "And just maybe I'll be better off too. I'll join if you'll have me."

Heth stuck out his hand for Lamartiere to shake. "Welcome aboard, kid," he said.

Stegner kicked *Hoodoo*'s skirt. "Now let's get this poor bitch patched up so we get the hell out of here, shall we?"

CULTURAL CONFLICT

Platoon sergeant Horthy stood with his right arm—his only arm—akimbo, surveying the rippling treetops beneath him and wishing they really were the waves of a cool, gray ocean. The trees lapped high up the sides of the basalt knob that had become Firebase Bolo three weeks before when a landing boat dropped them secretly onto it. Now, under a black plastic ceiling that mimicked the basalt to the eye of the Federation spy satellite, nestled a command car, a rocket howitzer with an air cushion truck to carry its load of ammunition, and Horthy's three combat cars.

Horthy's cars—except on paper. There Lieutenant Simmons-Brown was listed as platoon leader.

One of the long-limbed native reptiles suddenly began to gesture and screech up at the sergeant. The beasts occasionally appeared on the treetops, scurrying and bounding like fleas in a dog's fur. Recently their bursts of rage had become more common—and more irritating. Horthy was a short, wasp-waisted man who wore a spiky goatee and a drum-magazined powergun slung beneath his shoulder. His hand now moved to its grip . . . but shooting meant giving in to frustration, and instead Horthy only muttered a curse.

"You say something, Top?" asked a voice behind him. He turned without speaking and saw Jenne and Scratchard, his two gunners, with a lanky howitzer crewman whose name escaped him.

"Nothing that matters," Horthy said.

Scratchard's nickname was Ripper Jack because he carried a long knife in preference to a pistol. He fumbled a little nervously with its hilt as he said, "Look, Top, ah . . . we been talking and Bonmarcher here—" he nodded at the artilleryman "—he says we're not supporting the rest of the Regiment, we're stuck out here in the middle of nowhere to shoot up Federation ships when the war starts."

The sergeant looked sharply at Bonmarcher, then said, "*If* the war starts. Yeah, that's pretty much true. We're about the only humans on South Continent, but if the government decides it still wants to be independent and the Federation decides it's gotta have Squire's World as a colony—well, Fed supply routes pass through two straits within hog shot of this rock." Simmons-Brown would cop a screaming worm if he heard Horthy tell the men a truth supposed to be secret, but one way or another it wasn't going to matter very long.

"But Lord and *Martyrs*, Top," Bonmarcher burst out, "how long after we start shooting is it gonna be before the Feds figure out where the shells're coming from? Sure, this cap—" he thumbed toward the plastic supported four meters over the rock by thin pillars "—hides us now. But sure as death, we'll loose one off while the satellite's still over us, or the Feds'll triangulate radar tracks as the shells come over the horizon at them. Then what'll happen?"

"That's what our combat cars are for," Horthy said wearily, knowing that the Federation would send not troops but a salvo of their own shells to deal with the thorn in their side. "We'll worry about that when it happens. Right now—" He broke off. Another of those damned, fluffy reptiles was shrieking like a cheated whore not twenty meters from him.

"Bonmarcher," the sergeant said in sudden inspiration, "you want to go down there and do something about that noisemaker for me?" Two noisemakers, actually—the beast and the artilleryman himself for as long as the hunt kept him out of the way.

"Gee, Top, I'd sure love to get outa this oven, but I heard the lieutenant order . . ." Bonmarcher began, looking sidelong at the command car fifty meters away in the center of the knob. Its air conditioner whined, cooling Simmons-Brown and the radioman on watch within its closed compartment.

"Look, you just climb down below the leaf cover and don't loose off unless you've really got a target," said Horthy. "I'll handle the lieutenant."

Beaming with pleasure, Bonmarcher patted his sidearm to make sure it was snapped securely in its holster. "Thanks, Top," he said and began to descend by the cracks and shelvings that eternity had forged even into basalt.

Horthy ignored him, turning instead to the pair of his own men who had waited in silent concern during the exchange. "'Look, boys," the one-armed sergeant said quietly, "I won't give you a load of cop about this being a great vacation for us. But you keep your mouths shut and do your jobs, and I'll do my damnedest to get us all out of here in one piece." He looked away from his listeners for a moment, up at the dull iridium vehicles and the stripped or khaki crewmen lounging over them. "Anyhow, neither the Feds or the twats that hired us have any guts. I'll give you even money that one side or the other backs down before anything drops in the pot."

Scratchard, as lean and dark as Horthy, looked at the huge, blond Jenne. There was no belief on either face. Then the rear hatch of the command car flung open and the communications sergeant stepped out whooping with joy. "They've signed a new treaty!" he shouted. "We're being recalled!"

Horthy grinned, punched each of his gunners lightly in the stomach. "See?" he said. "You listen to Top and he'll bring you home."

All three began to laugh with released tension.

Hilf, Caller of the Moon Sept, followed his sept-brother Seida along the wire-thin filaments of the canopy. Their black footpads flashed a rare primary color as they leaped. The world was slate-gray bark and huge pearly leaves sprouting on flexible tendrils, raised to a sky in which the sun was a sizzling platinum bead. Both runners were lightly dusted with the pollen they had shaken from fruiting bodies in their course. The Tree, though an entity, required cross-fertilization among its segments for healthy growth. The mottled gray-tones of Seida's feathery scales blended perfectly with his surroundings, and his strength was as smooth as the Tree's. Hilf knew the young male hoped to become Caller himself in a few years, knew also that Seida lacked the necessary empathy with the Tree and the sept to hold the position. Besides, his recklessness was no substitute for intelligence.

But Seida was forcing Hilf to act against his better judgment. The creatures on the bald, basalt knob were clearly within the sept's territory; but what proper business had any of the Folk with rock-dwellers? Still, knowing that token activity would help calm his brothers, Hilf had let Seida lead him to personally view the situation. At the back of the Caller's mind was the further realization that the Mothers were sometimes swayed by the "maleness" of action as opposed to intelligent lethargy.

Poised for another leap, Hilf noticed the black line of a worm track on the bark beside him. He halted, instinctively damping the springiness of his perch by flexing his hind legs. Seida shrieked but fell into lowering silence when he saw what his Caller was about. Food was an immediate need. As Hilf had known, Seida's unfitness for leadership included his inability to see beyond the immediate.

The branch was a twenty-centimeter latticework of intergrown tendrils, leapfrogging kilometers across the forest. In its career it touched and fused with a dozen trunks, deep rooted pillars whose tendrils were of massive cross section. Hilf blocked the worm track with a spike-clawed, multi-jointed thumb twice the length of the three fingers on each hand. His other thumb thrust into the end of the track and wriggled. The bark split, baring the

hollowed pith and the worm writhing and stretching away
from the impaling claw. Hilf's esophagus spasmed once to
crush the soft creature. He looked up. Seida stuttered an
impoliteness verging on command: he had not forgotten
his self-proclaimed mission. The Caller sighed and followed
him.

The ancient volcanic intrusion was a hundred-meter
thumb raised from the forest floor. The Tree crawled
partway up the basalt, but the upper faces of the rock were
steep and dense enough to resist attachments by major
branches. Three weeks previously a huge ball had howled
out of the sky and poised over the rock, discharging other
silvery beasts shaped like great sowbugs and guided by
creatures not too dissimilar to the Folk. These had quickly
raised the black cover which now hung like an optical
illusion to the eyes of watchers in the highest nearby
branches. The unprecedented event had sparked the hot-
test debate of the Caller's memory. Despite opposition from
Seida and a few other hotheads, Hilf had finally convinced
his sept that the rock was not their affair.

Now, on the claim that one of the brown-coated invaders
had climbed out onto a limb, Seida was insisting that he
should be charged at once with leading a war party.
Unfortunately, at least the claim was true.

Seida halted, beginning to hoot and point. Even without
such notice the interloper would have been obvious to Hilf.
The creature was some fifty meters away—three healthy
leaps, the Caller's mind abstracted—and below the observ-
ers. It was huddled on a branch which acted as a flying
buttress for the high towers of the Tree. At near view it
was singularly unattractive: appreciably larger than one of
the sept-brothers, it bore stubby arms and a head less
regular than the smooth bullets of the Folk.

As he pondered, the Caller absently gouged a feather
of edible orange fungus out of the branch. The rest of the
aliens remained under their roof, equally oblivious to the
Folk and their own sept-brother. The latter was crawling
a little closer on his branch, manipulating the object he
carried while turning his lumpy face toward Seida.

Hilf, blending silently into the foliage behind his brother, let his subconscious float and merge while his surface mind grappled with the unpalatable alternatives. The creature below was technically an invader, but it did not seem the point of a thrust against the Moon Sept. Tradition did not really speak to the matter. Hilf could send out a war party, losing a little prestige to Seida since the younger brother had cried for that course from the beginning. Far worse than the loss of prestige was the risk to the sept which war involved. If the interlopers were as strong as they were big, the Folk would face a grim battle. In addition, the huge silver beasts which had whined and snarled as they crawled onto the rock were a dangerous uncertainty, though they had been motionless since their appearance.

But the only way to avoid war seemed to be for Hilf to kill his sept-brother. Easy enough to do—a sudden leap and both thumbs rammed into the brainbox. The fact Seida was not prepared for an attack was further proof of his unfitness to lead. No one would dispute the Caller's tale of a missed leap and a long fall. . . . Hilf poised as Seida leaned out to thunder more abuse at the creature below.

The object in the interloper's hand flashed. The foliage winked cyan and Seida's head blew apart. Spasming muscles threw his body forward, following its fountaining blood in an arc to the branch below. The killer's high cackles of triumph pursued Hilf as he raced back to the Heart.

He had been wrong: the aliens *did* mean war.

Simmons-Brown broke radio contact with a curse. His khakis were sweatstained and one of the shoulder-board chevrons announcing his lieutenancy was missing. "Top," he whined to Sergeant Horthy who stood by the open hatch of the command car, "Command Central won't send a space boat to pick us up, they want us to *drive* all the way to the north coast for surface pick-up to Johnstown. That's twelve hundred kilometers and anyhow, we can't even get the cars *down* off this Lord-stricken rock!"

"Sure we can," Horthy said, planning aloud rather than deigning to contradict the wispy lieutenant. Simmons-Brown was a well-connected incompetent whose approach to problem solving was to throw a tantrum while other people tried to work around him. "We'll link tow cables and . . . no, a winch won't hold but we can blast-set an eyebolt, then rappel the cars down one at a time. How long they give us till pick-up?"

"Fifteen days, but—"

A shot bumped the air behind the men. Both whipped around. Horthy's hand brushed his submachine gun's grip momentarily before he relaxed. He said, "It's all plus, just Bonmarcher. I told him he could shut up a couple of the local noisemakers if he stayed below the curve of the rock and didn't put a hole in our camouflage. The fed satellite isn't good enough to pick up small arms fire in this jungle."

"I distinctly ordered that no shots be fired while we're on detached duty!" snapped Simmons-Brown, his full mustache trembling like an enraged caterpillar. "Distinctly!"

Sergeant Horthy looked around the six blowers and twenty-three men that made up Firebase Bolo. He sighed. Waiting under commo security, between bare rock and hot plastic, would have been rough at the best of times. With Simmons-Brown added . . . "Sorry, sir," the sergeant lied straight-faced, "I must have forgotten."

"Well, get the men moving," Simmons-Brown ordered, already closing the hatch on his air-conditioning. "Those bastards at Central might just leave us if we missed pick-up. They'd like that."

"Oh, we'll make it fine," Horthy said to himself, his eyes already searching for a good place to sink the eyebolt. "Once we get off the rock there won't be any problem. The ground's flat, and with all the leaves up here cutting off light we won't have undergrowth to bother about. Just set the compasses on north and follow our noses."

"Hey, Top," someone called. "Look what I got!" Bonmarcher had clambered back onto the rock. Behind him, dragged by its lashed ankles, was a deep-chested reptile that had weighed about forty kilos before being decapitated. "Blew this monkey away my first shot," the artillery-man bragged.

"Nice work," Horthy replied absently. His mind was on more important things.

The world of the Moon Sept was not a sphere but a triangular section of forest. That wedge, like those of each of the twenty-eight other septs, was dominated by the main root of a Tree. The ground at the center was thin loam over not subsoil but almost a hectare of ancient root. The trunks sprouting from the edge of this mass were old, too, but not appreciably thicker than the other pillars supporting the Tree for hundreds of kilometers in every direction. Interwoven stems and branches joined eighty meters in the air, roofing the Heart in a quivering blanket of leaves indistinguishable from that of the rest of the forest. The hollow dome within was an awesome thing even without its implications, and few of the Folk cared to enter it.

Hilf himself feared the vast emptiness and the power it focused, but he had made his decision three years before when the Mothers summoned the previous Caller to the Nest and a breeder's diet. Hilf had thrust forward and used the flowing consciousness of the whole sept to face down his rivals for the Callership. Now he thumped to the hard floor without hesitation and walked quickly on feet and knuckles to the pit worn in the center of the root by millennia of Callers. His body prone below the lips of the blond rootwood, Hilf's right claw gashed sap from the Tree and then nicked his own left wrist. Sap and pale blood oozed together, fusing Caller and Tree physically in a fashion dictated by urgency. The intense wood grain rippled from in front of Hilf's eyes and his mind began to fill with shattered, spreading images of the forest. Each heartbeat sent Hilf out in a further surge and blending until every trunk and branch-bundle had become the Tree, each member of the Moon Sept had blurred into the Folk. A black warmth beneath the threshold of awareness indicated that even the Mothers had joined.

The incident trembled through the sept, a kaleidoscope more of emotion than pictures. Seida capered again, gouted and died in the invader's raucous laughter. Reflex stropped claws on the bark of a thousand branches. Response was the Caller's to suggest and guide, not to determine. The first blood-maddened reply by the sept almost overwhelmed Hilf. But his response had been planned, stamped out on the template of experience older than that of any living sept-brother—as old, perhaps, as the joinder of Folk and Tree. The alien nature of the invaders would not be allowed to pervert the traditional response: the remainder of Seida's hatching would go out to punish the death of their brother.

The pattern of the root began to reimpose itself on Hilf's eyes. He continued to lie in the hollow, logy with reaction. Most of the sept were returning to their foraging or play, but there were always eyes trained on the knob and the activity there. And scattered throughout the wedge of the Tree were thirty-seven of the Folk, young and fierce in their strength, who drifted purposefully together.

At the forest floor the raindrops, scattered by the triple canopy, were a saturated fog that clung and made breath a struggle. Horthy ignored it, letting his feet and sinewed hand mechanically balance him against the queasy ride of the air-cushion vehicle. His eyes swept the ground habitually. When reminded by his conscious mind, they took in the canopies above also.

The rain had slowed the column. The strangely-woven tree boles were never spaced too closely to pass the armored vehicles between them, but frequent clumps of spire-pointed fungus thrust several meters in the air and confused the aisles. Experience had shown that when struck by a car the saprophytes would collapse in a cloud of harmless spores, but in the fog-blurred dimness they sometimes hid an unyielding trunk behind them. The lead car had its driving lights on though the water dazzle made them almost useless, and all six vehicles had closed up more tightly than Horthy cared to see. There was little chance of a Federation ambush, but even a sudden halt would bring on a multiple collision.

The brassy trilling that had grown familiar in the past several hours sounded again from somewhere in the forest. Just an animal, though. The war on Squire's World was over for the time, and whether the Regiment's employers had won or lost there was no reason for Horthy to remain as tense as he was. Simmons-Brown certainly was unconcerned, riding in the dry cabin of his command car. That was the second vehicle, just ahead of Horthy's. The sergeant's wing gunners huddled in the fighting compartment to either side of him. They were miserable and bored, their minds as empty as their slack, dripping faces.

Irritated but without any real reason to slash the men to vigilance, Horthy glared back along his course. The stubby 150mm howitzer, the cause of the whole Lord-accursed operation, was the fourth vehicle. Only its driver, his head a mirroring ball behind its face shield, was visible. The other five men of the crew were within the open-backed turret whose sheathing was poor protection against hostile fire but enough to keep the rain out.

The ammo transporter was next, sandwiched between the hog and the combat car which brought up the rear of the column. Eighty-kilo shells were stacked ten high on its flat bed, their noses color coded with incongruous gaiety. The nearby mass of explosive drew a wince from Horthy, who knew that if it went off together it could pulverize the basalt they had been emplaced on. On top of the front row of shells where its black fuse winked like a Cyclops' eye was the gas round, a thin-walled cylinder of K3 which could kill as surely by touch as by inhalation. Everyone in the Regiment respected K3, but Horthy was one of the few who understood it well enough to prefer the gas to conventional weapons in some situations.

In part, that was a comment on his personality as well.

To Horthy's right, Rob Jenne began to shrug out of his body armor. "Keep it on, trooper," the sergeant said.

"But Top," Jenne complained, "it rubs in this wet." His

fingers lifted the segmented porcelain to display the weal
chafed over his floating ribs.

"Leave it on," Horthy repeated, gesturing about the fighting compartment crowded with ammunition and personal
gear. "There's not enough room here for us, even without
three suits of armor standing around empty. Besides—"

The gray creature's leap carried it skimming over Horthy
to crash full into Jenne's chest. Man and alien pitched over
the bulkhead. Horthy leaned forward and shot by instinct,
using his sidearm instead of the powerful, less handy,
tribarrel mounted on the car. His light finger pressure
clawed three holes in the creature's back as it somersaulted
into the ground with Jenne.

The forest rang as the transporter plowed into the stern
of the grounded howitzer. The gun vehicle seemed to crawl
with scores of the scale-dusted aliens, including the one
whose spear-sharp thumbs had just decapitated the driver.
Horthy twisted his body to spray the mass with blue-green
fire. The hog's bow fulcrummed in the soil as the transporter's impact lifted its stern. The howitzer upended, its
gun tube flopping freely in an arc while inertia vomited
men from the turret.

"Watch the bloody ammo!" Horthy shouted into his intercom as a tribarrel hosed one of the aliens off the transporter in a cloud of gore and vaporized metal. Ahead, the
command car driver had hit his panic bar in time to save
himself, but one of the long-armed creatures was hacking
at the vision blocks as though they were the vehicle's eyes.
The rear hatch opened and Simmons-Brown flung himself
out screaming with fear. Horthy hesitated. The alien gave
up its assault on the optical fibers and sprang on the
lieutenant's back.

Horthy's burst chopped both of them to death in a
welter of blood.

Only body armor saved the sergeant from the attack that
sledged his chest forward into the iridium bulkhead. He
tried to rise but could not against the weight and the shocks
battering both sides of his thorax like paired trip-hammers.

The blows stopped and the weight slid from Horthy's

back and down his ankles. He levered himself upright, gasping with pain as intense as that of the night a bullet-firing machine gun had smashed across his armor. Scratchard, the left gunner, grinned at him. The man's pale skin was spattered with the same saffron blood that covered his knife.

"They've gone off, Top," Scratchard said. "Didn't like the tribarrels—even though we didn't hit much but trees. Didn't like this, neither." He stropped his blade clean on the thighs of the beast he had killed with it.

"Bleeding martyrs," Horthy swore under his breath as he surveyed the damage. The platoon's own four blowers were operable, but the overturned hog was a total loss and the transporter's front fan had disintegrated when the steel ground-effect curtain had crumpled into its arc. If there was any equipment yard on Squire's World that could do the repairs, it sure as cop was too far away from this stretch of jungle to matter. Five men were dead and another, his arm ripped from shoulder to wrist, was comatose under the effects of sedatives, clotting agents, antibiotics, and shock.

"All plus," Horthy began briskly. "We leave the bodies, leave the two arty blowers too; and I just hope our scaly friends get real curious about them soon. Before we pull out, I want ten of the high explosive warheads unscrewed and loaded into the command car—yeah, and the gas shell too."

"Via, Top," one of the surviving artillerymen muttered, "why we got to haul that stuff around?"

"'Cause I said so," Horthy snarled, "and ain't I in charge?" His hand jerked the safety pin from one of the delay-fused shells, then spun the dial to one hour. "Now get moving, because we want to be a long way away in an hour."

The platoon was ten kilometers distant when the shock wave rippled the jungle floor like the head of a drum. The jungle had blown skyward in a gray puree, forming a momentary bubble over a five-hectare crater.

❖   ❖   ❖

The Moon Sept waited for twilight in a ring about the shattered clearing in which the invaders were halted. The pain that had slashed through every member of the sept at the initial explosion was literally beyond comparison: when agony gouged at the Tree, the brothers had collapsed wherever they stood, spewing waste and the contents of their stomach uncontrollably. Hours later the second blast tore away ten separate trunks and brought down a hectare of canopy. The huge silver beasts had shoved the debris to the side before they settled down in the new clearing. That explosion was bearable on top of the first only because of the black rage of the Mothers now insulating the Moon Sept from full empathy with their Tree; but not even the Mothers could accept further punishment at that level. Hilf moaned in the root-alcove, only dimly aware that he had befouled it in reaction. He was a conduit now, not the Caller in fact, for the eyeless ones had assumed control. The Mothers had made a two-dimensional observation which the males, to whom up and down were more important than horizontal direction, had missed: the invaders were proceeding toward the Nest. They must be stopped.

The full thousand of the Moon Sept blended into the leaves with a perfection achieved in the days in which there had been carnivores in the forest. When one of the Folk moved it was to ease cramps out of a muscle or to catch the sun-pearl on the delicate edge of a claw. They did not forage; the wracking horror of the explosions had left them beyond desire for food.

The effect on the Tree had been even worse. In multi-kilometer circles from both blast sites the wood sagged sapless and foliage curled around its stems. The powerguns alone had been devastating to the Tree's careful stasis, bolts that shattered the trunks they clipped and left the splinters ablaze in the rain. Only the lightning could compare in destructiveness, and the charges building in the uppermost branches gave warning enough for the Tree to minimize lightning damage.

There would be a further rain of cyan charges, but that

could not be helped. The Mothers were willing to sacrifice to necessity, even a Tree or a sept.

The four silvery beasts lay nose to tail among the craters, only fifty meters from the standing trunks in which the Folk waited. Hilf watched from a thousand angles. Only the rotating cones on the foreheads of each of the beasts seemed to be moving. Their riders were restive, however, calling to one another in low voices whose alien nature could not disguise their tension. The sun that had moments before been a spreading blob on the western horizon was now gone; invisible through the clouds but a presence felt by the Folk, the fixed Moon now ruled the sky alone. It was the hour of the Moon Sept, and the command of the Mothers was the loosing of a blood-mad dog to kill.

"Death!" screamed the sept-brothers as they sprang into the clearing.

There was death in plenty awaiting them.

The antipersonnel strips of the cars were live. Hilf was with the first body when it hurtled to within twenty meters of a car and the strips began to fire on radar command. Each of the white flashes that slammed and glared from just above the ground-effect curtains was fanning out a handful of tetrahedral pellets. Where the energy released by the powerguns blasted flesh into mist and jelly, the projectiles ripped like scythes over a wide area. Then the forest blazed as flickering cyan hosed across it.

The last antipersonnel charge went off, leaving screams and the thump of powerguns that were almost silence after the rattling crescendo of explosions.

The sept, the surprising hundreds whom the shock had paralyzed but not slain, surged forward again. The three-limbed Caller of the invaders shouted orders while he fired. The huge silver beasts howled and spun end for end even as Hilf's brothers began to leap aboard—then the port antipersonnel strips cut loose in a point-blank broadside. For those above the plane of the discharges there was a brief flurry of claws aimed at neck joints and gun muzzles tight against flesh as they fired. Then a grenade, dropped or jarred from a container, went off in the blood-slick

compartment of number one car. Mingled limbs erupted.
The sides blew out and the bins of ready ammunition gang-
fired in a fury of light and gobbets of molten iridium.

The attack was over. The Mothers had made the instant
assumption that the third explosion would be on the order
of the two previous—and blocked their minds off from a
Tree-empathy that might have been lethal. Without their
inexorable thrusting, the scatter of sept-brothers fled like
grubs from the sun. They had fought with the savagery of
their remote ancestors eliminating the great Folk-devouring
serpents from the forest.

And it had not been enough.

"Cursed right we're staying here," Horthy said in
irritation. "This is the only high ground in five hundred
kilometers. If we're going to last out another attack like
yesterday's, it'll be by letting our K3 roll downhill into those
apes. And the Lord help us if a wind comes up."

"Well, I still don't like it, Top," Jenne complained. "It
doesn't look natural."

Horthy fully agreed with that, though he did so in
silence. Command Central had used satellite coverage to
direct them to the hill, warning again that even in their
emergency it might be a day before a landing boat could
be cleared to pick them up. From above, the half-kilometer
dome of laterite must have been as obvious as a baby in
the wedding party, a gritty red pustule on the gray hide
of the continent. From the forest edge it was even stranger,
and strange meant deadly to men in Horthy's position. But
only the antipersonnel strips had saved the platoon the night
before, and they were fully discharged. They were left with
the gas or nothing.

The hill was as smooth as the porous stone allowed it to
be and rose at a gentle 1:3 ratio. The curve of its edge was
broken by the great humped roots that lurched and knot-
ted out of the surrounding forest, plunging into the hill at
angles that must lead them to its center. As Jenne had said,
it wasn't natural. Nothing about this cursed forest was.

"Let's go," Horthy ordered. His driver boosted the angle

and power of his drive fans and they began to slide up the hill, followed by the other two cars. Strange that the trees hadn't covered the hill with a network of branches, even if their trunks for some reason couldn't seat in the rock. Enough ground was clear for the powerguns alone to mince an attack, despite the awesome quickness of the gray creatures. Except that the powerguns were low on ammo too.

Maybe there wouldn't be a third attack.

An alien appeared at the hillcrest fifty meters ahead. Horthy killed it by reflex, using a single shot from his tribarrel. There was an opening there, a cave or tunnel mouth, and a dozen more of the figures spewed from it. "Watch the sides!" Horthy roared at Jenne and Scratchard, but all three powerguns were ripping the new targets. Bolts that missed darted off into the dull sky like brief, blue-green suns.

Jenne's grenade spun into the meter-broad hole as the car overran it. If anything more had planned to come out, that settled it. Scratchard jiggled the controls of the echo sounder, checked the read-out again, and swore, "Via! I don't see any more surface openings, Top, but this whole mound's like a fencepost in termite country!"

The three blowers were pulled up close around the opening, the crews awaiting orders. Horthy toothed his lower lip but there was no hesitation in his voice after he decided. "Wixom and Chung," he said, "get that gas shell out and bring it over here. The rest of you cover the forest—I'll keep this hole clear."

The two troopers wrestled the cylinder out of the command car and gingerly carried it to the lip of the opening. The hill was reasonably flat on top and the laterite gave good footing, but the recent shooting had left patches glazed by the powerguns and a film of blood over the whole area. The container should not have ruptured if dropped, but no one familiar with K3 wanted to take the chance.

"All plus," Horthy said. "Fuse it for ten seconds and drop it in. As soon as that goes down, we're going to hover over the hole with our fans on max, just to make sure all the gas goes in the right direction. If we can do them enough damage, maybe they'll leave us alone."

The heavy shell clinked against something as it disappeared into the darkness but kept falling in the passage cleared by the grenade. It was well below the surface when the bursting charge tore the casing open. That muted *whoomp* was lost in the shriek of Horthy's fans as his car wobbled on a column of air a meter above the hilltop. K3 sank even in still air, pooling in invisible deathtraps in the low spots of a battlefield. Rammed by the drive fans, it had permeated the deepest tunnels of the mound in less than a minute.

The rioting air blew the bodies and body parts of the latest victims into a windrow beside the opening. Horthy glanced over them with a professional concern for the dead as he marked time. These creatures had the same long limbs and smooth-faced features as the ones which had attacked in the forest, but there was a difference as well. The genitals of the earlier-seen aliens had been tiny, vestigial or immature, but each of the present corpses carried a dong the length and thickness of a forearm. Bet their girlfriends walk bow-legged, Horthy chuckled to himself.

The hill shook with an impact noticeable even through the insulating air. "Top, they're tunneling out!" cried the command car's driver over the intercom.

"Hold your distance!" Horthy commanded as five meters of laterite crumbled away from the base of the hill. The thing that had torn the gap almost filled it. Horthy and every other gunman in the platoon blasted at it in a reaction that went deeper than fear. Even as it gouted fluids under the multiple impacts the thing managed to squirm completely out. The tiny head and the limbs that waved like broomstraws thrust into a watermelon were the only ornamentation on the slug-white torso. The face was blind, but it was the face of the reptiloids of the forest until a burst of cyan pulped its obscenity. Horthy's tribarrel whipsawed down the twenty-meter belly. A sphincter convulsed in front of the line of shots and spewed a mass of eggs in jelly against the unyielding laterite. The blackening that K3 brought to its victims was already beginning to set in before the platoon stopped firing.

Nothing further attempted to leave the mound.

"Wh-what do we do now, Top?" Jenne asked.

"Wait for the landing boat," answered Horthy. He shook the cramp out of his hand and pretended that it was not caused by his panicky deathgrip on the tribarrel moments before. "And we pray that it comes before too bleeding long."

The cold that made Hilf's body shudder was the residue of the Mothers' death throes deep in the corridors of the Nest. No warmth remained in a universe which had seen the last generation of the Folk. The yellow leaf-tinge of his blast-damaged Tree no longer concerned Hilf. About him, a psychic pressure rather than a message, he could feel the gathering of the other twenty-eight septs—just too late to protect the Mothers who had summoned them. Except for the Moon Sept's, the Trees were still healthy and would continue to be so for years until there were too few of the Folk scampering among the branches to spread their pollen. Then, with only the infrequent wind to stimulate new growth, the Trees as well would begin to die.

Hilf began to walk forward on all fours, his knuckles gripping firmly the rough exterior of the Nest. "Top!" cried one of the invaders, and Hilf knew that their eyes or the quick-darting antennae of their silver beasts had discovered his approach. He looked up. The three-limbed Caller was staring at him, his stick extended to kill. His eyes were as empty as Hilf's own.

The bolt hammered through Hilf's lungs and he pitched backwards. Through the bloodroar in his ears he could hear the far-distant howl that had preceded the invader's appearance in the forest.

As if the landing boat were their signal, the thirty thousand living males of the Folk surged forward from the Trees.

LIBERTY PORT

Commandant Horace Jolober had just lowered the saddle of his mobile chair, putting himself at the height of the Facilities Inspection Committee seated across the table, when the alarm hooted and Vicki cried from the window in the next room, *"Tanks!* In the street!"

The three Placidan bureaucrats flashed Jolober looks of anger and fear, but he had no time for them now even though they were his superiors. The stump of his left leg keyed the throttle of his chair. As the fans spun up, Jolober leaned and guided his miniature air-cushion vehicle out of the room faster than another man could have walked.

Faster than a man with legs could walk.

Vicki opened the door from the bedroom as Jolober swept past her toward the inside stairs. Her face was as calm as that of the statue which it resembled in its perfection, but Jolober knew that only the strongest emotion would have made her disobey his orders to stay in his private apartments while the inspection team was here. She was afraid that he was about to be killed.

A burst of gunfire in the street suggested she just might be correct.

"Chief" called Jolober's mastoid implant in what he thought was the voice of Karnes, his executive officer. "I'm at the gate and the new arrivals, they're Hammer's, just came right through the wire! There's half a dozen tanks and they're shooting in the air!"

324

Could've been worse. Might yet be.

He slid onto the staircase, his stump boosting fan speed with reflexive skill. The stair treads were too narrow for Jolober's mobile chair to form an air cushion between the surface and the lip of its plenum chamber. Instead he balanced on thrust alone while the fans beneath him squealed, ramming the air hard enough to let him slope down above the staircase with the grace of a stooping hawk.

The hardware was built to handle the stress, but only flawless control kept the port commandant from up-ending and crashing down the treads in a fashion as dangerous as it would be humiliating.

Jolober was a powerful man who'd been tall besides until a tribarrel blew off both his legs above the knee. In his uniform of white cloth and lavish gold, he was dazzlingly obvious in any light. As he gunned his vehicle out into the street, the most intense light source was the rope of cyan bolts ripping skyward from the cupola of the leading tank.

The buildings on either side of the street enticed customers with displays to rival the sun, but the operators—each of them a gambler, brothel keeper, and saloon owner all in one—had their own warning systems. The lights were going out, leaving the plastic façades cold.

Lightless, the buildings faded to the appearance of the high concrete fortresses they were in fact. Repeated arches made the entrance of the China Doll, directly across the street from the commandant's offices, look spacious. The door itself was so narrow that only two men could pass it at a time, and no one could slip unnoticed past the array of sensors and guards that made sure none of those entering were armed.

Normally the facilities here at Paradise Port were open all day. Now an armored panel clanged down across the narrow door of the China Doll, its echoes merging with similar tocsins from the other buildings.

Much good that would do if the tanks opened up with their 20cm main guns. Even a tribarrel could blast holes in thumb-thick steel as easily as one had vaporized Jolober's knees and calves. . . .

He slid into the street, directly into the path of the lead tank. He would have liked to glance up toward the bedroom window for what he knew might be his last glimpse of Vicki, but he was afraid that he couldn't do that and still have the guts to do his duty.

For a long time after he lost his legs, the only thing which had kept Horace Jolober from suicide was the certainty that he had always done his duty. Not even Vicki could be allowed to take that from him.

The tanks were advancing at no more than a slow walk though their huge size gave them the appearance of speed. They were buttoned up—hatches down, crews hidden behind the curved surfaces of iridium armor that might just possibly turn a bolt from a gun as big as the one each tank carried in its turret.

Lesser weapons had left scars on the iridium. Where light powerguns had licked the armor—and even a tribarrelled automatic was light in comparison to a tank— the metal cooled again in a slope around the point where a little had been vaporized. High-velocity bullets made smaller, deeper craters plated with material from the projectile itself.

The turret of the leading tank bore a long gouge that began in a pattern of deep, radial scars. A shoulder-fired rocket had hit at a slight angle. The jet of white-hot gas spurting from the shaped-charge warhead had burned deep enough into even the refractory iridium that it would have penetrated the turret had it struck squarely.

If either the driver or the blower captain were riding with their heads out of the hatch when the missile detonated, shrapnel from the casing had decapitated them.

Jolober wondered if the present driver even saw him, a lone man in a street that should have been cleared by the threat of one hundred and seventy tonnes of armor howling down the middle of it.

An air-cushion jeep carrying a pintle-mounted needle stunner and two men in Port Patrol uniforms was driving alongside the lead tank, bucking and pitching in the current roaring from beneath the steel skirts of the tank's plenum chamber. While the driver fought to hold the light vehicle steady, the other patrolman bellowed through the jeep's loudspeakers. He might have been on the other side of the planet for all his chance of being heard over the sound of air sucked through intakes atop the tank's hull and then pumped beneath the skirts forcefully enough to balance the huge weight of steel and iridium.

Jolober grounded his mobile chair. He crooked his left ring finger so that the surgically redirected nerve impulse keyed the microphone implanted at the base of his jaw. "Gentlemen," he said, knowing that the base unit in the Port Office was relaying his words on the Slammers' general frequency. "You are violating the regulations which govern Paradise Port. Stop before somebody gets hurt."

The bow of the lead tank was ten meters away—and one meter less every second.

To the very end he thought they were going to hit him—by inadvertence, now, because the tank's steel skirt lifted in a desperate attempt to stop but the vehicle's mass overwhelmed the braking effect of its fans. Jolober knew that if he raised his chair from the pavement, the blast of air from the tank would knock him over and roll him along the concrete like a trashcan in a windstorm—bruised but safe.

He would rather die than lose his dignity that way in front of Vicki.

The tank's bow slewed to the left, toward the China Doll. The skirt on that side touched the pavement with the sound of steel screaming and a fountain of sparks that sprayed across and over the building's high plastic façade.

The tank did not hit the China Doll, and it stopped short of Horace Jolober by less than the radius of its bow's curve.

The driver grounded his huge vehicle properly and cut the power to his fans. Dust scraped from the pavement, choking and chalky, swirled around Jolober and threw him into a paroxysm of coughing. He hadn't realized that he'd been holding his breath—until the danger passed and instinct filled his lungs.

The jeep pulled up beside Jolober, its fans kicking up still more dust, and the two patrolmen shouted words of concern and congratulation to their commandant. More men were appearing, patrolmen and others who had ducked into the narrow alleys between buildings when the tanks filled the street.

"Stecher," said Jolober to the sergeant in the patrol vehicle, "go back there—" he gestured toward the remainder of the column, hidden behind the armored bulk of the lead tank "—and help 'em get turned around. Get 'em back to the Refit Area where they belong,"

"Sir, should I get the names?" Stecher asked.

The port commandant shook his head with certainty. "None of this happened," he told his subordinates. "I'll take care of it."

The jeep spun nimbly while Stecher spoke into his commo helmet, relaying Jolober's orders to the rest of the squad on street duty.

Metal rang again as the tank's two hatch covers slid open. Jolober was too close to the hull to see the crewmen so he kicked his fans to life and backed a few meters.

The mobile chair had been built to his design. Its only control was the throttle with a linkage which at high-thrust settings automatically transformed the plenum chamber to a nozzle. Steering and balance were matters of how the rider shifted his body weight. Jolober prided himself that he was just as nimble as he had been before.

—Before he fell back into the trench on Primavera, half wrapped in the white flag he'd waved to the oncoming tanks. The only conscious memory he retained of *that* moment was the sight of his right leg still balanced on the trench lip above him, silhouetted against the criss-crossing cyan bolts from the powerguns.

But Horace Jolober was just as much a man as he'd ever been. The way he got around proved it. And Vicki.

The driver staring out the bow hatch at him was a woman with thin features and just enough hair to show beneath her helmet. She looked scared, aware of what had just happened and aware also of just how bad it could've been.

Jolober could appreciate how she felt.

The man who lifted himself from the turret hatch was

under thirty, angry, and—though Jolober couldn't remember
the Slammers' collar pips precisely—a junior officer of some
sort rather than a sergeant.

The dust had mostly settled by now, but vortices still
spun above the muzzles of the tribarrel which the fellow
had been firing skyward. "What're you doing, you bloody
fool?" he shouted. "D'ye *want* to die?"

Not any more, thought Horace Jolober as he stared
upward at the tanker. One of the port patrolmen had
responded to the anger in the Slammer's voice by raising
his needle stunner, but there was no need for that.

Jolober keyed his mike so that he didn't have to shout
with the inevitable emotional loading. In a flat, certain
voice, he said, "If you'll step down here, Lieutenant, we
can discuss the situation like officers—which I am, and you
will continue to be unless you insist on pushing things."

The tanker grimaced, then nodded his head and lifted
himself the rest of the way out of the turret. "Right," he said.
"Right. I . . ." His voice trailed off, but he wasn't going to
say anything the port commandant hadn't heard before.

When you screw up real bad, you can either be afraid
or you can flare out in anger and blame somebody else.
Not because you don't know better, but because it's the
only way to control your fear. It isn't pretty, but there's
no pretty way to screw up bad.

The tanker dropped to the ground in front of Jolober
and gave a sloppy salute. That was lack of practice, not
deliberate insult, and his voice and eyes were firm as he
said, "Sir. Acting Captain Tad Hoffritz reporting."

"Horace Jolober," the port commandant said. He raised
his saddle to put his head at what used to be normal
standing height, a few centimeters taller than Hoffritz. The
Slammer's rank made it pretty clear why the disturbance
had occurred. "Your boys?" Jolober asked, thumbing toward
the tanks sheepishly reversing down the street under the
guidance of white-uniformed patrolmen.

"Past three days they have been," Hoffritz agreed. His
mouth scrunched again in an angry grimace and he said,
"Look, I'm real sorry. I know how dumb that was. I just . . ."

Again, there wasn't anything new to say.

The tank's driver vaulted from her hatch with a suddenness which drew both men's attention. "Corp'ral Days," she said with a salute even more perfunctory than Hoffritz's had been. "Look, sir, *I* was drivin' and if there's a problem, it's my problem."

"Daisy—" began Captain Hoffritz.

"There's no problem, Corporal," Jolober said firmly. "Go back to your vehicle. We'll need to move it in a minute or two."

Another helmeted man had popped his head from the turret—surprisingly, because this was a line tank, not a command vehicle with room for several soldiers in the fighting compartment. The driver looked at her captain, then met the worried eyes of the trooper still in the turret. She backed a pace but stayed within earshot.

"Six tanks out of seventeen," Jolober said calmly. Things *were* calm enough now that he was able to follow the crosstalk of his patrolmen, their voices stuttering at low level through the miniature speaker on his epaulet. "You've been seeing some action, then."

"Too bloody right," muttered Corporal Days.

Hoffritz rubbed the back of his neck, lowering his eyes, and said, "Well, running . . . There's four back at Refit deadlined we brought in on transporters, but—"

He looked squarely at Jolober. "But sure we had a tough time. That's why I'm CO and Chester's up there—" he nodded toward the man in the turret "—trying to work company commo without a proper command tank. And I guess I figured—"

Hoffritz might have stopped there, but the port commandant nodded him on.

"—I figured maybe it wouldn't hurt to wake up a few rear-echelon types when we came back here for refit. Sorry, sir."

"There's three other units, including a regiment of the Division Legere, on stand-down here at Paradise Port already, Captain," Jolober said. He nodded toward the soldiers in mottled fatigues who were beginning to reappear on the street. "Not rear-echelon troops, from what I've heard. And they need some relaxation just as badly as your men do."

"Yes, sir," Hoffritz agreed, blank-faced. "It was real dumb. I'll sign the report as soon as you make it out."

Jolober shrugged. "There won't be a report, Captain. Repairs to the gate'll go on your regiment's damage account and be deducted from Placida's payment next month." He smiled. "Along with any chairs or glasses you break in the casinos. Now, get your vehicle into the Refit Area where it belongs. And come back and have a good time in Paradise Port. That's what we're here for."

"*Thank* you, sir," said Hoffritz, and relief dropped his age by at least five years. He clasped Jolober's hand and, still holding it, asked, "You've seen service, too, haven't you, sir?"

"Fourteen years with Hampton's Legion," Jolober agreed, pleased that Hoffritz had managed not to stare at the stumps before asking the question.

"Hey, good outfit," the younger man said with enthusiasm. "We were with Hampton on Primavera, back, oh, three years ago?"

"Yes, I know," Jolober said. His face was still smiling, and the subject wasn't an emotional one any more. He felt no emotion at all . . . "One of your tanks shot—" his left hand gestured delicately at where his thighs ended "—these off on Primavera."

"Lord," Sergeant Days said distinctly.

Captain Hoffritz looked as if he had been hit with a brick. Then his face regained its animation. "*No*, sir," he said. "You're mistaken. On Primavera, we were both working for the Federalists. Hampton was our infantry support."

Not the way General Hampton would have described the chain of command, thought Jolober. His smile became real again. He still felt pride in his old unit—and he could laugh at those outdated feelings in himself.

"Yes, that's right," he said aloud. "There'd been an error in transmitting map coordinates. When a company of these—" he nodded toward the great iridium monster, feeling sweat break out on his forehead and arms as he did so "—attacked my battalion, I jumped up to stop the shooting."

Jolober's smile paled to a frosty shadow of itself. "I was successful," he went on softly, "but not quite as soon as I would've liked."

"Oh, Lord and Martyrs," whispered Hoffritz. His face looked like that of a battle casualty.

"Tad, that was—" Sergeant Days began.

"Shut it *off*, Daisy!" shouted the Slammers' commo man from the turret. Days' face blanked and she nodded.

"Sir, I—" Hoffritz said.

Jolober shook his head to silence the younger man. "In a war," he said, "a lot of people get in the way of rounds. I'm luckier than some. I'm still around to tell about it."

He spoke in the calm, pleasant voice he always used in explaining the—matter—to others. For the length of time he was speaking, he could generally convince even himself.

Clapping Hoffritz on the shoulder—the physical contact brought Jolober back to present reality, reminding him that the tanker was a young man and not a demon hidden behind armor and a tribarrel—the commandant said, "Go on, move your hardware and then see what Paradise Port can show you in the way of a good time."

"Oh, that I know already," said Hoffritz with a wicked, man-to-man smile of his own. "When we stood down here three months back, I met a girl named Beth. I'll bet she still remembers me, and the *Lord* knows I remember her."

"Girl?" Jolober repeated. The whole situation had so disoriented him that he let his surprise show.

"Well, you know," said the tanker. "A Doll, I guess. But believe me, Beth's woman enough for *me*."

"Or for anyone," the commandant agreed. "I know just what you mean."

Stecher had returned with the jeep. The street was emptied of all armor except Hoffritz's tank, and that was an object of curiosity rather than concern for the men spilling out the doors of the reopened brothels. Jolober waved toward the patrol vehicle and said, "My men'll guide you out of here, Captain Hoffritz. Enjoy your stay."

The tank driver was already scrambling back into her hatch. She had lowered her helmet shield, so the glimpse Jolober got of her face was an unexpected, light-reflecting bubble.

Maybe Corporal Days had a problem with where the conversation had gone when the two officers started talking like two men. That was a pity, for her and probably for Captain Hoffritz as well. A tank was too small a container to hold emotional trouble among its crew.

But Horace Jolober had his own problems to occupy him as he slid toward his office at a walking pace. He had his meeting with the Facilities Inspection Committee, which wasn't going to go more smoothly because of the interruption.

A plump figure sauntering in the other direction tipped his beret to Jolober as they passed. "Ike," acknowledged the port commandant in a voice as neutral as a gun barrel that doesn't care in the least at whom it's pointed.

Red Ike could pass for human, until the rosy cast of his skin drew attention to the fact that his hands had only three fingers and a thumb. Jolober was surprised to see that Ike was walking across the street toward his own brothel, the China Doll, instead of being inside the building already. That could have meant anything, but the probability was that Red Ike had a tunnel to one of the buildings across the street to serve as a bolthole.

And since all the *real* problems at Paradise Port were a result of the alien who called himself Red Ike, Jolober could easily imagine why the fellow would want to have a bolthole.

Jolober had gone down the steps in a smooth undulation. He mounted them in a series of hops, covering two treads between pauses like a weary cricket climbing out of a well.

The chair's powerpack had more than enough charge left to swoop him up to the conference room. It was the man himself who lacked the mental energy now to balance himself on the column of driven air. He felt drained—the tribarrel, the tank . . . the memories of Primavera. If he'd decided to, sure, but . . .

But maybe he was getting old.

The Facilities Inspection Committee—staff members, actually, for three of the most powerful senators in the Placidan legislature—waited for Jolober with doubtful looks. Higgey and Wayne leaned against the conference room window, watching Hoffritz's tank reverse sedately in the street. The woman, Rodall, stood by the stairhead watching the port commandant's return.

"Why don't you have an elevator put in?" she asked. "Or at least a ramp?" Between phrases, Rodall's full features relaxed to the pout that was her normal expression.

Jolober paused beside her, noticing the whisper of air from beneath his plenum chamber was causing her to twist her feet away as if she had stepped into slime. "There aren't elevators everywhere, Mistress," he said. "Most places, there isn't even enough smooth surface to depend on ground effect alone to get you more than forty meters."

He smiled and gestured toward the conference room's window. Visible beyond the China Doll and the other buildings across the street was the reddish-brown expanse of the surrounding landscape: ropes of lava on which only lichen could grow, where a man had to hop and scramble from one ridge to another.

The Placidan government had located Paradise Port in a volcanic wasteland in order to isolate the mercenaries letting off steam between battles with Armstrong, the other power on the planet's sole continent. To a cripple in a chair which depended on wheels or unaided ground effect, the twisting lava would be as sure a barrier as sheer walls.

Jolober didn't say that so long as he could go anywhere other men went, he could pretend he was still a man. If the Placidan civilian could have understood that, she wouldn't have asked why he didn't have ramps put in.

"Well, what *was* that?" demanded Higgey—thin, intense,

and already half bald in his early thirties. "Was anyone killed?"

"Nothing serious, Master Higgey," Jolober said as he slid back to the table and lowered himself to his "seated" height. "And no, no one was killed or even injured."

Thank the Lord for his mercy.

"It *looked* serious, Commandant," said the third committee member—Wayne, half again Jolober's age and a retired colonel of the Placidan regular army. "I'm surprised you permit things like that to happen."

Higgey and Rodall were seating themselves. Jolober gestured toward the third chair on the curve of the round table opposite him and said, "Colonel, your, ah—opposite numbers in Armstrong tried to stop those tanks last week with a battalion of armored infantry. They got their butts kicked until they didn't *have* butts any more."

Wayne wasn't sitting down. His face flushed and his short white mustache bristled sharply against his upper lip.

Jolober shrugged and went on in a more conciliatory tone, "Look, sir, units aren't rotated back here unless they've had a hell of a rough time in the line. I've got fifty-six patrolmen with stunners to keep order . . . which we do, well enough for the people using Paradise Port. We aren't here to start a major battle of our own. Placida needs these mercenaries and needs them in fighting trim."

"That's a matter of opinion," said the retired officer with his lips pressed together, but at last he sat down.

The direction of sunrise is also a matter of opinion, Jolober thought. It's about as likely to change as Placida is to survive without the mercenaries who had undertaken the war her regular army was losing.

"I requested this meeting—" requested it with the senators themselves, but he hadn't expected them to agree "—in order to discuss just that, the fighting trim of the troops who undergo rest and refit here. So that Placida gets the most value for her, ah, payment."

The committee staff would do, if Jolober could get them to understand. Paradise Port was, after all, a wasteland with a village populated by soldiers who had spent all the recent past killing and watching their friends die. It wasn't the sort of place you'd pick for a senatorial junket.

Higgey leaned forward, clasping his hands on the table top, and said, "Commandant, I'm sure that those—" he waggled a finger disdainfully toward the window "—men out there would be in better physical condition after a week of milk and religious lectures than they will after the regime they choose for themselves. There are elements—"

Wayne nodded in stern agreement, his eyes on Mistress Rodall, whose set face refused to acknowledge either of her fellows while the subject was being discussed.

"—in the electorate and government who would like to try that method, but fortunately reality has kept the idea from being attempted."

Higgey paused, pleased with his forceful delivery and the way his eyes dominated those of the much bigger man across the table. "If you've suddenly got religion, Commandant Jolober," he concluded, "I suggest you resign your current position and join the ministry."

Jobber suppressed his smile. Higgey reminded him of a lap dog, too nervous to remain either still or silent, and too small to be other than ridiculous in its posturing. "My initial message was unclear, madam, gentlemen," he explained, looking around the table. "I'm not suggesting that Placida close the brothels that are part of the recreational facilities here."

His pause was not for effect, but because his mouth had suddenly gone very dry. But it was his duty to—

"I'm recommending that the Dolls be withdrawn from Paradise Port and that the facilities be staffed with human, ah, females."

Colonel Wayne stiffened and paled.

Wayne's anger was now mirrored in the expression on Rodall's face. "Whores," she said. "So that those—*soldiers*—can disgrace and dehumanize real women for their fun."

"And kill them, one assumes," added Higgey with a touch of amusement. "I checked the records, Commandant. There've been seventeen Dolls killed during the months

Paradise Port's been in operation. As it is, that's a simple damage assessment, but if they'd been human prostitutes— each one would have meant a manslaughter charge or even murder. People don't cease to have rights when they choose to sell their bodies, you know."

"When they're forced to sell their bodies, you mean," snapped Rodall. She glared at Higgey, who didn't mean anything of the sort.

"Scarcely to the benefit of your precious mercenaries," said Wayne in a distant voice. "Quite apart from the political difficulties it would cause for any senator who recommended the change."

"As a matter of fact," said Higgey, whose natural caution had tightened his visage again, "I thought you were going to use the record of violence here at Paradise Port as a reason for closing the facility. Though I'll admit that I couldn't imagine anybody selfless enough to do away with his own job."

No, you couldn't, you little weasel, thought Horace Jolober. But politicians have different responsibilities than soldiers, and politicians' flunkies have yet another set of needs and duties.

And none of them are saints. Surely no soldier who does his job is a saint.

"Master Higgey, you've precisely located the problem," Jolober said with a nod of approval. "The violence isn't a result of the soldiers, it's because of the Dolls. It isn't accidental, it's planned. And it's time to stop it."

"It's time for us to leave, you mean," said Higgey as he shoved his chair back. "Resigning still appears to be your best course, Commandant. Though I don't suppose the ministry is the right choice for a new career, after all."

"Master Higgey," Jolober said in the voice he would have used in an argument with a fellow officer, "I know very well that no one is irreplaceable—but *you* know that I am doing as good a job here as anybody you could hire to run Paradise Port. I'm asking you to listen for a few minutes to a proposal that will make the troops you pay incrementally better able to fight for you."

"We've come this far," said Rodall.

"There are no listening devices in my quarters," Jolober explained, unasked. "I doubt that any real-time commo link out of Paradise Port is free of interception."

He didn't add that time he spent away from *his* duties was more of a risk to Placida than pulling these three out of their offices and expensive lunches could be. The tanks roaring down the street should have proved that even to the committee staffers.

Jolober paused, pressing his fingertips to his eyebrows in a habitual trick to help him marshal his thoughts while the others stared at him. "Mistress, masters," he said calmly after a moment, "the intention was that Paradise Port and similar facilities be staffed by independent contractors from off-planet."

"Which is where they'll return as soon as the war's over," agreed Colonel Wayne with satisfaction. "Or as soon as they put a toe wrong, any one of them."

"The war's bad enough as it is," said Rodall. "Building up Placida's stock of *that* sort of person would make peace hideous as well."

"Yes, ma'am, I understand," said the port commandant. There were a lot of "that sort of person" in Placida just now, including all the mercenaries in the line—and Horace Jolober back here. "But what you have in Paradise Port isn't a group of entrepreneurs, it's a corporation—a monarchy, almost—subservient to an alien called Red Ike."

"Nonsense," said Wayne.

"We don't permit that," said Rodall.

"Red Ike owns a single unit here," said Higgey. "The China Doll. Which is all he can own by law, to prevent just the sort of situation you're describing."

"Red Ike provides all the Dolls," Jolober stated flatly. "Whoever owns them on paper, they're his. And *everything* here is his because he controls the Dolls."

"Well . . ." said Rodall. She was beginning to blush.

"There's no actual proof," Colonel Wayne said, shifting his eyes toward a corner of walls and ceiling. "Though I suppose the physical traits are indicative . . ."

"The government has decided it isn't in the best interests of Placida to pierce the corporate veil in this instance," said Higgey in a thin voice. "The androids in question are shipped here from a variety of off-planet suppliers."

The balding Placidan paused and added, with a tone of absolute finality, "If the question were mine to decide—which it isn't—I would recommend searching for a new port commandant rather than trying to prove the falsity of a state of affairs beneficial to us, to Placida."

"I think that really must be the final word on the subject, Commandant Jolober," Rodall agreed.

Jolober thought she sounded regretful, but the emotion was too faint for him to be sure. The three Placidans were getting up, and he had failed.

He'd failed even before the staff members arrived, because it was now quite obvious that they'd decided their course of action before the meeting. They—and their elected superiors—would rather have dismissed Jolober's arguments.

But if the arguments proved to be well founded, they would dismiss the port commandant, if necessary to end the discussion.

"I suppose I should be flattered," Jolober said as hydraulics lifted him in the saddle and pressure of his stump on the throttle let him rotate his chair away from the table. "That you came all this way to silence me instead of refusing me a meeting."

"You might recall," said Higgey, pausing at the doorway. His look was meant to be threatening, but the port commandant's bulk and dour anger cooled the Placidan's face as soon as their eyes met. "That is, we're in the middle of a war, and the definition of treason can be a little loose in such times. While you're not technically a Placidan citizen, Commandant, you—would be well advised to avoid activities which oppose the conduct of war as the government has determined to conduct it."

He stepped out of the conference room. Rodall had left ahead of him.

"Don't take it too hard, young man," said Colonel Wayne when he and Jolober were alone. "You mercenaries, you

can do a lot of things the quick and easy way. It's different
when you represent a government and need to consider
political implications."

"I'd never understood there were negative implications,
Colonel," Jolober said with the slow, careful enunciation
which proved he was controlling himself rigidly, "in treating
your employees fairly. Even the mercenary soldiers whom
you employ."

Wayne's jaw lifted. "I beg your pardon, Commandant,"
he snapped. "I don't see anyone holding guns to the heads
of poor innocents, forcing them to whore and gamble."

He strode to the door, his back parade-ground straight.
At the door he turned precisely and delivered the broadside
he had held to that point. "Besides, Commandant—if the
Dolls are as dangerous to health and welfare as you say,
why are you living with one yourself?"

Wayne didn't expect an answer, but what he saw in
Horace Jolober's eyes suggested that his words might bring
a physical reaction that he hadn't counted on. He skipped
into the hall with a startled sound, banging the door behind
him.

The door connecting the conference room to the port
commandant's personal suite opened softly. Jolober did not
look around.

Vicki put her long, slim arms around him from behind.
Jolober spun, then cut power to his fans and settled his
chair firmly onto the floor. He and Vicki clung to one
another, legless man and Doll whose ruddy skin and beauty
marked her as inhuman.

They were both crying.

Someone from Jolober's staff would poke his head into
the conference room shortly to ask if the meeting was over
and if the commandant wanted nonemergency calls routed
through again.

The meeting was certainly over . . . but Horace Jolober
had an emergency of his own. He swallowed, keyed his
implant, and said brusquely, "I'm out of action till I tell
you different. Unless it's another Class A flap."

The kid at the commo desk stuttered a "Yessir" that was a syllable longer than Jolober wanted to hear. Vicki straightened, wearing a bright smile beneath the tear streaks, but the big human gathered her to his chest again and brought up the power of his fans.

Together, like a man carrying a moderate-sized woman, the couple slid around the conference table to the door of the private suite. The chair's drive units were overbuilt because men are overbuilt, capable of putting out huge bursts of hysterical strength.

Drive fans and power packs don't have hormones, so Jolober had specified—and paid for—components that would handle double the hundred kilos of his own mass, the hundred kilos left after the tribarrel had chewed him. The only problem with carrying Vicki to bed was one of balance, and the Doll remained still in his arms.

Perfectly still, as she was perfect in all the things she did.

"I'm not trying to get rid of you, darling," Jolober said as he grounded his chair.

"It's all right," Vicki whispered. "I'll go now if you like. It's all right."

She placed her fingertips on Jolober's shoulders and lifted herself by those fulcrums off his lap and onto the bed, her toes curled beneath her buttocks. A human gymnast could have done as well—but no better.

"What I *want*," Jolober said forcefully as he lifted himself out of the saddle, using the chair's handgrips, "is to do my job. And when I've done it, I'll buy you from Red Ike for whatever price he chooses to ask."

He swung himself to the bed. His arms had always been long—and strong. Now he knew that he must look like a gorilla when he got on or off his chair . . . and when the third woman he was with after the amputation giggled at him, he began to consider suicide as an alternative to sex.

Then he took the job on Placida and met Vicki.

Her tears had dried, so both of them could pretend they hadn't poured out moments before. She smiled shyly and touched the high collar of her dress, drawing her fingertip down a centimeter and opening the garment by that amount.

Vicki wasn't Jolober's ideal of beauty—wasn't what he'd *thought* his ideal was, at any rate. Big blondes, he would have said. A woman as tall as he was, with hair the color of bleached straw hanging to the middle of her back.

Vicki scarcely came up to the top of Jolober's breastbone when he was standing—at standing height in his chair—and her hair was a black fluff that was as short as a soldier would cut it to fit comfortably under a helmet. She looked buxom, but her breasts were fairly flat against her broad, powerfully muscled chest.

Jolober put his index finger against hers on the collar and slid down the touch-sensitive strip that opened the fabric. Vicki's body was without blemish or pubic hair. She was so firm that nothing sagged or flattened when her dress and the supports of memory plastic woven into it dropped away.

She shrugged her arms out of the straps and let the garment spill as a pool of sparkling shadow on the counterpane as she reached toward her lover.

Jolober, lying on his side, touched the collar of his uniform jacket.

"No need," Vicki said blocking his hand with one of hers and opening his trouser fly with the other. "Come," she added, rolling onto her back and drawing him toward her.

"But the—" Jolober murmured in surprise, leaning forward in obedience to her touch and demand. The metallic braid and medals on his stiff-fronted tunic had sharp corners to prod the Doll beneath him whether he wished or not.

"Come," she repeated. "This time."

Horace Jolober wasn't introspective enough to understand why his mistress wanted the rough punishment of his uniform. He simply obeyed.

Vicki toyed with his garments after they had finished and lay on the bed, their arms crossing. She had a trick of folding back her lower legs so that they vanished whenever she sat or reclined in the port commandant's presence.

Her fingers tweaked the back of Jolober's waistband and emerged with the hidden knife, the only weapon he carried.

"I'm at your mercy," he said, smiling. He mimed as much of a hands-up posture as he could with his right elbow supporting his torso on the mattress. "Have your way with me."

In Vicki's hand, the knife was a harmless cylinder of plastic—a weapon only to the extent that the butt of the short tube could harden a punch. The knife was of memory plastic whose normal state was a harmless block. No one who took it away from Jolober in a struggle would find it of any use as a weapon.

Only when squeezed after being cued by the pore pattern of Horace Jolober's right hand would it—

The plastic cylinder shrank in Vicki's hand, sprouting a double-edged 15cm blade.

"Via!" swore Jolober. Reflex betrayed him into thinking that he had legs. He jerked upright and started to topple off the bed because the weight of his calves and feet wasn't there to balance the motion.

Vicki caught him with both arms and drew him to her. The blade collapsed into the handle when she dropped it, so that it bounced as a harmless cylinder on the counterpane between them.

"My love, I'm *sorry*," the Doll blurted fearfully. "I didn't mean—"

"No, no," Jolober said, settled now on his thighs and buttocks so that he could hug Vicki fiercely. His eyes peered secretively over her shoulders, searching for the knife that had startled him so badly. "I was surprised that it . . . How *did* you get the blade to open, dearest? It's fine, it's nothing you did wrong, but I didn't expect that, is all."

They swung apart. The mattress was a firm one, but still a bad surface for this kind of conversation. The bedclothes rumpled beneath Jolober's heavy body and almost concealed the knife in a fold of cloth. He found it, raised it with his fingertips, and handed it to Vicki. "Please do that again," he said calmly. "Extend the blade."

Sweat was evaporating from the base of Jolober's spine, where the impermeable knife usually covered the skin.

Vicki took the weapon. She was so doubtful that her face showed no expression at all. Her fingers, short but perfectly formed, gripped the baton as if it were a knife hilt—and it became one. The blade formed with avalanche swiftness, darkly translucent and patterned with veins of stress. The plastic would not take a wire edge, but it could carve a roast or, with Jolober's strength behind it, ram twenty millimeters deep into hardwood.

"Like this?" Vicki said softly. "Just squeeze it and. . . ?"

Jolober put his hand over the Doll's and lifted the knife away between thumb and forefinger. When she loosed the hilt, the knife collapsed again into a short baton.

He squeezed—extended the blade—released it again—and slipped the knife back into its concealed sheath.

"You see, darling," Jolober said, "the plastic's been keyed to *my* body. Nobody else should be able to get the blade to form."

"I'd never use it against you," Vicki said. Her face was calm, and there was no defensiveness in her simple response.

Jolober smiled. "Of course, dearest; but there was a manufacturing flaw or you wouldn't be able to do that."

Vicki leaned over and kissed the port commandant's lips, then bent liquidly and kissed him again. "I told you," she said as she straightened with a grin. "I'm a part of you."

"And believe me," said Jolober, rolling onto his back to cinch up his short-legged trousers. "You're not a part of me I intend to lose."

He rocked upright and gripped the handles of his chair.

Vicki slipped off the bed and braced the little vehicle with a hand on the saddle and the edge of one foot on the skirt. The help wasn't necessary—the chair's weight anchored it satisfactorily, so long as Jolober mounted swiftly and smoothly. But it *was* helpful, and it was the sort of personal attention that was as important as sex in convincing Horace Jolober that someone really cared—*could* care—for him.

"You'll do your duty, though," Vicki said. "And I wouldn't want you not to."

Jolober laughed as he settled himself and switched on his fans. He felt enormous relief now that he had proved beyond doubt—he was sure of that—how much he loved Vicki. He'd calmed her down, and that meant he was calm again, too.

"Sure I'll do my job," he said as he smiled at the Doll. "That doesn't mean you and *me*'ll have a problem. Wait and see."

Vicki smiled also, but she shook her head in what Jolober thought was amused resignation. Her hairless body was too perfect to be flesh, and the skin's red pigment gave the Doll the look of a statue in blushing marble.

"Via, but you're lovely," Jolober murmured as the realization struck him anew.

"Come back soon," she said easily.

"Soon as I can," the commandant agreed as he lifted his chair and turned toward the door. "But like you say, I've got a job to do."

If the government of Placida wouldn't give him the support he needed, by the Lord! he'd work through the mercenaries themselves.

Though his belly went cold and his stumps tingled as he realized he would again be approaching the tanks which had crippled him.

The street had the sharp edge which invariably marked it immediately after a unit rotated to Paradise Port out of combat. The troops weren't looking for sex or intoxicants—though most of them would have claimed they were.

They were looking for life. Paradise Port offered them things they thought equaled life, and the contrast between reality and hope led to anger and black despair. Only after a few days of stunning themselves with the offered pleasures did the soldiers on leave recognize another contrast: Paradise Port might not be all they'd hoped, but it was a lot better than the muck and ravening hell of combat.

Jolober slid down the street at a walking pace. Some of the soldiers on the pavement with him offered ragged salutes to the commandant's glittering uniform. He returned them sharply, a habit he had ingrained in himself after he took charge here.

Mercenary units didn't put much emphasis on saluting and similar rear-echelon forms of discipline. An officer with the reputation of being a tight-assed martinet in bivouac was likely to get hit from behind the next time he led his troops into combat.

There were regular armies on most planets—Colonel Wayne was an example—to whom actual fighting was an aberration. Economics or a simple desire for action led many planetary soldiers into mercenary units . . . where the old habits of saluting and snapping to attention surfaced when the men were drunk and depressed.

Hampton's Legion hadn't been any more interested in saluting than the Slammers were. Jolober had sharpened his technique here because it helped a few of the men he served feel more at home—when they were very far from home.

A patrol jeep passed, idling slowly through the pedestrians. Sergeant Stecher waved, somewhat uncertainly.

Jolober waved back, smiling toward his subordinate but angry at himself. He keyed his implant and said "Central, I'm back in business now, but I'm headed for the Refit Area to see Captain van Zuyle. Let anything wait that can till I'm back."

He should have cleared with his switchboard as soon as he'd . . . calmed Vicki down. Here there'd been a crisis, and as soon as it was over he'd disappeared. Must've made his patrolmen very cursed nervous, and it was sheer sloppiness that he'd let the situation go on beyond what it had to. It was his job to make things simple for the people in Paradise Port, both his staff and the port's clientele.

Maybe even for the owners of the brothel: but it was going to have to be simple on Horace Jolober's terms.

At the gate, a tank was helping the crew repairing

damage. The men wore khaki coveralls—Slammers rushed from the Refit Area as soon as van Zuyle, the officer in charge there, heard what had happened. The faster you hid the evidence of a problem, the easier it was to claim the problem had never existed.

And it was to everybody's advantage that problems never exist.

Paradise Port was surrounded with a high barrier of woven plastic to keep soldiers who were drunk out of their minds from crawling into the volcanic wasteland and hurting themselves. The fence was tougher than it looked—it looked as insubstantial as moonbeams—but it had never been intended to stop vehicles.

The gate to the bivouac areas outside Paradise Port had a sturdy framework and hung between posts of solid steel. The lead tank had been wide enough to snap both gateposts off at the ground. The gate, framework and webbing, was strewn in fragments for a hundred meters along the course it had been dragged between the pavement and the tank's skirt.

As Jolober approached, he felt his self-image shrink by comparison to surroundings which included a hundred-and-seventy-tonne fighting vehicle. The tank was backed against one edge of the gateway.

With a huge *clang!* the vehicle set another steel post, blasting it home with the apparatus used in combat to punch explosive charges into deep bunkers. The ram vaporized osmium wire with a jolt of high voltage, transmitting the shock waves to the piston head through a column of fluid. It banged home the replacement post without difficulty, even though the "ground" was a sheet of volcanic rock.

The pavement rippled beneath Jolober, and the undamped harmonics of the quivering post were a scream that could be heard for kilometers. Jolober pretended it didn't affect him as he moved past the tank. He was praying that the driver was watching his side screens—or listening to a ground guide—as the tank trembled away from the task it had completed.

One of the Slammers' noncoms gestured reassuringly

toward Jolober. His lips moved as he talked into his commo helmet. The port commandant could hear nothing over the howl of the drive fans and prolonged grace notes from the vibrating post, but the tank halted where it was until he had moved past it.

A glance over his shoulder showed Jolober the tank backing into position to set the other post. It looked like a great tortoise, ancient and implacable, maneuvering to lay a clutch of eggs.

Paradise Port was for pleasure only. The barracks housing the soldiers and the sheds to store and repair their equipment were located outside the fenced perimeter. The buildings were prefabs extruded from a dun plastic less colorful than the ruddy lava fields on which they were set.

The bivouac site occupied by Hammer's line companies in rotation was unusual in that the large leveled area contained only four barracks buildings and a pair of broad repair sheds. Parked vehicles filled the remainder of the space.

At the entrance to the bivouac area waited a guard shack. The soldier who stepped from it wore body armor over her khakis. Her submachine gun was slung, but her tone was businesslike as she said, "Commandant Jolober? Captain van Zuyle's on his way to meet you right now."

Hold right here till you're invited in, Jolober translated mentally with a frown.

But he couldn't blame the Slammers' officer for wanting to assert his authority *here* over that of Horace Jolober, whose writ ran only to the perimeter of Paradise Port. Van Zuyle just wanted to prove that his troopers would be punished only with his assent—or by agreement reached with authorities higher than the port commandant.

There was a flagpole attached to a gable of one of the barracks. A tall officer strode from the door at that end and hopped into the driver's seat of the jeep parked there. Another khaki-clad soldier stuck her head out the door and called something, but the officer pretended not to hear. He spun his vehicle in an angry circle, rubbing its low-side skirts, and gunned it toward the entrance.

Jolober had met van Zuyle only once. The most memorable thing about the Slammers' officer was his anger—caused by fate, but directed at whatever was nearest to hand. He'd been heading a company of combat cars when the blower ahead of his took a direct hit.

If van Zuyle'd had his face shield down—but he hadn't, because the shield made him, made most troopers, feel as though they'd stuck their head in a bucket. That dissociation, mental rather than sensory, could get you killed in combat.

The shield would have darkened instantly to block the sleet of actinics from the exploding combat car. Without its protection . . . well, the surgeons could rebuild his face, with only a slight stiffness to betray the injuries. Van Zuyle could even see—by daylight or under strong illumination.

There just wasn't any way he'd ever be fit to lead a line unit again—and he was very angry about it.

Commandant Horace Jolober could understand how van Zuyle felt—better, perhaps, than anyone else on the planet could. It didn't make his own job easier, though.

"A pleasure to see you again, Commandant," van Zuyle lied brusquely as he skidded the jeep to a halt, passenger seat beside Jolober. "If you—"

Jolober smiled grimly as the Slammers' officer saw—and remembered—that the port commandant was legless and couldn't seat himself in a jeep on his air-cushion chair.

"No problem," said Jolober, gripping the jeep's side and the seat back. He lifted himself aboard the larger vehicle with an athletic twist that settled him facing front.

Of course, the maneuver was easier than it would have been if his legs were there to get in the way.

"Ah, your—" van Zuyle said, pointing toward the chair. Close up, Jolober could see a line of demarcation in his scalp. The implanted hair at the front had aged less than the gray-speckled portion which hadn't been replaced.

"No problem, Captain," Jolober repeated. He anchored his left arm around the driver's seat, gripped one of his chair's handles with the right hand, and jerked the chair into the bench seat in the rear of the open vehicle.

The jeep lurched: the air-cushion chair weighed almost as much as Jolober did without it, and he was a big man. "You learn tricks when you have to," he said evenly as he met the eyes of the Slammers' officer.

And your arms get very strong when they do a lot of the work your legs used to—but he didn't say that.

"My office?" van Zuyle asked sharply.

"Is that as busy as it looks?" Jolober replied, nodding toward the door where a soldier still waited impatiently for van Zuyle to return.

"Commandant, I've had a tank company come in shot to *hell*," van Zuyle said in a voice that built toward fury. "Three vehicles are combat lossed and have to be stripped—*and* the other vehicles need more than routine maintenance—*and* half the personnel are on medic's release. Or dead. I'm trying to run a refit area with what's left, my staff of twenty-three, and the trainee replacements Central sent over who haven't ridden in a panzer, much less pulled maintenance on one. And you ask if I've got time to waste on you?"

"No, Captain, I didn't ask that," Jolober said with the threatening lack of emotion which came naturally to a man who had all his life been bigger and stronger than most of those around him. "Find a spot where we won't be disturbed, and we'll park there."

When the Slammers' officer frowned, Jolober added, "I'm not here about Captain Hoffritz, Captain."

"Yeah," sighed van Zuyle as he lifted the jeep and steered it sedately toward a niche formed between the iridium carcasses of a pair of tanks. "We're repairing things right now—" he thumbed in the direction of the gate "—and any other costs'll go on the damage chit; but I guess I owe you an apology besides."

"Life's a dangerous place," Jolober said easily. Van Zuyle wasn't stupid. He'd modified his behavior as soon as he was reminded of the incident an hour before—and the leverage it gave the port commandant if he wanted to push it.

Van Zuyle halted them in the gray shade that brought sweat to Jolober's forehead. The tanks smelled of hot metal because some of their vaporized armor had settled back onto the hulls as fine dust. Slight breezes shifted it to the nostrils of the men nearby, a memory of the blasts in which it had formed.

Plastics had burned also, leaving varied pungencies which could not conceal the odor of cooked human flesh.

The other smells of destruction were unpleasant. That last brought Jolober memories of his legs exploding in brilliant coruscance. His body tingled and sweated, and his mouth said to the Slammers' officer, "Your men are being cheated and misused every time they come to Paradise Port, Captain. For political reasons, my superiors won't let me make the necessary changes. If the mercenary units serviced by Paradise Port unite and demand the changes, the government will be forced into the proper decision."

"Seems to me," said van Zuyle with his perfectly curved eyebrows narrowing, "that somebody could claim you were acting against your employers just now."

"Placida hired me to run a liberty port," said Jolober evenly. He was being accused of the worst crime a mercenary could commit: conduct that would allow his employers to forfeit his unit's bond and brand them forever as unemployable contract-breakers.

Jolober no longer was a mercenary in that sense; but he understood van Zuyle's idiom, and it was in that idiom that he continued, "Placida wants and needs the troops she hires to be sent back into action in the best shape possible. Her *survival* depends on it. If I let Red Ike run this place to his benefit and not to Placida's, then I'm not doing my job."

"All right," said van Zuyle. "What's Ike got on?"

A truck, swaying with its load of cheering troopers, pulled past on its way to the gate of Paradise Port. The man in the passenger's seat of the cab was Tad Hoffritz, his face a knife-edge of expectation.

"Sure, they need refit as bad as the hardware does," muttered van Zuyle as he watched the soldiers on leave with longing eyes. "Three days straight leave, half days after that when they've pulled their duty. But Via! I could use 'em here, especially with the tanks that're such a bitch if you're not used to crawling around in 'em."

His face hardened again. "Go on," he said, angry that Jolober knew how much he wanted to be one of the men on that truck instead of having to run a rear-echelon installation.

"Red Ike owns the Dolls like so many shots of liquor," Jolober said. He never wanted a combat job again—the thought terrified him, the noise and flash and the smell of his body burning. "He's using them to strip your men, everybody's men, in the shortest possible time," he continued in a voice out of a universe distant from his mind. "The games are honest—that's my job—but the men play when they're stoned, and they play with a Doll on their arm begging them to go on until they've got nothing left. How many of those boys—" he gestured to where the truck, now long past, had been "—are going to last three days?"

"We give 'em advances when they're tapped out," said van Zuyle with a different kind of frown. "Enough to last their half days—if they're getting their jobs done here. Works out pretty good.

"As a matter of fact," he went on, "the whole business works out pretty good. I never saw a soldier's dive without shills and B-girls. Don't guess you ever did either, Commandant. Maybe they're better at it, the Dolls, but all that means is that I get my labor force back quicker—and Hammer gets his tanks back in line with that much fewer problems."

"The Dolls—" Jolober began.

"The Dolls are clean," shouted van Zuyle in a voice like edged steel. "They give full value for what you pay 'em. And I've never had a Doll knife one of my guys—which is a curst sight better'n anyplace I been staffed with human whores!"

"No," said Jolober, his strength a bulwark against the Slammer's anger. "But you've had your men knife or strangle Dolls, haven't you? All the units here've had incidents of that sort. Do you think it's chance?"

Van Zuyle blinked. "I think it's a cost of doing business," he said, speaking mildly because the question had surprised him.

"No," Jolober retorted. "It's a major profit center for Red Ike. The Dolls don't just drop soldiers when they've stripped them. They humiliate the men, taunt them . . . and when one of these kids breaks and chokes the life out of the bitch who's goading him, Red Ike pockets the damage assessment. And it comes out of money Placida would otherwise have paid Hammer's Slammers."

The Slammers' officer began to laugh. It was Jolober's turn to blink in surprise.

"Sure," van Zuyle said, "androids like that cost a lot more'n gateposts or a few meters of fencing, you bet."

"He's the only source," said Jolober tautly. "Nobody knows where the Dolls come from—or where Ike does."

"Then nobody can argue the price isn't fair, can they?" van Zuyle gibed. "And you know what, Commandant? Take a look at this tank right here."

He pointed to one of the vehicles beside them. It was a command tank, probably the one in which Hoffritz's predecessor had ridden before it was hit by powerguns heavy enough to pierce its armor.

The first round, centered on the hull's broadside, had put the unit out of action and killed everyone aboard. The jet of energy had ignited everything flammable within the fighting compartment in an explosion which blew the hatches open. The enemy had hit the iridium carcass at least three times more, cratering the turret and holing the engine compartment.

"We couldn't replace this for the cost of twenty Dolls," van Zuyle continued. "And we're going to have to, you know, because she's a total loss. All I can do is strip her for salvage . . . and clean up as best I can for the crew, so we can say we had something to bury."

His too-pale, too-angry eyes glared at Jolober. "Don't talk to me about the cost of Dolls, Commandant. They're cheap at the price. I'll drive you back to the gate."

"You may not care about the dollar cost," said Jolober

in a voice that thundered over the jeep's drive fans. "But what about the men you're sending back into the line thinking they've killed somebody they loved—or that they *should*'ve killed her?"

"Commandant, that's one I can't quantify," the Slammers' officer said. The fans' keeping lowered as the blades bit the air at a steeper angle and began to thrust the vehicle out of the bivouac area. "First time a trooper kills a human here, that I *can* quantify: we lose him. If there's a bigger problem and the Bonding Authority decides to call it mutiny, then we lost a lot more than that.

"And I tell you, buddy," van Zuyle added with a one-armed gesture toward the wrecked vehicles now behind them. "We've lost too fucking much already on this contract."

The jeep howled past the guard at the bivouac entrance. Wind noise formed a deliberate damper on Jolober's attempts to continue the discussion. "Will you forward my request to speak to Colonel Hammer?" he shouted. "I can't get through to him myself."

The tank had left the gate area. Men in khaki, watched by Jolober's staff in white uniforms, had almost completed their task of restringing the perimeter fence. Van Zuyle throttled back, permitting the jeep to glide to a graceful halt three meters short of the workmen.

"The Colonel's busy, Commandant," he said flatly. "And from now on, I hope you'll remember that *I* am, too."

Jolober lifted his chair from the back seat. "I'm going to win this, Captain," he said. "I'm going to do my job whether or not I get any support."

The smile he gave van Zuyle rekindled the respect in the tanker's pale eyes.

There were elements of four other mercenary units bivouacked outside Paradise Port at the moment. Jolober could have visited them in turn—to be received with more or less civility, and certainly no more support than the Slammers' officer had offered.

A demand for change by the mercenaries in Placidan service had to be just that: a demand by *all* the mercenaries. Hammer's Slammers were the highest-paid troops here, and by that standard—any other criterion would start a brawl—the premier unit. If the Slammers refused Jolober, none of the others would back him.

The trouble with reform is that in the short run, it causes more problems than continuing along the bad old ways. Troops in a combat zone, who know that each next instant may be their last, are more to be forgiven for short-term thinking than, say, politicians; but the pattern is part of the human condition.

Besides, nobody but Horace Jolober seemed to think there was anything to reform.

Jolober moved in a walking dream while his mind shuttled through causes and options. His data were interspersed with memories of Vicki smiling up at him from the bed and of his own severed leg toppling in blue-green silhouette. He shook his head gently to clear the images and found himself on the street outside the Port offices.

His stump throttled back the fans reflexively; but when Jolober's conscious mind made its decision, he turned away from the office building and headed for the garish façade of the China Doll across the way.

Rainbow pastels lifted slowly over the front of the building, the gradation so subtle that close up it was impossible to tell where one band ended and the next began. At random intervals of from thirty seconds to a minute, the gentle hues were replaced by glaring, supersaturated colors separated by dazzling blue-white lines.

None of the brothels in Paradise Port were sedately decorated, but the China Doll stood out against the competition.

As Jolober approached, a soldier was leaving and three more—one a woman—were in the queue to enter. A conveyor carried those wishing to exit, separated from one another by solid panels. The panels withdrew sideways into the wall as each client reached the street—but there was always another panel in place behind to prevent anyone from bolting into the building without being searched at the proper entrance.

All of the buildings in Paradise Port were designed the same way, with security as unobtrusive as it could be while remaining uncompromised. The entryways were three-meter funnels narrowing in a series of gaudy corbelled arches. Attendants—humans everywhere but in the China Doll— waited at the narrow end. They smiled as the customers passed—but anyone whom the detection devices in the archway said was armed was stopped right there.

The first two soldiers ahead of Jolober went through without incident. The third was a short man wearing lieutenant's pips and the uniform of Division Legere. His broad shoulders and chest narrowed to his waist as abruptly as those of a bulldog, and it was with a bulldog's fierce intransigence that he braced himself against the two attendants who had confronted him.

"I am Lieutenant Alexis Condorcet!" he announced as though he were saying "major general." "What do you mean by hindering me?"

The attendants in the China Doll were Droids, figures with smoothly masculine features and the same blushing complexion which set Red Ike and the Dolls apart from the humans with whom they mingled.

They were not male—Jolober had seen the total sex-lessness of an android whose tights had ripped as he quelled a brawl. Their bodies and voices were indistinguishable from one to another, and there could be no doubt that they were androids, artificial constructions whose existence proved that the Dolls could be artificial, too.

Though in his heart, Horace Jolober had never been willing to believe the Dolls were not truly alive. Not since Red Ike had introduced him to Vicki.

"Could you check the right-hand pocket of your blouse, Lieutenant Condorcet?" one of the Droids said.

"I'm not carrying a weapon!" Condorcet snapped. His hand hesitated, but it dived into the indicated pocket when an attendant started to reach toward it.

Jolober was ready to react, either by grabbing Condorcet's wrist from behind or by knocking him down with the chair. He didn't have time for any emotion, not even fear.

It was the same set of instincts that had thrown him to his feet for the last time, to wave off the attacking tanks.

Condorcet's hand came out with a roll of coins between two fingers. In a voice that slipped between injured and minatory he said, "Can't a man bring money into the Doll, then? Will you have me take my business elsewhere, then?"

"Your money's very welcome, sir," said the attendant who was reaching forward. His thumb and three fingers shifted in a sleight of hand; they reappeared holding a gold-striped China Doll chip worth easily twice the value of the rolled coins. "But let us hold these till you return. We'll be glad to give them back then without exchange."

The motion which left Condorcet holding the chip and transferred the roll to the attendant was also magically smooth.

The close-coupled soldier tensed for a moment as if he'd make an issue of it; but the Droids were as strong as they were polished, and there was no percentage in being humiliated.

"We'll see about that," said Condorcet loudly. He strutted past the attendants who parted for him like water before the blunt prow of a barge.

"Good afternoon, Port Commandant Jolober," said one of the Droids as they both bowed. "A pleasure to serve you again."

"A pleasure to feel wanted," said Jolober with an ironic nod of his own. He glided into the main hall of the China Doll.

The room's high ceiling was suffused with clear light which mimicked daytime outside. The hall buzzed with excited sounds even when the floor carried only a handful of customers. Jolober hadn't decided whether the space was designed to give multiple echo effects or if instead Red Ike augmented the hum with concealed sonic transponders.

Whatever it was, the technique made the blood of even the port commandant quicken when he stepped into the China Doll.

There were a score of gaming stations in the main hall,

but they provided an almost infinite variety of ways to lose money. A roulette station could be collapsed into a skat table in less than a minute if a squad of drunken Frieslanders demanded it. The displaced roulette players could be accommodated at the next station over, where until then a Droid had been dealing desultory hands of fan-tan.

Whatever the game was, it was fair. Every hand, every throw, every pot was recorded and processed in the office of the port commandant. None of the facility owners doubted that a skewed result would be noticed at once by the computers, or that a result skewed in favor of the house would mean that Horace Jolober would weld their doors shut and ship all their staff off-planet.

Besides, they knew as Jolober did that honest games would get them most of the available money anyhow, so long as the Dolls were there to caress the winners to greater risks.

At the end of Paradise Port farthest from the gate were two establishments which specialized in the leftovers. They were staffed by human males, and their atmosphere was as brightly efficient as men could make it.

But no one whose psyche allowed a choice picked a human companion over a Doll.

The main hall was busy with drab uniforms, Droids neatly garbed in blue and white, and the stunningly gorgeous outfits of the Dolls. There was a regular movement of Dolls and uniforms toward the door on a room-width landing three steps up at the back of the hall. Generally the rooms beyond were occupied by couples, but much larger gatherings were possible if a soldier had money and the perceived need.

The curved doors of the elevator beside the front entrance opened even as Jolober turned to look at them. Red Ike stepped out with a smile and a Doll on either arm.

"Always a pleasure to see you, Commandant," Red Ike said in a tone as sincere as the Dolls were human. "Shana," he added to the red-haired Doll. "Susan—" he nodded toward the blond. "Meet Commandant Jolober, the man who keeps us all safe."

The redhead giggled and slipped from Ike's arm to Jolober's. The slim blond gave him a smile that would have been demure except for the fabric of her tank-top. It acted as a polarizing filter, so that when she swayed her bare torso flashed toward the port commandant.

"But come on upstairs, Commandant," Red Ike continued, stepping backwards into the elevator and motioning Jolober to follow him. "Unless your business is here—or in back?" He cocked an almost-human eyebrow toward the door in the rear while his face waited with a look of amused tolerance.

"We can go upstairs," said Jolober grimly. "It won't take long." His air cushion slid him forward. Spilling air tickled Shana's feet as she pranced along beside him; she giggled again.

There must be men who found that sort of girlish idiocy erotic or Red Ike wouldn't keep the Doll in his stock.

The elevator shaft was opaque and looked it from outside the car. The car's interior was a visiscreen fed by receptors on the shaft's exterior. On one side of the slowly rising car, Jolober could watch the games in the main hall as clearly as if he were hanging in the air. On the other, they lifted above the street with a perfect view of its traffic and the port offices even though a concrete wall and the shaft's iridium armor blocked the view in fact.

The elevator switch was a small plate which hung in the "air" that was really the side of the car. Red Ike had toggled it up. Down would have taken the car—probably much faster—to the tunnel beneath the street, the escape route which Jolober had suspected even before the smiling alien had used it this afternoon.

But there was a second unobtrusive control beside the first. The blond Doll leaned past Jolober with a smile and touched it.

The view of the street disappeared. Those in the car had a crystalline view of the activities in back of the China Doll as if no walls or ceilings separated the bedrooms. Jolober met—or thought he met—the eyes of Tad Hoffritz, straining upward beneath a black-haired Doll.

"*Via!*" Jolober swore and slapped the toggle hard enough to feel the solidity of the elevator car.

"Susan, Susan," Red Ike chided with a grin. "She will have her little joke, you see, Commandant."

The blond made a moue, then winked at Jolober.

Above the main hall was Red Ike's office, furnished in minimalist luxury. Jolober found nothing attractive in the sight of chair seats and a broad onyx desktop hanging in the air, but the decor did show off the view. Like the elevator, the office walls and ceiling were covered by pass-through visiscreens.

The russet wasteland, blotched but not relieved by patterns of lichen, looked even more dismal from twenty meters up than it did from Jolober's living quarters.

Though the view appeared to be panorama, there was no sign of where the owner himself lived. The back of the office was an interior wall, and the vista over the worms and pillows of lava was transmitted through not only the wall but the complex of rooms that was Red Ike's home.

On the roof beside the elevator tower was an aircar sheltered behind the concrete coping. Like the owners of all the other facilities comprising Paradise Port, Red Ike wanted the option of getting out fast, even if the elevator to his tunnel bolthole was blocked.

Horace Jolober had fantasies in which he watched the stocky humanoid scramble into his vehicle and accelerate away, vanishing forever as a fleck against the milky sky.

"I've been meaning to call on you for some time, Commandant," Red Ike said as he walked with quick little steps to his desk. "I thought perhaps you might like a replacement for Vicki. As you know, any little way in which I can make your task easier . . . ?"

Shana giggled. Susan smiled slowly and, turning at a precisely calculated angle, bared breasts that were much fuller than they appeared beneath her loose garment.

Jolober felt momentary desire, then fierce anger in reaction. His hands clenched on the chair handles, restraining his violent urge to hurl both Dolls into the invisible walls.

Red Ike sat behind the desktop. The thin shell of his

chair rocked on invisible gimbals, tilting him to a comfortable angle that was not quite disrespectful of his visitor.

"Commandant," he said with none of the earlier hinted mockery, "you and I really ought to cooperate, you know. We need each other, and Placida needs us both."

"And the soldiers we're here for?" Jolober asked softly. "Do they need you, Ike?"

The Dolls had become as still as painted statues.

"You're an honorable man, Commandant," said the alien. "It disturbs you that the men don't find what they need in Paradise Port."

The chair eased more nearly upright. The intensity of Red Ike's stare reminded Jolober that he'd never seen the alien blink.

"But men like that—all of them now, and most of them for as long as they live . . . all they really need, Commandant, is a chance to die. I don't offer them that, it isn't my place. But I sell them everything they pay for, because I too am honorable."

"You don't know what honor is!" Jolober shouted, horrified at the thought—the nagging possibility—that what Red Ike said was true.

"I know what it is to keep my word, Commandant Jolober," the alien said as he rose from behind his desk with quiet dignity. "I promise you that if you cooperate with me, Paradise Port will continue to run to the full satisfaction of your employers.

"And I also promise," Red Ike went on unblinkingly, "that if you continue your mad vendetta, it will be the worse for you."

"Leave here," Jolober said. His mind achieved not calm, but a dynamic balance in which he understood everything—so long as he focused only on the result, not the reasons. "Leave Placida, leave human space, Ike. You push too hard. So far you've been lucky—it's only me pushing back, and I play by the official rules."

He leaned forward in his saddle, no longer angry. The desktop between them was a flawless black mirror. "But the mercs out there, they play by their own rules, and they're not going to like it when they figure out the game you're running on them. Get out while you can."

"Ladies," Red Ike said. "Please escort the commandant to the main hall. He no longer has any business here."

Jolober spent the next six hours on the street, visiting each of the establishments of Paradise Port. He drank little and spoke less, exchanging salutes when soldiers offered them and, with the same formality, the greetings of owners.

He didn't say much to Vicki later that night, when he returned by the alley staircase which led directly to his living quarters.

But he held her very close.

The sky was dark when Jolober snapped awake, though his bedroom window was painted by all the enticing colors of the façades across the street. He was fully alert and already into the short-legged trousers laid on the mobile chair beside the bed when Vicki stirred and asked, "Horace? What's the matter?"

"I don't—" Jolober began, and then the alarms sounded: the radio implanted in his mastoid, and the siren on the roof of the China Doll.

"Go ahead," he said to Central, thrusting his arms into the uniform tunic.

Vicki thumbed up the room lights but Jolober didn't need that, not to find the sleeves of a white garment with this much sky-glow. He'd stripped a jammed tribarrel once in pitch darkness, knowing that he and a dozen of his men were dead if he screwed up—and absolutely confident of the stream of cyan fire that ripped moments later from his gun muzzles.

"Somebody shot his way into the China Doll," said the voice. "He's holed up in the back."

The bone-conduction speaker hid the identity of the man on the other end of the radio link, but it wasn't the switchboard's artificial intelligence. Somebody on the street was cutting through directly, probably Stecher.

"Droids?" Jolober asked as he mounted his chair and powered up, breaking the charging circuit in which the vehicle rested overnight.

"Chief," said the mastoid, "we got a man down. Looks bad, and we can't get medics to him because the gun's covering the hallway. D'ye want me to—"

"Wait!" Jolober said as he bulled through the side door under power. Unlocking the main entrance—the entrance to the office of the port commandant—would take seconds that he knew he didn't have. "Hold what you got, I'm on the way."

The voice speaking through Jolober's jawbone was clearly audible despite wind noise and the scream of his chair as he leaped down the alley staircase in a single curving arc. "Ah, Chief? We're likely to have a, a crowd control problem if this don't get handled real quick."

"I'm on the way," Jolober repeated. He shot onto the street, still on direct thrust because ground effect wouldn't move him as fast as he needed to go.

The entrance of the China Doll was cordoned off, if four port patrolmen could be called a cordon. There were over a hundred soldiers in the street and more every moment that the siren—couldn't somebody cut it? Jolober didn't have time—continued to blare.

That wasn't what Stecher had meant by a "crowd control problem." The difficulty was in the way soldiers in the Division Legere's mottled uniforms were shouting—not so much as onlookers as a lynch mob.

Jolober dropped his chair onto its skirts—he needed the greater stability of ground effect. "Lemme through!" he snarled to the mass of uniformed backs which parted in a chorus of yelps when Jolober goosed his throttle. The skirt of his plenum chamber caught the soldiers just above the bootheels and toppled them to either side as the chair powered through.

One trooper spun with a raised fist and a curse in French. Jolober caught the man's wrist and flung him down almost absently. The men at the door relaxed visibly when their commandant appeared at their side.

Behind him, Jolober could hear off-duty patrolmen scrambling into the street from their barracks under the port offices. That would help, but—

"You, Major!" Jolober shouted, pointing at a Division Legere officer in the front of the crowd. The man was almost of a size with the commandant; fury had darkened his face several shades beyond swarthiness. "I'm deputizing you to keep order here until I've taken care of the problem inside."

He spun his chair again and drove through the doorway. The major was shouting to his back, "But the bastard's shot my—"

Two Droids were more or less where Jolober had expected them, one crumpled in the doorway and the other stretched full length a meter inside. The Droids were tough as well as strong. The second one had managed to grasp the man who shot him and be pulled a pace or two before another burst into the back of the Droid's skull had ended matters.

Stecher hadn't said the shooter had a submachine gun. That made the situation a little worse than it might have been, but it was so bad already that the increment was negligible.

Droids waited impassively at all the gaming stations, ready to do their jobs as soon as customers returned. They hadn't fled the way human croupiers would have—but neither did their programming say anything about dealing with armed intruders.

The Dolls had disappeared. It was the first time Jolober had been in the main hall when it was empty of their charming, enticing babble.

Stecher and two troopers in Slammers' khaki, and a pair of technicians with a portable medicomp stood on opposite sides of the archway leading into the back of the China Doll. A second patrolman was huddled behind the three room-wide steps leading up from the main hall.

Man down, Jolober thought, his guts ice.

The patrolman heard the chair and glanced back. *"Duck!"* he screamed as Sergeant Stecher cried, *"Watch—"*

Jolober throttled up, bouncing to the left as a three-shot burst snapped from the archway. It missed him by little enough that his hair rose in response to the ionized track.

There *was* a man down, in the corridor leading back from the archway. There was another man firing from a room at the corridor's opposite end, and he'd just proved his willingness to add the port commandant to the night's bag.

Jolober's chair leaped the steps to the broad landing where Stecher crouched, but it was his massive arms that braked his momentum against the wall. His tunic flapped and he noticed for the first time that he hadn't sealed it before he left his quarters. "Report," he said bluntly to his sergeant while running his thumb up the uniform's seam to close it.

"Their officer's in there," Stecher said, bobbing his chin to indicate the two Slammers kneeling beside him. The male trooper was holding the female and trying to comfort her as she blubbered.

To Jolober's surprise, he recognized both of them—the commo tech and the driver of the tank which'd nearly run him down that afternoon.

"He nutted, shot his way in to find a Doll," Stecher said quickly. His eyes flicked from the commandant to the archway, but he didn't shift far enough to look down the corridor. Congealed notches in the arch's plastic sheath indicated that he'd been lucky once already.

"Found her, found the guy she was with and put a burst into him as he tried to get away." Stecher thumbed toward the body invisible behind the shielding wall. "Guy from the Legere, an El-Tee named Condorcet."

"The bitch made him do it!" said the tank driver in a scream strangled by her own laced fingers.

"She's sedated," said the commo tech who held her.

In the perfect tones of Central's artificial intelligence, Jolober's implant said, "Major de Vigny of the Division Legere requests to see you. He is offering threats."

Letting de Vigny through would either take the pressure off the team outside or be the crack that made the dam fail. From the way Central put it, the dam wasn't going to hold much longer anyhow.

"Tell the cordon to pass him. But tell him keep his head down or he's that much more t'clean up t'morrow," Jolober replied with his mike keyed, making the best decision he could when none of 'em looked good.

"Tried knock-out gas but he's got filters," said Stecher. "Fast, too." He tapped the scarred jamb. "All the skin absorbtives're lethal, and I don't guess we'd get cleared t' use 'em anyhow?"

"Not while I'm in the chain of command," Jolober agreed grimly.

"She was with this pongo from the Legere," the driver was saying through her laced fingers. "Tad, he wanted her so much, so fucking *much*, like she was human or something . . ."

"The, ah, you know. Beth, the one he was planning to see," said the commo tech rapidly as he stroked the back of the driver—Corporal Days—Daisy. . . . "He tried to, you know, buy 'er from the Frog, but he wouldn't play. She got 'em, Beth did, to put all their leave allowance on a coin flip. She'd take all the money and go with the winner."

"The bitch," Daisy wailed. "The bitch the bitch the bitch . . ."

The Legere didn't promote amateurs to battalion command. The powerful major Jolober had seen outside rolled through the doorway, sized up the situation, and sprinted to the landing out of the shooter's line of sight.

Line of fire.

"Hoffritz, can you hear me?" Jolober called. "I'm the port commandant, remember?"

A single bolt from the submachine gun spattered plastic from the jamb and filled the air with fresher stenches.

The man sprawling in the corridor moaned.

"I've ordered up an assault team," said Major de Vigny with flat assurance as he stood up beside Jolober. "It was unexpected, but they should be here in a few minutes."

Everyone else in the room was crouching. There wasn't any need so long as you weren't in front of the corridor, but it was the instinctive response to knowing somebody was trying to shoot you.

"Cancel the order," said Jolober, locking eyes with the other officer.

"You aren't in charge when one of my men—" began the major, his face flushing almost black.

"The gate closes when the alarm goes off!" Jolober said in a voice that could have been heard over a tank's fans. "And I've ordered the air defense batteries," he lied, "to fire on anybody trying to crash through now. If you want to lead a mutiny against your employers, Major, now's the time to do it."

The two big men glared at one another without blinking. Then de Vigny said, "Blue Six to Blue Three," keying his epaulet mike with the code words. "Hold Team Alpha until further orders. Repeat, hold Alpha. Out."

"Hold Alpha," repeated the speaker woven into the epaulet's fabric.

"If Condorcet dies," de Vigny added calmly to the port commandant, "I will kill you myself, sir."

"Do you have cratering charges warehoused here?" Jolober asked with no emotion save the slight lilt of interrogation.

"What?" said de Vigny. "Yes, yes."

Jolober crooked his left ring finger so that Central would hear and relay his next words. "Tell the gate to pass two men from the Legere with a jeep and a cratering charge. Give them a patrol guide, and download the prints of the China Doll into his commo link so they can place the charge on the wall outside the room at the T of the back corridor."

De Vigny nodded crisply to indicate that he too understood the order. He began relaying it into his epaulet while Stecher drew and reholstered his needle stunner and Corporal Days mumbled.

"Has she tried?" Jolober asked, waving to the driver and praying that he wouldn't have to . . .

"He shot at 'er," the commo tech said, nodding sadly. "That's when she really lost it and medics had to calm her down."

No surprises there. Certainly no good ones.

"Captain Hoffritz, it's the port commandant again," Jolober called.

A bolt spat down the axis of the corridor.

"That's right, you bastard, *shoot!*" Jolober roared. "You blew my legs off on Primavera. Now finish the job and *prove* you're a fuck-up who's only good for killing his friends. Come on, I'll make it easy. I'll come out and let you take your time!"

"Chief—" said Stecher.

Jolober slid away from the shelter of the wall.

The corridor was the stem of a T, ten meters long. Halfway between Jolober and the cross corridor at the other end, capping the T, lay the wounded man. Lieutenant Condorcet was a tough little man to still be alive with the back of his tunic smoldering around the holes punched in him by three powergun bolts. The roll of coins he'd carried to add weight to his fist wouldn't have helped; but then, nothing much helped when the other guy had the only gun in the equation.

Like now.

The door of the room facing the corridor and Horace Jolober was ajar. Beyond the opening was darkness and a bubble of dull red: the iridium muzzle of Hoffritz's submachine gun, glowing with the heat of the destruction it had spit at others.

De Vigny cursed; Stecher was pleading or even calling an order. All Jolober could hear was the roar of the tank bearing down on him, so loud that the slapping bolts streaming toward him from its cupola were inaudible.

Jolober's chair slid him down the hall. His arms were twitching in physical memory of the time they'd waved a scrap of white cloth to halt the oncoming armor.

The door facing him opened. Tad Hoffritz's face was as hard and yellow as fresh bone. He leaned over the sight of his submachine gun. Jolober slowed, because if he kept on at a walking pace he would collide with Condorcet, and if he curved around the wounded man it might look as if he were dodging what couldn't be dodged.

He didn't want to look like a fool and a coward when he died.

Hoffritz threw down the weapon.

Jolober bounced to him, wrapping the Slammers' officer in both arms like a son. Stecher was shouting, "Medics!" but the team with the medicomp had been in motion as soon as the powergun hit the floor. Behind all the battle was Major de Vigny's voice, remembering to stop the crew with the charge that might otherwise be set—and fired even though the need was over.

"I *loved* her," Hoffritz said to Jolober's big shoulder, begging someone to understand what he didn't understand himself. "I, I'd been drinking and I came back . . ."

With a submachine gun that shouldn't have made it into Paradise Port . . . but the detection loops hadn't been replaced in the hours since the tanks ripped them away; and anyhow, Hoffritz was an officer, a company commander.

He was also a young man having a bad time with what he thought was a woman. Older, calmer fellows than Hoffritz had killed because of that.

Jolober carried Hoffritz with him into the room where he'd been holed up. "Lights," the commandant ordered, and the room brightened.

Condorcet wasn't dead, not yet; but Beth, the Doll behind the trouble, surely was.

The couch was large and round. Though drumhead-thin, its structure could be varied to any degree of firmness the paying half of the couple desired. Beth lay in the center of it in a tangle of long black hair. Her tongue protruded from a blood-darkened face, and the prints of the grip that had strangled her were livid on her throat.

"She told me she loved *him*," Hoffritz mumbled. The commandant's embrace supported him, but it also kept Hoffritz from doing something silly, like trying to run.

"After what I'd done," the boy was saying, "she tells me she doesn't love me after all. She says I'm no good to her in bed, that I never gave her any pleasure at all. . . ."

"Just trying to maximize the claim for damages, son," Jolober said grimly. "It didn't mean anything real, just more dollars in Red Ike's pocket."

But Red Ike hadn't counted on Hoffritz shooting another merc. Too bad for Condorcet, too bad for the kid who shot him—

And just what Jolober needed to finish Red Ike on Placida.

"Let's go," Jolober said, guiding Hoffritz out of the room stinking of death and the emotions that led to death. "We'll get you to a medic."

And a cell.

Condorcet had been removed from the corridor, leaving behind only a slime of vomit. Thank the Lord he'd fallen face down.

Stecher and his partner took the unresisting Hoffritz and wrapped him in motion restraints. The prisoner could walk and move normally, so long as he did it slowly. At a sudden movement, the gossamer webs would clamp him as tightly as a fly in a spiderweb.

The main hall was crowded, but the incipient violence facing the cordon outside had melted away. Judging from Major de Vigny's brusque, bellowed orders, the victim was in the hands of his medics and being shifted to the medicomp in Division Legere's bivouac area.

That was probably the best choice. Paradise Port had excellent medical facilities, but medics in combat units got to know their jobs and their diagnostic/healing computers better than anybody in the rear echelons.

"Commandant Jolober," said van Zuyle, the Slammers' bivouac commander, "I'm worried about my man here. Can I—"

"He's not your man any more, Captain," Jolober said with the weary chill of an avalanche starting to topple. "He's mine and the Placidan courts'—until I tell you different. We'll get him sedated and keep him from hurting himself, no problem."

Van Zuyle's face wore the expression of a man whipping himself to find a deity who doesn't respond. "Sir," he said, "I'm sorry if I—"

"You did the job they paid you t'do," Jolober said, shrugging away from the other man. He hadn't felt so weary since he'd awakened in the Legion's main hospital on

Primavera: alive and utterly unwilling to believe that he could be after what happened.

"Outa the man's way," snarled one of the patrolmen, trying to wave a path through the crowd with her white-sleeved arms. "Let the commandant by!"

She yelped a curse at the big man who brushed through her gestures. "A moment, little one," he said—de Vigny, the Legere major.

"You kept the lid on good," Jolober said while part of his dazed mind wondered whose voice he was hearing. "Tomorrow I'll want to talk to you about what happened and how to keep from a repeat."

Anger darkened de Vigny's face. "I heard what happened," he said. "Condorcet was not the only human victim, it would seem."

"We'll talk," Jolober said. His chair was driving him toward the door, pushing aside anyone who didn't get out of the way. He didn't see them any more than he saw the air.

The street was a carnival of uniformed soldiers who suddenly had something to focus on that wasn't a memory of death—or a way to forget. There were dark undercurrents to the chatter, but the crowd was no longer a mob.

Jolober's uniform drew eyes, but the port commandant was too aloof and forbidding to be asked for details of what had really happened in the China Doll. In the center of the street, though—

"Good evening, Commandant," said Red Ike, strolling back toward the establishment he owned. "Without your courage, tonight's incident would have been even more unfortunate."

Human faces changed in the play of light washing them from the brothel fronts. Red Ike's did not. Colors overlay his features, but the lines did not modify as one shadow or highlight replaced another.

"It couldn't be more unfortunate for you, Ike," Jolober said to the bland alien while uniforms milled around them. "They'll pay you money, the mercs will. But they won't have you killing their men."

"I understand that the injured party is expected to pull

through," Red Ike said emotionlessly. Jolober had the feeling that the alien's eyes were focused on his soul.

"I'm glad Condorcet'll live," Jolober said, too tired for triumph or subtlety. "But you're dead on Placida, Ike. It's just a matter of how long it takes me to wrap it up."

He broke past Red Ike, gliding toward the port offices and the light glowing from his room on the upper floor.

Red Ike didn't turn around, but Jolober thought he could feel the alien watching him nonetheless.

Even so, all Jolober cared about now was bed and a chance to reassure Vicki that everything was all right.

The alley between the office building and the Blue Parrot next door wasn't directly illuminated, but enough light spilled from the street to show Jolober the stairs.

He didn't see the two men waiting there until a third had closed the mouth of the alley behind him. Indonesian music began to blare from the China Doll.

Music on the exterior's a violation, thought the part of Jolober's mind that ran Paradise Port, but reflexes from his years as a combat officer noted the man behind him held a metal bar and that knives gleamed in the hands of the two by the stairs.

It made a hell of a fast trip back from the nightmare memories that had ruled Jolober's brain since he wakened.

Jolober's left stump urged the throttle as his torso shifted toward the alley mouth. The electronics reacted instantly but the mechanical links took a moment. Fans spun up, plenum chamber collapsed into a nozzle—

The attackers moved in on Jolober like the three wedges of a drill chuck. His chair launched him into the one with the club, a meter off the ground and rising with a hundred and eighty kilos of mass behind the impact.

At the last instant the attacker tried to duck away instead of swinging at Jolober, but he misjudged the speed of his intended victim. The center of the chair's frame, between the skirt and the saddle, batted the attacker's head toward the wall, dragging the fellow's body with it.

Jolober had a clear path to the street. The pair of knifemen thought he was headed that way and sprinted in a desperate attempt to catch a victim who moved faster than unaided humans could run.

They were in midstride, thinking of failure rather than defense, when Jolober pogoed at the alley mouth and came back at them like a cannonball.

But bigger and heavier.

One attacker stabbed at Jolober's chest and skidded the point off the battery compartment instead when the chair hopped. The frame slammed knife and man into the concrete wall from which they ricochetted to the ground, separate and equally motionless.

The third man ran away.

"Get 'em, boys!" Jolober bellowed as if he were launching his battalion instead of just himself in pursuit. The running man glanced over his shoulder and collided with the metal staircase. The noise was loud and unpleasant, even in comparison to the oriental music blaring from the China Doll.

Jolober bounced, cut his fan speed, and flared his output nozzle into a plenum chamber again. The chair twitched, then settled into ground effect.

Jolober's mind told him that he was seeing with a clarity and richness of color he couldn't have equalled by daylight, but he knew that if he really focused on an object it would blur into shadow. It was just his brain's way of letting him know that he was still alive.

Alive like he hadn't been in years.

Crooking his ring finger Jolober said, "I need a pickup on three men in the alley between us and the Blue Parrot."

"Three men in the alley between HQ and the Blue Parrot," the artificial intelligence paraphrased.

"They'll need a medic." One might need burial. "And I want them sweated under a psycomp—who sent 'em after me, the works."

Light flooded the alley as a team of patrolmen arrived. The point man extended a surface-luminescent area light powered from a backpack. The shadows thrown by the meter-diameter convexity were soft, but the illumination was the blaze of noon compared to that of moments before.

"Chief!" bellowed Stecher. "You all right? Chief!" He wasn't part of the team Central vectored to the alley, but word of mouth had brought him to the scene of the incident.

Jolober throttled up, clamped his skirts, and boosted himself to the fourth step where everyone could see him. The man who'd run into the stairs moaned as the sidedraft spat grit from the treads into his face.

"No problem," Jolober said. No problem they wouldn't be able to cure in a week or two. "I doubt these three know any more than that they got a call from outside Port to, ah, handle me . . . but get what they have, maybe we can cross-reference with some outgoing traffic."

From the China Doll; or just maybe from the Blue Parrot, where Ike fled when the shooting started. But probably not. Three thugs, nondescripts from off-planet who could've been working for any establishment in Paradise Port *except* the China Doll.

"Sir—" came Stecher's voice.

"It'll keep, Sergeant," Jolober interrupted. "Just now I've got a heavy date with a bed."

Vicki greeted him with a smile so bright that both of them could pretend there were no tears beneath it. The air was steamy with the bath she'd drawn for him.

He used to prefer showers, back when he'd had feet on which to stand. He could remember dancing on Quitly's Planet as the afternoon monsoon battered the gun carriages his platoon was guarding and washed the soap from his body.

But he didn't have Vicki then, either.

"Yeah," he said, hugging the Doll. "Good idea, a bath."

Instead of heading for the bathroom, he slid his chair to the cabinet within arm's reach of the bed and cut his fans. Bending over, he unlatched the battery compartment—the knifepoint hadn't even penetrated the casing—and removed the powerpack.

"I can—" Vicki offered hesitantly.

"S'okay, dearest," Jolober replied as he slid a fresh pack from the cabinet into place. His stump touched the throttle, spinning the fans to prove that he had good contact, then lifted the original pack into the cabinet and its charging harness.

"Just gave 'em a workout tonight and don't want t' be down on power tomorrow," he explained as he straightened. Vicki could have handled the weight of the batteries, he realized, though his mind kept telling him it was ludicrous to imagine the little woman shifting thirty-kilo packages with ease.

But she wasn't a woman.

"I worry when it's so dangerous," she said as she walked with him to the bathroom, their arms around one another's waist.

"Look, for Paradise Port, it was dangerous," Jolober said in a light appearance of candor as he handed Vicki his garments. "Compared to downtown in any capital city I've seen, it was pretty mild."

He lowered himself into the water, using the bars laid over the tub like a horizontal ladder. Vicki began to knead the great muscles of his shoulders, and Lord! but it felt good to relax after so long. . . .

"I'd miss you," she said.

"Not unless I went away," Jolober answered, leaning forward so that her fingers could work down his spine while the water lapped at them. "Which isn't going to happen any time soon."

He paused. The water's warmth unlocked more than his body. "Look," he said quietly, his chin touching the surface of the bath and his eyes still closed. "Red Ike's had it. He knows it, I know it. But I'm in a position to make things either easy or hard, and he knows that, too. We'll come to terms, he and I. And you're the—"

"Urgent from the gate," said Jolober's mastoid implant.

He crooked his finger, raising his head. "Put him through," he said.

Her through. "Sir," said Feldman's attenuated voice, "a

courier's just landed with two men. They say they've got an oral message from Colonel Hammer, and they want me to alert you that they're coming. Over."

"I'll open the front door," Jolober said, lifting himself abruptly from the water, careful not to miskey the implant while his hands performed other tasks.

He wouldn't rouse the human staff. No need and if the message came by courier, it wasn't intended for other ears.

"Ah, sir," Feldman added unexpectedly. "One of them insists on keeping his sidearms. Over."

"Then he can insist on staying outside my perimeter!" Jolober snarled. Vicki had laid a towel on the saddle before he mounted and was now using another to silently dry his body. "You can detach two guards to escort 'em if they need their hands held, but *nobody* brings powerguns into Paradise Port."

"Roger, I'll tell them," Feldman agreed doubtfully. "Over and out."

"I have a fresh uniform out," said Vicki, stepping back so that Jolober could follow her into the bedroom, where the air was drier.

"That's three, today," Jolober said, grinning. "Well, I've done a lot more than I've managed any three other days.

"Via," he added more seriously. "It's more headway than I've made since they appointed me commandant."

Vicki smiled, but her eyes were so tired that Jolober's body trembled in response. His flesh remembered how much he had already been through today and yearned for the sleep to which the hot bath had disposed it.

Jolober lifted himself on his hands so that Vicki could raise and cinch his trousers. He could do it himself, but he was in a hurry, and . . . besides, just as she'd said, Vicki was a part of him in a real way.

"Cheer up, love," he said as he closed his tunic. "It isn't done yet, but it's sure getting that way."

"Good-bye, Horace," the Doll said as she kissed him.

"Keep the bed warm," Jolober called as he slid toward the door and the inner staircase. His head was tumbling with memories and images. For a change, they were all pleasant ones.

The port offices were easily identified at night because they *weren't* garishly illuminated like every other building in Paradise Port. Jolober had a small staff, and he didn't choose to waste it at desks. Outside of ordinary business hours, Central's artificial intelligence handled everything— by putting nonemergency requests on hold till morning, and by vectoring a uniformed patrol to the real business.

Anybody who insisted on personal service could get it by hammering at the Patrol entrance on the west side, opposite Jolober's private staircase. A patrolman would find the noisemaker a personal holding cell for the remainder of the night.

The front entrance was built like a vault door, not so much to prevent intrusion as to keep drunks from destroying the panel for reasons they'd be unable to remember sober. Jolober palmed the release for the separate bolting systems and had just begun to swing the door open in invitation when the two men in khaki uniforms, neither of them tall, strode up to the building.

"Blood and Martyrs!" Jolober said as he continued to back, not entirely because the door required it.

"You run a tight base here, Commandant," said Colonel Alois Hammer as he stepped into the waiting room. "Do you know my aide, Major Steuben?"

"By reputation only," said Jolober, nodding to Joachim Steuben with the formal correctness which that reputation enjoined. "Ah—with a little more information, I might have relaxed the prohibition on weapons."

Steuben closed the door behind them, moving the heavy panel with a control which belied the boyish delicacy of his face and frame. "If the colonel's satisfied with his security," Joachim said mildly, "then of course I am, too."

The eyes above his smile would willingly have watched Jolober drawn and quartered.

"You've had some problems with troops of mine today," said Hammer, seating himself on one of the chairs and rising again, almost as quickly as if he had continued to walk. His eyes touched Jolober and moved on in short hops that covered everything in the room like an animal checking a new environment.

"Only reported problems occurred," said Jolober, keeping the promise he'd made earlier in the day. He lighted the hologram projection tank on the counter to let it warm up. "There was an incident a few hours ago, yes."

The promise didn't matter to Tad Hoffritz, not after the shootings; but it mattered more than life to Horace Jolober that he keep the bargains he'd made.

"According to Captain van Zuyle's report," Hammer said as his eyes flickered over furniture and recesses dim under the partial lighting, "you're of the opinion the boy was set up."

"What you do with a gun," said Joachim Steuben softly from the door against which he leaned, "is your own responsibility."

"As Joachim says," Hammer went on with a nod and no facial expression, "that doesn't affect how we'll deal with Captain Hoffritz when he's released from local custody. But it does affect how we act to prevent recurrences, doesn't it?"

"Load file Ike One into the downstairs holo," said Jolober to Central.

He looked at Hammer, paused till their eyes met. "Sure, he was set up, just like half a dozen others in the past three months—only they were money assessments, no real problem.

"And the data prove," Jolober continued coolly, claiming what his data suggested but could *not* prove, "that it's going to get a lot worse than what happened tonight if Red Ike and his Dolls aren't shipped out fast."

The holotank sprang to life in a three-dimensional cross-hatching of orange lines. As abruptly, the lines shrank into words and columns of figures. "Red Ike and his Dolls—they were all his openly, then—first show up on Sparrowhome a little over five years standard ago, according to Bonding Authority records. Then—"

Jolober pointed toward the figures. Colonel Hammer put

his smaller, equally firm, hand over the commandant's and said, "Wait. Just give me your assessment."

"Dolls have been imported as recreational support in seven conflicts," said Jolober as calmly as if his mind had not just shifted gears. He'd been a good combat commander for the same reason, for dealing with the situation that occurred rather than the one he'd planned for. "There's been rear-echelon trouble each time, and the riot on Ketelby caused the Bonding Authority to order the disbandment of a battalion of Guardforce O'Higgins."

"There was trouble over a woman," said Steuben unemotionally, reeling out the data he gathered because he was Hammer's adjutant as well as his bodyguard. "A fight between a ranger and an artilleryman led to a riot in which half the nearest town was burned."

"Not a woman," corrected Jolober. "A Doll."

He tapped the surface of the holotank. "It's all here, downloaded from Bonding Authority archives. You just have to see what's happening so you know the questions to ask."

"You can get me a line to the capital?" Hammer asked as if he were discussing the weather. "I was in a hurry, and I didn't bring along my usual commo."

Jolober lifted the visiplate folded into the surface of the counter beside the tank and rotated it toward Hammer.

"I've always preferred nonhumans for recreation areas," Hammer said idly as his finger played over the plate's keypad. "Oh, the troops complain, but I've never seen *that* hurt combat efficiency. Whereas real women gave all sorts of problems."

"And real men," said Joachim Steuben, with a deadpan expression that could have meant anything.

The visiplate beeped. "Main Switch," said a voice, tart but not sleepy. "Go ahead."

"You have my authorization code," Hammer said to the human operator on the other end of the connection. From Jolober's flat angle to the plate, he couldn't make out the operator's features—only that he sat in a brightly illuminated white cubicle. "Patch me through to the chairman of the Facilities Inspection Committee."

"'Senator Dieter?" said the operator, professionally able to keep the question short of being amazement.

"If he's the chairman," Hammer said. The words had the angry undertone of a dynamite fuse burning.

"Yessir, she is," replied the operator with studied neutrality. "One moment please.

"I've been dealing with her chief aide," said Jolober in a hasty whisper. "Guy named Higgey. His pager's loaded—"

"Got you a long ways, didn't it, Commandant?" Hammer said with a gun-turret click of his head toward Jolober.

"Your pardon, sir," said Jolober, bracing reflexively to attention. He wasn't Hammer's subordinate, but they both served the same ideal—getting the job done. The ball was in Hammer's court just now, and he'd ask for support if he thought he needed it.

From across the waiting room, Joachim Steuben smiled at Jolober. That one had the same ideal, perhaps; but his terms of reference were something else again.

"The senator isn't at any of her registered work stations," the operator reported coolly.

"Son," said Hammer, leaning toward the visiplate, "you have a unique opportunity to lose the war for Placida. All you have to do is *not* get me through to the chairman."

"Yes, Colonel Hammer," the operator replied with an aplomb that made it clear why he held the job he did. "I've processed your authorization, and I'm running it through again on War Emergency Ord—"

The last syllable was clipped. The bright rectangle of screen dimmed gray. Jolober slid his chair in a short arc so that he could see the visiplate clearly past Hammer's shoulder.

"What is it?" demanded the woman in the dim light beyond. She was stocky, middle-aged, and rather attractive because of the force of personality she radiated even sleepless in a dressing gown.

"This is Colonel Alois Hammer," Hammer said. "Are you recording?"

"On *this* circuit?" the senator replied with a frosty smile. "Of course I am. So are at least three other agencies, whether I will or no."

Hammer blinked, startled to find himself on the wrong end of a silly question for a change.

"Senator," he went on without the hectoring edge that had been present since his arrival. "A contractor engaged by your government to provide services at Paradise Port has been causing problems. One of the Legere's down, in critical, and I'm short a company commander over the same incident."

"You've reported to the port commandant?" Senator Dieter said, her eyes unblinking as they passed over Jolober.

"The commandant reported to me because your staff stonewalled him," Hammer said flatly while Jolober felt his skin grow cold, even the tips of the toes he no longer had. "I want the contractor, a nonhuman called Red Ike, off-planet in seventy-two hours with all his chattels. That specifically includes his Dolls. We'll work—"

"That's too soon," said Dieter, her fingers tugging a lock of hair over one ear while her mind worked. "Even if—"

"Forty-*eight* hours, Senator," Hammer interrupted. "This is a violation of your bond. And I promise you, I'll have the support of all the other commanders of units contracted to Placidan service. Forty-eight hours, or we'll withdraw from combat and you won't have a front line."

"You *can't*—" Dieter began. Then all muscles froze, tongue and fingers among them, as her mind considered the implications of what the colonel had just told her.

"I have no concern over being able to win my case at the Bonding Authority hearing on Earth," Hammer continued softly. "But I'm quite certain that the present Placidan government won't be there to contest it."

Dieter smiled without humor. "Seventy-two hours," she said as if repeating the figure.

"I've shifted the Regiment across continents in less time, Senator," Hammer said.

"Yes," said Dieter calmly. "Well, there are political consequences to any action, and I'd rather explain myself to my constituents than to an army of occupation. I'll take care of it."

She broke the circuit.

"I wouldn't mind getting to know that lady," said Hammer, mostly to himself, as he folded the visiplate back into the counter.

"That takes care of your concerns, then?" he added sharply, looking up at Jolober.

"Yes, sir, it does," said Jolober, who had the feeling he had drifted into a plane where dreams could be happy.

"Ah, about Captain Hoffritz . . ." Hammer said. His eyes slipped, but he snapped them back to meet Jolober's despite the embarrassment of being about to ask a favor.

"He's not combat-fit right now, Colonel," Jolober said, warming as authority flooded back to fill his mind. "He'll do as well in our care for the next few days as he would in yours. After that, and assuming that no one wants to press charges—"

"Understood," said Hammer, nodding. "I'll deal with the victim and General Claire."

"—then some accommodation can probably be arranged with the courts."

"It's been a pleasure dealing with a professional of your caliber, Commandant," Hammer said as he shook Jolober's hand. He spoke without emphasis, but nobody meeting his cool blue eyes could have imagined that Hammer would have bothered to lie about it.

"It's started to rain," observed Major Steuben as he muscled the door open.

"It's permitted to," Hammer said. "We've been wet be—"

"A jeep to the front of the building," Jolober ordered with his ring finger crooked. He straightened and said, "Ah, Colonel? Unless you'd like to be picked up by one of your own vehicles?"

"Nobody knows I'm here," said Hammer from the doorway. "I don't want van Zuyle to think I'm second-guessing him—I'm not, I'm just handling the part that's mine to handle."

He paused before adding with an ironic smile, "In any case, we're four hours from exploiting the salient Hoffritz's company formed when they took the junction at Kettering."

A jeep with two patrolmen, stunners ready, scraped to a halt outside. The team was primed for a situation like the one in the alley less than an hour before.

"Taxi service only, boys," Jolober called to the patrolmen. "Carry these gentlemen to their courier ship, please."

The jeep was spinning away in the drizzle before Jolober had closed and locked the door again. It didn't occur to him that it mattered whether or not the troops bivouacked around Paradise Port knew immediately what Hammer had just arranged.

And it didn't occur to him, as he bounced his chair up the stairs calling, "Vicki! We've won!" that he should feel any emotion except joy.

"Vicki!" he repeated as he opened the bedroom door. They'd have to leave Placida unless he could get Vicki released from the blanket order on Dolls—but he hadn't expected to keep his job anyway, not after he went over the head of the whole Placidan government.

"Vi—"

She'd left a light on, one of the point sources in the ceiling. It was a shock, but not nearly as bad a shock as Jolober would have gotten if he'd slid onto the bed in the dark.

"Who?" his tongue asked while his mind couldn't think of anything to say, could only move his chair to the bedside and palm the hydraulics to lower him into a sitting position.

Her right hand and forearm were undamaged. She flexed her fingers and the keen plastic blade shot from her fist, then collapsed again into a baton. She let it roll onto the bedclothes.

"He couldn't force me to kill you," Vicki said. "He was very surprised, very. . . ."

Jolober thought she might be smiling, but he couldn't be sure since she no longer had lips. The plastic edges of the knife Vicki took as she dressed him were not sharp enough for finesse, but she had not attempted surgical delicacy.

Vicki had destroyed herself from toes to her once-perfect face. All she had left was one eye with which to watch Jolober, and the parts of her body which she couldn't reach unaided. She had six ribs to a side, broader and flatter than those of a human's skeleton. After she laid open the ribs, she had dissected the skin and flesh of the left side farther.

Jolober had always assumed—when he let himself think about it—that her breasts were sponge implants. He'd been wrong. On the bedspread lay a wad of yellowish fat streaked with blood vessels. He didn't have a background that would tell him whether or not it was human normal, but it certainly was biological.

It was a tribute to Vicki's toughness that she had remained alive as long as she had.

Instinct turned Jolober's head to the side so that he vomited away from the bed. He clasped Vicki's right hand with both of his, keeping his eyes closed so that he could imagine that everything was as it had been minutes before when he was triumphantly happy. His left wrist brushed the knife that should have remained an inert baton in any hands but his. He snatched up the weapon, feeling the blade flow out—

As it had when Vicki held it, turned it on herself.

"We are one, my Horace," she whispered, her hand squeezing his.

It was the last time she spoke, but Jolober couldn't be sure of that because his mind had shifted out of the present into a cosmos limited to the sense of touch: body-warm plastic in his left hand, and flesh cooling slowly in his right.

He sat in his separate cosmos for almost an hour, until the emergency call on his mastoid implant threw him back into an existence where his life had purpose.

"All units!" cried a voice on the panic push. "The—"

The blast of static which drowned the voice lasted only a fraction of a second before the implant's logic circuits shut the unit down to keep the white noise from driving Jolober mad. The implant would be disabled as long as the jamming continued—but jamming of this intensity would block even the most sophisticated equipment in the Slammers' tanks.

Which were probably carrying out the jamming.

Jolober's hand slipped the knife away without thinking—with fiery determination not to think—as his stump kicked the chair into life and he glided toward the alley stairs. He was still dressed, still mounted in his saddle, and that was as much as he was willing to know about his immediate surroundings.

The stairs rang. The thrust of his fans was a fitful gust on the metal treads each time he bounced on his way to the ground.

The voice could have been Feldman at the gate; she was the most likely source anyway. At the moment, Jolober had an emergency.

In a matter of minutes, it could be a disaster instead.

It was raining, a nasty drizzle which distorted the invitations capering on the building fronts. The street was empty except for a pair of patrol jeeps, bubbles in the night beneath canopies that would stop most of the droplets.

Even this weather shouldn't have kept soldiers from scurrying from one establishment to another, hoping to change their luck when they changed location. Overhanging façades ought to have been crowded with morose troopers, waiting for a lull—or someone drunk or angry enough to lead an exodus toward another empty destination.

The emptiness would have worried Jolober if he didn't have much better reasons for concern. The vehicles sliding down the street from the gate were unlighted, but there was no mistaking the roar of a tank.

Someone in the China Doll heard and understood the sound also, because the armored door squealed down across the archway even as Jolober's chair lifted him in that direction at high thrust.

He braked in a spray. The water-slicked pavement didn't affect his control, since the chair depended on thrust rather than friction—but being able to stop didn't give him any ideas about how he should proceed.

One of the patrol jeeps swung in front of the tank with
a courage and panache which made Jolober proud of his
men. The patrolman on the passenger side had ripped the
canopy away to stand waving a yellow light-wand with
furious determination.

The tank did not slow. It shifted direction just enough
to strike the jeep a glancing blow instead of center-punching
it. That didn't spare the vehicle; its light frame crumpled
like tissue before it resisted enough to spin across the
pavement at twice the velocity of the slowly advancing tank.
The slight adjustment in angle did save the patrolmen, who
were thrown clear instead of being ground between
concrete and the steel skirts.

The tank's scarred turret made it identifiable in the light
of the building fronts. Jolober crooked his finger and shouted,
"Commandant to Corporal Days. For the *Lord's* sake, trooper,
don't get your unit disbanded for mutiny! Colonel Hammer's
already gotten Red Ike ordered off-planet!"

There was no burp from his mastoid as Central retrans-
mitted the message a microsecond behind the original. Only
then did Jolober recall that the Slammers had jammed his
communications.

Not the Slammers alone. The two vehicles behind the
tank were squat armored personnel carriers, each capable
of hauling an infantry section with all its equipment.
Nobody had bothered to paint out the fender markings of
the Division Legere.

Rain stung Jolober's eyes as he hopped the last five
meters to the sealed façade of the China Doll. Anything
could be covered, could be settled, except murder—and
killing Red Ike would be a murder of which the Bonding
Authority would have to take cognizance.

"Let me in!" Jolober shouted to the door. The armor was
so thick that it didn't ring when he pounded it. "Let me—"

Normally the sound of a mortar firing was audible for a
kilometer, a hollow *shoomp!* like a firecracker going off in
an oil drum. Jolober hadn't heard the launch from beyond
the perimeter because of the nearby roar of drive fans.

When the round went off on the roof of the China Doll,

the charge streamed tendrils of white fire down as far as the pavement, where they pocked the concrete. The snake-pit coruscance of blue sparks lighting the roof a moment later was the battery pack of Red Ike's aircar shorting through the new paths the mortar shell had burned in the car's circuitry.

The mercs were playing for keeps. They hadn't come to destroy the China Doll and leave its owner to rebuild somewhere else.

The lead tank swung in the street with the cautious delicacy of an elephant wearing a hoopskirt. Its driving lights blazed on, silhouetting the port commandant against the steel door. Jolober held out his palm in prohibition, knowing that if he could delay events even a minute, Red Ike would escape through his tunnel.

Everything else within the China Doll was a chattel which could be compensated with money.

There was a red flash and a roar from the stern of the tank, then an explosion muffled by a meter of concrete and volcanic rock. Buildings shuddered like sails in a squall; the front of the port offices cracked as its fabric was placed under a flexing strain that concrete was never meant to resist.

The rocket-assisted penetrators carried by the Slammers' tanks were intended to shatter bunkers of any thickness imaginable in the field. Red Ike's bolt-hole was now a long cavity filled with chunks and dust of the material intended to protect it.

The tanks had very good detection equipment, and combat troops live to become veterans by observing their surroundings. Quite clearly, the tunnel had not escaped notice when Tad Hoffritz led his company down the street to hoo-rah Paradise Port.

"Wait!" Jolober shouted, because there's always a chance until there's no chance at all.

"Get out of the way, Commandant!" boomed the tank's public address system, loudly enough to seem an echo of the penetrator's earth-shock.

"Colonel Hammer has—" Jolober shouted.

"We'd as soon not hurt you," the speakers roared as the

turret squealed ten degrees on its gimbals. The main gun's
bore was a 20cm tube aligned perfectly with Jolober's eyes.

They couldn't hear him; they wouldn't listen if they
could; and anyway, the troopers involved in this weren't
interested in contract law. They wanted justice, and to them
that didn't mean a ticket off-planet for Red Ike.

The tribarrel in the tank's cupola fired a single shot.
The bolt of directed energy struck the descending arch
just in front of Jolober and gouged the plastic away in
fire and black smoke. Bits of the covering continued to
burn, and the underlying concrete added an odor of hot
lime to the plastic and the ozone of the bolt's track
through the air.

Jolober's miniature vehicle thrust him away in a flat arc,
out of the door alcove and sideways in the street as a
powergun fired from a port concealed in the China Doll's
façade. The tank's main gun demolished the front wall with
a single round.

The street echoed with the thunderclap of cold air filling
the track seared through it by the energy bolt. The pistol shot an instant earlier could almost have been a pro-
leptic reflection, confused in memory with the sun-bright
cyan glare of the tank cannon—and, by being confused,
forgotten.

Horace Jolober understood the situation too well to
mistake its events. The shot meant Red Ike was still in the
China Doll, trapped there and desperate enough to issue
his Droids lethal weapons that must have been difficult
even for him to smuggle into Paradise Port.

Desperate and foolish, because the pistol bolt had only
flicked dust from the tank's iridium turret. Jolober had
warned Red Ike that combat troops played by a different
rulebook. The message just hadn't been received until it
was too late. . . .

Jolober swung into the three-meter alley beside the
China Doll. There was neither an opening here nor
ornamentation, just the blank concrete wall of a fortress.

Which wouldn't hold for thirty seconds if the combat
team out front chose to assault it.

The tank had fired at the building front, not the door. The main gun could have blasted a hole in the armor, but that wouldn't have been a large enough entrance for the infantry now deploying behind the armored flanks of the APCs.

The concrete wall shattered like a bomb when it tried to absorb the point-blank energy of the 20cm gun. The cavity the shot left was big enough to pass a jeep with a careful driver. Infantrymen in battle armor, hunched over their weapons, dived into the China Doll. The interior lit with cyan flashes as they shot everything that moved.

The exterior lighting had gone out, but flames clawed their way up the thermoplastic façade. The fire threw a red light onto the street in which shadows of smoke capered like demons. Drips traced blazing lines through the air as they fell to spatter troops waiting their turn for a chance to kill.

The assault didn't require a full infantry platoon, but few operations have failed because the attackers had too many troops.

Jolober had seen the equivalent too often to doubt how it was going to go this time. He didn't have long; very possibly he didn't have long enough.

Standing parallel to the sheer sidewall, Jolober ran his fans up full power, then clamped the plenum chamber into a tight nozzle and lifted. His left hand paddled against the wall three times. That gave him balance and the suggestion of added thrust to help his screaming fans carry out a task for which they hadn't been designed.

When his palm touched the coping, Jolober used the contact to center him, and rotated onto the flat roof of the China Doll.

Sparks spat peevishly from the corpse of the aircar. The vehicle's frame was a twisted wire sculpture from which most of the sheathing material had burned away, but occasionally the breeze brought oxygen to a scrap that was still combustible.

The penthouse that held Ike's office and living quarters was a squat box beyond the aircar. The mortar shell had detonated just as the alien started to run for his vehicle.

He'd gotten back inside as the incendiary compound sprayed the roof, but bouncing fragments left black trails across the plush blue floor of the office.

The door was a section of wall broad enough to have passed the aircar. Red Ike hadn't bothered to close it when he fled to his elevator and the tunnel exit. Jolober, skimming again on ground effect, slid into the office shouting, "Ike! This—"

Red Ike burst from the elevator cage as the door rotated open. He had a pistol and eyes as wide as a madman's as he swung the weapon toward the hulking figure in his office.

Jolober reacted as the adrenaline pumping through his body had primed him to do. The arm with which he swatted at the pistol was long enough that his fingers touched the barrel, strong enough that the touch hurled the gun across the room despite Red Ike's deathgrip on the butt.

Red Ike screamed.

An explosion in the elevator shaft wedged the elevator doors as they began to close and burped orange flame against the far wall.

Jolober didn't know how the assault team proposed to get to the roof, but neither did he intend to wait around to learn. He wrapped both arms around the stocky alien and shouted, "Shut up and hold still if you want to get out of here alive!"

Red Ike froze, either because he understood the warning—or because at last he recognized Horace Jolober and panicked to realize that the port commandant had already disarmed him.

Jolober lifted the alien and turned his chair. It glided toward the door at gathering speed, logy with the double burden.

There was another blast from the office. The assault team had cleared the elevator shaft with a cratering charge whose directed blast sprayed the room with the bits and vapors that remained of the cage. Grenades would be next, then grappling hooks and more grenades just before—

Jolober kicked his throttle as he rounded the aircar. The fans snarled and the ride, still on ground effect, became greasy as the skirts lifted undesirably.

The office rocked in a series of dense white flashes. The room lights went out and a large piece of shrapnel, the fuze housing of a grenade, powdered a fist-sized mass of the concrete coping beside Jolober.

His chair's throttle had a gate. With the fans already at normal maximum, he sphinctered his skirts into a nozzle and kicked again at the throttle. He could smell the chair's circuits frying under the overload as it lifted Jolober and Red Ike to the coping—

But it did lift them, and after a meter's run along the narrow track to build speed, it launched them across the black, empty air of the alley.

Red Ike wailed. The only sound Horace Jolober made was in his mind. He saw not a roof but the looming bow of a tank, and his fears shouted the word they hadn't been able to get out on Primavera either: "*No!*"

They cleared the coping of the other roof with a click, not a crash, and bounced as Jolober spilled air and cut thrust back to normal levels.

An explosion behind them lit the night red and blew chunks of Red Ike's office a hundred meters in the air.

Instead of trying to winkle out their quarry with gunfire, the assault team had lobbed a bunker-buster up the elevator shaft. The blast walloped Jolober even though distance and the pair of meter-high concrete copings protected his hunching form from dangerous fragments.

Nothing in the penthouse of the China Doll could have survived. It wasn't neat, but it saved lives where they counted—in the attacking force—and veteran soldiers have never put a high premium on finesse.

"You saved me," Red Ike said.

Jolober's ears were numb from the final explosion, but he could watch Red Ike's lips move in the flames lifting even higher from the front of the China Doll.

"I had to," Jolober said, marvelling at how fully human the alien seemed. "Those men, they're line soldiers. They think that because there were so many of them involved, nobody can be punished."

Hatches rang shut on the armored personnel carriers.

A noncom snarled an order to stragglers that could be heard even over the drive fans.

Red Ike started toward the undamaged aircar parked beside them on this roof. Jolober's left hand still held the alien's wrist. Ike paused as if to pretend his movement had never taken place. His face was emotionless.

"Numbers made it a mutiny," Jolober continued. Part of him wondered whether Red Ike could hear the words he was speaking in a soft voice, but he was unwilling to shout.

It would have been disrespectful.

Fierce wind rocked the flames as the armored vehicles, tank in the lead as before, lifted and began to howl their way out of Paradise Port.

"I'll take care of you," Red Ike said. "You'll have Vicki back in three weeks, I promise. Tailored to *you*, just like the other. You won't be able to tell the difference."

"There's no me to take care of any more," said Horace Jolober with no more emotion than a man tossing his uniform into a laundry hamper.

"You see," he added as he reached behind him, "if they'd killed you tonight, the Bonding Authority would have disbanded both units *whatever* the Placidans wanted. But me? Anything I do is my responsibility."

Red Ike began to scream in a voice that became progressively less human as the sound continued.

Horace Jolober was strong enough that he wouldn't have needed the knife despite the way his victim struggled.

But it seemed like a fitting monument for Vicki.

STANDING DOWN

"Look, I'm not about to wear a goon suit like that, even to my wedding," Colonel Hammer said, loudly enough to be heard through the chatter. There were a dozen officers making last-minute uniform adjustments in the crowded office and several civilians besides. "Joachim, where's Major Pritchard? I want him in the car with us, and it's curst near jump-off now."

Joachim Steuben was settled nonchalantly on the corner of a desk, unconcerned about the state of his dress because he knew it was perfect—as always. He shrugged. "Pritchard hasn't called in," the Newlander said. His fine features brightened in a smile. "But go ahead, Alois, put the armor on."

"Yes indeed, sir," said the young civilian. He was holding the set of back-and-breast armor carefully by the edges so as not to smear its bright chrome. Rococo whorls and figures decorated the plastron, but despite its ornateness, the metal/ceramic sandwich beneath the brightwork was quite functional. "Really, the image you'll project to the spectators will be ideal, quite ideal. And there couldn't be a better time for it, either."

Lieutenant Colonel Miezierk frowned, wrinkling his forehead to the middle of his bald skull. He said, "Yes Colonel. After all, Mr. van Meter's firm studied the matter very carefully and I think—" Joachim snickered; Miezierk's scalp reddened but he went on "—that you ought to follow his advice here."

"Lord!" Hammer said, but he thrust his hands through the armholes and let Miezierk lock the clamshell back.

Someone tapped on the door. A lieutenant was leaning over the front desk, combing his hair in the screen of the display console. He cursed and straightened so that the door could open to admit Captain Fallman. The Intelligence captain was duty officer for the afternoon, harried by the inevitable series of last-minute emergencies. "Colonel," he said, "there's a Mr. Wang here to see you."

"Lord curse it, Fallman, he can wait till tomorrow!" Hammer blazed. "He can wait till Hell freezes over. Miezierk, get this bloody can off me, it's driving the stylus in my pocket clear through my rib cage."

"'Sir, we can take the stylus—" Miezierk began.

"Sir, he's from the Bonding Authority," Fallman was saying. "It's about President Theismann's—death."

Hammer swore, brushing the startled Miezierk's hands away. The room grew very silent. "Joachim what's in the office next door?" Hammer asked.

"Dust, three walls, and some stains from the Iron Guards who decided to make a stand there," the Newlander replied.

"Bring him next door, Captain, I'll talk to him there," Hammer said. He met his bodyguard's eyes. "Come along too, Joachim."

At the door the colonel paused, looking back at his still-faced officers. "Don't worry," he said. "Everything's going to work out fine."

The closing door cut off the babble of nervous speculation from within.

A moment after Hammer and his aide had entered the side office, Captain Fallman ushered in a heavy Oriental. Joachim bowed to the civilian and closed the door, leaving the duty officer alone in the hallway.

An automatic weapon had punched through the outer wall of the office, starting fires which the grenade thrown in a moment later had snuffed. There was still a scorched-plastic aflterstench mingling with that of month-dead meat. Joachim had been serious about the Iron Guards.

"I'm Hammer," the colonel said, smiling but not offering the Authority representative his hand for fear it might be refused.

"Wang An-wei," said the Oriental, nodding curtly. He held a flat briefcase. It seemed to be more an article of dress than a tool he intended to use this morning. "I was sent here as Site Officer when Councillor Theismann—"

"President Theismann, he preferred," interjected Hammer. He seated himself in feigned relaxation on a blast-warped chair.

Wang's answering smile was brief and as sharp as the lightning. "He was never awarded the title by a quorum of the Council," the Terran said. "As you no doubt are aware, Site Officers are expected to be precise. If I may continue?"

Hammer nodded. Steuben snickered. His left thumb was hooked in the belt which tucked his tailored blouse in at the waist, but his right hand dangled loose at his side.

"When Councillor Theismann hired you to make him dictator," Wang continued coolly. "Naturally I have been investigating the death of your late employer. There have been—and I'm sure you're aware of this—accusations that you murdered Councillor Theismann yourself in order to replace him as head of the successful coup."

The Site Officer looked at the men in turn. The two Slammers looked back.

"I started with the autopsy data. In addition, I have interrogated the Councillor's guards, both his personal contingent and the platoon of—White Mice—on security detail here at Government House." Wang stared at Hammer. "I assume you were informed of this?"

Hammer nodded curtly. "I signed off before they'd let you mind-probe my men."

"I used mechanical interrogation on all troops below officer rank involved," Wang agreed, "as your bond agreement specifies the Site Officer may require." When Hammer made no reply, he continued, "The evidence is uncontroverted that Councillor Theismann, accompanied by you, Colonel—" Hammer nodded again "—stepped out onto his balcony and was struck in the forehead by a pistol bolt."

Wang paused again. The room was very tense. "The pistol must have been fired from at least a kilometer away. Because of the distance and the fact that fighting was going on at several points within the city, I have reported to my superiors that it was a stray shot, and that the Councillor's death was accidental."

Joachim's fingers ceased toying with the butt of the powergun holstered high on his right hip. "We were clearing some of van Vorn's people out of the Hotel Zant," he said. "Pistol and submachine gun work. There might have been a stray shot from that. It'd be very difficult to brain a man that far away with a pistol, wouldn't it?"

"Impossible, of course," Wang said. His gaze flicked to Steuben's ornate pistol, flicked up to the bodyguard's eyes. For the first time the Oriental looked startled. He looked away from Steuben very quickly and said, "Since the investigation has cleared you, and your employment has ended for the time, I'll be returning to Earth now. I wish you good fortune, and I hope we may do business again in the near future."

Hammer laughed, clapping the civilian on the shoulder with his left hand while their right hands shook. "That's all over, Mr. Wang. The Slammers're out of the merc business for good, now. But I appreciate your wishes."

Wang turned to the door, smiling by reflex. He looked at Joachim's face again: the Cupid grin and unlined cheeks; the hair which, though naturally graying, still fell across the Newlander's forehead in an attractive page-boy; and the eyes. Wang was shivering as he stepped into the hall.

Danny Pritchard stood outside the door watching the Site Officer leave. He was dressed in civilian clothing.

Spaceport buses did not serve the cargo ships for the man or two they might bring, so Rob Jenne hiked toward the barrier on foot. At first he noticed only that the short man marching toward the terminal from the other recently landed freighter was also missing an arm. Then the other's crisp stride rang a bell in Jenne's mind. He shouted, "Top! Sergeant Horthy! What the hell're *you* doing here?"

Horthy turned with the wary quickness of a man uncertain as to any caller's interest. At Jenne's grin he broke into a smile himself. The two men dropped their bags and shook hands awkwardly, Jenne's left in Horthy's right. "Same thing you're doing, trooper," Horthy said. The Magyar's goatee was white against his swarthy skin, but his grip was as firm as it had been when Rob Jenne was Horthy's right wing gunner. "Comin' here to help the colonel put some backbone in this place. You don't know how glad I was when the call came, snake."

"Don't I though?" Jenne murmured. Side by side, talking simultaneously, the two veterans walked toward the spaceport barrier. There was already a line waiting at the customs kiosk. Jenne knew very well what his old sergeant meant. Seven years of retirement had been hard on the younger man, too. He hadn't lacked money—his pension put him well above the norm for the Burlage quarrymen to whom he had returned—but he was useless. To himself, to Burlage, to the entire human galaxy. Jenne had shouted for joy when Colonel Hammer summoned all pensioned Slammers who wanted to come. The Old Man needed supervisors and administrators, now. It didn't matter any more that gaseous iridium had burned off Jenne's right arm, right eye, and his gonads; it was enough that Hammer knew where his loyalties lay.

A gray bus with wire-mesh windows and SECURITY stencilled on its side pulled up to the barrier. The faces and clothing of the prisoners within were as drab as the air cushion vehicle's exterior. A guard wearing the blue of the civil police stepped out and walked to the barrier. His submachine gun was slung carelessly under his right arm.

Horthy nudged his companion. "It's a load a' politicals for the Borgo Mines," he muttered. "Bet they're bein' hauled out on the ship that brought me in. *And* I'll bet that bus'll be heading back to wherever the colonel is, just as quick as it unloads. Let's see if that cop'll offer us a ride, snake."

As he spoke, the Magyar veteran stepped to the waist-high barrier. The customs official bustled over from his kiosk and shouted in Horthy's face. Horthy ignored him. The official unsnapped the flap of his pistol holster. Other travellers waiting for entry scattered, more afraid of losing their lives than their places in line. Jenne, his good eye flashing across the tension, knowing as well as any man alive that his muscles were nothing to the blast of a powergun, cursed and closed the Magyar's rear.

A second bus, civilian in stripes of white and bright orange, pulled up behind the prison vehicle. The policeman turned and waved angrily. The bus hissed and settled to the pavement despite him. The policeman fumbled with his submachine gun.

A shot from the bus cut him down.

A man with a pistol swung to the loading step of the striped vehicle. He roared, "Just hold it, everybody. We got a load of hostages here. Either we get out of here with our friends or nobody gets out!"

The customs official had paused, staring with his mouth open and his fingers brushing the butt of the gun whose existence he had forgotten. Horthy, behind him, drew the pistol and fired. The rebel doubled over, his jacket afire over his sternum. Someone aboard the civilian bus screamed. Another gun fired. Horthy was prone, his pistol punching out windows in answer to the burst that had sawed the customs official in half.

Rob rolled over the barrier, coming up with the guard's automatic weapon.

The striped bus was moving, dragging the fallen gunman's torso on the concrete. The ex-tanker's mind raced in the old channels. The fans of the bus were not armored like those of a military vehicle. Rob aimed low. A powergun bolt sprayed lime dust over his head and shoulders. His own burst ripped across the plenum chamber. The driving fans disintegrated, flaying the air with steel like a bursting shell. The bus rolled over on its left side. Metal and humans screamed together. A gray-suited prisoner jumped from the door of the government bus. Horthy shot her in the face.

The ruptured fuel cell of the overturned vehicle ignited. The explosion slapped the area with a pillow of warm air. The screaming took a minute to die. Then there was just the rush of wind feeding the fire, and the nearing wail of sirens.

Jenne's cheek and shoulder-stub were oozing where the concrete had ground against them. He rose to his knees, keeping his eye and the submachine gun trailed on the gray bus. No one else was trying to get out of it. The police could sort through whatever had happened inside in their own good time.

Horthy stood, heat rippling from the barrel of the weapon he had appropriated. He glanced at the mangled customs official as if he would rather have spit on the body. "Oh, yes," the veteran said. "They need us here, trooper. They need people to teach 'em the facts of life."

"Pritchard, where the Hell have you been?" Hammer demanded, pretending that he did not understand the implications of his subordinate's business suit.

"I need to talk to you, Colonel," the brown-haired major said.

Hammer stood aside. "Then come on in. Joachim, we'll join the group next door in a moment. Wait for us there, if you will."

Pritchard took a step forward. He hesitated when he realized that Joachim was not moving. The Newlander had been as relaxed as a sunning adder during the interview with Wang An-wei. Now he was white and tense. "Colonel, he's a traitor to you," Joachim said. "He's going to walk out." His voice was quiet but not soft.

"Joachim, I told you—"

"You don't talk to traitors, Colonel. What you do to traitors—" The Newlander's hand was dipping to his gun butt. Hammer grappled with him. He was not as fast as his aide, but he knew Joachim's mind even better than the gunman did himself. The extra fraction of a second saved Pritchard's life.

The two men stood, locked like wrestlers or lovers. Pritchard did not move, knowing that emphasizing his presence would be the worst possible course under the circumstances. Hammer said, "Joachim, are you willing to shoot me?"

The bodyguard winced, a tic that momentarily disfigured his face. "Alois! You know I wouldn't. . . ."

"Then do as I say. Or you'll have to shoot me. To keep me from shooting you."

Hammer stepped away from his aide. Joachim lurched through the doorway, bumping Pritchard as he passed because his eyes had filled with tears.

Pritchard swung the door shut behind him. "I told you last week I was going to resign from the Slammers, sir."

Hammer nodded. "And I told you you weren't."

Pritchard looked around at the dust and rubble of the room, the bloodstains. "I've decided there's been enough killing, Colonel. For me. We're going somewhere else."

"Danny, the killing's over!"

The taller man gave a short snap of his head. He said, "No, it'll never be over—not any place you are." He spread his hands, then clenched them. He was staring at his knuckles because he would not look at his commander. "Right now we're chasing van Vorn's guards like rabbits, shooting 'em down or sticking 'em behind wire where they're not a curse a' good to you or themselves or this planet."

He faced Hammer, the outrage bubbling out at a human being, not the colonel he had served for all his adult life. "And the ones we kill—doesn't every one a' them have a wife or a brother or a nephew? And they'll put a knife in a Slammer some night and be shot the same way because of it!"

"All right," said Hammer calmly. "What else?"

"How about the Social Unity Party, then?" Pritchard blazed. "Maybe the one chance to get this place a work force that *works* instead of the robots the Great Houses've been trying to make them. And does anybody listen? Hell, no! The Council tinkers with the franchise to make sure they don't get a majority of the Estates-General; van Vorn outlaws the party and makes their leaders terrorists instead of politicians. And you, *you* ship them off-planet to rot in state-owned mines on Kobold!"

"All right," Hammer repeated. He sat down again, his stillness as compelling as that of the shattered room around him. "What would you do?"

Pritchard's eyes narrowed. He stretched his left hand out to the wall, not leaning on it but touching its firmness, its chill. "What do you care?" he asked quietly. "I didn't say the Slammers couldn't keep you in power here the rest of your life. I just don't want to be a part of it, is all."

Without warning, Hammer stood and slammed his fist into the wall. He turned back to his aide. His bleeding knuckles had flecked the panel more brightly than the remains of the Iron Guards. "Is that what you think?" he demanded. "That I'm a bandit who's found himself a bolt hole? That for the past thirty years I've fought wars because that's the best way to make bodies?"

"Sir, I . . ." But Pritchard had nothing more to say or need to say it.

Hammer rubbed his knuckles. He grinned wryly at his subordinate, but the grin slipped away. "It's my own fault," he said. "I don't tell people much. That's how it's got to be when you're running a tank regiment, but . . . that's not where we are now.

"Danny, this is my *home*." Hammer began to reach out to the taller man but stopped. He said, "You've been out there. You've seen how every world claws at every other one, claws its own guts too. The whole system's about to slag down, and there's nothing to stop it if *we* don't."

"You don't create order by ramming it down peoples' throats on a bayonet! It doesn't work that way."

"Then show me a way that *does* work!" Hammer cried, gripping his subordinate's right hand with his own. "Are things going to get better because you're sitting on your butt in some farmhouse, living off the money *you* made killing? Danny I *need* you. My *son* will need you."

Pritchard touched his tongue to his lips. "What is it you're asking me to do?" he said.

"Do you have a way to handle the Unionists?" Hammer shot back at him. "And the Iron Guards?"

"Maybe," Pritchard said with a frown. "Amnesty won't be enough—they won't believe it's real, for one thing. But a promise of authority . . . administrative posts in education, labor, maybe even security—that'd bring out a few of the Unionists because they couldn't afford not to take the chance. Most of the rest of them might follow when they saw you really were paying off."

The brown-haired man's enthusiasm was building without the hostility that had marked it before. "The Guards, that'll be harder because they're rigid, most of them. But if you can find some way to convince them there's nothing to gain by staying out, and—Hell, there'll be counter-protests, but work the ones who turn over their guns into the civil police. Not in big dollops, but scattered all over the planet. They'll feel more secure that way, and you can keep an eye on them easier anyhow."

Hammer nodded. "All right, bring me a preliminary assessment of both proposals by, say, 0800 Tuesday. No, make that noon, you're going to waste the rest of today watching a wedding from the front row. You'll have the backing you'll need, but these are *your* projects—I've got too much blood on my hands to run them." His eyes held Pritchard's. "Or don't you have the guts to try?"

The taller man hesitated, then squeezed Hammer's hand in return. "I rode your lead tank," he said. "I ran your lead company. If you need me now, you've got me." His face clouded. "Only, Colonel—"

Hammer tightened. "Spit it out."

"I'm not ashamed of anything. But I swore to Margritte I'd never wear another uniform or carry another gun. And I won't."

Hammer cleared his throat. "Right now I don't need a major as much as I do a conscience," he said. He cleared his throat again. "Now let's go. We've got a wedding to get to."

Cosimo Barracks was a fortress in the midst of estates which had belonged for three hundred years to the family of the late President van Vorn. The Slammers had bypassed

Cosimo in the blitzkrieg which replaced van Vorn with Theismann, their employer. But now, a month after van Vorn had poisoned himself in Government House and three weeks after someone else had burst Theismann's skull with a powergun, the fortress still refused to surrender. Sally Schilling, leading a "battalion" made up of S Company and six hundred local recruits, was on hand to do something about the situation.

A burst of automatic fire combed the rim of the dugout, splashing Captain Schilling with molten granite. "Via!" she snapped to the frightened recruit. "Keep your coppy head down and don't draw fire."

The sergeant who shared the dugout with Schilling and the recruit shook his own head in disgust. In her mind, Schilling seconded the opinion. To police a planet, Hammer needed more men than the five thousand he had brought with him. He wanted to give the new troops at least a taste of combat in the mopping-up operations. Schilling could understand that desire, but it was a pain in the ass trying to do her own job and act as baby-sitter besides.

She looked again through the eyepiece of her periscope. The machine gun had ceased firing, though cyan flickers across the perimeter showed someone else was catching it. The Iron Guards were political bullies rather than combat soldiers, but their fortress here was as tough as anything the Slammers had faced in their history. The fiber-optics periscope showed Cosimo Barracks only as a rolling knob. The grass covering the rock was streaked yellow in fans pointing back to hidden gunports. The ports themselves were easy enough targets, but the weapons within were on disappearing carriages and popped up only long enough to fire. The rest of the fortress, with an estimated five hundred Iron Guards plus enough food, water and ammunition to last a century, was deep underground.

Schilling glanced down at her console. On it Cosimo Barracks showed as a red knot of tunnels drawn from plans found in Government House. "Sigma Battalion," she said, "check off." Points of green light winked on the screen, an emerald necklace ringing the fortress. Each point was a squad guarding nearly one hundred meters of front. That was adequate; the infantry was on hand primarily to prevent a breakout.

"Fire Central," Schilling said, "prepare Fire Order Tango-Niner."

"Ready," squawked the helmet.

"Ma'am," said the recruit, "w-why don't the tanks attack instead of us?"

"Shut it off, boy!" the sergeant snapped.

"No, Webbert, we're supposed to be teaching them," Schilling said. She gestured toward the knob. The recruit automatically raised his head. Webbert shoved him back down before another burst could decapitate him. The captain sighed. "Mines're as thick up there as flies on a fresh turd," she said, "and they've got more guns in that hill than the light stuff they've been using on us. Besides, *we* aren't going to attack."

The recruit nodded with his mouth and eyes both wide open. He began to rub the stock of his unfamiliar power-gun.

"Fire Central, execute Tango-Niner," Schilling ordered.

"On the way."

Nothing happened. After a long half minute, the recruit burst out, "What went wrong? Dear Lord, will they make us charge—"

"Boy!" the sergeant shouted, his own knuckles tight on his weapon.

"Webbert!"

The sergeant cursed and turned away.

Schilling said, "The hogs're a long way away. It takes time, that's all. Everything takes time."

"Shot," said the helmet. Five seconds to impact. The sky overhead began to howl. The recruit was trembling, his own throat working as if to scream along with the shells.

The explosions were almost anticlimactic. They were only a rumbling through the bedrock, more noticed by one's feet than one's ears. Schilling, at the periscope, caught the spurts of earth as the first penetrator rounds struck. The detonations seconds later were lost in the shriek of further shells landing on the same points. Each tube's first shell ripped sod to the granite. The second salvo struck gravel; the third, sand. By the tenth salvo, the charges were bursting in the guts of Cosimo Barracks, thirty meters down. A magazine went off there, piercing earth and sky in a cyan blast that made the sun pale.

"Not an oyster born yet but a starfish can drill a hole through it," muttered Webbert. He had been a fisherman long years before when he saw one of Hammer's recruiting brochures.

"Sigma One, this is Sigma Eight-Six," said the helmet. "Our sensors indicate all three fortress elevators are rising."

With the words, circuits of meadow gaped. "Sigma Battalion," Schilling said as she rose and aimed over the lip of the dugout, "time to earn our pay. And remember— no prisoners!"

Because of the way the ground pitched, it was hard for the captain to keep her submachine gun trained on the rising elevator car. But there were eight hundred guns firing simultaneously at the three elevator heads. The bolts converged like suns burning into the heart of the hillside.

"They were sending up their families!" the recruit suddenly screamed. "The children!"

Sally Schilling slid a fresh gas cylinder in place in the butt of her weapon, then reached for another magazine as well. "They had three months to turn in their guns," she said. "Half the ones down there were troops we beat at Maritschoon and paroled. So this was the second time, and I'm not going to have my ass blown away because I gave somebody three chances to do it. As for the families, well . . . there's a couple thousand more of van Vorn's folks mooching around in the Kronburg, and they won't know it was an accident: when word of this gets around, the ones that're still out are going to think again."

The fortress guns had fallen silent as the elevator cars rose. Now a few weapons opened up again, but in long, suicidal bursts which flailed the world until the Slammers' fire silenced them forever.

❖   ❖   ❖

President van Vorn's Iron Guards had planned to use
the garage beneath Government House for a last stand;
which in a manner of speaking was what they did. The
political soldiers had naively failed to consider gas. The
Slammers introduced KD7 into the forced ventilation system, then spent three days neutralizing the toxin before
they could safely enter the garage and remove the bloated
corpses. Now the concrete walls, unmarred by shots or
grenade fragments, echoed to the fans of two dozen combat
cars readying for the parade.

"There's three layers a' gold foil," the bald maintenance chief was saying as he rapped the limousine's
myrmillon bubble. "That'll diffuse most of a two see-
emma bolt, but the folks, they'll still be able to *see* you,
you see?"

"What I don't see is my wife," Hammer snapped to the
stiff-faced noble acting as the Council's liaison with their
new overlord. "She's agreed, I've agreed. If you think that
the Great Houses can back out of this now—"

"Colonel," interrupted Pritchard, pointing at the closed
car which was just entering the garage. The armored doors
to the mews slammed shut behind the vehicle, cutting off
the wash of sunlight which had paled the glow strips by
comparison. The car hissed slowly between armored vehicles
and support pillars, coming to a halt beside Hammer and
his aides. Two men got out, dressed in the height of con-
servative fashion. The colors of Great Houses slashed their
collar flares. A moment later, a pair of women stepped out
between them.

One of them was sixty, as tall and heavy as either of
the men. Her black garments were as harsh as the glare
she turned on Hammer when he nodded to her.

The other woman was short enough to be petite. It was
hard to tell, however, because she wore a dress of misty,
layered fabric which gave the impression of spiderweb but
hid even the outline of her body. The celagauze veil hanging
from her cap-brim blurred her face similarly. Before any
of those around her could interfere, she had reached up
and removed the cap.

"Anneke!" cried the woman in black. One of the escorting nobles shifted. Danny Pritchard motioned him back, using his left hand by reflex.

Anneke sailed the cap into the intake of a revving combat car. Shreds of white fabric softened the floor of the garage. "What, Aunt Ruth?" she asked. Her voice was clearly audible over the fans and the engines. "That's the idea, isn't it? Prove to the citizens that the Great Houses are still in charge because the colonel is marrying one of us? But then they've got to see who I am, don't they?"

Hammer stepped forward. "Lady Brederode," he said, repeating his nod. The older woman looked away as if Hammer were a spot of offal on the pavement. "Lady Tromp."

Anneke Tromp extended her right hand. She had fine bones and skin as soft as the lining of a jewelry box. The fingernails looked metallic.

The colonel knelt to kiss her hand, the gesture stiffened by his armor. "Well, Lady Tromp," he said, "are you ready?"

The woman smiled. Hammer became the commander again. He waved dismissingly toward his bride's aunt and escort. "I've made provisions for your seating at the church," he said, "but you'll not be needed for the procession. Lady Tromp will ride in my vehicle. We'll be accompanied by majors—that is, by Major Steuben and Mr. Pritchard."

Anneke nodded graciously to the aides flanking Hammer. Unexpectedly, Joachim giggled. His eyes were red. "Your family and I go back a long way, Lady," he said. "Did you know that I shot your father on Melpomene? Between the eyes, so that he could see it coming."

The colonel's face changed, but he grinned as he turned. He threw an arm around his bodyguard's shoulders. "Joachim," he said, "let's talk in the car for a moment." Steuben looked away, blazing hatred at everyone else in the room, but he followed his commander into the soundproofed compartment.

As the car door thudded shut, Anneke Tromp stepped idly to Pritchard's side. She was still smiling. Without looking at the limousine's bubble, she said, "That's a very jealous man, Mr. Pritchard. And jealous not only of me, I should think."

Danny shrugged. "Joachim's been with the colonel a long time," he said. "He's not an . . . evil . . . man. Just loyal."

"A razor blade in a melon isn't evil, Mr. Pritchard," the woman said, gesturing as though they were discussing the markings of the nearest combat car. "It's just too dangerous to be permitted to exist."

Pritchard swallowed. Part of his duties involved checking the roster of veterans returning to the colors. He was remembering a big man with an engaging grin—as good a tank commander as had ever served under Pritchard, and the lightest touch he knew on the trigger of an automatic weapon. "We'll see," Danny said without looking at the woman.

"When I was a little girl," she murmured, "my father ruled Friesland. I want to live to see my son rule."

The car door opened and both men got out. "Joachim has decided to ride up front with the driver instead of with us in back," Hammer said with a false smile. He held the door. "Shall we?"

Pritchard sat on a jump seat across from Hammer and Lady Tromp. The armored bubble was cloudy, like the sky on the morning of a snowstorm. Hammer touched a plate on the console. "Six-two," he said. "Move 'em out."

Fans revved. The garage door lifted and began passing combat cars out into the mews. Hammer's driver slid the limousine into the line of cars waiting to exit. More armored vehicles edged in behind them. They accelerated up the ramp and into the Frisian sunlight. The whole west quarter of Government House had burned in the fighting, darkening the vitril panels there.

Pritchard leaned forward. "You don't really think that you can turn Friesland around, much less the galaxy?" he asked.

Hammer shrugged. "If I don't, they'll at least say that I died trying."

The limousine glided through the archway into Independence Boulevard. Tank companies were already closing either end of the block, eight tanks abreast. The panzers had been painted dazzlingly silver for the celebration. The combat cars aligned themselves in four ranks between the double caps of bigger vehicles, leaving the limousine to tremble alone in the midst of the waves of heavy armor. Hammer's breastplate was a sunblazed eye in the center of all.

On the front bench beside the driver, Joachim was trying nervously to scan the thousands of civilians. He knew that despite the armored bubble, the right man could kill Hammer as easily as he himself had murdered Councillor Theismann. He wished he could kill every soul in the crowd.

Pritchard checked the time, then radioed a command. The procession began to slip forward toward the throngs lining the remaining three kilometers of the boulevard, all the way to the Church of the First Landfall.

"I've been a long time coming back to Friesland," said Hammer softly. He was not really speaking to his companions. "But now I'm back. And I'm going to put this place in order."

Anneke Tromp touched him. Her glittering fingernails lay like knife blades across the back of his hand. "*We're* going to put it in order," she said.

"We'll see," said Danny Pritchard.

"Hammer!" shouted the crowd.

"Hammer!"

"Hammer!"

"Hammer!"